STAR WARS®

KNIGHT ERRANT

BY JOHN JACKSON MILLER

Star Wars: Knight Errant
Star Wars: Lost Tribe of the Sith: The Collected Stories
Star Wars: Kenobi
Star Wars: A New Dawn
Overdraft: The Orion Offensive

STAR WARS®

KNIGHT ERRANT

JOHN JACKSON MILLER

BALLANTINE BOOKS • NEW YORK

Star Wars: Knight Errant is a work of fiction. Names, places, and incidents either are products of the author's imagination or are used fictitiously.

Copyright © 2011 by Lucasfilm Ltd. & ® or ™ where indicated. All Rights Reserved. Used Under Authorization.

Excerpt from *Star Wars: The Old Republic: Deceived* © 2011 by Lucasfilm Ltd. & ® or ™ where indicated. All Rights Reserved. Used Under Authorization.

Published in the United States by Del Rey, an imprint of The Random House Publishing Group, a division of Random House, Inc., New York.

DEL REY is a registered trademark and the Del Rey colophon is a trademark of Random House, Inc.

This book contains an excerpt from *Star Wars: The Old Republic: Deceived* by Paul S. Kemp. This excerpt has been set for this edition only and may not reflect the final content of the forthcoming editon.

ISBN 978-0-345-52264-1

Printed in the United States of America

www.starwars.com
www.fateofthejedi.com
www.delreybooks.com

9 8 7 6 5 4

To Meredith,
intrepid and wise

ACKNOWLEDGMENTS

Knight Errant began life when Dark Horse Comics editor Randy Stradley suggested I develop a comic-book series following a lone Jedi Knight in Sith space during the Dark Ages of the Republic a thousand years before *The Phantom Menace*. At the same time I was developing Kerra Holt and her world, Lucasfilm fiction editor, Sue Rostoni, approached Del Rey editor Shelly Shapiro with the idea of my creating an original novel using the same character and milieu. The resulting comics and prose novel developed in parallel; while this original novel follows the events of the first comics story line, both works stand alone.

In addition to Randy and Shelly my appreciation goes to my comics editor, David Marshall, who helped hone the original concept, and artists Federico Dallocchio and Michael Atiyeh who influenced the design of many characters. At Lucasfilm, the advice of Sue Rostoni, Leland Chee, and Pablo Hidalgo proved invaluable; my appreciation also goes to Jason Fry and Daniel Wallace, for their cartographic assistance. Finally, I owe special thanks to my wife, Meredith Miller, and assistant, T. M. Haley, for their proofreading (and patience).

If you are interested in more of Kerra Holt's adventures, check out the *Knight Errant* comics and collected editions available from Dark Horse.

THE STAR WARS LEGENDS NOVELS TIMELINE

BEFORE THE REPUBLIC
37,000–25,000 YEARS BEFORE STAR WARS: A New Hope

c. 25,793 *YEARS BEFORE STAR WARS: A New Hope*

Dawn of the Jedi: Into the Void

OLD REPUBLIC
5000–67 YEARS BEFORE STAR WARS: A New Hope

Lost Tribe of the Sith: The Collected Stories

3954 *YEARS BEFORE STAR WARS: A New Hope*

The Old Republic: Revan

3650 *YEARS BEFORE STAR WARS: A New Hope*

The Old Republic: Deceived
Red Harvest
The Old Republic: Fatal Alliance
The Old Republic: Annihilation

1032 *YEARS BEFORE STAR WARS: A New Hope*

Knight Errant
Darth Bane: Path of Destruction
Darth Bane: Rule of Two
Darth Bane: Dynasty of Evil

RISE OF THE EMPIRE
67–0 YEARS BEFORE STAR WARS: A New Hope

67 *YEARS BEFORE STAR WARS: A New Hope*

Darth Plagueis

33 *YEARS BEFORE STAR WARS: A New Hope*

Cloak of Deception
Darth Maul: Shadow Hunter
Maul: Lockdown

32 *YEARS BEFORE STAR WARS: A New Hope*

> ### STAR WARS: EPISODE I
> ### THE PHANTOM MENACE

Rogue Planet
Outbound Flight
The Approaching Storm

22 *YEARS BEFORE STAR WARS: A New Hope*

> ### STAR WARS: EPISODE II
> ### ATTACK OF THE CLONES

22–19 *YEARS BEFORE STAR WARS: A New Hope*

> ### STAR WARS: THE CLONE WARS

The Clone Wars: Wild Space
The Clone Wars: No Prisoners

Clone Wars Gambit
Stealth
Siege

Republic Commando
Hard Contact
Triple Zero
True Colors
Order 66

Shatterpoint
The Cestus Deception
MedStar I: Battle Surgeons
MedStar II: Jedi Healer
Jedi Trial
Yoda: Dark Rendezvous
Labyrinth of Evil

19 *YEARS BEFORE STAR WARS: A New Hope*

> ### STAR WARS: EPISODE III
> ### REVENGE OF THE SITH

Kenobi
Dark Lord: The Rise of Darth Vader
Imperial Commando 501st

Coruscant Nights
Jedi Twilight
Street of Shadows
Patterns of Force

The Last Jedi

10 *YEARS BEFORE STAR WARS: A New Hope*

The Han Solo Trilogy
The Paradise Snare
The Hutt Gambit
Rebel Dawn

The Adventures of Lando Calrissian
The Force Unleashed
The Han Solo Adventures
Death Troopers
The Force Unleashed II

REBELLION
0–5 YEARS AFTER
STAR WARS: A New Hope

Death Star
Shadow Games

0

STAR WARS: EPISODE IV
A NEW HOPE

Tales from the Mos Eisley Cantina
Tales from the Empire
Tales from the New Republic
Scoundrels
Allegiance
Choices of One
Honor Among Thieves
Galaxies: The Ruins of Dantooine
Splinter of the Mind's Eye
Razor's Edge

3 YEARS AFTER *STAR WARS: A New Hope*

STAR WARS: EPISODE V
THE EMPIRE STRIKES BACK

Tales of the Bounty Hunters
Shadows of the Empire

4 YEARS AFTER *STAR WARS: A New Hope*

STAR WARS: EPISODE VI
THE RETURN OF THE JEDI

Tales from Jabba's Palace

The Bounty Hunter Wars
The Mandalorian Armor
Slave Ship
Hard Merchandise

The Truce at Bakura
Luke Skywalker and the Shadows of
Mindor

NEW REPUBLIC
5–25 YEARS AFTER
STAR WARS: A New Hope

X-Wing
Rogue Squadron
Wedge's Gamble
The Krytos Trap
The Bacta War
Wraith Squadron
Iron Fist
Solo Command

The Courtship of Princess Leia
Tatooine Ghost

The Thrawn Trilogy
Heir to the Empire
Dark Force Rising
The Last Command

X-Wing: Isard's Revenge

The Jedi Academy Trilogy
Jedi Search
Dark Apprentice
Champions of the Force

I, Jedi
Children of the Jedi
Darksaber
Planet of Twilight
X-Wing: Starfighters of Adumar
The Crystal Star

The Black Fleet Crisis Trilogy
Before the Storm
Shield of Lies
Tyrant's Test

The New Rebellion

The Corellian Trilogy
Ambush at Corellia
Assault at Selonia
Showdown at Centerpoint

The Hand of Thrawn Duology
Specter of the Past
Vision of the Future

Scourge
Survivor's Quest

THE STAR WARS LEGENDS NOVELS TIMELINE

NEW JEDI ORDER
25–40 YEARS AFTER
STAR WARS: A New Hope

The New Jedi Order
Vector Prime
Dark Tide I: Onslaught
Dark Tide II: Ruin
Agents of Chaos I: Hero's Trial
Agents of Chaos II: Jedi Eclipse
Balance Point
Edge of Victory I: Conquest
Edge of Victory II: Rebirth
Star by Star
Dark Journey
Enemy Lines I: Rebel Dream
Enemy Lines II: Rebel Stand
Traitor
Destiny's Way
Force Heretic I: Remnant
Force Heretic II: Refugee
Force Heretic III: Reunion
The Final Prophecy
The Unifying Force

35 YEARS AFTER STAR WARS: A New Hope

The Dark Nest Trilogy
The Joiner King
The Unseen Queen
The Swarm War

LEGACY
40+ YEARS AFTER
STAR WARS: A New Hope

Legacy of the Force
Betrayal
Bloodlines
Tempest
Exile
Sacrifice
Inferno
Fury
Revelation
Invincible

Crosscurrent
Riptide
Millennium Falcon

43 YEARS AFTER STAR WARS: A New Hope

Fate of the Jedi
Outcast
Omen
Abyss
Backlash
Allies
Vortex
Conviction
Ascension
Apocalypse

X-Wing: Mercy Kill

45 YEARS AFTER STAR WARS: A New Hope

Crucible

A long time ago in a galaxy far, far away . . .

PROLOGUE

With each stroke of his pen, the old Sullustan discovered the creator of the universe.

Lord Daiman was relatively young, as humans went. And yet Gub Tengo found his liege again and again as he worked through the stack of crumpled flimsiplast cels. Shipping invoices. Engineering schematics. Restaurant receipts. Gub couldn't read the words, but he could sometimes tell what they were about from the pictures. All were dated long before—sometimes centuries before—Daiman came to power on Darkknell. Yet all, somehow, presaged His Lordship's rise.

It was an amazing thing, Gub thought, riffling the thin sheets of acrylic, stuck together from age. Documents on such mundane matters—and yet they all were part of creation: Daiman's creation. Gub shook the glow lamp he had been allotted and brought it nearer to the text. Yes, the prophetic symbols were there again, hiding. It was Gub's job to make them apparent to all.

He quietly thanked Daiman for that. At sixty, Gub was lucky to be of any service—especially after losing the use of his legs in a vat collapse during Lord Chagras's reign. That should have been the end of his usefulness. But years earlier, Gub had worked in a bioweapons factory, injecting spores with poison. It had been a short step from that meticulous work to using a chemical stylus—and such a skill was always handy on Daiman's capital world.

On taking power, Daiman had ordered the Aurebesh letters that spelled his name altered to reflect his mark on existence. Two flag-like strokes would be added to the characters not just when they were written in the future, but also everywhere they had previously appeared. And *altered* wasn't the right word, because—as Daiman had put it—the "new" characters had always existed. Mere organics simply couldn't see them. Making them visible now wasn't alteration—it was *revelation*.

The change was instantaneous for the vast majority of written words in Daiman's domain, all electronically stored. But manual attention was required for signs and labels—as well as for the relatively few physical documents the culture had generated. Thus, Gub and thousands of craftsbeings like him on Darkknell and elsewhere had been tasked with "revealing" the letters that had always been there.

It might have been easier simply to destroy the earlier materials; most flimsiplasts dissolved eagerly in water. But Gub knew that wasn't the point. If, as Daiman's Sith adepts said, the universe had been created twenty-five years before, when Daiman was born, all "older" matter must have been created by him, as well—including this advertisement. If a ragged sheet depicting pictures of shoes held within it the marks of Daiman, then it was not an advertisement, but a holy artifact. Destroying it would be sacrilege worthy of the Great Enemy.

Daiman's signature was everywhere in the galaxy—even in the sky above. The pages from the past were just another piece of that ubiquity. They had to look the part.

Zeroing in on the circular, Gub found one of the letters he was seeking in the caption for a gray boot. Another *aurek*. Gub sighed and rubbed the electrostatic pen against his knee to charge it. He knew the importance of his job, but he still tired of seeing the pesky vowels. The added flags—his supervisor called them *kerns*—that created the holy letter *aurek-da* flew to the left of the character, almost always butting up against the adjacent figure. But if Daiman didn't intend for the characters to run together, then Gub must do his best to see that the transformed, revealed characters didn't, either.

In matters of creation, neatness counted.

And so, the old Sullustan sat in his tiny apartment in the Iridium Quarter, his day a slurry of *dorn-da*s and *enth-da*s that often stretched far into night, as it had tonight. Gub seldom wondered what happened to the reams of completed flimsiplast he'd returned over the years. He assumed the documents went right back to where they'd been found, although he could tell from the stains and smell that some of them had been in landfills, waiting for expulsion into the nearest star. Who kept track of what needed to be returned where? What kind of a job must *that* be? Gub couldn't imagine.

It didn't matter, so long as he'd done *his* part for divine revelation. His work concerns were only in meeting his quota and pleasing a passive-aggressive inspector. His real worries he saved for his dwindling food ration, forced to serve three, and for his orphaned granddaughter Tan, sleeping in the other room, her future unknown.

And increasingly, he worried over the caregiver he'd recently hired for the two of them. Unreasonable, brash—and, unbeknownst to him, at that moment across town working toward the ultimate destruction of Lord Daiman, forger of alphabets and creator of the universe.

Part One

THE DAIMANATE

CHAPTER ONE

In Sith space, everyone is a slave. It was a funny thing about a bunch whose credo included a line about their "chains being broken," Narsk thought. They were always careful to leave plenty of chains intact for everyone else.

Still, some people were more enslaved than others. It paid to be special, to be good at something. Life was less unpleasant then. And for the *really* special? One had one's choice of masters—not that the options were that appealing.

Narsk Ka'hane's own specialty had brought him to Darkknell, seat of power for Daiman, self-declared Sith Lord and would-be godling. Narsk had first used a stealth bodysuit to harvest rimebats from caverns on Verdanth, and what he was doing now wasn't much different. True, the Bothan couldn't imagine anyone back home clinging upside down to a rope in a high-security tower's ventilation system—but then, not everyone could be special.

What *was* different now was the stealth suit. The Sith warring in the region hadn't focused much on advancing stealth technology over the last few decades; they were only after bigger explosions. That was fine with Narsk. The bodysuit he wore was the top of a Republic line never seen in the Grumani sector. He didn't know how his supplier had acquired a Cyricept Personal Concealment

System, Mark VI—or even whether the previous five versions were any good. Narsk just knew he'd never gotten so far on an assignment so easily.

Almost a shame, given all the preparation he'd put in. He'd arrived in Xakrea, Darkknell's administrative capital, weeks earlier to establish his cover identity. Locating the target was simple enough; the lopsided pyramid known colloquially as the Black Fang was visible from most of town. He'd carefully studied traffic patterns around the obsidian edifice and noted the shift changes of the sentries guarding the few openings. Within a month, he'd located every route into and out of the colossal house of secrets.

And then he had walked right in.

The Mark VI could do for tradecraft what hyperdrive did for space travel, Narsk thought. Electronic baffles worked into the suit's skin at a molecular level warped and bent electromagnetic waves around the wearer. Sound, light, comms—the Mark VI dodged them all. And Cyricept had thought of everything. A breath filter matched exhalations to room temperature and humidity. Special goggles permitted Narsk to see out, despite the fact that no light was reaching his eyes. They'd even supplied a similarly cloaked pouch for carry-along items. If Narsk wasn't exactly invisible, he took an attentive eye to spot, especially in the dark.

But attentiveness, Narsk had found, was not a gift that "Lord Daiman, creator of all," had seen fit to bestow on his sentries. As elsewhere, the peculiar Lord's adepts had rounded up menacing-looking characters and proceeded to overdress them. There wasn't a bruiser so tough he couldn't be made to look silly when strapped into gilded armor and wrapped in a burgundy skirt. One poor Gamorrean—his squat, lumbering green body particularly at odds with his finery—across town had looked ready to cry.

So while Narsk had brought his needler and extra rounds on every trip to the research center, he'd never needed them. The Mark VI had gotten him to the door, but the sentries had actually opened it for him, allowing him inside when they entered themselves. "When your job's to make sure nothing ever happens," he'd once heard, "you begin to see nothing happening even when something's going on." By now, his thirteenth and final trip inside, Narsk believed it. Many of the secrets of the Black Fang—officially, the Daimanate Dynamic Testing Facility (Darkknell)—rested comfortably in the memory of the datapad in his pouch.

Lord Odion would be pleased.

That wasn't always a good thing, Narsk knew: Daiman's older brother got most of his thrills from death and destruction. The whole sorry war smacked of a psychological study. Daiman was the spoiled kid who thought he was the only person in the universe who mattered; Odion was the jealous sibling, reacting to his loss of uniqueness by trashing the playpen. If Daiman thought he created everything, Odion believed it was his destiny to destroy everything. Half of Odion's adepts were part of a death cult, flitting around his evil light hoping to cash out in his service. Ralltiiri glowmites were less suicidal.

Fortunately, Narsk didn't have to adopt their ways to take their assignments. Not many of them, anyway.

Reaching a juncture in the ventilation system, Narsk felt the whole building wheeze around him. Frigid air chuffed past, cooling the facility for today's big test. The Mark VI responded, matching the surrounding temperature while somehow keeping frost from accumulating on the suit's surface. The Republic designers were good, Narsk thought. *Too bad they can't fight. Or won't.*

Cutting the cable, Narsk settled gently onto the vent cover. The main testing center below was the only important room he hadn't entered, if only because his quarry hadn't been moved here yet. But there it was, its metallic bulk just visible through the icy slats at his feet.

Convergence.

In Daiman's conflict with Odion, the great capital ships that once dominated Sith battles with the Republic had sat largely out of play. Neither had a clear idea how many great ships his brother had, and while Odion would have happily taken his chances in a huge engagement, Daiman was unwilling to oblige. The result had been a series of strokes and counterstrokes, where the winning factor wasn't the amount of firepower as often as it was the ability to project different kinds of strength quickly. The field of battle changed constantly.

The Convergence Tactical Assault Vehicle had chucked thousands of years of military science in favor of Daiman's idea of the moment: one-ship-fits-all. Like Narsk's stealth suit, *Convergence* was intended to do everything. Twice the size of a starfighter, the craft served as a small troop transport, capable of delivering eight to ten warriors through hyperspace. It also sported weapons systems allowing it to play the role of fighter or bomber depending on the situation. Daiman foresaw a time when millions of the vessels would propel him to his rightful place, ruling the galaxy.

Daiman's engineers, meanwhile, had foreseen only a never-ending nightmare. And their prediction, spoken only to themselves, had thus far come closest to reality. Peering down into the chamber, Narsk could see why. Mounted onto a colossal testing arm was the ugliest contraption he'd ever seen. *Convergence* was a hundred-ton expression of one man's moods, changeable and conflicting.

Daiman had demanded that the vessel keep to the tri-pronged dart aesthetic of his starfighters, but the wings and color scheme were about all that the pregnant monster had in common with those sleek ships. Designers had saddled the forward section with a hulking crew compartment that was still less than comfortable: room for nine passengers, but only if six stood the entire way. The engines, enlarged on two earlier occasions, seemed nonetheless outmatched. A missile battery pointed nowhere in particular. And a massive nacelle ran along the underside, last vestige of an earlier plot to convert the ship into a tracked vehicle for use on land. Narsk imagined they still kept the wheels somewhere in the building, anticipating Daiman's frequent changes of mind.

Endless engineering for an endless war. Narsk thought it something a child would design. Yet despite it all, there was still something worth stealing. For all their troubles, Daiman's designers had lucked upon some worthwhile advances. Some of the composite work on the hull had shown fruit, and the turbolaser energy efficiency was as good as anyone in the sector had seen.

Useful facts, especially to his employer. Self-styled though he was, Lord Odion was a proper mimic when it came to technology. Narsk had been assigned to pick *Convergence*'s secrets clean. With any luck, Odion's massive floating factory, The Spike, would soon be churning out better weapons systems using the ideas.

Narsk had stolen most of the data at his leisure, thanks to Daiman's sudden decision to add riot-control features to the ship. Now he was back for the last morsel: the energy shield package. Over the past week, Daiman's researchers had exposed its shields to sonic waves, electronic emissions, and blazing heat, adjusting the ship's software package as needed. This test, designed to evaluate shield performance in atmospheres, was the one Narsk had been waiting for. The *Convergence* prototype had been married to a huge rotating arm, a centrifuge designed to simulate performance at sublight speeds. On less secret vehicles, this kind of testing was done in the air—but, Narsk imagined, the researchers probably worried the thing would never fly anyway. He was glad he hadn't been ordered to steal the ship itself!

A buzzer sounded. The massive torus began to move, sleepily dragging the bulk of *Convergence.* Narsk's attention was below, nearer the hub. The observers monitoring outside wouldn't have a visual on the gargantuan motor, or the space around it.

Narsk heaved himself over the edge, timing his drop to allow him to land on the gargantuan arm itself. Touching metal for a moment, he lithely tumbled backward off the rotating bar toward the floor below. He immediately went flat, mashing his furry face to the ribbed decking of the testing chamber. Less than a meter stood between the floor and instant decapitation.

Just another day working for the Sith, Narsk thought, adjusting his mask's visor to accommodate for the sudden, whirring darkness. Regaining his bearings, he shimmied toward the motor housing at the room's center. There, in the motionless base, was what he was expecting to find: a live control panel, intended for use only when the centrifuge wasn't in motion.

Narsk studied the display. Telemetry from the test streamed to the hub through an insulated cable snaking along the great arm's length to *Convergence.* Seeing information cascade across the small screen, Narsk reached in his pouch for the datapad, packed neatly on top. A simple interface established, he began downloading the results from this and every previous shield test on the prototype. It was as easy as he'd been told. It helped to know the odd Odionite hiding within Daiman's technical ranks.

They're all odd, Narsk thought. *But never mind.*

Download complete, he squinted at the display, taking precious extra time to make sure he was seeing what he was supposed to. Deciphering the Daimanite alphabet didn't help. *What a pain in the—*

Another buzzer, barely audible, alerted him that the

prototype had reached full speed. Soon it would be starting its long deceleration. He had to go. But first he needed to leave his parting gift, in exchange for all the information he had stolen. Gingerly reaching into the pouch, Narsk removed the cargo he'd been toting: baradium thermal charges. They'd gotten dearer on Darkknell recently, forcing Narsk to smuggle in his own—hardly a comfortable experience given the explosives' testiness. Just a few charges attached to the centrifuge's base would be enough to disable part of the testing center and take out the prototype, too, as soon as Narsk activated the remote detonator.

It would make for a pretty explosion, he thought, but he'd be too far away to see it. He was already on his way out, slinking into a narrow drain used for runoff from weather-related tests. Too slick and vertical to be a route into the center, it was a remarkably convenient way out. Sliding down in darkness, Narsk smiled. He'd never gotten within twenty meters of *Convergence*—and yet he had everything needed to build his own.

As if anyone would want it!

When Lord Chagras's holdings were broken up, young Daiman had been quick to seize Darkknell. There was little question why. The aesthetics did more to sell his vision of godhood than an army of statues—although he had that, too. The planet's main sun, Knel'char I, provided residents with a sickly light that led scientists to worry it might throw off its hydrogen core at any time. But it was the two younger, brighter stars slowly circling each other in an outer orbit that were the real attraction. With only just enough mass to support fusion, Knel'char II and III were too remote to destabilize Darkknell's orbit or even affect the weather. But they were always visible somewhere on the planet, day or night.

The suns watched Darkknell—*literally*, residents said.

For the azure and golden orbs resembled nothing more than the mismatched eyes of Daiman himself! Thus the so-called creator of all forever watched his fearful subjects from the skies, ensuring that no treason could ever fester under his gaze.

Unless the planet happened to be facing the other way. Looking up from the roof of the airspeeder factory next door to the testing center, Narsk chortled. Moments before, the "eyes" had risen above the Black Fang, in advance of impending dawn—which left half the planet's residents unmolested by any stellar voyeur. Astronomical details didn't matter, of course. People in the Grumani sector had lived under Sith rule for so long, they'd believe anything. Narsk had always assumed that Daiman had altered his irises to match the stars, but Odion had sworn the brat's off-putting eyes were natural.

Whatever the truth, it was a good ploy. Filtered through the polluted haze of the capital, the stars made for an arresting spectacle. And if anyone snickered at the time of the year when the stars' orbits made their creator appear cross-eyed, well, that was what Daiman's Correctors were for.

Pulling the mask back from his hairy pointed ears, Narsk was thankful the Correctors weren't here now. The Mark VI had performed well, but even Cyricept couldn't shield him from a large number of people searching with the dark side of the Force. Narsk knew mental rituals for maintaining a low profile, but getting into and out of the testing center had kept him pretty busy. It was good that Daiman had pulled most of the Correctors back to his headquarters in advance of some new plan against Odion. Narsk didn't wonder much about what it was. The Sanctum Celestial was someone else's assignment.

Narsk removed his gloves and placed them with the goggles and mask in his bag, just beside the detonator.

He'd wait to trigger the explosives until he was on the freighter taking off. He already had the travel authorization under his cover identity. He raked tan claws through matted facial fur; even with the suit's cooling system, he was soaked. He breathed deeply. Too many trips into dark spaces. It was good to be done with Darkknell.

Making his way toward the side of the roof where his clothes were hidden, Narsk thought about what the completed job would actually mean. Money wasn't significant in many Sith territories; units of exchange didn't even exist in Odion's realm. Possessions, likewise, were difficult to accumulate in a region where borders were impermanent and safety was fleeting.

No, in Sith space, people were measured by their options. By the little degrees of freedom they were allowed to have—and by the mobility they *had* to have when things fell apart. It wasn't enough to find a reasonably nonmurderous despot to nuzzle up against. Sith Lords fell as quickly as they rose. The only way to survive was to be valuable to many Sith at once. With this feat, Narsk's reputation would grow—a reputation that would keep the Bothan out of chains no matter what came.

It was the most that anyone living in Sith space could hope for, he thought. *Or want.*

"You have something I want" came a low female voice from behind.

Corrector!

Narsk tumbled forward even as he heard the lightsaber hum to life behind him. It *had* to be a Corrector; none of Daiman's sentries carried lightsabers. But Narsk wasn't bothering to look. He was already over the side of the rooftop, angling toward the ledge that ran the length of the factory. Padded boots ground against durasteel as he found his balance and sprang into a headlong run.

His pursuer remained above, dashing quickly along

the roof edge. Narsk worried that his speed wouldn't be enough, especially with his legs already aching from exertions in the testing center. He fumbled for the pouch, still pulling against his arm as he ran. He reached—and reached again. The needler was . . . where?

The bottom of the bag, blast it!

No time to go searching, not with the end of the ledge ahead and footfalls growing nearer above. More factory buildings stretched into the distance, leading farther away from the Black Fang. Narsk leapt the few meters to the cornice of the next building. It would be a much longer jump from the Corrector's rooftop, but Narsk wasted no hope on his pursuer giving up.

Sure enough, glancing back, he spied a shadowy bipedal form sailing through the air, easily crossing the distance between the structures. Only a Sith with Force skills could have made that leap, Narsk thought. Such were the Correctors, elite officers charged with repairing those elements of creation that didn't suit Daiman's liking. Narsk didn't want to know what the revision process was like.

The new ledge went a short distance before turning. Narsk skidded as he rounded the corner. It was narrower on this side, just half a meter separating the wall from a six-story drop to the alley. The Bothan didn't slow down at all, though every step tested fate. The stealth suit's boots weren't made for this, he knew—but there was no question of recovering his street clothes back on the rooftop. He just needed time to get to a place where he could don the suit's mask and gloves and reboot the stealth system.

Narsk shot another look back. His assailant was a female humanoid, close to his height and weight. That wasn't much cause for relief, though. If it came to a physical showdown, he wouldn't last against a Sith adept of any size. And at least against a larger pursuer, he might be able to use his nimbleness to his advantage. But this Corrector had matched him leap for leap.

At least her lightsaber was out of sight; he'd heard it, but he'd never seen it. She must have doused the thing immediately as soon as the run began, Narsk guessed. Puzzling.

Why hasn't backup arrived? Where are the klaxons?

Narsk had just begun to wonder when salvation appeared to him, shining through the skylight of the smaller building below. It was the answer—if only he could get down there. Without thinking twice, he bounded from the corner and tucked his body into a tight ball, steeling himself. The Mark VI wasn't a suit of armor, but as he fell he hoped it might offer some defense against the shiny membrane, seemingly hurtling toward him.

Ker-rash! Shards of shoddy transparisteel exploded downward as he fell, offering less resistance than he'd expected. The same couldn't be said, though, for the permacrete floor. And any hope Narsk had for a controlled landing ended when he hit the surface . . . and he proceeded to slide a dozen meters through a puddle of golden goo before finally slamming into a wall.

Uncurling, Narsk squinted through the pain and looked around. The place was what he'd thought it was. Incomplete speeder bike bodies dangled from pulleys on chains, swaying as they worked their way toward a shower of paint. The whole place reeked with the pungent lacquer, wafting in steamy sheets. Narsk saw droids on duty so covered with spray, they could barely move. Evidently, there *was* a place in the Daimanate too toxic even for his slaves!

Narsk struggled to stand. Where was the Corrector? Not above him, he saw. She hadn't been dressed like the ones he'd seen in public. Did Daiman have some new kind of secret police? Why didn't she follow him down?

Do they worry about getting messy?

An idle and foolish thought—and one he paid for immediately as he lost his footing in the greasy runoff and planted his chin onto the floor. The junk was in his fur now: more of that blasted gilt Daiman liked to see on everything.

Rising, Narsk realized it was also covering a good part of the stealth suit. There was no sense activating it; it'd need to be wiped completely clean before it could fool anyone. But he'd had no choice. Craning his neck, he scanned the rafters for the reason he entered.

There it was, high in the rafters: a fully assembled speeder bike, glistening and dry, hanging from the end of a chain. Moving more carefully this time, Narsk pushed past a loader droid on his way to a gantry ladder. Looking up again—still no Corrector—he made for the top step and waited for the conveyer to bring it past.

A short jump—but slipping in the slop atop the ladder, Narsk nearly missed it altogether. Clawing frantically, he finally locked an elbow around the rocking frame and joined his hands, hoisting himself onto the seat.

Safely astride the vehicle, Narsk ripped the protective coverings from the control display. Yes, the speeder would operate, but it barely had enough fuel to make the edge of Xakrea. That didn't really matter. The Corrector would definitely have brought in support by now; Narsk would reach safety in the next few minutes, or not at all. Opening his bag, he found the needler. It was right on top of his other goods, easily reachable. Narsk sighed. *Terrific.* Switching the hand-built weapon's setting to fire acid-filled darts, he drew a bead on the pulley above and fired.

Moments later, bleary-eyed workers departing from the Personal Transport Assembly Shop looked up to see a golden blur rocketing through an open fourth-story window. Narsk tucked his body tightly against the speeder's frame. The chain, still attached to the vehicle, whipped behind like a mosgoth's tail, smashing against a nearby building as he turned for the main avenue.

No time to worry about that. Narsk allowed the wind to replace the gunk in his lungs. He'd never considered Xakrea's air to be fresh before now. Manufacturers' Way stretched ahead, leading toward Little Duros and a thousand places where he could lose himself. The only thing behind him was the Black Fang, its outline lit by the twin stars above. Seeing no Corrector, he turned his attention back to the street ahead.

He should have looked up.

The woman hurtled down from a skybridge crossing the thoroughfare, far above. Seeing her falling, her arms and hands outstretched, Narsk instinctively mashed the throttle. A sudden *thump* jerked the speeder from behind, nearly causing him to slip off again. Seizing a single handlebar with both hands, Narsk forced the speeder bike out of its turn and angled back into the open.

Narsk looked behind him. He'd momentarily thought she'd landed on the vehicle, but there was no sign of her. Maybe she'd made a grab for the seat and slipped to her doom. *About time for it to inconvenience someone else,* he thought. Only, the speeder was still shimmying to and fro. Something was impeding his control. Narsk looked around again—

—and found her, behind and below, clinging to the end of six meters of chain still attached to the speeder. She'd looped a length of it around her arm, and was now riding it like a tether. By the blur of streetlights far beneath, Narsk could see her starting to climb toward him.

The Sith and their chains!

"That's enough!" Finding his needler, Narsk locked his knees against the speeder frame and released the handlebars. With one hand on the chassis, Narsk reached behind and started firing. Darts lanced through the exhaust trail, just missing his stowaway, who angled her body to avoid them. The projectiles' paths terminated out of sight far below on the street.

Narsk swore. A needler was the wrong weapon—but he couldn't very well bring a blaster to a spy mission. Scanning the dial, he found a setting he could use. The pulse-wave darts would detonate seconds after they cleared the barrel, delivering most of their force in her direction. She was nearly to the back of the speeder now, grasping for a handhold. Narsk reset his weapon, steadied himself . . .

. . . and gaped as his pursuer vanished into the darkness. Puzzled, Narsk squinted for a second—only to go flying himself, as the nose of the speeder caromed off a sturdy metal obstacle: another skybridge! The bottom of the speeder smacked the outer guardrail, throwing the entire vehicle end-over-end. Sky and bridge spun consecutively before Narsk's eyes, before blending together in agonizing darkness.

She was human, after all. Narsk awoke to the sight of her as, lit by the burning wreckage of the speeder bike, the woman crossed the wide skybridge toward him. A young adult, dark-complexioned, with short-cropped black hair; a few odd wisps of it blew in the wind. Clad in a laborer's tawny work shirt and dark canvas pants, she blended with the night—and unlike Narsk, she didn't appear any worse for the landing. She hadn't been trying to climb onto the speeder, he realized as he struggled to get to his knees. She'd seen the bridge up ahead, and had been readying to drop away to safety.

Now she strode confidently toward him, looking determined and holding her unlit lightsaber. Forcing himself to stand, Narsk fell on his hairy face. His right leg was sprained, perhaps broken.

And the needler was gone.

Narsk squirmed in panic as he heard the familiar hum from above. He clawed at the roadbed, desperate to avoid the moment he'd so often delayed. This had always been a danger; the risk that came with being special. All those jobs, and any one could have ended like this, with a flash of crimson—

Green.

Green!

Narsk's eyes widened. The lightsaber was green.

"Jedi?" Narsk rolled over and looked at the woman's eyes. Hazel. Wide, alert, focused—but on the right side of madness.

A Jedi. He couldn't believe his luck. A Jedi? *Here?*

He'd heard a single Jedi had recently been on the loose in Sith space. One who had challenged Odion during the Chelloa affair—and who had lately given Daiman fits. Narsk had never met any Jedi, but he knew their reputation—and he knew he never could have hoped to have been discovered by anyone better on Darkknell.

"You're her," Narsk began. "Aren't you? You're *Kerra Holt.*"

The woman didn't answer. Kneeling, she frisked him. In no position to resist, Narsk scanned her face more closely. Yes, it matched the images he'd seen. He licked his pointed teeth. He knew what to do.

"I'm on your side," Narsk said. "I want to destroy Daiman, too."

Ignoring him, the woman pawed at the stealth suit. Amazingly to Narsk—and seemingly so to her—the Mark VI had no rips, although it now had grit to go with its golden splotches. Stepping away with Narsk's pouch, she found the datapad inside.

Eyes skimming the screen, she spoke. "You work for Lord Odion."

Narsk was startled. Her voice was low and rough, not

much more than a whisper. "Odion?" he responded. "What makes you think that? Maybe I'm a revolutionary."

"There are no revolutionaries on Darkknell," she said, voice rising as she deactivated the datapad. "And if there were, they wouldn't be stealing military secrets." Holding the datapad where Narsk could see it, she casually flipped the device into the air and bisected it with a sudden flick of her lightsaber.

Narsk gulped. *All that work!*

"All that work *for Odion*," she said, catching his thought.

"Yes," he said. No sense denying it now, he realized; he might as well hit her with some truth. "I *was* working for Odion. But I'm not an Odionite. It's just a job."

"That's worse," Kerra said, looking down. "You're an *enabler*." She nearly spat the word, causing Narsk to flinch. She yanked his bag from the ground and stepped back.

Narsk forced himself to stand, painful as it was. "Fine," he said, clearing his throat. "You've denied Odion the knowledge. But the important thing is to deny Daiman the knowledge—*and* the warship he's building. And we can do that. Look here, I can show you—"

Narsk stepped toward her and his bag, only to have her raise the lightsaber between them again. "I don't work with Sith," she said.

"I told you, I'm not Sith." He gestured toward the pouch. "Look in the bag. You'll see."

The human deactivated her weapon and reached inside. Seeing her recognize the detonator control for what it was, Narsk flashed a toothy smile. "You see? We have the chance to do something important against Daiman." He began to reach for the controller. "And all I ask is that I be allowed time to—"

"No." In a single, liquid motion, the woman looked

back up Manufacturers' Way, pointed the detonator, and pressed the button.

A flash and a rumble came from the far end of the avenue. Two kilometers away, the opaque skin of the Black Fang heaved for a split second before erupting outward. Metal shards ripped free from the structure, desperate to escape. Thunder followed fire, more than enough noise and light to wake all Xakrea.

Narsk brought a bruised hand to his long nose in horror. *They must have powered up the centrifuge again,* he thought. Fully armed and fueled, *Convergence* would have exploded in an outward spiral. He'd thought that was a possibility before he planted his explosives, but he had always planned to be aboard a freighter lifting off from Darkknell before pressing the button.

Not gawking like an idiot on a skybridge with a Jedi.

"You fool!" Narsk yelled. "Do you realize what you've done?"

The woman regarded the blaze with mild satisfaction. "Yes."

Narsk wilted, forgetting the pain in his leg. He looked to the rooftop plazas at either end of the skybridge. No authorities were here yet, but they soon would be. And still, the Jedi seemed pleased with herself.

Idiot, Narsk thought. *No wonder the Sith ran the Jedi out of the Outer Rim.* He barked at her. "Is that it? Are we done here?"

"No," she said, igniting her lightsaber and waving it in his direction. *"Strip."*

The woman neatly slipped the folded Mark VI back into Narsk's bag—although neither suit nor bag was particularly neat anymore, smeared and stinking of paint. "You've really made a mess of this thing," she said. "Is this stuff permanent?"

"I don't know," Narsk snarled. He didn't care about

the suit anymore. The real authorities were out, screaming in their airspeeders toward the cauldron that was the testing center. And here he was: naked, but for his shorts, sitting in a garbage bin in a shadowy section of the plaza. The woman had marched him there, taken the stealth suit, and bound his wrists.

It was not where he wanted to be with Sith on the way.

"How can you do this? You *know* what they'll do to me if they catch me!" Seeing her beginning to close the lid, Narsk grew more frantic. "You can't do this! You Jedi are supposed to be about fair play and decency! *You're supposed to be a Jedi!*"

The woman paused. "What?" Kerra Holt said, suddenly miffed. "I'm not *locking* it."

The lid snapped shut above him.

CHAPTER TWO

"I declare the dawn."

With Daiman's words, the sun rose.

"I declare the dawn now, as I did, standing in the waters of darkness long ago." The voice grew louder as it wafted through the streets of Xakrea, beckoning to dayshift workers leaving for the transit hubs. Their liege had prepared another day for them.

Seventy meters tall, the image of Daiman looked down upon his works and smiled. Colossal holographic hands opened just as the first rays of Knel'char I crested the city skyline. Product of sixty-four holoprojectors—and easily the single largest nonmilitary consumer of energy on Darkknell—the sparkling image rendered the giant in surprising detail. Above were the confident, piercing eyes, blue and amber, just like the stars, and the short crop of fair, golden hair. Even the talons molded to the fingertips of his right hand appeared in shimmering relief. The imaging specialists had done their work well.

Seven marble statues depicting Daiman's rise to power and prominence ringed the image's base. Huge themselves—yet dwarfs next to the crackling titan above—each stone figure looked down one of Xakrea's major avenues, radiating from the central plaza. *Daiman's Rise* faced Celestial Way, gazing the long kilometers toward the palace. *Daiman at Chelloa* triumphantly faced

Mining Way, home to many of Darkknell's processing plants. Daiman's voice seemed to come from all the statues in unison. *"I have decided the sun will shine for twenty-three hours today, with nine hours of night to follow. The warmth of summer I give to you, and light from the heavens."*

Kerra Holt was impressed. She thought the display could have been more effective only had several of the city blocks not been burning to the ground as the holograph spoke.

Hood pulled over her head, Kerra slipped from one doorway to another as she made her way back home. It had been a mistake, allowing the chase with the Bothan to carry so far down Manufacturers' Way. To get home, she had to pass what was left of the Black Fang. What had been a lopsided pyramid was now a tangle of molten girders, with blazes still raging on many levels.

"My cosmic eyes will rest upon the people of the southlands today, but know that I am with you always," Big Daiman said. *"You are The Encumbered. You are arms of my creation, extensions of my will. You know your functions."* As far as Kerra could tell, those functions right now seemed to be running around in confusion and screaming at random passersby. At least, that's what Daiman's sentries were doing. Normally stern and forbidding agents of order were dashing back and forth across the plaza, unsure of what to do without divine guidance.

"Never forget, my will is . . . ."

No one heard what Daiman's will was, because the blazing research center chose that moment to tip completely over in an exhausted faint. By the time those around recovered their feet—and their hearing—the loudspeakers throughout Xakrea had gone silent.

They'd heard it all before. Kerra used to hear the spiel every morning on the way to her job at the munitions plant, before she moved to later shifts. On all the worlds of the Daimanate, listeners were assured: Daiman controlled everything that happened in his realm.

Those listeners might be less sure if they were on the plaza this morning, Kerra thought. One of Daiman's thugs was on fire. She recognized him. A terror in her neighborhood for as long as she'd resided there, now the hulking guard staggered about, screaming in pain. Kerra froze for a moment, unsure of what to do. Evil minion or no, the creature was suffering.

She stepped into the street, only to be knocked aside by the advance of three of his fellow sentries. Remembering her cover identity, Kerra began to exhale, relieved that someone else had gone to help him.

Nope, they shot him. Seeing the thug fall dead at his would-be rescuers' feet, Kerra rolled her eyes and retreated into an alley. Sith space was like this everywhere: a place of sudden violence—almost completely devoid of compassion or remorse. She'd never understand it. But she didn't have to understand it to win her fight.

And now she had a stealth suit.

A cracked window heaved upward. Lithely, Kerra slipped back into her home of the past few weeks. The only things inside were a pair of bedrolls, her duffel, and a stand for the portable glow lamp she had to share with Gub Tengo's young granddaughter. From the look of the crumpled blankets in the corner, Tan was already gone for the morning. The room wouldn't have been big enough for a closet back in the Jedi academy, a place where the students were preparing to live with no possessions. Here on Darkknell, it had to accommodate two.

Setting down the Bothan's pouch, Kerra peeked through the open doorway into the main room. The old Sullustan was there, asleep in his chair again before a mass of documents. His arm stuck out at a right angle, his worn hand shaking as his fingers clutched an invisible pen.

Kerra edged into the room long enough to douse the glow lamp and push him back from the table. Flimsiplast cels fluttered to the floor. Kerra winced. Every part of Gub's job was insane. Not just what he had to do—but how *much* of it he had to do. On other worlds with long rotational periods, societies made some allowances for species that were used to standard-length days. Not so for Daiman's realm. The Sith Lord saw a day with thirty-two hours as a chance to get in another work shift.

Stealing back into her chambers, Kerra hung the ragged sheet that served as a door and reached for the gold-stained bag. For all the technology it contained, the Bothan's bodysuit had folded up nicely. The label was just inside the seam. CYRICEPT.

Kerra hadn't been gone that long from Republic space, but somehow, seeing something as simple as a familiar commercial trade name felt refreshing. And a stalwart firm, at that. As the Sith had advanced farther on the Outer Rim, other corporations had tried to deal with the new "locals," usually to their ultimate regret. The more vital to Republic security a company was, the more the Defense Ministry usually had to cajole it to relocate. But Cyricept had repeatedly pulled its operations back from the frontier without being asked. Maybe it was because their whole stealth-systems business was about staying low and keeping out of trouble. Whatever the reason, Kerra was overjoyed to see the suit now, even in its despoiled condition. Her supplies from the Republic were limited to the clothes she wore and the lightsaber in her knapsack.

That was never supposed to have been the case. Jedi Master Vannar Treece's venture into Daiman's space was supposed to have been a surgical strike: short and well supplied. An inspiring figure, Treece had led volunteers into Sith space several times, taking upon himself missions the larger Jedi Order could no longer perform. The

Sith in the outer reaches had grown so robust that the Republic, already weakened by the Candorian plague, had largely written off everything beyond an inner security cordon. It had even deactivated the interstellar relays that allowed communications with the outside. Whole swaths of space lay abandoned.

The Republic government and the Jedi Order weren't against Treece's raids. The need for them was obvious. But the woman who headed both bodies, Chancellor Gennara, knew well that her fearful people wouldn't tolerate her sending large groups of Jedi Knights on offense when all were needed to protect the home front. Treece had cleverly found a way around that. Each standard year, Jedi Knights had been serving three months on law-and-order patrol and nine months at the frontier. But sixteen days were allotted for travel between those assignments, a figure that remained the same even as the boundaries of the Republic contracted. And, as in peacetime, the travel arrangements remained in the hands of individual Jedi Knights.

That had given Treece an opening. There were enough Jedi volunteers in transit at any moment that Treece could usually get a team of them to rendezvous at a jumping-off point. That allowed a few days for a quick raid—usually one where no casualties were expected—before the Jedi returned to their designated duties.

The results of Treece's raids generally pleased the Chancellor. The morale boost came cheaply; all ships and munitions involved came from private contributions. It was a much different reaction than Jedi Knight Revan had received, centuries earlier, in his own extracurricular efforts against the Mandalorians. But the circumstances, Kerra recalled, were different. The Sith were evil; the Mandalorians just had an attitude problem.

The logistics were complicated, but Vannar Treece had someone he could rely on in Kerra. Vannar—she had always been on a first-name basis with him—had rescued her from Aquilaris years earlier, just after that planetary paradise fell to forces led by the future Lord Odion. Vannar, sensing the child Kerra's potential as both a Jedi and a motivated opponent of the Sith, became her sponsor and mentor. She had lost her family, but found a cause.

Kerra always wondered if he'd given her the work because he'd thought it would be therapeutic for her. No matter—it was. At twelve, she coordinated travel assignments for volunteers. At fourteen, she helped him raise donations. In the last three years, she'd taken charge of outfitting each group, making sure everything from blaster power cells to medpacs were aboard ship in abundance. In a short time, Kerra had learned everything necessary to run a volunteer paramilitary organization—all while working to become a Jedi Knight.

It had been a busy adolescence.

But she'd never joined any of the raids herself. Vannar had forbidden that while she was still a Padawan. Returning to Sith space was too emotional a mission for her, and Vannar knew it. So for years, she'd lived vicariously through him and his allies, taking some solace in the knowledge that she, in some small way, was helping the people she'd left behind.

When Kerra became a Jedi Knight the day before her eighteenth birthday, Vannar had remained reluctant to send her into action. But a dire warning from Sith space had taken that decision from him. Vannar called upon every Jedi available for a vital mission on extremely short notice. Kerra was available—and, as it proved, essential.

Kerra had found the addition of fieldwork to her duties enormously satisfying. All those forgotten, busy weeks preparing the way for others to strike at the Sith suddenly gained amplified meaning. Now *she* was the weapon, finally to be used in places she'd fled from when powerless.

If anything, she prepared even harder for the mission. With Vannar and the other volunteers at her side, she'd have everything she needed.

Today, on Darkknell, what she needed was *them*. And they were gone forever.

The mission at Chelloa had been a disaster. Everyone had been lost. *Everyone*. Daiman's forces hadn't even been the cause. Vannar's team had become trapped in the madness that was Sith space. The problem with making only occasional forays into the region was they didn't know what they didn't know. Vannar had valued surprise in ensuring that his Jedi Knights got in and out quickly and safely. But he'd forgotten that *he* could be surprised, too.

Only Kerra had survived, with none of the weapons, medicine, or supplies she had so carefully gathered. They, and the starship they'd arrived in, had disappeared into a sea of fire. Kerra didn't even know how to get home. She'd memorized the hyperspace route they'd taken into Daiman's territory, but that terminated at the planet they'd raided, a place now under such heavy guard she could never return to it.

She'd been tempted to end her own journey soon afterward. Residents lived in constant despair, and meeting both Daiman and Odion confirmed for her that things could never improve. Death was better than survival for those living underfoot—and, perhaps, for a Jedi alone. Better to go down fighting.

It had taken making friends here—including one surprising, selfless individual—to change Kerra's trajectory. "You're no good to us dead," Vannar had always told her. That applied, too, to the people living under Sith rule. She was no good to *them* dead, either. Suicide-by-Sith wasn't the answer. She had to live.

In a curious way, Kerra's change of heart had been like another Vannar Treece raid. It stabbed into the darkness

that had clouded her soul and offered hope. Defeating
the Sith wasn't the point; helping the people was. Fighting Sith was certainly one way the Jedi could help the
downtrodden, but it wasn't the only way. Yes, the people
needed bold, dramatic acts of the Vannar variety, but
they also needed more than gestures. They needed things
that did immediate good: a tall order for a team of Jedi,
much less one acting alone. She'd have to manufacture
her own opportunities. That required a plan.

Planning, she was good at.

Kerra was already in Daiman's realm; he became the
first target. Her feelings against Odion were stronger, but
for that reason she didn't trust them. Anger over her childhood's premature end had already led her astray once.
Daiman was younger, and while he wasn't as physically
powerful as his monstrous sibling, he was, in his own way,
just as much of a threat.

Daiman was a creature utterly without empathy. At
the academy, Kerra had studied the notion of solipsism
as it related to Sith teachings; none other than Darth
Ruin had expounded upon it years before. Sith philosophy promoted the glorification of self and the subjugation of others. The young lord took it to a deranged
extreme, declaring that existence was some game constructed by—what? Some version of himself on a higher
plane, pitting Daiman's mortal body against artificial ob-
stacles it had dreamed up, like physics, and evil siblings.
Daiman's empire depended on the labor of others, but the
lives of the others didn't matter to him.

The parasite needed to be separated from the host. But
first, its spread had to be contained.

Kerra found a good target in the munitions industry,
which allowed Daiman both to wage war and to oppress
people on multiple worlds at once. It was better than
striking at the military directly. Even if she somehow
found a way to land a devastating blow, her worry was

that Odion or another opportunistic neighbor might pour across the cosmic border, hurting more innocents still. Better to rot Daiman's system from within, leaving the illusion of strength to his peers but an empty shell inside. By the time the regime collapsed, she hoped, most of the civilians would be out of harm's way.

Her weeks since losing her Master on Chelloa had included strikes against weapons plants on a string of worlds. In some cases, she'd been able to free the slave laborers and their families, but those opportunities had grown less frequent as she'd approached the center of Daiman's realm. In the metropolis, there was no wilderness into which freed natives could flee. But Darkknell was obviously her ultimate goal. By striking Daiman's military research efforts here, she could still factories on a dozen worlds at once.

She'd arrived on Darkknell as she had on the other worlds, disguised as an itinerant laborer on assignment. She'd blanched at that more than once. Disguise wasn't her forte. Persuasion, mesmerism, misdirection—these were skills for a Jedi who couldn't master a lightsaber or blaster, not for an accomplished fighter like Kerra. Vannar had used those ploys only to achieve military surprise; Kerra could hardly stomach going through her daily life undercover. But she'd had little choice. Daiman might doubt her sentience, but he knew she was part of the great game he'd devised for himself—and his Force-sensitive Correctors would be able to sense her presence. She had to be on her guard at all times.

It had been happenstance that she'd spotted the Bothan while scouting the Black Fang herself, nights earlier. The spy was good, but he'd gotten too comfortable, selecting the same nearby rooftop to change into his stealth gear. She'd simply waited for her chance. His sabotage of the building was a terrific bonus, especially as it came at an hour when only Daiman's true believers would be inside.

She was almost sorry to leave the spy to his fate, but no ally of Odion could be a friend of hers. Odion was both brutal and insipid. It was no wonder half his followers were suicidal.

Kerra scraped at the fabric of the stealth suit. Tiny raised lines crisscrossed its surface, leaving countless pits in between for its spectral baffles. Most of the paint clung to the ribbed fabric, she saw. It would be a problem. With his main military research lab in flames, Daiman would be doubly on his guard—enough so to make her next move impossible without artificial help. But the suit wouldn't be much in the invisibility department without a proper cleaning.

She flipped the suit inside out. A manufacturer's label, but no care instructions. *That would be too easy,* she thought. She was hardly in a position to call the manufacturer. Maybe she could ask someone at work, down at the—

"*What are you doing here?*"

Kerra yanked the fabric close to her chest as she recognized her host's voice. "Just . . . just about to do some laundry," she said, folding the suit over quickly and jamming it behind her bedroll. She turned to find Gub standing in the doorway, curtain clenched in his fist. *So much for privacy.* "What can I do for you?"

"I remembered I had a message for you," Gub growled. His voice was a gravel road, aggravated by years with a tiny water ration. "But my granddaughter said you weren't here." Droopy eyebrows flared into a weak scowl. "You went *out.*"

He says that like it's a bad word, Kerra thought. *Well, maybe here, it is.* "I . . . was called for the wraith-watch," she said. It was what they called it down at the munitions plant—the one shift with no daylight, whatever the season. During sharply tilted Darkknell's winter solstice, it was the morbid middle third of a twenty-four-hour night. "I had to go in."

"That's a lie!" Gub yanked at the curtain, ripping it free from the doorjamb. It fell to the duracrete floor.

Kerra edged backward, almost as wary of the little creature's wrath as she was of any Sith Lord. They'd had their bad moments since she'd turned up here offering to tutor his granddaughter for room and board. She was desperate not to let this moment get out of hand. "Oh?" she finally asked.

"Yes," he said, staring her down before finally kneeling to pick up the sheet. "I know that isn't true, young human, because the message was from someone at your work—someone *on* the wraithwatch, asking you to come in this morning. You clearly could not have already been there."

Kerra sighed. Daiman allowed his slaves no communications devices; couriers handled everything, even if it meant productivity suffered by messages being delayed. The odds of someone showing up while she was out skulking were long, but evidently not long enough. Kerra searched for words. She didn't want to use the Force to persuade Gub; not when they lived together. He'd figure that out eventually, and she was trying to use the Force as little as possible so as not to attract the Correctors' attention. But she couldn't see what else to do.

"It isn't the first time," Gub said, folding the sheet over his arm. "Tan sleeps in the same room with you. She knows you leave at night. The girl's been covering for you—"

"Master Tengo, don't blame—"

"She imagines you have some great romance going," he continued. "Why anyone would choose to bring more people into this world is beyond me!"

Kerra stood and managed a blush. *Okay, that's my way out.* "I—I'm sorry. It won't happen again."

Gub straightened on his leg braces. Looking at Kerra, he exhaled audibly. "Well, we're all to suffer, now. You have to leave to work your shifts—and I expect you back here to tutor Tan as you're supposed to, when she gets home from *her* work." At twelve, Tan only had to work eight hours a day. "And think about me! I shall have to make my own breakfast!"

At that, the Sullustan hobbled out, taking her door with him.

Kerra plopped back down on her bed cushion and rubbed her temples. More insanity. Shaking her head, she looked at her duffel—and gulped. The handle of her lightsaber gleamed in the low light. She'd never stuffed it all the way into the bag on entering. She slapped it fully inside, then punched the bag a couple of times for good measure.

One more day without sleep. One more day under-cover. And probably a lot more days than that before she could do anything substantive against Daiman. She might never survive at this rate.

"You'll know which skills you need when you need them," Vannar had always said. Well, he was right about that. Kerra's worry was that she didn't have those skills at all.

Or the patience.

CHAPTER THREE

"You understand why we're doing this, Brigadier Rusher," the factory administrator said. "We're loyal Daimanites, through to the core. And that's why we want to make sure we serve His Lordship in the best way possible."

The redheaded human in the entry hall rocked back and forth on shined boots. "Of course."

Administrator Lubboon stared out the apartment window at the dense smoke hanging over the city. "I've been running the Plasteelworks here on Darkknell since the days of Lord Chagras . . . or those are the memories that have been given to me by Lord Daiman. I'm the first Duros to hold such a position. And I've never been a shirker. Daiman created The Encumbered to serve him, and serve him we do." The tall green figure turned and gestured to his furnishings. "I may live better than many, but it makes no difference to me whether my son was created for a place on my production line—or on the front lines of battle. I know why we exist."

"Oh, of course." Brigadier Jarrow Rusher looked to the wall and smirked. It was a different story in every Sith Lord's territory, but he'd forgotten what a weird customer Daiman was, sowing the fantasy that all creation was the figment of his warped imagination. Rusher had scars older than Daiman's twenty-five years, but never mind: those were apparently figments of *his* imagination. *Maybe all those city blocks on fire when I landed were hallucinations, too.*

"But we know our child has talent," Lubboon continued, crossing to the divan and placing his hand on his wife's shoulder. "And that means—that *must* mean—that a position with you is what His Lordship intended for our son. It would be a waste of material otherwise." He looked up, tentatively. "Don't you agree, General?"

"Oh, yes." Turning to face the couple, Rusher spoke in his best sales voice. "That's exactly why you want your son in Rusher's Brigade, Master Lubboon. There's no place better for someone to find his potential." He fingered his lapel, subtly angling the silver pins on his trench coat so that they glinted in the warm light. The Duros had brought out the extra lumens today, he saw. Indoor light was rationed on Darkknell as everything else—even for the relatively well off.

"We really would like our son to be in a place that challenges him," the prim Duros woman said, pressing green fingers to green cheeks. "*Offworld.*"

Twirling the brassy knob atop his wooden walking stick, Rusher smiled. They'd reached that part. "Of course. And you're probably asking whether going with us is safe." He turned to the caf dispenser, meticulously set out before him. "Well, I'm not going to lie," he said, pouring himself a drink. "We're at war—and in war, people get hurt. But if you have to be on a battlefield, ma'am, there's no better place to be than next to a laser artillery piece."

The brigadier elaborated on the quality of his armaments, drawing pictures in the air with a gloved hand. He'd known recruiters who brought formal holographic presentations, but it never seemed necessary to Rusher. When people in Sith space saw a ruddy, reasonably young man with all the limbs he was born with in charge of a military outfit, they inferred some level of competence—or luck.

And if that failed, he had a bigger gun. Now it was time to use it.

"What's more," he said, "our shipboard fatalities in transit are zero. No one dies on the way to the fight. No one." He raised the cup to his lips and paused deliberately before continuing. "It's because there are no Sith aboard."

The Lubboons gasped. *"None?"*

"No adepts, no adherents, no lieutenants, no grunts. We're *specialists,* Administrator. Independent militia units like ours are the fasteners that hold His Lordship's whole military scheme together."

Pairs of bulbous red eyes locked on each other before returning to him. "We've never heard of such a thing. No Sith?"

Rusher sipped cloudy liquid from the cup. Surprisingly, there was a taste to it. "Look, you operate a factory here on Darkknell. Of course, you've got your Daimanite authorities looking over your shoulder all the time, to ensure your progress, check quality, and all that. You wouldn't have it any other way, I'm sure." He waved in the general direction of the spaceport. "But the Kelligdyd Five Thousand cannon is an advanced piece of weaponry. It takes skilled squads of merc—of *specialists* to land them on the battlefield, assemble them, and put them into action."

Setting the cup down, he took the walking stick in both hands. "One bonding pin out of place, one power coupler misconnected, and you've got seventeen tons of *scrap* just sitting out there. So we're our own judges of quality. If we don't do the work right on our own? We're already *dead.*" Rusher rapped his cane on the floor to punctuate the statement.

"Oh, my!"

Rusher grinned. He hadn't needed the cane for years, but the public liked it. Same for the early gray in his sideburns and beard. "But we do the work right, ma'am. Like I say, we're experts. We don't need babysitting. We're not a regular part of Daiman's structure at all." He caught himself. "Which, uh . . . is, of course, how he intends it. Being the creator, and all."

The male Duros sank to the couch beside his wife in disbelief. Rusher could see the words passing silently between them: *No Sith.*

Rusher chuckled. *Right on target. Again.* "And our ship? Why, it's a pleasure palace. You saw *Diligence* on her approach over Xakrea this morning. There isn't a better vessel in the sector."

"I'm sure we wouldn't know. But if you say so—"

"I do. Many do. I built her myself, you know. I've got people who never want to leave—which is why openings are so few." Rusher turned to see an oval-shaped human in the doorway. "Ah. This is Dackett, our ship's master. He'll be taking care of your son until he's assigned. Assigned to one of our gun squads—or, perhaps, to my headquarters unit."

"Headquarters?" The Lubboons audibly cooed. "Is that possible? I mean, he's a bright boy . . ."

"Then there's no telling how far he'll go," Rusher said. Staying out of the main room, Dackett merely nodded, oversized ears crested with tufts of white hair. Rusher heard someone approach from the Lubboons' bedchambers. "Ah. Here comes our soldier now, I think?"

Taller even than his parents, teenage Beadle Lubboon strode confidently into the room, wearing a fresh pair of neatly pressed work dungarees, standard uniform for youth laborers. Nodding to his parents, he offered a mock salute to the visitors and leaned against the caf cart—which promptly gave way under his weight, collapsing along with the gawky kid and several pots of beige water.

Administrator Lubboon looked at his son, mortified, as his wife knelt to help pick up the wreckage. "Bound for your headquarters unit," Dackett whispered to Rusher in the doorway.

"We'll be lucky if he doesn't take out the whole ammo magazine," Rusher replied.

Shooing his aide to the outer hall, Rusher gave the Lubboons some time to compose their child. But, turning back, he saw there wasn't enough time in Darkknell's ridiculous day to manage that trick. While his mother dabbed at the stains on his shirt with her handkerchief, Beadle tried to extricate his hand from a tin carafe. The operation took nearly a minute, time during which the administrator's face grew longer than it already was. "Sorry about that, sir," the squirming boy said.

"You should see what happens to my setup when the bombs start falling," Rusher said, summoning the smile again. "And tell your parents not to worry. Like Garbelian said at Averam: 'War ain't a talent show.' "

The Lubboons didn't bother to confer. "I think we're settled on this, Brigadier Rusher," the father said. "Our boy will be in good hands."

Rusher beamed. "Very glad." He slapped a hand on young Beadle's shoulder. "Welcome to the team," he said, shaking the boy's still-dripping hand vigorously. In the same movement, he edged Beadle aside and looked directly at the administrator. "There's just the matter of terms."

The elder Lubboon straightened. "I was expecting this."

"You manage Daiman's hydraulic lift factory. *Diligence* needs some new drives. We need four or five—"

"*Six!*" came a voice from the hallway.

"—we need *six* new drives, for our off-loading assemblies." Rusher gently but forcibly sat Beadle down on the couch and continued to speak over the teenager's head. "They're key to getting *Diligence* safely off Darkknell—*with your son, of course.*"

"Of course," Administrator Lubboon said, drily. "It will be . . . difficult. All we produce is for Daiman, of course."

"And that's who we're fighting for." *This is how it works,* he didn't add. He didn't need to.

Five minutes later, Rusher eased out of the Lubboons' apartment, walking stick at his side. Dackett was in the hall, waiting for him. Rusher tossed him the cane. "Nice enough place," he said.

"Them that has, sir, them that has." Dackett smirked. "Daiman lets them live like that?"

"Guess he throws a few crumbs to the true believers. And a good thing—for us." Rusher nabbed the datapad from Dackett's waistcoat pocket and located an address. "You'll have what you need by nightfall—whenever the blazes that is around here."

Rusher began walking down the hall when the ship's master called out. "Oh, yeah—there's something else."

"What is it?"

"Novallo just called from *Diligence,*" Dackett said. "She's chased down that problem on the port landing assembly. Wasn't the gimbals after all—we need the hydraulic accumulator on that side changed out before we lift off again."

"A complete replacement?" Rusher scratched his beard. "She can't jerry-rig something?"

"Negative."

"Pricey."

"Yeah."

"Tell her it's covered," Rusher said, cocking an eyebrow as he turned back toward the apartment door. "Let's see if they've got any other kids."

Narsk woke up.

That fact alone meant they didn't know who he was. The fact that he still didn't know *where* he was, though, meant he was in very deep trouble.

The Jedi had been true to her word. She hadn't locked the garbage bin. That hadn't made it any easier to get out of, though, with his hands bound behind his back. It had taken painful minutes to force his way out, and even then he'd landed on his bad leg clambering down. His cry had attracted the attention of Daiman's sentries, checking out the speeder bike debris on the nearby skybridge. Bound and half naked, Narsk wasn't likely to escape attention.

Daiman's thugs had rounded up a number of individuals from the streets of Xakrea in the hours following the destruction of his testing center. Narsk had met some when they were hauling him away in the transport. Most were homeless invalids, unable to work; Daiman usually didn't bother to liquidate those.

As the first day had passed, he'd grown more confident. They'd all gone to the sentry station on Administrative Way for questioning, where a Corrector had interviewed each of the bystanders. Several vagrants were chucked down the front stairs of the station to the street, excused from further questioning. Narsk had hoped they'd do the same with him.

Waiting for his reprieve, he'd finally given in to sleep that evening. A mistake. For later that night, he'd woken not in the seamy cell of the station, but strapped to a stone table wet with sweat in a marble-walled room. He was almost relieved when four of Daiman's burgundy-clad Correctors entered. It meant he was still on Darkknell. He'd had a nightmare of being found by Odion, furious over his failure to rescue the secrets of the late, lamented *Convergence*. No wonder he'd awakened with drenched fur.

Correctors buzzed in and out of the room through portals visible to him only as black spots at the edge of his vision. The straps were so tight he couldn't turn his head—and it was what was inside his head that held their interest.

Narsk couldn't imagine how he could have confused the Jedi with a Corrector. The Correctors walked around broadcasting their presence through the Force, making sure he knew they had the ability to enter his mind at will. The Jedi, meanwhile, hadn't put any mental pressure on him at all, probably for fear of being spotted—by Correctors.

But she would have seen them coming, Narsk thought. *No wonder she's been able to hide here.*

The Correctors departed for a moment, allowing him to think more freely about what had happened. How long had the Jedi been shadowing him? She had to be Kerra Holt. Had she just happened upon him? Had she told anyone else he was there? Did they have her now? The answers mattered. She could give him away.

"*You,*" an Arkanian-accented voice said. Narsk rolled his bloodshot eyes back to see the purple cowl of one of the Correctors who'd interviewed him before. "You were found in Manufacturers' District without leave, without clothes."

"I told you," Narsk said, "I was mugged. It's why I don't have my work permit on me." He repeated yet again the details of his cover identity. *Machine tool operator. Transferred from Nilash. Trying to arrive at work early.* The words seemed to form a structure of their own in his mind, a protective surface covering his true mission—and the truer, more secret mission beneath that one. Narsk saw the Arkanian's white, iris-less eyes widen as the Corrector leaned over him. Another mental invasion was about to begin.

Suddenly the familiar figure leaned back, to be replaced by another, just out of his sight, behind the head of the table. "This is the one?"

"As my lord knows."

As my lord knows. Narsk lurched against the restraints, nearly cracking his clavicle. *Lord Daiman!*

"There is something in you," said the same voice from the sunrises and sunsets. Golden talons molded to human fingertips scraped the side of Narsk's face. "There is something in you. It must come out."

The Correctors had rifled through Narsk's mind in anger. That was an assault he was mentally prepared for. Compartmentalization exercises had helped him to bury what was important; in their eagerness to prove their dominance, the Sith adepts had missed everything important. But Daiman seemed indifferent, casually riffling through Narsk's mind with all the interest of a window-shopper.

I created this mind, Daiman seemed to say. The unspoken words echoed in Narsk's flared ears. Daiman believed he had created Narsk's mind, just as he might have programmed a droid—and while he might not have immediate access to all the information in the Bothan's head, the Sith Lord felt perfectly within his rights to go looking for it now.

An unbidden image appeared in Narsk's mind. Dark hair. Brown skin. Glistening, determined eyes. And *green light*—

"The Jedi!"

Daiman released his mental hold on Narsk, who had never once seen his captor. "The errant Knight is here," Daiman said, startled. "On Darkknell!"

Narsk's whiskers bristled upward. For the first time since the night before, something in the mess had worked to his advantage. *They haven't caught her yet. Maybe they won't.*

"Yes," Narsk said, panting, his mouth dry. "It was a woman with a lightsaber." His eyes narrowed. "I feared to tell you, my lord. Her presence here—I didn't understand it. It frightened me. I tried to run when I saw her. Tried to warn someone . . ." The story flowed seamlessly into his tale of a random attack. His shame, he said, had prevented him from revealing all before. Such a person should never have bested a true Daimanite.

Daiman stepped back from the table. Narsk hoped he was considering the story. It was almost too much to hope for to be set free. But if there was anyone he needed to convince, Daiman was the one.

Narsk's heart fell when another Corrector entered from another portal. The spy heard Daiman inquire, "What is it?"

"As my lord knows," the new Corrector said, using what Narsk imagined was a standard form for addressing the theoretically omniscient, "a package has just been discovered on a rooftop near the testing center. It was hidden beneath a vent cover. A bundle containing clothes and a travel permit. The holo-imprint matches the prisoner. As my lord knows."

"So he had been near the testing center. Kilometers from where he was found?"

"As my lord knows."

The shadow of Daiman fell on Narsk again. Only this time, the shadow was not cast by light, but by darkness. Narsk struggled. He'd been told he could only protect his secrets from Daiman with a wall of will, a defiant insistence that his brain was his, and his alone.

You're not sentient, Daiman said in his mind. *Don't pretend to be.*

Narsk screamed.

*   *   *

"They're here for the girl!"

Kerra froze on the steps when she heard her neighbor's voice. Tall, shadowy figures had just entered Gub Tengo's apartment at the far end of the long basement hall. She couldn't make out any details about them, but they'd certainly attracted the attention of the other residents, still buzzing in the halls. *They're here for the girl.*

Not waiting to inquire, Kerra twirled and dashed back up the steps to the streets. None of it made sense. She hadn't felt any malevolent presence while entering the borrat warren that was Gub's apartment block. And Daiman's Correctors weren't exactly keeping a low profile. Far from it.

She'd seen them, earlier, in the transport station, making examples of the poor wretches they'd rousted from the factories. They'd been doing it for five days, at every shift change so the commuters could see. None of the harassed had anything to do with the destruction of the testing center, but she figured Daiman probably knew that. Two of the "Faulty Encumbered" had been ripped from her own workplace earlier in the day. One had recently criticized the work schedule; the other, a Snivvian grandmother, had accidentally used an offhand expression invoking the spirits of her ancestors. Both were candidates for a public form of "correction" involving alternating bouts of mental and physical abuse. Spectacle always served Daiman when something went wrong.

Kerra had wanted to leap the platform and do something, there and then, but she'd learned her lesson since Chelloa. Gub and Tan didn't deserve to be endangered over something they knew nothing about. It had been risky even moving in with them. After arriving on Darkknell, she'd looked for someone who needed a boarder; then, their home had seemed the perfect cover. But now, as she ducked outside, it felt like the worst idea ever. She couldn't make this mistake again.

Vannar had said it: *"Keep saying 'next time,' Kerra, and someday there might not be one waiting."*

Kerra doubled back behind the apartment building, an iridium-processing plant long since retired. The idea of using an old factory for housing always seemed noxious to her, but she was glad of the place now, with its many ways in and out. The two ankle-level windows of Gub's place lay ahead, just behind the sad little gnawroots he'd planted to supplement their rations. Kerra had never entered this way in daylight before, but there wasn't any choice.

Seeing Tan absent, Kerra slipped in and examined her duffel. Yes, everything was still there. Fingering her lightsaber, she listened for the voices beyond the recently replaced privacy curtain. Gub was out there, along with someone else—voices excited, but not distressed. Tucking the weapon into the deep pocket inside her work vest, she allowed herself to breathe. *Maybe it's not so bad after—*

"Hey!"

The curtain jerked back, causing Kerra to reach abruptly for the bulge in her vest. Wide black eyes peered up at her from waist level. Kerra relaxed as she recognized her young charge. "You scared me, Tan."

"I didn't know you were home," the Sullustan girl said, "but I'm glad you are." Normally a bundle of energy, Tan was nearly bursting today, her young jowls curled upward in absolute joy. "They're here! They're here for *me*!"

Kerra could only look down in puzzlement as the girl grabbed her by the wrist and yanked her into the main room. Seven eyes suddenly stared back. Old Gub stood before two taller beings in the doorway. A male Gran peered at her curiously, his trio of dark eyes curling on leathery stalks. The other, an Ishi Tib female, gave a squawk of mild surprise, her lidless yellow eyes shining in the low light. Both, Kerra noticed, wore blinking cybernetic implants at their temples.

"Pardon me," Gub grumbled, turning away from the visitors. He glared at Kerra. "What were you doing in there? I didn't see you come in!"

"Didn't you?" Kerra changed the subject, hoping he would forget. "Who are your guests?" She bowed her head toward the visitors.

The Gran seemed pleased, leaf-like ears wiggling above his implants. "Ah. You must be the tutor." His face curled into a tiny smile, about the most his narrow snout could manage. "Ler-Laar Joom, at your service—and my colleague is Eraffa. We're from Industrial Heuristics."

Kerra looked at the badge proffered by the Gran. "You're salespeople?"

"Certainly not," Ler-Laar said. Beside him, the star-faced Ishi Tib gurgled something like a guffaw. Somehow, the cybernetic devices were allowing them to communicate.

Gub, unhappy at the interruption, glared at Kerra. "They're the reason I took you in, human. They're talent scouts," Gub said, "here to see Tan."

Talent scouts. The stresses of the previous minutes evaporating, Kerra's eyes narrowed. The twelve-year-old Sullustan spent her mornings in one of Daiman's scavenge plants, disassembling the technological detritus of decades past for salvage. But even the supervisor at that miserable place had noticed Tan's acuity with electronics, loaning the girl operator's guide datapads found in Republic wrecks to peruse. With Gub too busy discovering the creator of the universe in scraps from the trash, he'd hired Kerra to teach Tan how to read. Any advance in her skills might mean a softer future. Assembling blasters, perhaps.

These visitors, however, had more in mind. Kerra looked more closely at the Ishi Tib's badge, of a kind she'd never seen before. The identification allowed newcomers to move about on Darkknell; it would be worth getting hold of one, she thought. She'd never heard of Industrial Heuristics, either. Daiman dissolved most corporations he captured, but she'd seen a few commercial names operating in his space. This was a new one.

"Our headquarters is in Lord Bactra's region," Ler-Laar said, sensing her confusion. "Lord Daiman has generously provided a dispensation allowing us to recruit in his territory."

Not for nothing, Kerra thought. "You're taking Tan away?"

"We mean to *transform* Tan." The jade-skinned Ishi Tib squawked something in evident agreement.

"This morning," Ler-Laar went on, "at her place of work, we evaluated her proficiency on the advice of her superiors. And we have determined to a mathematical certainty her talent, her destiny. That which makes her special." The Gran clasped his bony hands together. *"Bombsights."*

"Bombsights?"

"Yes. Lord Daiman's fighters use precision-guided munitions—but for the most part, the guidance comes from the weapons themselves. To keep the vehicles small and nimble, as few systems are built on board as possible."

That much is true, Kerra thought, rolling her eyes. She'd ridden in one of Daiman's flying death traps soon after her arrival in Sith space. She was surprised he'd bothered with oxygen.

The Gran continued, "Generally, gravity-assisted bombs are smart enough to find their targets on their own—but in the presence of electronic countermeasures, it can help to have manual guidance." Ler-Laar gestured to Tan, now blushing so hard her skin had turned a pale brown. "Tan will join an offworld team devoted to developing the next generation of optics."

"For Daiman?" Kerra asked.

"For whomever he chooses," Ler-Laar said. "She is his to dispose of, of course." The Gran rambled about Industrial Heuristics' long history in the sector, and how the company had proudly supplied a long list of Sith Lords over the years. He seemed thrilled that Daiman would be added to the list. "Your leader supplies us the raw materials. We finish the product."

"What product?"

"Why, Tan is the product. Properly educated, that is." He rested his bony hand on Tan's head. "Industrial Heuristics is, in its own way, another factory. We manufacture intellects."

Tan smiled up at the visitors, and then at Kerra. The youngling was ecstatic. "This is what I've always wanted, Kerra! What we've been working toward!"

Kerra had never known of any specific goal Tan was working toward; she'd just assumed literacy was good in and of itself. But the girl acted as if she'd been reprieved from a death sentence. Maybe she had.

At the same time, though, it seemed like another kind of prison to Kerra. And so, it seemed, to Gub.

"Bombsights." Gub stared at his granddaughter, his eyes weary. "That's all she'll learn about? Only that?"

The Ishi Tib trilled an answer, which Ler-Laar translated. "An engineer is a part like any other," he said. "Specialized. Devoted to a specific function. Replaceable, should the need arise." Tan would learn her specialty in a setting with other handpicked students who would form her work group in later life. "There isn't any need for her to learn about anything else." The Gran chuckled. "You wouldn't try to boil water with a blaster."

Kerra steamed. It was all so backward. Tan would be doomed to a life little different from Gub's, putting Daiman's imprint on the past. Almost anything in the "next generation of optics," she estimated, would have been discovered long ago. Discovered, and lost, in the interminable years of conflict during which countless universities, corporations, and scholars had been lost. They were constantly trying to rediscover knowledge they, themselves, had destroyed.

"Where would she go?" Gub asked, looking down.

Not seeming to understand why it mattered, the Gran explained that his company had education centers throughout Bactra's space—as well as some mobile centers. "Of course, after . . . *recent events* here, Tan might well find an opening closer to home." Daiman had proclaimed publicly that the Black Fang had been demolished to make way for a new and better research center. Even if the ongoing public inquisition suggested otherwise, Daiman might well be in the market for more brainpower.

"It's what His Lordship intends," Gub said. Limping across the room, he took his granddaughter's hands in his. The old man trembled, holding back tears. "You will go."

Kerra shot the scouts a look as the Sullustans embraced. As far as they were concerned, Tan didn't have an option. They wanted her. She *would* go. And right away. The Ishi Tib waved off Gub's efforts to give his granddaughter anything to take along. The recruits were being taken to a staging area at the spaceport, Ler-Laar said; transports had already been sent for. Whatever facility she went to would have everything she'd ever need.

And it will be all she'll ever have, Kerra thought. But as she'd seen every day, life under Sith rule was a constant negotiation. The only way to improve things was on the margins. "Take care," she said, hugging a tearful but happy Tan in the doorway. *May the Force be with you. Let it be with something, out here, for a change.*

Gub lingered, sad and small, in the doorway. Outside, neighbors parted and watched, amazed, as one of their own escaped.

"She'll remain a slave," Kerra whispered behind her landlord's back.

"But she'll have an easier time of it," Gub responded. In a year, Tan would be thirteen—and obligated to work three shifts daily if she wanted to be fed at all. There was no guarantee her next assignment wouldn't be more dangerous. She could even wind up drafted. A safer monotony wasn't a bad thing, especially if it was somewhere else. The old man straightened, his leg braces creaking. "She'll have an easier time of it," he said again, almost to himself. "As will I."

Limping back inside, he found Kerra's curtain again. A stiff yank brought it down for the second time in a week.

The message was clear. "You want me to go?"

Gub looked up at her, fat eyes communicating the obvious. The child was gone. Kerra was no longer necessary. He took the curtain—now a sheet again—and draped it across the chair where he did his work.

Kerra looked blankly into the darkened room. *Evicted from a closet.*

"Come now," the old man said, depositing himself in his seat before the desk. "Now you will be able to work a third eight-hour shift—and qualify for a room and ration of your own."

But, of course, Kerra needed her nights.

"I'm . . . glad I was able to help, Master Tengo," she said to his back. "I'll be out in the morning."

"Tonight," he said, charging his pen against his knee.

CHAPTER FOUR

"We're racing against time, here! Step it up!"

Scratching his muscled neck, Jarrow Rusher squinted up at the crane. They were losing the sun—the one sun that did anything, anyway. Daiman's "eyes" had set earlier, beyond the smokestacks west of the parade grounds. Now the cannoneer was watching major surgery on the vessel that was his livelihood—and facing the prospect that the operation might have to be completed in the dark.

Squatting on what once had been a bolo-ball field, *Diligence* resembled nothing more than a mammoth, two-clawed crustacean. Two colossal retro-rockets provided the ship with its footing, each engine the center of a cluster of four giant cargo modules. Large X's when viewed from above, the cargo clusters were joined together by the oversized fuselage of the crew section—

—or at least, that was how things were *supposed* to be. At the moment, Rusher's precious warship was in two pieces, while his team levered up three thousand metric tons of metal to make room for the new hydraulic accumulator unit the Lubboons had sent over. But the old one had to be dealt with first.

"Watch out!"

A steel cable snapped with an earsplitting *crack*, causing the mass of metal bound to the crane to dangle wildly. Seconds later the remaining cable gave out, rocketing around the pulley and flinging outward, bisecting a metal scaffold in the process. The crane's lopsided cargo fell to the ground, burying itself in the turf and just missing Rusher's chief machinist.

At least it was the old unit, Rusher thought. He scanned the scrambling crowd. "Who set that rig?"

"Rookie!"

Rusher didn't need to hear any more than that—and he didn't need to look. It had made some sense, initially. The new hydraulic module had bought Beadle Lubboon a place in the crew, after all, and the Duros teen had assured them that he'd worked with the equipment in his parents' factory. But it was looking less like a bargain for Rusher all the time.

The new recruit scurried past in his too-small fatigues, offering something between a wave and a shrug. "Sorry, Captain."

"That's *Brigadier.*"

Trooper Lubboon was already out of earshot, slamming the door to the portable refresher set up at the field's edge. The team had learned earlier in the day that stress did something vile to the boy's stomach. This evening was having much the same effect on Rusher, standing in the long shadows cast by his disjointed creation. If the playing field had ever been under the lights, it wasn't anymore. Soon the only illumination would be what they could generate themselves—and, of course, from those fool holographic statues at the four corners of the field.

It was a crazy idea, mounting a full-sized troop transport ship on top of a couple of cargo haulers. But the daring design of *Diligence* had made Rusher something of a legend in Sith artillery circles. Most methods of cannon deployment in the sector involved shipping guns and their operators separately. That was dangerous on several scores. Often, one or the other wouldn't make it to the battlefield. Or worse, the crews would have to traverse contested ground to reach their weapons. Frequently, artillery pieces were simply dropped from space, with no provision for retrieval. That had been good for scroungers like Rusher, but it was hardly efficient.

Some pieces *were* carried aboard ships with their operators, but the guns tended to be small. Weapons could be disassembled, but as Rusher had seen, another problem came in: most ships unloaded down a single ramp, causing traffic jams as workers got parts into position. Rusher had longed to combine the large, automated cargo pods dropped from orbit with a vessel hauling the gunnery crews.

No such ship had existed in Sith space—until Rusher, a few years after leaving Beld Yulan's crew, built it himself. Salvaging a Devaronian cruise liner, Rusher and a sleepless work team mounted the massive ship atop a superstructure bridging two cargo pod clusters. Their modules opened outward in four directions, allowing eight crews to off-load weapons simultaneously. "Down, gun, and done," he'd called it. Few crews were faster than Rusher's Brigade.

They'd even solved the problem of shipping long guns by mounting the barrels outside the ship, jutting outward from the cargo pods. That didn't do much for the ship's appearance, and there were few city platforms wide enough to accommodate *Diligence* with all the metal prods sticking out. On the other hand, as Rusher had once observed, in Sith space it didn't hurt to appear to be bristling with guns. That the guns were nonfunctioning parts of cannons yet to be assembled was their little secret.

"That's better," Rusher said, seeing Prenda Novallo and her engineers hoist the new hydraulic unit into place. He retreated to the sidelines. They were literal this time, but Rusher usually stood there anyway for these kinds of jobs. It was easier on the nerves. Dackett, Novallo—he'd been blessed on the maintenance side of things. No one knew better how to run an artillery carrier in all of Sith space than his crew. And they'd kept him free.

Free enough, anyway.

Rusher looked to the rumbling skies. More warships were arriving. Independents, like him. There were even a couple of corporate transports mixed in that he didn't recognize. He swore. Something was going on. He'd put in at Darkknell for refit and recruiting, not to take on a new mission right away. People just didn't show up on a Sith Lord's homeworld unbidden. Not if they wanted to be able to leave.

"That's Mak Medagazy," called a voice from behind as a Toong battle droid carrier soared overhead through the darkness. Master Dackett pointed to the vessel, lighting on the other side of the field. "What's this about?"

"I've seen what you've seen," Rusher said. It was a problem with working for Daiman. Normally, the chiefs of mercenary vessels would gather at local cantinas and compare notes. But Daiman had dismantled most services that marketed to the public, unwilling to waste entertainments on those who existed to provide *him* entertainment. He'd wiped out a key source of information—and a lot of good cantinas to boot.

Stepping into the light of one of the holostatues, Dackett made his report on the refit. *Diligence*'s unusual configuration put extreme stresses on its frame when landing in high-gravity environments; functioning hydraulic systems were vital. "We'd like another two weeks to get the whole thing done right."

"Two weeks." Rusher looked again to the darkening skies, filled with lights from descending vehicles. "Well, do what you have to. As long as we don't hear from His Craziness, we should be—"

"Lord Daiman speaks!" thundered a voice from above.

Startled, Rusher and his aide looked to the holographic statue behind them. Three times life-sized, the figure of Daiman had ceased its automated posturing and was now addressing them. Specifically, *him.* "Jarrow Rusher is destined for the Sanctum Celestial, tomorrow at noon."

Rusher shot a glance to the dark wall of the palace, looming to the northwest. "Do you have a mission for—"

"Jarrow Rusher is destined for the Sanctum Celestial, tomorrow at noon. Meet your destiny." At that, the holographic statue was as it had been before, depicting Daiman looking thoughtful and complicated.

"I regret to inform you, the mission has been scrubbed," Dackett said.

"So much for your two weeks." Rusher looked at Dackett. "Think he heard me?"

"I doubt it. But who knows?"

It would certainly be an excellent way for Daiman to impress his omniscience upon his people, Rusher thought. Eavesdrop on everyone electronically, and then use his virtual personage on every street corner to react. It would be right up there with some of the more effective totalitarian states he'd read about. But, like his aide, Rusher doubted it. He'd never met the young lord, but he'd known people who had. Spying on everyone sounded like too much work for someone like Daiman. If you didn't think anyone else existed, why bother?

Dackett clapped his datapad against his artificial hand. "Right, then. I'll tell Novallo she's working through the night."

"Tell you what, Dackett," Rusher said. "I'll finish the welding. *You* visit His Lordship."

"No, sir," the older man said, his gapped tooth whistling. "Every band has a front man. I just play the pretty music."

Rusher chuckled. *Front man?* Maybe. But even for the

so-called independents, someone else always called the tune.

When she was a child, Kerra had visited the chilly polar regions of Aquilaris—about the only place on the planet where the weather wasn't gorgeous constantly. Even that had been beautiful, with whitecaps cresting one after another in the fjords.

She had spied a lone quadractyl, an oceangoing avian creature more at home in warmer climes, afloat in the crashing surf. At first, she thought the animal was in trouble. A whitecap would wash over it, forcing it underwater. Seconds later it would resurface, soggy and closer to shore, just in time to be struck by the next icy wave. It didn't seem to be making any attempt to fly away, preferring, it seemed, to ride along and take what fate—or the planet's three moons—had in store for it.

Having watched Sith slaves from Chelloa to Darkknell deal with their lives, Kerra began to think that was what was happening here, too. The people who lived in this sector were like the wretched quadractyl, being buffeted by one violent wave of Sith conquerors after another. Blow followed upon blow. And yet the people, like the animal, rode it out.

Some in the Republic felt that the people who lived under Sith rule didn't deserve saving, because they hadn't acted to free themselves. It was clear to Kerra those people had never seen Sith oppression up close, or they would have understood how wrong they were. The power imbalance between master and slave was just too great. There was no practical way for those under Daiman's heel to band together—and in fact, gathering together had the effect of making them more vulnerable, rather than more powerful. No uprising was possible.

And yet, kneeling in the darkness of her soon-to-be-former room, Kerra wondered if she'd just seen resistance in action. Parents in the Daimanate were willing to endure more hardship for themselves if it meant their children might migrate to a position that was marginally better. Decades of oppression had forced on them such a long view of life that even the smallest step was a mighty leap to freedom.

Maybe that quadractyl was where it was because it *had* acted—acted to send its chicks south. It just didn't have anything left to save itself.

But Kerra had escaped once. And she wouldn't stay now.

Peeking outside to confirm that Gub was at his desk, Kerra pulled the folded stealth suit from beneath her bedroll. It was pristine. She'd been given a solvent by one of her friends at work. Ostensibly intended to clean a piece of furniture, the fluid had worked marvelously on the Mark VI. It had taken meticulous effort, mostly after Tan had gone to sleep each night. But the suit was necessary. Essential, in fact, for realizing the value of what she'd gained through her *other* job on Darkknell.

Kerra pulled the drawstring on the duffel bag. Lifting her few personal items from the top, she emptied the sack onto her pillow. Pouches of glistening gel tumbled into a pile. *Baradium nitrite.* Enough explosive to send the universe's would-be creator on a journey of discovery—through the stratosphere.

She'd brought the explosive out of the factory a little at a time, in disposable squeeze food packets. It had been easy enough; she was supposed to bring her own lunch and pack out her trash. In its fluid form, it was less prone to accidental detonation than other explosives, and she probably didn't have enough to pull off what the Bothan had done at the Black Fang. But as a Jedi alone heading up against a Sith Lord, she knew it didn't hurt to have backup.

She hadn't known what to do with it all, before the other day. Daiman himself had given her the key, in his vain insistence that everyone hear his voice daily. On one other world, she'd heard his message declaring the sunrise. Listening again the last two days, she'd heard it again: the same phrasing as offworld, except for the parts about the day's duration. Surely, he didn't record different ones for every world he held—and she wasn't aware of any communications network in Sith space that equaled the one that the Republic had deactivated on the Outer Rim. Both meant that Daiman's voice was being simulated, and simulated locally on each world.

Obvious, really, but she'd never thought about the corollary. If Daiman vanished tomorrow, the rival Sith Lords whose rampage she feared might not find out about it for a long time. Daiman's Correctors would want to keep their jobs, which meant they would pretend nothing had changed.

But in fact, something would have changed, Kerra thought as she refilled the bag and cinched it shut. Life wouldn't improve dramatically, but a Daimanate without a Daiman would be something that would help many people at once.

Kerra took a last look around the room and stood to depart. Daiman *would* vanish tomorrow.

And it was about blasted time.

There were worse things than death.

Narsk's aunt had told him that, raising him alone on Verdanth. Near the juncture of three sectors and situated on a major hyperspace lane, the planet was desired by many a petty princeling. Indeed, several had declared themselves Sith Lords immediately upon taking the green world, as if the title *conqueror of Verdanth* meant anything. It usually didn't. Verdanth's masters seldom lived long. But they always survived long enough to do serious damage to the population of the world, a diverse patchwork of transplanted peoples.

The Bothan community on Verdanth had suffered less than others, if only because of the species' penchant for intrigues. More stubborn races had refused to submit when the Sith first invaded; their survivors saw each successive wave as something to be resisted with all means. A noble thought. But ownership of Verdanth was changing almost annually. Defiance of all invaders earned only extinction. The Bothans, meanwhile, submitted freely to whichever Sith warlord they estimated had the upper hand. Their instincts were so good, observers said, that one could track the balance of power in the system simply by looking at who had the most Bothans in his or her camp.

Being on the losing side meant death. But that wasn't the worst part, as his aunt had put it: it meant that you'd *guessed wrong*.

Understanding the relationships between others and accurate reckonings of power and where it lay: these were the things that made one a Bothan. Narsk's aunt once described a tribe of feral Bothans, found untold years after a crash on a deserted planet. They had no spoken language, but they could rank with exactitude the numbers of various kinds of predators in their surroundings. To be a Bothan was to be always on the lookout.

Narsk had taken those lessons to heart. While a slave for successive Sith Lords on Verdanth, he'd managed to find chores that bettered his perceptions. The sloppy job of harvesting rimebats led to assignments tracking escapees. Those led to missions as a nonmilitary scout and, finally, a saboteur. All the time, he'd kept his eyes on the Sith players, in the best traditions of his people.

The quandary came when two particularly pugnacious rivals chose to settle the ownership of the planet in a duel that left them both dead. The resulting power vacuum put many Bothans off kilter. There was no reason to expect Verdanth would stay free from Sith rule for more than a few weeks at most, and yet the planet-bound Bothans had no real way of gauging the relative strengths of powers yet unseen. The only real way to know which Sith Lord to back was to strike out into space personally and have a look.

Narsk did. And never returned.

He'd found a wondrously complicated political scene. A patchwork of dominions and dependencies, ruled by despots with secret connections and histories of betrayal. It could keep an industrious Bothan busy for a lifetime.

For Narsk, it had. And now, it was all over—because he wasn't on the lookout.

The Jedi was a wild card, but he should've known she was there. He'd been on Darkknell a month, assessing the potential hazards. Even if only one person on Darkknell knew she was there, *he* should have been the one.

He noted, ironically, that he probably *had* been the first to know she was there. But that information had come too late to be useful. And now that Daiman had, through him, become the second to know, Narsk wondered why he was still alive.

He'd remained on the slab for days without food, tasting water when a torture session involved it. Daiman knew now that Narsk was an agent for Odion. Once Narsk realized that secret was gone, he'd relaxed his defenses, allowing the Sith Lord to see everything in his memories since his arrival on Darkknell. The assumption of the cover identity, the scouting of the testing center, the many forays inside. That was a tactic he'd been taught, too. Once a secret lost its value as a secret, it could be used to shield other truths. He'd flooded Daiman with details that didn't matter anymore.

It seemed to have worked. Apparently satisfied, Daiman

had left him alone. Several times the young Sith had sensed the importance of a female human in Narsk's memories—but from his remarks, Daiman had always assumed it was the Jedi. Daiman was no better than the sentries, Narsk thought. *They only see what they're looking for.*

Now, though, Narsk saw only imminent death. He had nothing more to give—nothing he would give, anyway. His execution was at hand. Four Correctors entered the room, releasing him from the table and shifting his limp, half-clothed body to a circular metal frame. His feet and ankles were fastened to its perimeter, splaying his body across its width. The Correctors tipped the device on its side, wheeling Narsk down one of the narrow darkened hallways.

With nothing to support his neck, Narsk's head hung backward as the frame rolled. Dizzily, he saw a blur of light ahead. His eyes adjusting, Narsk realized it was a wide indoor area with a skylight above. With a bump, the Correctors rolled his circular rack onto a small platform built to lift something in antigrav suspension.

Lofted into the air by an unseen force, Narsk saw the people in attendance and realized that his aunt had been right. He'd guessed wrong. It was not an execution. And there *were* things worse than death.

He had become a stage prop.

CHAPTER FIVE

The young lord shimmered, resplendent in his plumage. Daiman's preference for shining attire was well known—but today's coppery cape had something extra going for it. Every time the Sith Lord stepped between his viewers and the skylight above, small prisms in the great folds of the garment refracted the noon sun, throwing brilliant-colored light all around the Adytum.

And here, in this enormous heptagonal shrine within the Sanctum Celestial, *everyone* was beneath Daiman. Seven crystal catwalks led to a suspended platform in the center, directly beneath the skylight. Each of the seven midair entrances sat in the middle of an alabaster column, curling upward toward the ceiling and forming, with the skylight, a replica of Daiman's sun-and-tentacles emblem. The walls between bore ornate relief carvings of Daiman throughout history and prehistory. So did the floor, where those waiting attendance alternately looked up at their lord and down at their feet, to keep from tripping on the uneven surface.

Only Narsk was close to Daiman's level, but the Bothan didn't feel very honored. After the Correctors had used the antigrav generator to lift his circular prison several meters in the air, they'd done something to apply some spin. Now Narsk tumbled gyroscopically in the air meters above the others, in the space between two of

Daiman's catwalks. It'd been like this all day: bouts of violent rotation punctuated by occasional slowdowns during which his body was right-side up. Narsk supposed it was to keep him from passing out. For the first time since his imprisonment, he was glad he hadn't been fed.

The brief respites had given him a chance to survey the hall, though, and those inside. Daiman had stalked the catwalks for hours, seemingly brooding on some aspect of creation or another. Occasionally, he retired to the oversized plush mass, more a bed than a throne, resting in the middle of the suspended platform. Narsk thought he sat like a youngling, his legs curled up underneath as he idly kicked the ends of the cape. *No, not a child,* Narsk thought. *An adolescent.*

Beyond a few aggravated sighs, Daiman had said nothing at all. He had, however, vanished twice into one of the exits for a wardrobe change. Narsk figured something must be about to happen. The sighs were becoming more like groans, and each outfit had been more outrageous than the last.

There must be company coming, Narsk thought. *I can't believe this is what he wears around the house.*

The audience below had gotten no more attention from Daiman than Narsk had. There were Correctors there, and a few elite sentries. They stood, waiting silently on their master—as did a Woostoid woman Narsk took to be Daiman's aide-de-camp. Narsk didn't recognize her, but no spy could ever keep track of Daiman's palace lineup. She certainly hadn't been hired for her charm, he saw, every time he revolved to face her. Orange-skinned with bound magenta hair, the spindly thing looked like a black hole was sucking her face from within. All the engineering teams in the sector couldn't construct a smile out of that raw material.

Narsk couldn't figure it. Daiman seemed to prize beauty in his household. But then he had another thought: *It must be this way when you're in love with yourself.*

"I heard that, spy!"

Narsk's frame whirled around long enough to give him a glimpse of Daiman at the edge of the platform, raising his talon-tipped hand. Seconds later all Narsk saw was blue pain, as Force lightning wracked his shaking body. As the attack subsided, rivulets of energy crackled off the side of the rack.

"You think you've hurt me, don't you? *Don't you?*" Cape billowing, Daiman stalked the edge of his platform. Below, several listeners on the lower floor stumbled, trying to keep up with him. "You haven't hurt me at all," he railed. "In fact, my little nothing, you haven't changed my course a whit."

Narsk found his mouth too dry after the attack to respond—but it was just as well. There was no right answer.

"No, you and the Jedi woman have given me *exactly* what I wanted. I just didn't realize it at the time," Daiman said, kneeling and eyeing Narsk. "I don't always see the plan I started with until later—but I always do."

Already dizzy, Narsk shook his head. How did Daiman's followers stand such doubletalk?

"Uleeta!" Daiman called. "Is the connection ready?"

Beneath, the Woostoid spoke. "As my lord knows, the heretic Bactra awaits on the priority channel." The woman, Narsk saw, never faced Daiman when addressing him. Instead, she craned her neck and directed her bulbous ebony eyes toward the skylight, as if Daiman were living in the rafters somewhere. *Well, he kind of is,* Narsk thought.

Uleeta glanced at her handheld control pad and looked up again. She spoke cautiously, as if fearful to offend. "Bactra . . . likes to be called *Lord*. As my—"

"What he likes is pointless. Activate it."

"Activating. Should we remove the prisoner?"

"No."

The answer sent a chill shot back down Narsk's back. Whatever was about to happen, it didn't matter if he knew about it. He was still dead.

The rafters of a Sith Lord's entry hallway were not the place to be pawing at one's armpits. And yet, Kerra couldn't stop herself. It was good that getting inside the Sanctum Celestial was so easy, because she'd had to fight a small war just to get into the stealth suit.

The skintight garment was functioning properly; it had gotten her past eight sentry posts so far. But there wasn't anything comfortable about it. The planners at Cyricept had thought of a lot of things, but making one size fit all species and genders wasn't among them. The Bothan had been slightly shorter, and while Kerra wasn't overly endowed, she'd had to take extreme measures to get the fasteners closed. If she had to die somewhere, she'd already be mummified.

On the other hand, there was too much room in the mask, where the Bothan's hairy snout had been. She'd folded part of the fabric inside and pinned it in order to cinch the mask closed, leaving a bizarre chevron-shaped beak above the mouthpiece. She was positively thrilled no one could see her.

Now, as Kerra crept from alcove to alcove, every step reminded her why Jedi didn't wear bodysuits. Her regular clothes, stuffed in the tote bag just beneath the explosives, were loose fitting and comfortable. Kerra doubted she'd have wanted the suit even if it were in her size, but she also knew she never would have gotten far without it. She'd broken into Sith strongholds before, but keeping Daiman and his Correctors from noticing her through the Force took extra concentration. The suit was her edge.

She just wanted her edge to stop digging into her mid-section.

Kerra had only ever seen Daiman's stronghold from a distance, its obsidian walls tracing long lines around Xakrea's centermost point. Tall pylons flanked a gate-way on each of the seven sides; Kerra had simply picked the nearest. She'd wondered once why Daiman didn't have some towering, vertical roost from which to survey his surroundings, as he had on Chelloa. A co-worker at the plant had explained that since Daiman had created Darkknell, he had no need to look down on it. Kerra had barely stifled her laughter then. *So he's got a wall. If we don't exist, why does he need it?*

She'd imagined the walls enclosed some kind of open space—perhaps a courtyard or a lake, with a smaller castle somewhere within. Instead, she'd found that the great gateway was actually a door. The walls weren't a divider, but the outsides of the largest building she'd ever encountered.

The structure was recent, raised in the few years since Daiman's ascension to power. Kerra was flabbergasted. So much of Xakrea was old, dating back to previous Sith Lords and before. What had Daiman put his build-ing resources into? The biggest shrine to arrogance ever, easily surpassing for scale and gaudiness any of the in-dustrialists' mansions she'd visited when raising money for Vannar. Those people's homes were temples to their own achievement, but only in a figurative sense. Daiman's actually came with bas-reliefs of himself creating the uni-verse.

And yet, changing her route to avoid yet another hall of mirrors—no telling what those would do to the stealth suit—Kerra found the place strangely empty. It was a temple without worshippers. Enormous ball-rooms and dining halls had clearly never seen a dancer or a diner. If Daiman wanted ostentation, he seemed not to understand what it was for.

It pained her to see it all now, to think of the people whose lives were wasted in erecting the place. Kerra had forgiven the lip service given in public to Daiman's creatorhood, but she'd never understood why so many people she'd met also did so in private. Gub, for one. He was more than twice the Sith Lord's age. She wondered if there was a specific day on which everyone on Darkknell stopped rolling their eyes when they spoke of Daiman's myth. It must have been some long time earlier. It always confused her. If no one else but Daiman existed, as his thinking went, why would he go to the trouble to indoctrinate anyone? Why would he care?

She'd only met Daiman once, but she knew enough from their short exchange to guess. Daiman could see into the minds of others using the Force, but he didn't take that for proof that they were independent beings. He assumed that any contrary thoughts in their heads were part of the galactic puzzle he'd created for himself to correct. It was just one more thing to fix, another victory condition to satisfy. He wanted the droids around him to *know* they were droids: organic or otherwise. And if that meant spending five years building an atrium that took five minutes to traverse—so be it. Even if the builders were the only others who would ever see inside.

Interesting as Daiman's home was as a psychological study, it was ruination for Kerra's plans. Feeling for the baradium nitrite in the pouch, she looked around in exasperation. Even if she could find Daiman, she'd need a shuttle of the stuff to bring this place down!

Hearing activity atop a stone staircase, Kerra slipped over the banister and dropped into a crawl space. They weren't sentries, this time, but soldiers. About a dozen figures of various species, all in different forms of military dress, followed a protocol droid down the steps into an atrium.

Certainly not Daiman's usual high-fashion troopers. Kerra gawked, unseen, at the ragtag bunch. What would possess any band of mercenaries to work for a schizophrenic monomaniac? It didn't matter. Inside the mask, she smiled. *Take me to your leader.*

"Nice to see you through something other than a rangefinder," Rusher said, jabbing the Toong with a gloved hand. "Eating pretty well over on the Gevarno Loop, I see."

Olive and ovoid, Mak Medagazy smirked. "Haven't had to face *you* in a while, R-r-rusher," he said, massive belly wobbling as he extended a long, thin arm to the brigadier. "Kept the replacement costs d-d-down."

Having spent their working lives trying to kill one another, not all the militia leaders in the subsector got along. But Mak was easy to like. Because he was a droid-runner, casualties were never personal for him. And perhaps to avoid the characteristic Toong nervous stutter, he always kept his remarks short, offending few.

Not so for some of the others in the party, Rusher saw. Like Kr'saang the Togorian, who insisted on being called that, as if anyone could miss a two-and-a-half-meter mound of hairy anger. The feral-looking mercenary insisted on pushing his way to the front of the group, nearly bowling over their electronic guide in the process.

"What's the hurry, Tog?" Rusher asked again. The Sith Lord's house was endless; the meet could be kilometers away.

Kr'saang snarled, whiskers flaring on either side of his angular muzzle. "Waste your own time, human—not mine!" Leader of a brigade of shock troops, Kr'saang complained again about being called to a briefing in person. "Foolishness."

"Then why are you here? Got to be other Sith Lords who can keep your muzzle full of chow."

Several mercenaries edged back from Rusher, in case the black-furred giant snapped. But Kr'saang kept walking. "My business." Emerald eyes glared back at Rusher. "I sure know why *you're* here, rock-thrower. Daiman won't fight Bad Brother Odion one-on-one. He's looking for somebody even more gutless to make him look good."

"Well, he has you there," Mak said, giant lip curling.

Rusher didn't push it. He already knew why most of them were there. Several of the indies had lately come from the service of the other side. The brigadier had been smarter than they were in that regard. It was Odion-avoidance that had sent Rusher into business for himself, years earlier.

Beld Yulan had been everything a mentor should be. A fine artilleryman, he'd also cultivated an interest in military history among his recruits. Young Rusher had learned not just about the engagements, but the reasons why they were fought—and how, in many cases, the decisions of a single person could have led to different outcomes. Rusher would've stayed aboard *Perspicacity* forever, had Yulan not lost his children to the plague on Fostin IX. The general's mourning became depression, culminating with a "religious conversion": he'd become an Odionite, a member of the dread Lord's death-seeking cult.

Rusher had begun to suspect when the general started throwing caution to the wind, committing squads to ever-more-dangerous assignments. The force's "lurch ratio," or percentage of warriors left stranded, had gone skyward, with hundreds of troops abandoned to their fates. Finally, when Yulan announced that the brigade would be taking a job from Lord Odion, Rusher had seen enough. At least Daiman believed in a tomorrow— if only so he could have a chance to take credit for its arrival. If even steely operators like Kr'saang were coming to that realization, things must be getting bad indeed on the other side.

"Hold here," the droid said, pausing in a chandelier-filled room. Gilded double doors sat beneath a marbled arch in the eastern wall. "His Lordship is in conference with his other creations, but your time will come."

Sad Toong eyes rolled toward Rusher. "G-g-good to know," Mak said.

"Yeah, I feel blessed."

The mercs had stopped short of the grand entryway, jabbering and drooling at the riches of the anteroom. Statues, paintings, chandeliers: surely more wealth than they had ever seen, Kerra figured. Still, they'd brought her to the right place. She'd been cautious not to dip into the Force for anything, but she couldn't miss the evil taint that lay ahead. It could only be Daiman and his closest aides.

But there was no easy frontal assault, not with the crowd of warriors and sentries lingering there. Slipping past the rearmost member of the party—a fortyish red-bearded human in a trench coat, not entirely oafish looking—Kerra made for a narrow spiral staircase at the left side of the room.

Upstairs, the steps finished in a candlelit hallway, leading toward a bright opening. Hearing voices, Kerra edged toward it, cautiously.

There he was, at the end of a long, crystalline catwalk: Little Daiman himself, announcer for the morning rush hour. It looked like his rumpus room on Chelloa, only grander—and suspended above the ground by pathways that formed a seven-pointed star. It was, by far, the strangest room she'd seen in the building.

And *what* was he wearing?

Kerra knelt in the doorway and breathed lightly. Her

respiration didn't make the slightest difference inside the Mark VI, but it didn't matter. She'd found the center of the madness, right where she left it, with Daiman. And for a change, Daiman's taste in architecture would serve her. If she could walk to the central platform, Kerra thought, her homemade bomb might have more than its explosive impact. It might well churn the crystal catwalk and platform into a million splinters. The shape of the room and ceiling might well focus the impact, giving her a running chance to escape.

That was worth the risk.

Reflexively, she looked to see who else was present. The aides she expected, of course, all slavering below. And just to the right of her catwalk something else floated: the Bothan spy, strapped to a rotating wheel. She'd expected to find him here, although she was surprised to see that he still seemed to be in one piece.

For a while, anyway. *Tough week to be you.*

There was something else, just on the far side of Daiman's perch, that had his full attention. With a start, she recognized the hologram: another Sith Lord! The Quermian, Lord Bactra, towered in the life-sized image, his shriveled white head craning on his long, narrow neck. She'd studied him, back in the Republic. What did Daiman have going on with someone like Bactra?

Whatever it was, it wouldn't be going on for long. Steeling herself, Kerra stood and took a step onto the catwalk.

"It is refreshing to see the Lord Daiman again," the flickering Quermian said, "especially after the troubles you've described." The image of Lord Bactra brought his azure fingers the meter and a half up to his lofty chin and smiled. The skinny titan kept his second pair of arms within the folds of his rich cloak.

For one of the sector's smarter Sith Lords, Narsk

thought, Bactra was doing a good job of playing dumb. So far, in this conversation, he'd professed to know nothing about the destruction of the testing center on Darkknell. That surely wasn't so. The mess at the Black Fang could have been seen from orbit, Narsk guessed, and even Sith who weren't open enemies kept an eye on one another's affairs. "I assume the figure I see there is the perpetrator?"

"The saboteur is here." Daiman directed the hovering holocam to take a shot of Narsk in his spinning prison. "Do you recognize him?"

"Bothan. No, I don't," Bactra said, lipless mouth never changing its shape. "But their kind tends to meddle in things that are above them."

Narsk swallowed, or tried to. The only things above him at the moment were his feet.

And meddling, he knew, was something Ayanos Bactra worked at doing without ever seeming to take a side. He'd stayed out of the conflict between Odion and Daiman, both of whose territories bordered his own. In fact, Narsk knew, the ancient Quermian had gone out of his way to avoid destructive battles with most of his neighbors, preferring, instead, to accumulate more intangible holdings: corporations. Several of the interstellar firms that had continued to operate in the sector under Sith rule were headquartered in Bactra's space.

Quietly, Bactra's influence among his neighbors had grown. A less thoughtful strategist might have become a supplier to one side or another, but Bactra understood that clumsy partisanship would have earned him enmity. A Sith expected an arms dealer to sell secretly to all sides, so Bactra did it openly and equally. And when contested worlds fell and their manufacturing interests fled, Bactra's space just happened to be there as a convenient haven. Chaos served Bactra.

As it was serving him now. "I . . . gather that the sabotage creates a *weakness* in your technical capacity, Lord Daiman."

"Purely temporary." Daiman lay back on the plush bed, staring at the skylight.

"Of course. But it is a problem in the near term," Bactra said. "Consider what you could do if you held the solution—as I do."

"Industrial Heuristics?"

"The one." Narsk knew that Daiman had recently begun allowing Bactra's firm to recruit in his territory, in exchange for some of the fruits of research his people produced. Now Bactra offered Daiman something more immediate. "From what your aides told mine, you're prepared to consider a further expansion of our franchise."

"I don't see a better way," Daiman said. "There are reports my brother is considering building a second factory complex, even larger than The Spike." He sat up, his cape a crumpled mass. "An arxeum is the answer. I require one—delivered."

The rotation slowing, Narsk considered what he'd just heard. He recognized the name. Arxeums were an Industrial Heuristic invention: giant mobile universities dedicated to the war-making sciences. Students sometimes spent their entire working lives aboard a single arxeum, churning out new military designs. The clever aspect was the mobile part. By making arxeums spaceworthy, the company had made it possible for the valuable facilities to move, should conditions warrant.

But what Daiman was suggesting was new. Industrial Heuristics turned students into researchers in a lot of places, but all were in Bactra's realm. Daiman was asking for the outright purchase of a working arxeum, shipped directly into his space. No information sharing, this time; Daiman's people would be building weapons directly for him.

Not bad, Narsk thought. The Black Fang had taken years to build, and seconds to destroy. Daiman had just figured out how to replace it in days. What price must that come at?

Bactra was ready with the answer. "I require passage across your territory to strike at Vellas Pavo. Temporary; we do not intend to hold the world. Six weeks should suffice."

Daiman stared. Vellas Pavo was unoccupied by any Sith Lord, Narsk knew. The Sith Lord looked to his Woostoid aide, down below. "Why does he want this?"

"Gadolinium," Uleeta replied, temporarily muting the conversation. "As my lord knows, Bactra controls three of the four largest superconductor interests in the sector. The fourth sources most of its gadolinium from Vellas Pavo." By striking at the mining operations, Uleeta explained, Bactra expected to take out a competitor. "As my lord knows."

Daiman sneered. "Bactra hasn't changed. Play for third, hope to win."

"My lord knows."

Daiman stood from the bed and approached the holographic image. "You have your passage," he said. "But I would want to unite the recruits your firm has already found here with the facility as quickly as possible, that they may begin work. Is there a suitable frontier world for the rendezvous?"

Bactra paused, referring to something off to the side. "We have a number of facilities that could reach your territory quickly. There is one near Tergamenion. Alphoresis. Gazzari . . ."

"Gazzari. That sounds well."

Narsk's prison suddenly sped up again. This time, when the rack turned him upside down, it stayed there, whirling him faster and faster. Fighting against passing out, Narsk looked for a fixed point to focus on. All he

could find was one of the seven darkened doorways leading from the Adytum, a blot behind the crystal railing of
the catwalk. The faster his prison rotated, the faster the
doorway flickered, until the vision of it persisted. The
doorway—and something just inside. An outline. A figure.

Narsk blinked, sure he was hallucinating. He'd only
seen something like it once before, in the Black Fang
whenever he looked at his own hands . . .

The Jedi!

"Jedi?" Daiman looked back from the hologram with a
start. He scanned the faces of his followers below. "Which
one of you—?" Daiman's voice trailed off. "Never mind."

Turning the Bothan upright again, the rack slowed.
Narsk swallowed, taking care to shield his thoughts.
The Jedi had the stealth suit. And she'd come here, of all
places!

The Jedi had come here for some reason—and what
was more important, only he knew about it. The young
lord had known for several days that Narsk had used a
stealth suit to enter the testing center, and that the Jedi
had taken it. The fact that she was here meant that even
with that knowledge, Daiman had no proof against it.

For the first time since his capture, Narsk managed the
tiniest smile. What might a word of warning mean now,
coming from a condemned prisoner?

I might get out of this yet.

CHAPTER SIX

Kerra was glad for the stealth suit for one thing: no one could hear her swearing.

Certain now of her invisibility, she stood gawking in the doorway. The place was impossible. There was no way she could reach Daiman's loft-like platform at the center of the great room to deposit the explosives. Even if she could stay hidden within the Force from him and the Correctors below, Daiman's silly cape was throwing all kinds of light everywhere. She had no idea what the effect would be on the Mark VI.

That left affixing the explosive packets to something physical and tossing them inside. But she wasn't sure she could get clear if she just tossed them over the side of the catwalk and ducked back outside. She wanted to stop Daiman, but she wasn't going to throw her life away.

And Bactra's appearance had thrown *her*. Kerra wanted to end Daiman's oppression. But, she realized while standing in the doorway, there was another reason she'd come to Sith space. She wanted to *understand*. What was it that made brother fight brother here, destroying the lives of countless innocents underfoot? What was the role of the other would-be Sith Lords? Could they stop this madness between Daiman and Odion, or were they just making it worse?

Kerra cocked her head. The mask had provisions so

she could see and hear what was going on outside, but she needed a straight shot at the speakers. Daiman kept moving—and the hologram was on the far side of the platform. That's the side she needed to be on.

She ran back down the hallway she'd entered through. There were six other entrances to Daiman's room at this level. There had to be some route to one of the doors at the other side. But where?

Blast!

Facing the doorway again, Narsk squinted. He couldn't see the Jedi anymore, but that didn't mean anything. That he'd seen her at all was an accident: a trick of the light, generated by the freak combination of his motion and the crystal walkway between them.

Behind him, the conversation with Bactra was ending in a deal. Daiman mentioned his plans to travel aboard his flagship to Gazzari to meet the mobile research center. Hearing Daiman end the call, Narsk steeled himself to raise his voice. One way or another, this might be made to serve his—

Whulp!

Suddenly Narsk plummeted. The metal frame he was bound to bounced once on a cushion of antigrav force and struck the floor. Two Gamorrean sentries stepped to either side, guiding the prison, wheel-like, toward an exit. "Get him out of here," he could hear Daiman say from behind.

Tumbling, Narsk watched helplessly as a crowd of others filtered into the Adytum, past him. Strange faces—alien species he rarely saw in the Daimanate.

"Wait!" he croaked, his dry throat too raw for his voice to carry far. *"Wait!"*

Rusher didn't think long about the torture device being wheeled past him, or the poor soul strapped to it. Other

Sith Lords liked to do things for show, and Daiman certainly seemed to fit the breed. Rusher looked mildly back at the chattering Bothan as the door closed behind him. *Rough day to be you, pal.*

More interesting was what lay ahead. The Sith Lord stood suspended on his crystal platform, gesticulating before a huge planet hanging in the air before him. It was a holographic image, five meters wide. Motioning, Daiman wheeled the cloudy gray world around, reaching in occasionally to touch the image with his talon-tipped fingers. At every brush, a light burst from the surface of the pseudo-planet.

Cauldron of creation, Rusher thought, looking around the heptagonal temple. Everything he'd heard about Daiman was true.

"The specialist battalions." Daiman addressed the company of generals without looking at them. "You will depart Darkknell at sunset, each jumping to different destinations. In four days, you will reassemble here, on Gazzari." Daiman spun the virtual globe again and gave it a shove. The holographic world danced through the air before drifting to the marble floor, just ahead of Rusher and company. The lights shining through the clouds were each marked with unit names in Daiman's alphabet. "You will deploy your forces at the locations being shown to you now. Memorize them."

Kr'saang the Togorian peered at the hologram. "This is where we're setting up. Where's the enemy?"

"Odion will arrive thereafter," Daiman said offhandedly. "I have arranged for it."

The Nosaurian, another gunnery leader, emitted a series of warbling squawks. Rusher didn't know the language, but he figured the question. "How do we know he won't bomb us from orbit before he lands?"

Reacting to a nod from Daiman, the Woostoid woman stepped beside the floating image. "Lord Daiman created

Gazzari to be a volcanic world, shrouded in a cloud of metallic ash. Your emplacements will be quite invisible when the Great Enemy arrives." Beneath the haze, Gazzari's pockmarked surface was ridden with lofty ridges overlooking wide rills, providing excellent spots to set up for an ambush.

Sounds like a lovely place, Rusher thought. He and the others only had a minute to study their assigned locations before the image vanished.

"Ambush. That's about what I expected." Kr'saang turned on a massive clawed foot and began walking toward the exit.

Daiman looked down, clearly puzzled. "What?"

The Togorian turned back and stuck out his armored chest. "It's what I expected from you. Like on Chelloa. Odion's people are still talking about that one." Rusher noticed others stepping back from the Togorian. It seemed a good idea.

But Daiman reacted mildly. "You expect fairness, do you?"

"I expect a straight-up fight—but I heard you don't do those. Looks like they're right." He reached for the gilded doorknob.

A spray of multicolored light flashed against the door in front of Kr'saang. Turning his head, he saw Daiman's lustrous cape thrown in the air, catching the sunlight from above. Its owner, freed, hurtled downward toward the floor. Kr'saang pivoted, reaching for a blade hidden in his belt—only to see a flash of crimson ahead of him. Before he hit the ground, Daiman quartered the massive alien with two great strokes of his lightsaber.

For several moments, Daiman looked down in seeming fascination at the disgusting remains at his feet. Finally, he looked up. "Where's my cape?"

Daiman's attendants sprang to his side, delivering the

requested garment as he deactivated his lightsaber. "What was he?"

"Kr'saang," Uleeta said. "He led shock troopers, as my lord knows. Specialist Unit Two Hundred Seven, in our accounting. His transport, the *Dar'oosh*, is at the north end of the old parade grounds."

"Send Correctors there and induct the lot."

Rusher winced. Kr'saang's warriors had just become part of Daiman's slave army.

"I'm telling you, there's a Jedi here! I have to talk to Lord Daiman!"

The sentries didn't speak. The burly Gamorreans simply continued to wheel the imprisoned Narsk down a hallway, ignoring his every plea. Narsk wondered for a moment if this was why he got into the Black Fang so easily. *Does Daiman only hire the deaf?*

More likely, he thought as he heard their guttural grunts, they simply didn't understand Basic. He tested the theory with a remark about Gamorrean females. A further stream of insults confirmed it. There was literally no talking to them.

Leaving the main thoroughfare, the guards rolled Narsk's prison down a side hallway. Darkness lay ahead. For a time, Narsk felt only the bumps of the tiles as his prison rumbled onward. *Back to the dungeon,* he assumed.

Then he was alone.

Narsk blinked. The Gamorreans had parked his wheel against a wall and wandered off. The Bothan craned his neck forward and behind, straining to see anything down the hallway. Nothing.

For five minutes.

"Just leaving me? Fine!" If this was a new kind of torture, it was working. Narsk ranted. Days with no food and only enough water to keep him talking. Days of mental invasions from the monomaniac and his minions. And today, spinning on display like a child's toy. All of it came pouring, foully, out of the Bothan's mouth—

—until an unseen hand clasped his muzzle shut. A foreign thought touched his mind.

Shut up.

Startled, Narsk felt the wheel turning again. Propelled seemingly by nothing at all, the frame rolled down the darkened hall and through an open doorway into a deserted service passage. The door closed behind, leaving him in a small, dim maintenance area. An unused scullery for one of the countless dining rooms he'd been wheeled past, he expected.

The wheel stopping gently against a wall, Narsk smiled. "You've come to return my property, I hope."

"That depends," Kerra said, removing her mask, "on what you tell me. *And how quickly you tell it.*"

The remains of the Togorian oozed untouched on the temple floor. Daiman donned his cape, unconcerned; the generals parted to let him pass. "You will deploy to Gazzari in four days," he resumed. "More vessels will arrive. Remain in your positions. You will not disturb them." With a wave of his hand, more holograms appeared, depicting several ships.

Rusher studied them. There were four personnel transports, each labeled with the corporate logo of Industrial Heuristics, and a much larger structure. A floating cluster of connected towers, the city-in-miniature also bore the climbing-arrow logo that symbolized the "manufacturer of intellects." He'd heard of the firm, back when working in Bactra's territory. A few on his crew had even learned their trades there. "An arxeum," he spoke aloud. "Some kind of war college, isn't it?"

"And our personnel to be trained within it. They will

arrive first, before the facility. And, then," Daiman said confidently, "Odion will arrive."

Rusher flinched. *Why?*

"He will come to destroy the facility Bactra sends. Or he will try. He will certainly know of it." Daiman didn't say how. "And he will know we are sending our bright young prospects there to meet it. Industrial Heuristics has been recruiting openly on Darkknell for days—and my brother is known to have spies here," Daiman said, waving offhandedly toward the entrance. "You met one as you entered."

"You're using the training center as bait," Rusher said, looking down at his walking stick. The knob atop it glinted as he twirled it in place. "And . . . *the students*."

"Yes." Daiman returned to the center of the room. "He will not attack when the facilities are in Bactra's hands. He'll wait until the delivery is made, so the loss will impact me and not Bactra."

It was a standard move for Odion, Daiman said, but as ever, he was the better gamesman. "He must see the recruits waiting on the ground to seal the illusion."

"What do we do if he doesn't take the b-b-bait?" Mak stammered.

"He will. I have arranged for it."

Daiman gestured, and a shining staircase descended from the crystal platform at the center of the room. Setting foot upon it, he was interrupted by a statement from behind: "I'm not sure I like this."

Daiman stopped climbing. "What?"

"I said I'm not sure I like this," Rusher said, grasping the walking stick more tightly. Spying Mak's wild expression, he shrugged. *No, I don't know what I'm doing, either.* "You're taking younglings on the battlefield, and you're expecting them to be taken out."

"And I'm expecting you to do as you're told."

Daiman crooked his head slightly in irritation. "Who *are* you?"

"Brigadier Jarrow Rusher. I carry eight battalions running medium artillery, laser and missile. I've worked jobs for you for years," he said. "But I'm an independent operator—"

Daiman's response dropped below freezing. "As you've just seen, there is no such thing."

Rusher swallowed. He could feel the Sith Lord's supplicants glaring at him—and it didn't help that the other generals were edging out of the way. *Some colleagues.* "We're not part of your army, Lord Daiman."

"That can be corrected," Daiman said. To one side, the violet-clad Correctors took a step forward. He waved them off. This moment was his. "I created you, *Brigadier,*" the young Sith said, raising his metal-tipped hand. "You will function as I desire."

Yanked by an unseen power, Rusher rose several meters into the air. The walking stick clattered to the marble beneath as Rusher's gloved hands clutched at his neck, just above his collar. There was nothing there, but he could feel the presence of Daiman's hand. Even the false fingertips, clawing at the back of his neck. Shaking, Rusher coughed and kicked—and tried to speak.

"I'm . . . just doing . . . *what you created me to do . . .*"

The pressure subsided slightly. Still suspended in midair, Rusher watched Daiman step toward him. Mismatched eyes looked up. "What?"

Rusher's mind racing, his mouth moved to match. "Having autonomous forces was *your* idea. We were created for the purpose. *Your* purpose!"

Daiman lowered his hand, and his victim dropped violently to the floor. Blond eyebrows tilted in amusement. "*Tell* me the purpose," Daiman said, smirking.

Ignoring the shooting pain in his shin from the rough

landing, Rusher fought to get to his knees. "We look different. You can't send your regular forces ahead to Gazzari without him sensing a trap—"

"Any ship can be disguised!"

"—and the truth is," Rusher said, shifting gears, "you'd rather rent than own!"

"What in blazes are you talking about?"

"I'm saying you've got more important things to think about," Rusher said, getting to his feet. "There are too many details to running an artillery brigade—"

"Details I have designed!"

"And that's the problem," Rusher said, searching for his retail smile. "You worked so many complexities into this universe, Lord Daiman, that it's hard for us *lesser beings* to cope. Not all organics are up to it." He slapped his chest. "You created us specialists to manage these systems—and our own affairs—for greater efficiency. We're like anything else you created to work your will," he said, "just a little different."

Rusher watched the Sith Lord, burning eyes still set on him. They really did look like the double stars outside. The brigadier stepped over to retrieve his cane. "And you know what's really amazing?" he asked. "It all *works*. The variety you've designed into the universe is really something. Genius, really." He looked back at Daiman. "*As my lord knows.*"

Daiman stood stone-silent amid the generals and Correctors.

At last, he spoke. "You have your assignments. Prepayments of ordnance and fuel are already being delivered to your ships." He turned back toward the stairs. "Leave me."

The sentries opened the doors outward. The generals didn't waste any time stepping over the Togorian's remains.

*   *   *

"Where'd you *go?*"

Kerra lifted her mask and faced the Bothan, still bound to the round frame. He seemed perturbed by her disappearance; as annoyed as she'd been at his unwillingness to talk, earlier. He'd only agreed to trade information for his freedom, and only after he was freed. "I'm not in the business of helping Jedi," he'd said.

I'm not in the business of freeing Sith spies, she'd thought.

Hearing approaching voices, she'd headed back into the hallway just in time to see Daiman's procession depart the heptagonal temple, heading in the opposite direction.

If Daiman was at the front, she hadn't been able to see him. But where else would he be? "Where is he going?"

"I can answer that," the spy replied. "And you know how."

Kerra groaned. Seeing no alternative, she came to a decision. "Hold on."

"Wait! *Whulp!*"

Kerra started the wheel moving again, careful not to upset anything as she rolled it through the storage area. The kitchen outside looked as though it had never produced a meal, and yet the larder was fully stocked with fresh food and shining cooking implements. *While everyone outside works three shifts for a ration,* she thought.

"Is this really necessary? Cut me down from this thing!"

"Just let me do this. There's a way out of here, but you're in no shape for sneaking around," she said. "Now, about Daiman?"

The Bothan fumed. "He's going to Gazzari," he said, finally. "Aboard *Era Daimanos.*"

"Gazzari?" Kerra's brow furrowed. She thought back on the intelligence reports she'd seen in the Republic.

The world sat in a wedge of Daiman's space between Bactra's territory and Odion's. "Does this have to do with what's going on with Bactra?"

"Yes," he said.

"And that is?"

"Only once we're outside."

Kerra slid up to a window and looked out. There was the flagship *Era Daimanos*, parked on a rooftop within the compound. The boarding ramps were down on the vessel, and she saw the massive rear engines outgassing. It was a ship preparing to travel.

Kerra opened her pouch. The explosives were there, beneath her clothes and lightsaber. Yes, she thought, it might be easier to do away with Daiman aboard a ship. As inviting a target as the temple had been, she'd still have the problem of escaping from what was, in effect, Corrector Central. How much easier would it be to decapitate the regime from the comfort of a life pod, on the way to someplace else?

It'd be nice to do something easy. For a change.

Sealing the pouch, she returned to the Bothan's torture wheel. He saw her coming. "I'll tell you the rest, but you have to take me with you. Wherever you're going." The spy's voice stirred with emotion, as it had back on the plaza, nights earlier. "I owe Daiman now, Kerra. You *must* take me."

"Nope."

"What?"

Kerra kicked open a door and grabbed the side of the wheel. "I don't work with Sith. And I don't work with people who work with Sith."

"This again? I don't—"

"I told you, there's only one way to get you out of here," she said, releasing the great wheel and walking toward a corrugated metal door. With a heave, she forced it open, revealing a long stone trough leading downward. Down, and out of Daiman's compound, terminating in the mountainous refuse pile that abutted the south wall.

"No!" Seeing the long chute below, the spy writhed. "Don't!"

"If it's any consolation," she said, "I don't think those bonds of yours will survive the landing. I don't know why, but it looks like the guards loosened them." She positioned the circular rack on the open ledge.

His eyes burned with anger. "You'll regret this, Jedi. I'm not what you think I am!"

"So long."

She gave the wheel a shove.

Only Mak had bothered to wait for Rusher. Using the cane for real, this time, Rusher stepped past the sentries at the gate and looked up at the black wall behind him. Daiman's favorite suns had just set, he saw. *Diligence*'s crew wouldn't have much time to get packed up to move. Master Dackett wasn't going to like this at all.

There wasn't any thought of not taking the assignment. Not if Rusher ever wanted to set foot in Daiman's space again. And one never knew. If Daiman's gambit proved successful, it might *all* be Daiman's space before too long.

Mak looked up at the human and smirked. "Really, Rusher. *'You'd rather rent than own'*?"

"It's what came to me," Rusher said, stretching his bruised leg. Just a little sprain; he'd walk it off. "It's not my line. Admiral Veltraa said it about irregular units, back in the ancient times," Rusher said. *A little history comes in handy.*

"I thought you'd converted for a mo-mo-moment."

"Don't worry, Mak. I'm not about to start wearing gold armor and chanting."

Suddenly the two heard a bloodcurdling scream from

off to the right. Scanning the ramparts, Rusher saw nothing as the cry trailed off into silence. He cinched up his trench coat. "Crazy place."

"And that Daiman's the craziest of all," Mak said, covering his mouth. "Not much to like about this b-b-business."

"Oh, I don't know," Rusher said, straightening his collar. "We get to face Odion. His death-cultists *want* to be blown up. Makes for a short workday."

Era Daimanos was Daiman's flagship in the classic naval sense. Kerra had seen larger, more powerful vessels in the young lord's fleet; *Era* was more a cross between a battleship and a pleasure yacht. But *Era* bore Lord Daiman, and that unlucky fact gave it its distinction.

It had been surprisingly simple for her to reach the ship before Daiman's entourage. Giving up on navigating the labyrinthine palace, Kerra had found her way to the rooftop. It had been an easy traverse from there in the stealth suit. By the time the first train of bearers arrived with Daiman's luggage, she was already safely on board, hiding in a service area beneath a deck grating.

The service tunnel was a close fit, but she'd found several passages branching from it to other areas of the ship. She'd been relieved to find one leading to an unused galley, as it meant she could take her time and pick her moment. And in the tunnel, she wouldn't need the stealth suit every minute of the day. She hoped Daiman wasn't bringing many adepts sensitive to feelings of hate, because she was coming to absolutely loathe the accursed suit.

Settling in near a grating, Kerra turned up the suit's audio sensors. She could just make out Daiman and the Woostian aide, passing somewhere in the company of his sentries.

"—as my lord knows, the Bothan spy is missing," she

said. "The Gamorreans left him as instructed. He was not there when they returned."

"Your lord knows," Daiman said to his aide. "I knew he'd find a way, once we left him alone. An intrepid little beast. Quite entertaining."

Beneath the floor, Kerra pursed her lips. She'd thought the Gamorreans had loosened the Bothan's bonds before they'd left him alone. It didn't make much sense.

Hearing the engines of the vessel throttle up, Kerra strained to catch Daiman's final comment before he went out of earshot: "All proceeds according to my design."

Kerra looked at the explosives sitting inside her bag and smiled. *Just wait, Dark Lord. Let's see you design your way out of this!*

CHAPTER SEVEN

The tortured ground pointed up; turrets of Sarrassian iron pointed out, and down. Standing in the spotters' nest atop *Diligence*'s hull, Rusher regarded the sight with pride, wondering if this was how gardeners felt.

Of course, he planted death, rather than life. But in Sith space, that seemed to fit.

Hours earlier, it had been a rusty ridge, untouched by organics. Now cannon barrels lined the eastern edge of the bowl valley, the weapons planted just inside the stalagmite line by his busy crews. Taking macrobinoculars from one of his aides, Rusher looked along the ridgeline. There were the Nosaurian's long Brock-Eight cannons, just going in to the north. Lower down, Mak was positioning his droids as best he could, given the many crevasses in the landform.

Rusher had seldom deployed in such challenging terrain. The "valley" was actually an ancient crater several kilometers across; their ridge was part of the eastern wall, broken several times by tectonic action and meteor strikes. The curious stone shards rising from the ridge had made finding an elevated place to land *Diligence* difficult. Rusher guessed they came from acid rain, generated by the same volcanoes whose smoke gave Gazzari its low ceiling. Weather seemed to come in only two kinds here: rain, or ashfall. Watching blackened motes flutter by, he was thankful they'd gotten here during the latter. Rain that could give a crater teeth was something he didn't want to be out in.

Below, he saw what the combination of the two had wrought. The floor of the crater was a tarry slick, a featureless sheen stretching to the corresponding ridge far away. Daiman had perched his vessel on the northern crater wall; even now, his elite troops were setting up temporary structures down in the valley. Or trying to. The surface slurry looked ankle-deep. Rusher could see the Daimanites struggling in the terrain.

But the idea was pretty clever, Rusher thought. By raising decoy tents and depots there, Daiman stood a chance of convincing anyone landing that the terrain was manageable. Lost moments in the valley would give his irregulars the advantage. The planet looked as if it had been created specifically with an ambush in mind.

Of course, Daiman would say he'd done exactly that, Rusher thought, rubbing his neck.

He turned his attention back to his own forces. Rusher treated deployments like a science, but visually they had the artistic appeal of a dance. They'd parked *Diligence* in a clearing behind stone spires a couple of meters high, just tall enough to screen their cargo operations. Landing on flat ground to permit easier unloading, they'd activated the precious hydraulic lifts to tilt the nose of the crew compartment downward, providing Rusher's rooftop command center a better angle on the valley.

Now, before any enemies were even in the system, the real operation was under way. With the ramps on *Diligence*'s two cargo-cluster feet petaled outward, all eight battalions hit the ground simultaneously. Squads of rifle-toting troopers emerged first, setting a perimeter. Scouts followed on their speeder bikes, examining terrain and checking for mines.

Then the majors—Rusher always fancied the old Republic ranks—emerged with their headquarters units, conferring electronically about deployment zones with their spotter counterparts on *Diligence*'s roof. The big machines came last, wheeling out the bases of the larger pieces and bringing down the long barrels from their stowage spaces outside the ship's hull.

There were no assembly workers in Rusher's Brigade. No gunners, either, for that matter. As specialists went, Rusher was a committed generalist. Every laborer who built the weapons was also rated to operate them, and anyone who wanted the fun of firing one had to build the emplacement beforehand and tear it down after the party ended. Artillery pieces were complicated enough that an intimate understanding of them was necessary at every step, from assembly to use to retrieval. It was something he'd learned from old Yulan, back in better days. If a turbolaser blast took out half your people, you didn't want to lose the only ones who knew how to shoot back. Or how to lift off in a hurry.

Still, there was the occasional irreplaceable component. Rusher saw his, perched down on the cargo support and screaming inaudibly at teams on the ground. Master Ryland Dackett was the reason things looked choreographed rather than chaotic. He'd spent his life helping Sith shoot Sith. Enough, Rusher imagined, to qualify as an honorary Jedi. He was getting results, as usual. Everything was moving nicely. Engineer Novallo was out giving *Diligence*'s clubbed feet a once-over. Tun-Badon, the creepy Sanyassan running Serraknife Battalion, was scaring the blazes out of his team; no wonder they were always the first to finish deploying. This could be done in record time, despite the terrain.

A light on the northern crater wall caught Rusher's attention. He redirected the macrobinoculars to see Daiman emerging from *Era Daimanos*. Gone was the spectral cape from days before. Today's Daiman was downright demure, decked out in a royal blue flak jacket and leather leggings that tucked into knee-high boots. *Dressed for a fight,* Rusher thought. *Or maybe the weather's just too rotten for the draperies.*

Scanning away from Daiman's departing entourage, Rusher thought for a moment he spied movement beneath one of the flagship's cargo ramps. Something seemed to stir there in the falling ash, almost like a frosted phantom.

Zeroing in, he looked again. Nothing.

Rusher rapped the macrobinoculars twice against the railing. "Get these checked," he said, passing them to an aide. "If there's one thing I'll need today, it's eyes that work!"

It had been the most frustrating journey Kerra had endured since arriving in Sith space. Hearing Daiman board his starship while on Darkknell, she'd assumed she'd be able to find him later just by looking for the biggest room. Not so. *Era Daimanos* lacked any lavish pleasure dome like the one in his Xakrean compound.

She'd heard a rumor on the work line that Daiman didn't care for spaceflight. She couldn't imagine him having a weak stomach; maybe the so-called creator of the cosmos simply felt inadequate actually seeing it up close. That was as good an explanation as any for the fact that there was no hint of Daiman in any of the major cabins with views to the outside. He didn't seem the sort to cocoon himself in a meditation chamber, but after the third day and night, she'd actually begun searching rooms that small.

Again, no luck. *Maybe he stores himself in deep freeze to stay all shiny,* she'd thought.

Worse, while the service tunnels were both deserted and

extensive, the one place they *didn't* seem to go was toward the reactors. Then again, that might have been for the best. *Era* was well fixed for kitchens, but it came up short in the life pod department. Evidently, Daiman's life was the only one that mattered. There was no easy way to blow up the ship and escape.

So she'd waited. The baradium nitrite packs were swiftly becoming the most traveled explosives in the history of guerrilla warfare.

By the fourth day, when *Era* had groaned to a landing, Kerra was afraid Daiman wasn't on the ship at all. It had been a relief, on finally reaching a cargo ramp, to see Daiman's seven-tentacled sun standard hanging outside. Several hundred meters across Gazzari's surface, another stood before a canvas dome erected in a forest of jagged pillars. Kerra had seen several of Daiman's aides milling about—and, finally, the popinjay himself. The headquarters dome was well within the power of her explosives to destroy. Looking toward the eastern ridge of the crater, she'd seen several more ships parked in the highlands. Lots of options for escape. Things were finally breaking her way.

Or so it had seemed. Now, on the ground, Kerra realized the destination was more aggravating than the flight. The Mark VI, which had kept her alive throughout her exploration of Daiman's Darkknell castle, was almost entirely useless here. The fine particles of volcanic dust drifting through the air found something to love about the suit. Or maybe about Kerra. For whatever reason, the ash only clung to her while the suit was activated.

It made the "stealth suit" nothing of the kind. After five minutes walking around on Gazzari, she'd look like a short Talz—covered with white dust instead of fur, and with a clipped mask instead of a weird proboscis.

I don't care if they see me, Kerra thought, ducking

beneath the cargo ramp. *I'm not going to die wearing this thing!*

Crouching in the shadows after her impromptu wardrobe change, Kerra thanked the Force for her freedom. It was good to be back in her old brown-and-black outfit again, augmented with her gun belt and lightsaber. And something new: the bandolier she'd fashioned aboard ship for carrying the explosive packets. One wire running to a receiver triggered the whole thing. Folding the stealth suit into the now-empty pouch, Kerra strapped the pack around her shoulders and stood.

Her bones ached from days in cramped compartments. Her hair, once fine, was a dirty clump. She'd had to wear the Mark VI just to get to the refresher stations aboard ship. Food had been whatever she could abscond with.

It had to end.

She bolted from beneath the ramp into the open. Time to join the fight.

"How're we doing, Dackett?" Rusher said, amused. It hardly seemed necessary to ask.

"We can't get Kelli Two-Five out of the hold," the ship's master said, stubbing out a smoldering cigarra. "Some idiot loaded it wrong back on Whinndor." Dackett slapped his datapad, jowls shaking as he did. He'd just climbed the six ladder flights to the rooftop without complaint, stopping only to relight. The man was a marvel.

Rusher was almost afraid to ask how old Dackett was. He knew the ship's top noncom went all the way back to the days before Lord Mandragall, but "born during an artillery barrage—and conceived there, too," was Dackett's only line on the score. A pulse cannon was just a giant puzzle to him; he'd helped assemble his first ion cannon when he was seven, alongside his father and stepmother. Rusher didn't know how many battles lay between then and his own first meeting with Dackett, but the brigadier never would have gone into business for himself without him. They'd started with a single gun crew and "Bitsy," a long-barreled heavy laser cannon salvaged from some old derelict. They could barely get her into the hold of their transport back then.

Now they ran a crew of nearly three thousand—and according to Dackett's report, nearly everyone was in position, having constructed dozens of guns less than fifteen minutes after pads-down. "Still a few problems with the bulk loaders we salvaged," Dackett said. "But, you know, the port hydro's runnin' like a dream. Your Duros boy's folks came through."

"You're welcome," Rusher said.

"Yeah, well, Novallo didn't get everything on her list, now, did she?"

Rusher smiled. "Is it my fault the kid was an only child?"

"I'm wishin' his parents had taken a vow of chastity." Dackett gestured toward the starboard side.

Rusher pointed the new pair of macrobinoculars. There, beyond one of the cargo ramps, sat Beadle Lubboon in a tracked power-loader vehicle, hopelessly mired in the brackish mud. "I didn't think there was any of that guck up here on the ridge."

"He found it."

The teenager poked tentatively at controls, one after another, to no avail.

Rusher snorted. The recruit had been a total disaster. Most crew slots they'd traded for equipment had netted them something. Few lived long in Sith space with no skills whatsoever. Beadle's talent must have been stealth, Rusher thought. His virtues had, thus far, escaped all notice.

"Good day, sir!" Beadle yelled, standing in his driver's seat and saluting the ship.

"Right," Rusher nodded, flashing the kid half a grin

before turning to Dackett. "Please tell me you've already got that pod unloaded."

Dackett shrugged. "Breathe, Brig. All that's left on that side is the Kelligdyd we can't get out of the hold anyway. I wouldn't put the kid on anything that mattered." The master ambled back toward the hatch leading down. "Oh, and we should be fully deployed in . . . about a minute."

"Will you marry me, Master Dackett?"

"Three wives is enough, sir," Dackett said. "But if one of them dies, I'll let you know."

Era Daimanos brought more people than Kerra had imagined. Hundreds of troopers crisscrossed the edge of the valley and erected defensive positions. She'd had a lot of ground to cover unseen, but the rock spires had offered inviting shadows. Gazzari didn't seem to have day and night so much as it had blankets of gray clouds alternating with waves of fire-lit black smoke.

Slipping from pillar to pillar, Kerra grinned. She loved hunting at night. The winding path to the command dome was working out to be closer to half a kilometer, but at least she was—

"Hey!"

Kerra looked up to see the glistening black eyes of a Nautolan trooper. One of Daiman's soldiers, the green-skinned bruiser held a blaster rifle loosely in one hand—and a container of spice tightly in the other.

Without thinking, Kerra grabbed the surprised trooper's head-tentacles with either hand and yanked, pulling his head into her launching knee. The drug and weapon both flying from the brute's hands, Kerra drove her shoulder into his armored midsection, toppling him. Staying atop his crashing form, Kerra jammed a tentacle into his gaping mouth, stifling his cry.

The Nautolan's right hand slapped violently in the

gravel, searching. Kerra found her weapon first. She ignited her lightsaber—and deactivated it again within the same second.

Kerra looked in all directions as life drained from the guard. No one had heard, and she hadn't had to resort to use of the Force. Breathing, she returned her gaze to the body in the dirt. The guard hadn't been trying to recover his rifle, but the little container of spice.

Dragging the body into a crevice between broken stone pillars, Kerra lifted the warrior's rifle and resumed her circuitous trek to the dome. There were sentries out front, but none behind, where the canvas structure abutted the rocky spires. Light inside casting outsized shadows on the fabric, Kerra could tell that two people were within.

Patting the explosives on her bandolier anxiously, Kerra bit her lip. This wasn't close enough. And she had to know *who* was in the mega-tent. She'd seen Daiman enter the dome earlier, but that was before her wardrobe change.

Creeping behind the structure, she saw an opportunity. While the workers had cleared some of the ground for Daiman's command tent, the surface was still uneven enough that light slipped from gaps underneath. Edging toward the dome, Kerra took the sentry's rifle and slipped the muzzle beneath the canvas.

"You're breathing. I didn't tell you to."

Hearing the Sith Lord's voice, Kerra froze.

"I am sorry, my lord."

The respondent's voice was scratchy and female. Kerra lifted the fabric as much as she dared. It was the Woostoid woman she'd seen earlier, in Daiman's palace. Wearing a silken white dress, she sat atop a silver trunk, staring mindlessly into the bright glow lamp at the center of the room.

His back to Kerra, Daiman stood behind the woman. He was now in a black sleeveless tunic, and his biceps shone with sweat. Kerra could never let herself forget that, for one seemingly sedentary, he was an energetic and dangerous fighter. Daiman's focus was entirely on his aide, his hands digging into her purple hair. "Time to try it again, Uleeta."

Kerra rocked back, nauseated. The last thing she wanted to see was pre-battle action in a Sith warlord's boudoir. But what she heard from the Woostoid regained her attention.

"Flesh is an atrocity," Uleeta chanted.

"Flesh is a prison," Daiman said, digging into her purple scalp. He didn't appear to be wearing the talons. "I exist beyond. Form is a prison to keep me from achieving all my mind imagines. But I can transcend the rules I have created—with the dark side of the Force. *My* Force."

"We are The Encumbered," she chanted.

"You are without the light," Daiman intoned. "You have form, but not spirit. You are a husk." He brought his hands around, raking urgently at her temples. "I knew that the first time I saw into another mind. But if I am to transcend, I must expand my reach."

"I am nothing. There is no Uleeta. Only an agency of Daiman."

"You are nothing—and you are Daiman. I will see with your eyes. Breathe with your lungs. Now."

Kerra recoiled. If this was seduction, it was the worst date she'd ever seen. But she continued to look. The woman was shaking, now, under the Sith Lord's concentration. Kerra could feel the waves of Force streaming off them. The aide's heart was nearly as black as Daiman's. And yet she was letting down all her defenses, burying her will to serve as a conduit for his power. Uleeta's right hand, clasped in her lap, trembled and lifted into the air before the light.

"Very good. My will raises your hand," Daiman said. *"My hand."*

"As my lord knows," Uleeta said.

"I did not will you to speak."

The woman went immediately silent. From behind, Daiman gripped her skull harder, growing frustrated. "No—it isn't true. This isn't real. *I'm* not the one raising your hand!"

Uleeta paused before speaking. "You have told me to, lord. I am doing it."

"*You* do not exist in this. My will should activate your motion directly," Daiman said, releasing his hold on her. "And look!" He grabbed the Woostian's wrist. "A pulse. Your heart is beating!" Offended, he glared at her. "And you're *breathing*! I'm not willing this. I should be in control!"

"I am sorry, Lord Daiman," Uleeta said. "These things are autonomous—"

"There is no autonomy! Not unless I say so!"

The Woostoid aide burst into tears, hiding her face.

Kerra caught a flash of the woman's emotions, still unshielded. True shame. Kerra shifted her weight on the rocks. The moment was horrific—and yet, spellbinding. The woman didn't appear to have suffered physically, but she seemed to shrink as Daiman glared at her.

"It's always the same," he said, simmering. "I can animate still objects. I can persuade you to act. But I can't act through you." Daiman shoved his sobbing aide violently off the trunk and opened it. "I *know* this can work. I know it," he said, rifling through the chest.

The woman spoke, weakly. "The holocrons tell of Karness Muur, an ancient Sith Lord who could enthrall entire populations, making them an extension of his will. He was even developing a method to move his own consciousness from one organic form into another."

Daiman towered over the woman, crumpled on the floor. "It's so obvious," he raved. "Why else would I have planted such information in the past, if it weren't the key to my escape from this—this *prison*?"

"Through victory, my chains are broken."

"The Force shall free me," Daiman said, completing the Sith Code. "Get up. There's time before the ambush. We'll try again."

That does it! Kerra yanked back the rifle and skittered away from the canvas. Furious, she lifted the bandolier over her head. *I don't care who finds me. I'm blowing this freak sky-high!*

"Command, Recon Knife-Two!"

Rusher tapped his helmet comlink. "Go, Knife-Two."

"Aerial contact arriving, two seventy mark."

"Mark, recon." Rusher looked above the grumbling volcanoes beyond the far crater wall. There was movement in the clouds. "Stay cool, brigade. This is only Party Guest One."

They'd arrived suddenly, their screaming thrusters reaching Kerra's ears the moment she'd knelt over the explosives. Daiman's "ambush" comment and the presence of the armed welcoming party had led her to expect Odion's forces, although why they'd willingly come to such a place was beyond her. But the vessels soaring over the western crater wall looked nothing like warships.

Kerra slipped the bandolier over her shoulder and crept away from the dome, climbing toward a protected perch higher on the ridge. Looking down, she saw four transports hovering over the center of the valley, their retro-rockets sending circular ripples across the pudding that served for ground.

She'd seen Daiman's personnel transports before, on

Chelloa. These looked more like commercial vehicles. And the markings weren't Daiman's at all. Instead of his symbol, the tail fins of each transport bore insignias she couldn't quite make out. Vertical lines—or perhaps arrows.

Where have I seen those before? Kerra blinked through the ash. To her left, flashes came from the eastern crater ridge. Macrobinoculars—and plenty of them—were trained on the new arrivals. *What I wouldn't give for a pair now!*

Rusher spotted the new contact just as his crew did. They could hardly miss it. The skies wrenched with something new, something much larger, descending into the valley.

He shook the ash from his hair. It was helmet time for the brigadier, too. Daiman may not have created the universe, Rusher thought, but he certainly ran things to the minute. "That's Guest Two, crew. We're on the timer!"

"What in blazes is *that*?"

Kerra spoke aloud for the first time since her encounter with the Bothan, days earlier. There was obviously something the spy hadn't told her.

At first glance, she'd thought it was nine different vehicles, descending through the clouds in perfect formation. She'd soon realized it was all one vessel, with nine building-like assemblies the size of city blocks connected into a grid by colossal crossbars. And *city* was the right term, for as the vessel continued to fall, she realized how vertical the thing actually was, with towers rising from the base structure. Kerra rubbed her eyes in disbelief. It was one of the largest vessels she'd seen in Sith space, comparable in size to Daiman's mobile munitions factories.

Kerra gawked as the vehicle—if that was what it was—hovered above the crater floor. Nine mighty engines pummeled the surface, exposing the rock beneath the goo. Finding a spot northeast of the crater's center, the complex eased downward, sinking heavily into the remaining muck.

Silence. The Jedi shot one look down the hill to Daiman's forces near the temporary buildings, followed by another glance at the eastern wall. None of Daiman's people seemed to be reacting, anywhere.

The first movement came, in fact, from the four transports. Parked a kilometer to the west of the monstrous new arrival, the ships all put down their landing ramps, at the same moment. Kerra watched as figures began streaming out of the transports. Straining to see, she finally gave up and crept downward to a closer vantage point. At least so far, Daiman's forces on the ground were facing the center of the bowl, paying no mind to the hills.

Squinting from her new location, Kerra saw hundreds of beings assembling in rows outside the transports. But the ranks weren't orderly, and the figures weren't in military dress. Members of dozens of air-breathing species milled about, kicking and playing in the mud—

Younglings!

There were hundreds of them. Youths and teenagers, with some young adults mixed in, all in slave dungarees. All looking excitedly at the sky, the far-off volcanoes, and the giant new city that had followed them into the crater. Each of its nine towers terminated just beneath the low overhanging clouds, each sporting the same three-arrow logo, now clearly visible to Kerra.

"No," she said, standing and nearly giving herself away. "Oh, no!"

She remembered where she'd seen the logo: on the Ishi Tib's badge, days before, on Darkknell. And scanning the crowd, she felt a familiar presence. Focusing, she saw exactly what she feared: an animated Sullustan girl, obviously excited about her first visit to another planet.

Of all places and times—Tan Tengo was here!

"Facility down, Brigadier!"

So that's an arxeum, Rusher thought. *Big.* He opened his helmet comlink. "That's the last of our party, Rushies. Look alive!" This was happening quickly. A voice on another band had just told him what he needed to hear. "Daiman called, people. Our crashers are at the edge of the system."

Rusher had guessed right. Daiman had hidden a surveillance probe in the nebula surrounding Gazzari's parent star. The cosmic display made for a pretty sight and a fine place to watch for sudden arrivals. The rest of Daiman's force, both his ground regulars and his attack fleet, were set to leap in from hyperspace as soon as they got word of Odion's arrival. It was up to Daiman's escort and the specialists on the crater rim to keep Bad Brother occupied until then. "Weapons live, brigade! Confirm!"

"Coyn'skar, live!"

"Serraknife, live!"

"Dematoil, live!"

One by one, all eight battalions—all named for the exotic ancient weapons etched on their helmets—checked in. Rusher had found the names in his studies, names connecting his troopers with the past. It was a tough thing, nearly dying for a different Sith Lord every year. It helped to have a connection to something.

Snapping the visor down on his helmet, Rusher pointed toward a technician looking back at him from a hemispheric window in *Diligence*'s hull. Responding to the gesture, the tech threw a switch—and the entire vessel hummed as the ship's energy shield came alive. *Diligence* made too nice a target, sitting there amid the emplacements. The invisible shield wouldn't stop a projectile, but it might dissipate some of the other fire directed their way. Rusher expected plenty. His flak jacket had been on, beneath his overcoat, since touchdown.

"Guns hot," he called. "Rusher out." Looking down again at the four transports, with their passengers gathering outside, he reactivated the comlink. "And if anyone targets within a klick of those kids, I'll strap them to Bitsy and pull the trigger myself!"

"No! No!"

She recognized the visitors' garments, now. These were all factory workers—slaves from Darkknell and other planets—recruited by Industrial Heuristics. Adolescents, like Tan. Led by droid minders, the group made its way slowly through the sludge toward the giant facility.

There's still time before the ambush. Daiman had said it in the dome—and she could see Daiman's forces readying lower down the north crater wall. There were more forces in the highlands to the east. Who knew how many blasters, how much artillery might be trained on the innocents?

And why? She'd thought before there was no reason for Odion's forces to come here, not into what was so obviously a trap. There wasn't anything here worth fighting over. At least not until the monster city-ship showed up—

No.

Kerra bolted down the hillside, uncaring. This was wrong, all wrong. In minutes Daiman had turned Gazzari from a useless rock into a vital strategic target. And the target was her friend, tromping around down there in the ashen mud with her companions and laughing.

Daiman had baited a trap for Odion on Chelloa by using the explosive baradium mines as the lure. This time the bait was live.

The fastest way down the cliffside led away from Daiman's dome. It wasn't important now. Kerra launched down a rocky incline toward the crater floor, attracting the attention of two Sith soldiers at the perimeter. The armored warriors barely had time to look in her direction before she cut them down with a flash of brilliant green. Kerra stood revealed.

"Jedi?" came a stunned voice from higher on the ridge. *"Jedi!"*

Kerra bolted into the valley, boots slapping against the ocher mud as she made for the temporary buildings. She hadn't heard blasterfire yet, but she would. The transports were a good way off, but she still had the first warrior's rifle. Maybe she could drive the crowds back onto the transports.

Lurching into the clear, Kerra tripped over her feet and slammed into the tarry surface. She looked up, stunned. Nothing had interfered with her progress; the ground was featureless in all directions. She listened again for blaster-fire . . .

. . . and instead felt a stinging pain near her heart.

Ignoring the throbbing, Kerra tried to crawl across the blackened field. For a moment, she thought exhaustion from the past few weeks' exertions had finally overtaken her. But hearing the rumbling above, she knew better.

Or worse.

Kerra opened her mind to the Force. Discretion didn't matter; Daiman's forces, including any Correctors present, already knew she was here. And if they were here now, they were probably feeling the same crushing pressure she was. Something was approaching. A psychic black hole, drawing in all that existed and destroying everything it encountered. It was a feeling she'd first felt on Aquilaris, the day she lost her family—and again on Chelloa, the day she lost Master Treece and the other Jedi, her second family. It was why Daiman's forces weren't shooting at her now. They'd gotten the word. They'd sensed his presence, just as she had.

Vannar Treece's killer was here.

Lord Odion had arrived.

CHAPTER EIGHT

"It's a trap, Lord Odion!"

"Of course it's a trap," boomed the stentorian voice from above. "The little snot doesn't operate any other way."

Narsk looked up at Odion and marveled. Daiman's older sibling truly was his antithesis, both philosophically and aesthetically. Where would-be creator Daiman surrounded himself with light, destroyer Odion sat at the center of a sphere of darkness, lit only by holograms depicting the ships outside. *Sword of Ieldis* had one of the stranger bridge designs Narsk had ever seen. A great uncomfortable throne of Mandalorian iron sat on a pedestal suspended meters above the ship's crew, themselves arranged in concentric circles beneath their lord. Some facing inward, to serve him; the rest facing outward, scanning the space outside.

Sword had come crashing out of hyperspace, hurtling into the Gazzari system at a speed that unnerved Narsk. It was just another day in Odion's service. His flagship named to honor an ancient Sith warlord, Odion styled himself the barbarian king. Heavy battle armor hid a bulkier form, exposing only his hairless, burn-scarred head. Narsk thought it unlikely that true barbarian kings wore their armor all the time, but Odion seemed unbound by convention. Or much else.

"Of course, Bothan, if it is a trap, we could send *you* down first." Odion glared down, ruby light from his left cybernetic eye pulsating in the blackness. "It ought to take you just a few minutes to bollix things up entirely!"

Narsk froze in his seat, searching for meaning in his employer's scowl. Seconds later, Odion quaked with laughter, the sound amplified by his surgically implanted mouthpiece. Narsk bristled. The worst was the silence from the rest of the crew, unwilling or simply too afraid to join in their master's laughter. *Sword*'s bridge had all the warmth of a polar icecap.

Even before Darkknell, working for Odion had been a barefoot dance on the long edge of a vibrosword. But Narsk had to return, even without the *Convergence* data he'd been sent to steal. Daiman had left Narsk alive for one reason: to arrange the upcoming battle. A battle that Odion desired more than a thousand datapads packed with secret schematics.

Narsk was now certain Daiman had wanted him to deliver Odion the news of the deal for Bactra's arxeum. He'd had plenty of time to think back on it hiding in the cargo ship leaving the Daimanate. Daiman had kept Narsk in his presence long enough to hear everything that transpired with Bactra. Even the rotation of his gyroscopic prison, he'd realized, had been programmed to slow down whenever anything important was said.

And the Jedi woman was right. The Gamorrean sentries *had* loosened his bonds before abandoning him in the darkened hallway. If she hadn't come along, he would have escaped himself.

As Daiman expected.

It also explained, he knew now, why it had been such a simple matter to emerge from the Darkknell junkyard and find offworld transit heading in the right direction. The freighter he'd chosen had hopped to a neutral planet, one that just happened to see regular visitors from the

Odionate. In two standard days, Narsk had found himself back before Odion.

Narsk's homecoming was harsh but brief compared with the punishment he had endured at Daiman's hands. Narsk had destroyed the Black Fang, after all; if he hadn't pushed the button, he'd planted the charges. And while he hadn't mentioned the Jedi's role in that—or his escape—he had described her presence on Darkknell, something that interested Odion immensely. Odion had kept him alive throughout the battle preparations, just to hear more about the dark-haired Jedi running amok in Daiman's territory.

As ridiculous as Daiman seemed at times, he'd definitely thought things through. He had given Narsk the kind of information that negated all of his previous failures for Odion, thus ensuring Narsk would deliver it. And he had engineered a situation that was obviously a trap, and yet irresistible to his older sibling. Daiman had avoided direct confrontations ever since the loss of Chelloa. Odion would take any chance for a fight, regardless of the danger.

"Scan for Daiman's forces," Odion said as *Sword* decelerated, its ungainly, chunky form reaching the edge of the planetary nebula.

"Daiman's forces are not in the system," screeched a voice from the grave—or somewhere near to it. Jelcho, one of Odion's Givin navigators, showed his fright-mask face. It turned Narsk's stomach.

"No, Boy-boy's here," Odion said, sniffing. "He's on Gazzari, like the bumbler said." The main body of Daiman's space forces had made a public show of being elsewhere during the last couple of days; Daiman, likewise, hadn't covered his tracks about coming to this frontier world with a light escort. "Someone else is in the nebula," Odion barked. "Tighten the scan."

Jelcho turned his empty eye sockets back toward the

monitor. Narsk was glad. He hated the Givin. An entire species with holes in their heads, and yet they made up the bridge crew. Diversity meant nothing in Odion's service. He liked his spies Bothan, his engineers Verpine, and his navigators Givin—a curious species capable of calculating hyperspace jumps in their withered heads.

The holographic visuals surrounding Odion refreshed. He gestured to a small flotilla, loitering beyond Gazzari's sun. "Who's that?"

Jelcho had the answer. "Lord Bactra's fleet."

"Moving?"

Jelcho paused as another Givin whispered into his earhole. "If our scans on entering the system are correct, they have just delivered the arxeum to Gazzari's surface. They appear to be departing."

"They're not being very quick about it," Odion growled. He waved a massive gauntleted hand, activating an unseen system. "Who's that over there?" he called into the darkness. "Identify yourself!"

Cold moments passed before the holographic image of Lord Bactra materialized in the space before him. "It is Bactra, Lord Odion. My greetings to you." The flickering Quermian shifted, uneasily. "We are . . . literally just *passing through*."

"That's a lie. I know what you were delivering to the brat!"

"And it is delivered," Bactra promptly responded. "What happens to the arxeum now is no concern of mine." His enormous neck dipped, bringing his icy smile into focus. "Of course, if *you* should like to employ Industrial Heuristics' services yourself, I am sure something can be—"

Odion cut off the transmission. "Wretched little trader." Despite the years of uneasy peace between them, his distaste for the Quermian's ways was well known.

Another Givin bleated. "I have firing solutions on the Bactranites, Lord Odion."

"Forget it. Pleasure first."

Narsk watched through the bridge window as they passed Bactra's ships, still dallying before their scheduled engagement on Vellas Pavo. Maybe they simply wanted to watch a good fight. While none of Bactra's affair, the result would certainly alter the balance of power in the region. Bactra would be interested in that.

Knowing Daiman as Narsk did, it could always be something else. He wondered: Had Daiman secretly gotten Bactra to renounce his neutrality, adding to the ambush? If so, the Quermian hadn't brought enough forces for it. Bactra's dozen ships might suffice to escort an arxeum or destroy some gadolinium mines, but Odion had brought a quarter of his home fleet, even now forming an orbital perimeter around Gazzari.

And the master of destruction had brought something else, just now exiting hyperspace behind them. "It's here," Odion said, rising with a clank. "Thunderers, to their transports. Jelcho, you're with me." Pausing on the opaque catwalk leading out of his personal planetarium, Odion shot a wicked look down at Narsk. "You, too, bumbler."

Narsk jolted upright in his seat. "Why me?"

"I might need you to blow up something else of Daiman's." Black teeth showed through curling lips. "Or if the Jedi wench is here, maybe you can let *her* destroy it for you . . . again!"

Kerra got to her knees just in time. Blasterfire from Daiman's ridgeline encampment raked the pasty soil, spraying ash all around her. She could see Daiman's forces scrambling toward their heavy artillery, and while she now knew that the firepower wasn't intended for her, at least a few sentries were still after her. Finding her feet, Kerra made a dash for the cover of a temporary building.

Glimpsing through a window, Kerra saw what she expected: nothing at all. It was all a lure. The little outpost on the crater. The students. And now the towering Industrial Heuristics facility, just arrived. All of it was designed to attract Odion to Gazzari, so the forces on the crater walls could put him into a cross fire.

Could Odion really be so stupid, so desperate for battle as to walk into such a place?

Yes, she thought. That was definitely his presence she sensed entering orbit. And the rumbling of the clouds above meant more than rain. She looked urgently to the west. Clusters of students still marched across the ebon valley toward the facility, seemingly heedless of anything that had transpired between her and Daiman's sentries.

Time was running out. Kerra bolted into the open.

"Command, Recon Ripper-Two! Additional contact!"

"I see it, Rip-Two," Rusher said, doing his best to track the lone female figure on the poisoned plain. The brown-clad woman was making a headlong run for the protean mass of transport passengers, a kilometer away—and Daiman's thugs on the ridge were taking potshots at her. "I don't know who she is—or what she's trying to prove. But she's not our problem."

"Not on the surface, Brigadier! Additional contact in the air, sky-high!"

Reflexively, Rusher lifted the macrobinoculars to look up, before realizing he didn't need them to see what was descending. It was the last thing he expected to see here. And the one thing he never wanted to see.

"Death Spiral!"

*   *   *

Everywhere on the crater floor, beings looked up in awe. That included Kerra, halfway to the groups of children, watching the shadow pierce the haze above.

The form falling through the clouds was a featureless truncated cone, several hundred meters in height. Braking rockets allowed the monstrous obsidian shape to settle on the surface just southwest of the crater's center, equidistant from the transports and the big facility that had arrived before it.

Within a second of planting itself in the similarly colored surface, the towering cone shuddered. With a clatter drawing shrieks of surprise and horror from the mob of students, the device shed its outer casings, ejecting mammoth metal panels to the ground.

For it was a *device* that remained. Kerra recognized it immediately from the history holos. *A Death Spiral*. Developed by Lord Chagras years earlier, it had been conceived as a siege tower in reverse. From its base to its tapering top were more than a dozen concentric rings of blaster turrets and missile launchers, all able to rotate independently. Dropped in the middle of a location under siege, a Death Spiral—named for the rotating levels giving the illusion that the cone was screwing itself into the ground—was designed to fire in all directions at once.

The late Chagras had built several of the devilish devices on a smaller scale; Vannar had barely survived to tell of his encounter with one. Those towers had been controlled remotely. But Odion's version was so large, Kerra saw, that there were actual crews on each level, operating the guns. The huge base, too, served as its own transport and armory, wide doors lower down opening to release scores of airspeeders, speeder bikes, and three-legged armored transports.

Above, Odion's troop transports descended. Kerra

shuddered. It had been exactly like this on Chelloa: Odion, invading from the sky with a contraption of death. There was no mistaking it. This was nothing of Daiman's. Odion's symbol, imprinted on the transports, said it all. Seven chevrons in a circle, pointed outward, on a black field. Arrows reaching outward—but being swallowed from behind by an ever-expanding void.

With an ear-piercing groan, the Spiral's turrets began to move and fire. The void was expanding.

"Quickfire, quickfire!"

Rusher gripped the railing as brilliant streaks erupted along the ridge on either side of him. In just a few minutes, the once-deserted crater floor had become a busy place. It was about to become a hot one, too. Laserfire from Rusher's unit pounded the murderous pillar, towering to the southwest. Seconds later, the Nosaurian's crew opened up from farther along the ridge. Rusher smirked. The Rushies were first on target again.

Some target. Yulan had spoken of Death Spirals, but Rusher had never seen one. And no one had ever seen one like this. The tower must have kept the fabricators on The Spike busy for months. As the flashes dissipated, Rusher could see the Spiral's rings continuing to move, firing at Daiman's forces to the north.

That wasn't good. "Sergeant Wenna'lah! Target damage assessment!"

Rusher barely heard the spotter's voice over the din of another round of outgoing energy. "Damage zero, command."

"*Zero?*"

"Energy shield went live the second the target landed."

Rusher swore. They'd had a clear shot while the beast was descending, but Daiman's signal had ordered them to hold their fire. The young lord was waiting for Odion to make his appearance. Now that he had, somewhere out there in that swarm of transports disgorging his crack Thunder Guard troops, it was too late. Rusher's most potent weapons were out of play.

"Ripper and Sat'skar! Projectile only, on the tower!" The two battalions had the largest number of proton mortar launchers.

"No shot from the north," called a voice back. Ripper Battalion was on the upper flank, partially screened from the Death Spiral by the buildings of the arxeum.

"Aim high and lob 'em over!" Rusher rolled his eyes skyward. To clear the arxeum, they'd be firing into the clouds. *Looks like rain.* "Energy weapons crews, target Bad Brother's vehicles and personnel. Rolling barrage—don't let 'em cross!" Odion's forces were moving, now, fanning out. The fliers would be the first across, reaching the arxeum, the transports, and the students if Daiman's ground troops didn't get there first.

The students! Rusher urgently scanned the field. The adolescents had broken from the semi-orderly companies the minder droids had organized, and were stampeding as a crazed mass back toward the transports. The Death Spiral hadn't begun firing in their direction yet, but he didn't put it past Odion.

And Rusher's employer had put them in this position. *And you went along, to save your neck,* Rusher thought. *Stars help them.*

To the south, the rings of the Death Spiral lined up, their guns unleashing their deadly potential. "Give me that blasted fire on the tower, now!"

Skrra-aakt!

Narsk folded his furry ears over and mashed his hands down upon them. Odion's crew hadn't bothered to supply him with a helmet, but this close to the Death Spiral, the Bothan found himself wishing for earplugs.

"That's the way!" yelled Lord Odion, standing in the

open drop-gate of the hovering transport. Looking glee-fully at the spitting tower, he pulled his cybernetically at-tached comlink closer to his lips. "Do it! Again!"

Another shrill, piercing scream from above—and to the north, Narsk saw another of the Industrial Heuristics transports explode. Shrapnel showered the ashen mulch for hundreds of meters around, just short of the mob of teenagers. With a third volley destroying another trans-port, the trapped students turned again in panic, flowing like mercury back toward the arxeum.

Field trip's over, kids, Narsk thought. *Sorry.*

Clinging inside the doorway, Narsk watched as Odion gave a booming battle cry and bounded to the surface. Other similarly armored members of the Thunder Guard followed, leaving only himself, Jelcho, and the command crew aboard.

"Look over there!"

Narsk turned to see flashes of artillery fire coming from hidden positions on the crater wall, far to the east. They weren't Daiman's regulars; those were all coming down into the fray from the northern ridge. He thought back to the mercenaries he'd passed on the way out. *Part of Daiman's preparations, no doubt.*

Watching several Thunderers blown to pieces ahead of Odion, Narsk spoke his mind. "This is ridiculous! He knew what was down here. Why didn't he just bombard the crater from orbit?"

"Lord Odion wanted to be sure of the Petulant One's presence before dispatching him to the void," Jelcho said. The Givin joined him at the edge of the transport's tailgate, his bony knuckles clasped together excitedly. There was almost color in his freakish face, Narsk saw. *Almost.*

Narsk found the Givin noxious—and obnoxious. First among Odion's death cultists, they seemed to have noth-ing in their skinless heads beyond a desire to finish decomposing, once and for all. "My people would prefer that our lord slew us, of course," Jelcho nattered. "But we will happily accept reaching the void through the agency of Death's brother."

Narsk glared. "How about Death's furry pal?"

"What?"

"Nothing." Narsk wished for something to hit Jelcho in the face with, if only to improve his appearance. But Odion had made Jelcho his babysitter for the duration; the wraith was the closest excuse Odion had to an aide-de-camp. Odion had the simplest power structure of any Sith Lord he'd met. There were no ranks whatsoever, and none of Daiman's regimentation, either. Unlike Daiman, Odion knew others existed—and feared them. He kept potential rivals from rising by making sure everyone reported to him.

In practice, the result was chaos. Odion's empire devoured worlds like a space slug, using neither finesse nor, often, good sense. The competent were neutralized or paralyzed. And those closest to Odion were the ones who cared least for their own survival, because so few survived around him very long.

That worked well enough for Narsk, as an outsider. It allowed him to treat Odion's underlings any way he wished. None had any power over him—except to nauseate.

"Jelcho!" one of the pilots called from the back. "*Sword of Ieldis* just called. Daiman's fleet just arrived from hyperspace! They're engaging our forces now!"

So that's the ploy, Narsk thought. *Get Odion here, and don't let him leave.*

The edges of Jelcho's mouth curled, lending a macabre aspect to his anatomically permanent frown. He embraced the Bothan. "This truly is the day!" he trilled. "And you, Bothan spy, made this all possible."

Narsk shrank from the insipid touch. "Would it be

all right if I had a blaster? I promise I won't go anywhere."

The Death Spiral spat again, demolishing the last Industrial Heuristics transport. Kerra slid in the muck,
stopping just in time to avoid being struck by flaming
debris.

It had been wrong to come this way. She'd hoped to
herd at least some of the students aboard one of the
transports, but Odion's hateful machine hadn't left them
anything. The youthful gaggle had dispersed now, running pell-mell across the northern surface of the crater.
At least Daiman's warriors hadn't charged the field yet,
or they'd be caught in the middle.

Right now, Daiman was letting others do his fighting.
Several cadres of battle droids rushed the valley from the
east, engaging Odion's Thunderers—and then there was
that artillery. Running again, Kerra thanked the Force
for whomever Daiman had on that eastern ridge. Inten-
tionally or not, their shells were screening the fleeing
refugees from Odion's charge.

But it couldn't last for long. Looking south, she saw
that the Death Spiral had the eastern emplacements ze-
roed in. She wouldn't have enough time to intercept the
crowd unless—

Blasterfire suddenly raked the ground ahead of her.
Kerra leapt to the side, tumbling in the greasy soil. The
flanking edge of Odion's first wave of swoop bike riders
soared past, with three of the armored warriors breaking
off to circle her. Parrying blaster shots with her lightsaber,
Kerra closed with the nearest rider and pounced. Slashing
the front control rods from the vehicle, Kerra twirled underneath, watching rider and vehicle plummet downward
into an explosive crash.

She spun and spun again as the remaining riders
closed with her, trying to get a bead on her while mov-

ing. The first rider, a Rodian, lost balance when a deflected blaster bolt knocked him from his seat; the second lost her helmeted head to Kerra's lightsaber.

Ignoring the departing wave of fliers, Kerra approached the fallen Rodian. Armored as one of Odion's Thunderers, he gurgled in agony as Kerra stepped over his body to reach his stalled bike.

"Yeah, that's bad," Kerra said, righting the handlebars. "Trust me, you died for a reason."

"Kellies inoperable, command!"

"Blast!" Lights were going off the board one after another. Now Rusher's best battalion was without its strongest weapons. "Pull out the Gweiths, Tun-Badon—and join in on the tower!"

The leader of Serraknife wouldn't take that well, he knew; the Gweith Brothers concussion missile launchers were some of the slowest-loading pieces in the arsenal, with a fire/disable rating in the planetary core. You could paint a peace mural on them between shots. But he also knew Major Tun-Badon would already be on the job.

Between blasts, word had come from the bridge that Daiman's fleet had arrived and was engaging Odion's forces in orbit. It couldn't have mattered less to *Diligence*, doing its best to stay horizontal with all the impacts.

"We're dialed in!" someone yelled over the comlink. Rusher couldn't make out the call signal.

"Repeat! Whose battalion was that? Which battalion?"

Seeing the flares of energy lancing from the Death Spiral, Rusher realized the answer.

All of them.

The signal was unmistakable. Even in the din of battle, Narsk had felt and heard it: a gentle buzz, in the back of his head.

It had been delivered by a tiny implant at the base of

his skull, hidden so well that Daiman's scans had never found it. Narsk knew instantly what the signal meant.

His true master was calling. He had to respond.

Narsk searched the ready room of the transport. The implant was simply an alert device; he'd have to make the contact. Any communications device would work, so long as it could reach space. Finding a spare portable commset out of sight of the crew, Narsk sat down and activated it.

Static. He scowled. It was the Death Spiral's energy shield, most likely. Since receiving the news about Daiman's fleet, the nervous transport pilot had parked closer to the tower's base for protection. Narsk figured the untested device was interfering with subspace transmissions inside its protected radius. His implant had gotten its signal—but, as he knew, it was from a technology beyond even the capacities of Odion's builders to foul up.

Narsk stood, feeling the pain of the past week's ordeal. There was no choice. He'd have to go out. Slipping the commset into a backpack, he made for the exit. At least the nasty Givin didn't seem to be—

"Where are you going?"

Narsk sighed. He couldn't even run onto a battlefield without permission.

Steeling his stomach, Narsk looked directly at the Givin's face. "I . . . I've decided you're right, Jelcho." He pointed outside, where Odion and his Thunderers were dashing between mortar strikes to eviscerate mercenary infantry coming down from the eastern hills. "Seeing all this, I just have to get out and take part."

"Would that I could!"

Narsk stared. "Well, why not?" Wincing inside, he took the navigator by the chitinous arm.

"I cannot," Jelcho said. "Lord Odion wanted me here.

If the operation should fail, his transport will need a navigator."

"Failure? What're you talking about?" Narsk stepped down onto the crater's surface and waved toward the carnage. "Odion's changing the map of this place. This is the big showdown. And you're telling me you don't want to be in on it?"

Tentatively, like a wistful bride, Jelcho set a boot gently on the battleground. Another foot followed. The Givin rasped, a full breath coming from deep inside his bony carcass. "There is *so* much void."

No need to waste any, freak. Grabbing a pair of blasters from the transport, Narsk returned to Jelcho and spun him by the shoulder. There, a short distance away, sat open airspeeder bays at the bottom of the groaning Death Spiral. "There's your speeder. Here's your gun." He slapped the blaster into the Givin's hands. "Claim some void."

Narsk took his new blaster and began walking around the Death Spiral to the south. It'd be quieter and safer there, with the tower between him and Daiman's forces. He had no desire for a reunion.

Feeling someone looking at him, Narsk turned. The Givin stood limply, gaping.

"Now what?" Narsk could barely be heard over the sound of the tower's rotating, blasting rings.

"A strange thing, Bothan spy," the Givin yelled. Jelcho's triangular eye holes seemed to sag a little. "When you spoke earlier of Odion bombing the crater—you said '*he*' instead of '*we*.' Isn't Odion's glory your own?"

"Shut up and go shoot something!" *Before I shoot you,* he felt like adding.

Rusher looked around. There was suddenly plenty of room atop the hull. Each battalion kept three dedicated spotters on the command platform, but with Serraknife, Flechette, and Sat'skar all out of action, their minders had gone down to manage recovery ops.

Not that those who remained were able to do much. The ridge hadn't turned out to be such a good place to set up, after all. Every impact on the hillside rattled upward through *Diligence,* nearly knocking the spotters' helmets sideways. And smoke on the range was so thick now they couldn't see their own teams.

Rusher checked the command board on the railing. The display showed five good lights, two north and three south. His battalions were still giving their all, the fires of perdition soaring from the ridge down into the valley. But Odion's forces in the Death Spiral had them dialed in.

In a blinding flash, a part of the ridge to the north vanished, sending debris skyward. Rusher's command crew shielded themselves as the shock pummeled *Diligence,* followed by a shower of rocks. No energy shield was going to do much against an avalanche from the air.

"I've lost Rantok Battalion!" Ignoring the fall of pebbles, the lead Rantok spotter bounded from his elevated chair and followed his aide toward the ladder.

Rusher grabbed the third spotter, a young human, by the arm. "Stay here. You're on evac watch now. Port side!"

The pink-faced spotter, all of sixteen, nodded. Rusher headed for the other side. The mission now would be mapping optimum routes back to *Diligence.* It didn't do any good for a team to head back to its designated cargo ramp for boarding if there was an impact crater in the way.

Hanging across the railing, Rusher scanned the haze below. He wouldn't be able to check the paths from every ramp; the cameras on *Diligence*'s belly hadn't worked in years. But he could get direct visuals on the others. A roiling pit had opened near the foot of Starboard Three. That was out. But at least Starboard Two looked nominal—

Rusher lowered the macrobinoculars and squinted. Beadle Lubboon, helmet askew and shaking nervously, was driving away from the ramp aboard his tracked cargo crawler. Haphazardly fastened to a chain behind was the long barrel of Kelligdyd 25, the laser cannon infamously loaded up wrong on Whinndor. The Duros recruit had somehow gotten the recalcitrant cannon out of the hold and was dragging it behind, its mass leaving a gouge in the volcanic dirt.

"Kid! Kid!" Rusher could barely hear his own yells. But the newbie didn't seem to be in his right mind, from the look of him. The boy was ducking as low as he could while still seeing over the hauler's hood. Green knuckles had gone pale on the steering yoke.

Rusher pounded his fist against his helmet. He didn't need this now!

Across the valley, the Death Spiral winked—and the whole of *Diligence* moved, actually lifting a few meters off the surface before slamming back to the ground. Wrapping his arm around the railing, Rusher looked back. The young spotter had gone over the side, as well as two of the remaining officers who weren't strapped into chairs. Rusher scrambled to the forward railing and looked down. It had been a glancing blow, leveling a zone just to the south of the ship's perch. But he could tell from the redundant command board that the ship's energy shield was gone. And what else?

Rusher activated his helmet comlink. "Dackett! What have we got?"

There was no response from down below. He called again, only to hear a voice he wasn't familiar with from down on the ridge.

"Master Dackett's down!"

Rusher swallowed hard. Looking back at the decimated spotter crew, he made for the ladder. Rusher's Brigade was breaking.

Riding the speeder bike like a bantha rancher, Kerra shepherded the younglings forward. The transports ablaze, she had to get them to the far side of the giant Industrial Heuristics facility. Turbolaser fire was lancing out in several directions from Odion's cone of death, including over the students' heads. Those barrages targeted Daiman's positions on the northern ridge; more blasts raked the grounds to the east, cutting down a charging cadre of war droids.

Most of its fire, though, was directed at the nearest target: the corporate pseudo-city at the crater's center. One of the nine towers had already imploded and fallen, kicking up a mass of debris that helped screen her crowd's movements.

Kerra had led a charge of Jedi back on Chelloa. This was nothing like it. There were hundreds of students, perhaps more than a thousand—all streaming chaotically across the shuddering, sloppy ground. She kept her lightsaber aloft and pointed, serving as a visual beacon driving the refugees onward. But no refuge was to be had. A few dozen students, seeing the rising towers of the facility, ran toward imagined shelter, only to veer back in panic as another tower on the southern side collapsed.

And still, Odion's troops bolted ahead, ripping into Daiman's forces, which now charged senselessly from the northern ridge toward the Death Spiral. Kerra laced back and forth through the rushing crowd, working to keep stragglers from being cut off. Some aliens couldn't run at all, she saw—and many, like Tan, could go only as fast as their little legs could take them. Angling the larger exodus toward the quieter ground halfway between

Daiman's northern and eastern positions, she gunned the swoop on a wide sweep, circling the laggards.

Blasterfire arced behind her neck. Kerra swerved. One of Daiman's Vodran troopers, legless and bleeding in the muck, lay on his chest firing at Kerra with his rifle. Kerra squeezed the throttle, only to have the bolts follow her, glancing off the back of the bike.

"They're attacking you, idiot! Why are *you* attacking *me?*"

Seeing the children charge before her, Kerra slammed the swoop into reverse. Blaster bolts flying past her, she flipped backward off the swoop and thudded on top of Vodran's armored back. As the warrior tried to roll over and raise his rifle, Kerra screamed in anger and stabbed downward.

Withdrawing the blade, Kerra gnashed her teeth and stepped off the body. Deactivating her lightsaber, she shot a glance back to the ridge. She'd hoped Daiman was getting a part of it, but the command dome was still there, almost taunting her. They'd probably have an energy field over the encampment now. Her next thought was of the explosives she'd slaved to accumulate and haul halfway across the Daimanate—to the back door of the creator of chaos. *Explosives already behind any energy screen protecting Daiman.*

Kerra's eyes narrowed. *Do it,* a voice said. *End it.*

Standing beside where the swoop had come to rest in the gray mud, Kerra pictured herself back at the dome, just an hour earlier, lifting the bandolier over her shoulder. She should have finished him then.

You can finish it. From here. End it.

Reaching in her backpack, Kerra found the detonator. Confirming from the display that she was in range, she focused her eyes back on the dome. In one instant all her exasperation, all her anger welled up. She saw the dome as she wanted to see it, destroyed, with the oppressor gone and her troubles ended. She saw what she'd seen down Manufacturers' Way when she destroyed the Black Fang, using the same remote control. In that moment, she saw an ending.

What she did not see—or even notice—in that moment, was her bandolier of explosives, still draped across her chest, where they'd been since she'd mindlessly put them on, back on the ridge an hour earlier.

CHAPTER NINE

"Kerra! *Kerra!*"

Her thumb poised over the red button on the detonator, Kerra looked down. Amid the slower refugees, one small figure had stopped. Tan Tengo looked up at Kerra, black eyes just as tearful as they'd been the day they'd parted on Darkknell. "Kerra, what are you doing? What are you doing *here*?"

The Jedi lowered the detonator control. She'd asked herself the same question so many times in the last few weeks. Now she asked it of herself again—and almost involuntarily patted the bandolier wrapped around her body. *What are you doing?*

"Gah!" With a start, Kerra pitched the detonator away, pulling her hands back to her chest. For a second, amid all the sounds of warfare, she listened for herself breathing. *What was I thinking?*

Tan padded over and picked up the control. "You lost your thingie," she squeaked. "Are you—are you a Jedi?"

Kerra sighed and hugged her former student and took the detonator back. "Yeah," she said, "I think so." Still grasping the quivering Tan, Kerra looked back toward the Death Spiral. She knew what had just happened. Odion used his peculiar Force abilities to drive others toward acts of self-destruction. Either in his name—as his charging warriors were now demonstrating—or not.

Daiman's forces on the ridge had broken ranks, goaded into a suicidal charge just as she had been. It was probably the same psychic message.

Tan cried. "Our school—our arxeum. They're destroying it! Why are they doing that?" She looked toward the sea of students beginning to coalesce in a nook where the northeastern crater wall bowed inward. "Why are they trying to kill us, Kerra? What did we do?"

"Nothing," Kerra said, ire rising again. She looked back at Odion's vile tower, now reducing the buildings at the center of the arxeum—so *that's* what the thing was—to molten slag. "It's what I'm *going* to do that they've got to worry about."

Releasing Tan, Kerra turned to see another of Odion's speeder bike riders charging her, mounted blasters firing. Standing her ground, Kerra simply raised her hands in the air . . .

. . . and shoved downward, slamming an invisible weight to the ground. The Odionite's speeder bike went out from under him, crashing into the crater floor a meter from her feet. Kerra strode toward the dazed rider and delivered a resounding crack to his jaw.

A Givin. Kerra had seen Givin during her ill-advised foray to The Spike, weeks earlier, but she had no idea Odion was using them for cannon fodder. The creature wasn't even armored beyond his natural exoskeleton.

"Hide behind my bike, Tan," Kerra said, putting the Givin's grounded vehicle into hover mode. She pulled the unconscious rider from the ground by his spindly arms. "It'll only be a minute, I promise!"

Concussion missiles screaming overhead, Rusher forced himself to focus on the debris-strewn path. There was more incoming than outgoing, he figured, by a three-to-one margin. Whenever that happened for any stretch of time, the battle was over, even for a gunner with a full crew.

And his wasn't. It had come apart so quickly. There were others here: all the specialists from that day in Daiman's temple, minus the unlucky Togorian. And yet they seemed to be suffering even worse. He still saw some weak fire coming from the Nosaurian's position up the line, but he couldn't see Medagazy's droids at all.

His people back on *Diligence* had told him Dackett had left with a recovery team to try to bring back anything from Tun-Badon's battalion, from guns to the Sanyassan himself. *Always worried about the lurch ratio,* Rusher thought. *Leave no one behind.* Dackett must not have known that Serraknife Battalion's entire chunk of ridge was already destroyed. Communications had gone to blazes, along with discipline. That usually happened around the same time.

Rusher looked to a rise in the ridge, just ahead. The formation wasn't there before; much of what lay beyond had given way, and the rest of it was smoking. Stabbing at the ground with his walking stick, he propelled himself forward, fearing what he'd see on the other side of the divide.

"Sir! Sir!"

Rusher gaped as he crested the hill. There was the death and destruction he'd expected, worse than he'd seen in his career. Hillside and weaponry had changed places, leaving the odd metal spar—and organic limb—jabbing up from the sizzling rubble. But his eyes fixed on the one thing moving. Beadle Lubboon's cargo crawler trundled through the smoke, puttering between impact craters. In place of the gun barrel from earlier, the Duros recruit had chained a makeshift stretcher to the back.

"I have Master Dackett, sir!"

"I can see that!"

Forgetting the pain in his leg, Rusher dashed around the crawler to the litter. Dackett was there, bloody clothing shredded.

Beadle called from ahead. "I saw him when I went over the hill with the gun, sir!"

Rusher knelt beside the stretcher. Looking behind, he saw a long trail gouged in the gravel and snaking out of sight. He doubted repulsorlifts could handle this terrain. "Kind of a bumpy ride, Ryland."

Dackett grabbed Rusher's collar with a bruised right hand. "Shoot me, Brig, before he kills me!"

Rusher looked at Dackett's other arm. It was down near his feet, set at the end of the litter. "I brought it back myself," Dackett coughed. "Never leave anything behind—"

Another turbolaser blast struck the ridge, lower down. Tossing his cane aside, Rusher clambered back to the cargo crawler. He opened a bin inside the vehicle's door and pulled out a medpac.

"Oh, that's where it was," Beadle said, still frozen at the control yoke.

"That's where it was," Rusher said, scrambling back.

Rusher found a spot in the folds of Dackett's neck and injected a painkiller. Dazed, the veteran babbled, apologizing for leaving the ship. "Getting too old, I guess—takin' chances I shouldn't." Rusher looked around. Everyone on the team, it seemed, was acting with abandon today. The Duros boy included. Something felt wrong about Gazzari. They had to get away.

"Give me a hand, kid!"

Ripping his fingers from the control yoke, the Duros bounded from his seat and stumbled to the surface. Together with Rusher, he helped lift the hefty victim into the crawler's passenger seat. "Don't forget the arm," Dackett ordered woozily.

"Yes, sir. I mean, no, sir," the Duros said.

With Beadle perched awkwardly on the hood, Rusher settled into the driver's seat and reached for the control yoke. Imprints of the recruit's fingers were there, worn deep into the plastoid. Rusher shook his head. He'd had driven Dackett through half a kilometer of the most pockmarked terrain on the ridge, under fire. "Kid, what possessed you to come all the way down here to get him?"

The Duros looked down, embarrassed. "He was the only person I knew, sir."

Rusher laughed, despite himself—but only for a moment. Crowning the hill, he saw his worst fears realized. Before leaving *Diligence*, he'd called a general retreat, using the battalions nearest the ship on either side to screen the movements of the forces coming from farther away. But the blazing wreckage strewn ahead was all that was left of the screeners and the screened.

"Outfit status!"

"One battalion aboard," crackled the reply over the comlink. "Two still out and stragglers, north and south—"

Rusher couldn't hear the rest. From far away on the crater floor, the Death Spiral fired again and again, banks of turrets on different levels targeting all along the crater wall. They didn't have *Diligence* in their sights yet; Rusher doubted they could *see* it, with all the dust and ash in the air. But they were doing a great job of picking off any of his forces trying to return to it. The only possible haven for the remains of the brigade might as well have been light-years away.

And what's my top speed? Four kilometers an hour? Rusher stood up in his seat and scowled. There was no way through. No way for anyone.

"So much for working for the creator of the universe," he snarled, sitting down and slamming the vehicle into gear. "No miracles here!"

*   *   *

Crouching behind the frame of a crashed airspeeder, Narsk looked at the comm unit. And looked again. Such timing. This would be the strangest thing ever to happen in the history of organized warfare—or even war between Sith Lords.

But the message he had received from space was clear—as was his mission. He had a signal to send to the combatants on Gazzari. Odion—*and* Daiman.

He would have the passcode. They would have to accept his word. But looking at the Death Spiral hurling energy at the dwindling forces on the crater wall, Narsk wondered if any present would hear his message. Searching, he found a pair of macrobinoculars near the corpse of the speeder's Odionite pilot. Even if the Death Spiral weren't throwing off interference, were Odion and Daiman even listening?

Scanning across the field, he found them. They weren't hard to miss. Daiman stood atop a hover platform on the northern ridge of the crater, lightsaber lit. His own forces were gathered beneath, a mix of soldiers and the accursed Correctors, wielding their own weapons. Less than a kilometer away, Odion's Thunderers crashed toward them, having broken the ambush. The man himself rode above them, carried atop a flying skiff. Force lightning flashed in the destroyer's hands as he approached his long-desired confrontation.

No, they definitely won't listen, Narsk thought. And probably no one in the space battle raging above would hear his call, either. He turned his macrobinoculars to the east, where the expensive arxeum had been reduced almost entirely to slag. It wouldn't be long now before the Death Spiral found the mass of refugees, scattering to the east—

Narsk blinked. No mistake: a green lightsaber. The Jedi. She was astride a swoop bike carrying some youngling, directing traffic. *Insane.* Black hair came and went from his view as she alternated her gaze between them and the Death Spiral. But she wasn't looking at its towering heights, now firing fruitlessly at Daiman's shielded platform. Rather, she stared at something closer to its base.

Narsk shifted his view to the left, across an endless stretch of body-strewn muck. The Odionites had cleared the entire area surrounding the conical weapons platform, an area now being traversed by a single speeder bike. Coming from the Jedi's position, the grayish flier was traveling beneath the energy shield on a direct course back to the Death Spiral's speeder bays. Narsk tightened his focus.

Jelcho.

The unconscious Givin was slumped over the handle-bars of the speeder bike, hurtling at full speed, its accelerator jammed. Moving his scope, Narsk saw that Jelcho was attached to the vehicle by something dark. A bandolier, lined with small, silvery pouches.

Just before the helpless rider reached the tower, Narsk scanned back across the crater to see a vision from the past: Kerra Holt, squeezing something. His detonator.

Narsk dived behind the tipped body of the airspeeder. *This'll be bad.*

The base of the Death Spiral disappeared with a blinding flash, sundering the massive structure. A shattering crack emanated from the epicenter, shaking the floor of the crater and throwing Odion's rearmost echelons into the air. To the north, the blast wave knocked both Sith Lords from their aerial perches, depositing them violently upon their respective coteries below.

The quake drove all others in the crater to the ground—even the students herded near the northeastern wall. Kerra looked back in fear. She'd gotten them well enough away from the blast zone, but the ringed tower was wrenching itself into bits as it collapsed, throwing shrapnel in all directions.

Then, seeing the debris fall short of the mob, Kerra sat back on the bike and smiled gently. Daiman's plant had produced the baradium nitrite for use against Odion. She'd just used it as it was intended, but in a way the so-called creator had never imagined!

"What in blazes was that?" Even Dackett, in his pharmaceutical haze, felt the tremor rattling through the cargo crawler's frame.

"Our miracle," Rusher said, mouth dry. The turrets that had been firing on the ridge were now spiraling for real, far over the crater's edge. Not waiting for the echoes to die, he pulled the helmet mike to his lips. "That's our cue. All units, recall and board!"

Reactivating the cargo crawler, Rusher looked back at the pillar of fire and marveled. *Where had Daiman pulled that trick from?* Many more moments like this, and he'd become a believer himself!

Narsk slid out from beneath the body of the airspeeder. The shock wave had lifted the car and thrown it into the southern wall of the crater, picking Narsk up in transit. The Bothan found himself upside down in the front seat, the crumpled dashboard having taken most of the impact.

Staggering to his feet, he swore. Everything hurt again—but he'd picked the right time to take his call. The Death Spiral had collapsed into its own metallic funeral pyre, a miniature volcano added to Gazzari's complement. Jelcho had found his void, thanks to the Jedi. *If only the pleasure had been mine,* Narsk thought, stumbling painfully away. *From orbit.*

He found the comm unit not far from the wreck. Its casing was cracked, but it otherwise appeared functional. Narsk activated it. He could make his call. And maybe now, the Sith Lords might even be listening.

Kerra stood on her bike, her lightsaber pointed straight ahead as she flew over the student body. She yelled to one side and the other in every language she could remember; on the back of the seat, little Tan did the same. "To the east! To the hills!"

The Sith Lords behind had momentarily ceased their battle to regroup, but they would eventually recover—and the victor would have the students. Refuge now could only exist in one place, Kerra realized. Something had to have brought all those war droids and cannons to the battle.

"Kerra, there's a path!"

Kerra thanked the Force for the Sullustan's sharp vision. The bombardment had collapsed the ridge in places, but some of the graded pathways the battle droids had paved to reach the crater floor remained. She couldn't tell what lay above in the smoke, but it had to be better than staying here.

"Everyone, climb!"

The ship's master was safely aboard. Rusher had seen the Duros recruit and Dackett up the ramp before returning to the surface. Coyn'skar and Zhaboka battalions had already returned; amazingly, with most of their equipment. But Team Ripper was still out there, returning from the northernmost position through the mess Beadle had wandered into. The Death Spiral was gone, but Odion's forces were not. Rusher would wait as long as he could, but not a second longer.

He looked down. Gazzari had been a disaster right up there with Serroco. He'd always wanted a piece of military history. Now he had it—if anyone on the world survived to tell about it. Three thousand soldiers had awakened under his command that morning. If a thousand remained, he would be relieved.

No, not relieved. Nothing would heal this wound. He'd been lucky, so far. All these years, and never the big wipeout, until today. So many were gone. Tun-Badon, and his Serraknifes. The Sat'skars. The Dematoils. And now Dackett was fighting for his life. There wasn't any coming back from this for Rusher, not for a gunner with only half a—

Through the swirling dust, Rusher saw the long barrels of the Kelligdyds above the northern fold of the ridge. The Rippers had made it! Rusher trotted forward, stepping around debris as the machines came across the rise on their repulsorlifts. Elated, Rusher patted the backs of the bewildered, battered troopers running beside.

"Load up, folks! Pick any cargo ramp. We've got eight of them, no . . ."

He stopped. Standing at the crest of the crumbling formation, Rusher looked down upon a multitude. Students from the Industrial Heuristics transports swarmed up the hill, inundating his beleaguered forces.

Rusher rocked back, raising his cane in a futile attempt to bar the way. "Now wait!" Younglings and adolescents from practically every species in the Daimanate flooded past, pouring over the hill toward *Diligence* and its "eight ramps, no waiting."

Amazed, Rusher looked toward one of his armored gunners, doing her best to keep moving. "Zeller! Did you bring these people?"

"Negative, Brigadier. They came with *her*!"

Rusher looked back to the horizon. Pulling up the rear was a brown-clad human woman on a speeder bike, chivvying the refugees along. Young, but older than most of the students—and holding a lightsaber.

Zeller lifted her sidearm and gestured toward the ship's ramps. "You want us to turn them back?" Rusher's sentries stood at the ramps, holding their rifles and looking urgently toward him for guidance. The students were almost to the ship.

Rusher removed his helmet and rubbed his eyes. "I think we're outnumbered." He didn't honestly expect his people to turn back a bunch of kids fleeing a war zone. But the woman on the speeder bike was another story. The stragglers all ahead of her, she deactivated her lightsaber.

"Right," Rusher said. Throwing the headgear to the ground, he began to march over the hill toward her, flanked by Zeller and three of her crewmates.

The running refugees simply parted, flowing around him. Rusher ignored them, too. "Hold on right there! Who are you? What are you trying to prove?"

"And you are . . . ?" The woman's voice was husky, matching her dark features.

"Jarrow Rusher. *Brigadier* Rusher." He pointed down the hill. "That's my ship."

"Aha. Kerra Holt," she said, stepping off the bike. She pointed in the same direction. "That's our ship."

"Like blazes it is," Rusher said, "What's this about?"

"What do you mean, what's it about?" Kerra said, lifting the young Sullustan off the bike. "I should think it's obvious." She jabbed a thumb over her right shoulder toward the crater floor. The fireworks were beginning again, with Daiman's and Odion's personal forces engaging directly. "You're here. We're here. We're leaving."

"We're a military vehicle on assignment," Rusher said, trying to block her path.

"Not anymore," she replied, bowling past him.

Rusher's troopers to either side started to move, but he bolted first, following the young woman. "I don't think you understand, girl. We may not have room for . . . how many have you got here?"

"I didn't have time for a head count."

Neither did I. Rusher shot a glance at *Diligence.* The crowd had reached the ramps, streaming up all of them, past the cannons waiting outside to be loaded. The woman stopped, staring at the main body of the ship perched above the twin cargo landers. "That looks to me like a spaceliner."

"It was!"

"Good," she said, adjusting her backpack. "It is again."

Rusher grabbed at her jacket. The leather was worn and dingy, caked—as she was—with the ashfall. Intense hazel eyes glared back at him. Not the perverse golden irises of Sith Lords, but just as bright. "No Sith on my ship!"

"Do I look Sith to you?"

"You look crazy. That's enough!"

Kerra yanked free from the brigadier's hold. "You see a lot of Sith carrying green lightsabers?"

"Depends on who they kill!" Rusher knew plenty of Sith who had collected them, back when Jedi had still been active out here.

Fingering her unlit weapon, the woman stopped and studied Rusher's face. "You work for Daiman. I've seen you before—in his palace."

Rusher stared. "I can't imagine how."

"No, you probably can't," she said. Watching the lines of students moving up the ramps into *Diligence,* she gestured for the Sullustan girl to step to her side. "These people are from Daiman's territory. He brought them here."

"I know."

"Well, now you can take them out of here," she said. "Before they get killed."

"I sympathize. But we're only here to provide fire support against Odion," Rusher said, straightening. Would Daiman really send someone to test him in the middle of a war? He wasn't going to get caught. "He doesn't bring us here to evac civilians."

"You don't look like you're providing fire support. You look like you're leaving." The woman gestured beyond the throng, where the remaining soldiers of Ripper Battalion were breaking down its artillery pieces. Turning back, she approached Rusher. Boot-to-boot with him, she looked urgently into his eyes. "Look, take them out anyway. You already know: if he approves, Daiman will tell you it was his intention all along."

Rusher blinked. *She's met Daiman all right.* The woman was barely half his age, maybe a little older. What was she doing out here? She wasn't one of Daiman's people, not dressed this way. And worried about the kids?

Can she actually be a Jedi?

Kerra stepped away to where the Sullustan was helping the smallest refugees toward the cargo ramp. Seemingly satisfied with their movement, she looked back to Rusher. "Look, if you don't want me aboard, I'll stay." She shot a glance toward the ascending crowd. "Just get them away from here."

A screeching sound from high above preempted Rusher's response. Through roiling clouds now beginning to spill their polluted rain, those outside *Diligence* saw ever-darkening shadows. *Several* shadows. Rusher's shoulders sagged. "Now what? This place is busier than a spaceport!"

"You're not wrong," Kerra said, pointing up.

Two huge warships pierced the clouds, descending toward opposite ends of the crater. Rusher recognized one as part of Daiman's attack force; the other sported an Odionite symbol. Separated by mere kilometers, the two vessels hovered over the crater. Facing each other—and waiting. "That . . . doesn't look like air support."

"No," Kerra said, biting her lip. "Something has changed."

"Not changed enough." Looking fruitlessly for his helmet, Rusher reached into his pocket for his spare comlink. "Novallo, are we in shape to move?"

His foulmouthed engineer responded with several epithets regarding the new guests in the accessways.

"I'll take that as a yes. Light her up." He turned to Zeller. "Push everyone into the barracks and tell them to hunker down."

Rusher turned back to see Kerra kneeling next to the Sullustan. "Don't worry, Tan. This man will take you out of here." She grasped the girl's tiny hands. "I'll find a way out of here, too."

"Yeah, kid. Don't worry. She will," Rusher said. Tossing his cane up the ramp, he scooped up Tan and addressed his remaining ground crew. "Forget the equipment. Get these stragglers on!"

Kerra lingered outside, watching the general and his tearful, writhing cargo disappear up the ramp. Taking a deep breath, she turned back to look at the new arrivals setting down in the crater.

"What are you gawking at?" Rusher stood on the ramp. "I said you'd find a way. You might be suicidal like an Odionite, but you sure don't work for Daiman." He pointed. "Come on. Carry someone!"

Narsk looked at the descending Sith vessels and smiled. He had made his call, as ordered—and they'd heard his message all right. Now events had been set in motion; the Battle of Gazzari would end far differently than either Odion or Daiman had imagined.

After the past couple of weeks, it was nice to be the puppeteer for a change.

Making his way to one of Odion's transports, he cast his eye across the rainy battlefield. So many lives. So much material. The corpses and wreckage would just be another layer in the ooze soon. He was overjoyed to be leaving. It would be a simple matter to get back to *Sword of Ieldis*.

But that would end his sojourn here. He'd studied the schematics of Odion's flagship while aboard, earlier. Once back aboard it, a one-person, hyperspace-capable fighter would be within easy reach.

And then, to his *real* master's side.

CHAPTER TEN

"Something's wrong!"

There were actually quite a lot of things wrong, from Kerra's standpoint on the "bridge" of *Diligence*. For a warship, the command deck looked ridiculous. She'd been joking outside about the main fuselage resembling a commercial liner. Now, inside, she could see that was exactly what it was. Posh bridge chairs bore the emblems of a cruise line from the Republic colonies; judging from them, *Diligence*'s crew compartment had evidently begun life as *Vichary Telk* out of Devaron. How had it wound up out here, toting artillery for Sith?

But that wasn't the problem that had caused her to open her mouth for the first time since reaching orbit. Standing on plush carpet long since beaten into submission by combat boots, Kerra studied the conflagration raging outside the viewport. Odion's hulking capital ships vied with Daiman's smaller destroyers and snub-fighter fleets for control of Gazzari; from the number of flaming derelicts, the battle had been raging for some time. And judging from the near hits *Diligence* had experienced during the ascent, it was clear neither side was yet willing to yield a cubic meter of space to the transit of the other.

So why had the two big cruisers, the ones that had arrived while *Diligence* was loading, been allowed to descend earlier, unmolested?

During liftoff, she'd gone to one of the lower viewports hoping to see the results of Daiman's duel with Odion, postponed by her destruction of the Death Spiral. Instead, she'd seen the lone Odionite and Daimanate cruisers settling closer to the surface, with no one taking a shot at either. And she'd seen none of the telltale signs of the final, fraternal showdown.

Kerra walked down the soft steps to the railed-off command pit. The place was ludicrous. No tactical setup here; the bridge was designed so tourists could walk around the perimeter of the deck and look out to space— or down to observe the captain and his crew doing their work, like figures in a museum display. She found Rusher there, leaning over a crewmate and looking generally dumbfounded. "Captain, something's wrong!"

"Yes, it is," Rusher said. "I'm a brigadier." Without asking her pardon, Rusher pushed past Kerra to another command station. "The zoo's closed. Visit when we're not being pursued."

"Pursued?" The design of the ship made it impossible to see aft from the bridge, and Kerra hadn't noticed anything resembling a tactical map. "You mean, by Odion?"

"I mean, by everyone," Rusher said, looking up at her. Lit by the screens below, he looked older than she'd remembered. "Odion's people think we're with Daiman. Which we *were*—only Daiman wasn't expecting us to pull out, so the ships he's brought in don't know *what* we are," he said. He flipped sweat from his short mop of auburn hair. "There isn't exactly anyone running traffic control right now."

"They just took out *Remorseless*," his Mon Cal navigator reported.

"See?" The general winced. "It's not just us. That was

an infantry carrier. All the irregs coming off the ridge are getting it."

Kerra walked back up the steps to the huge observation window on the starboard side. The battle was dazzling, almost too much for the human mind to process. *Vichary Telk*'s tourists had never seen a sight like this from here. With *Diligence* weaving, it was difficult to find a steady point of reference. Except for one . . .

"Wait," she said. Squinting, Kerra saw a small flotilla of ships hanging in the nebula near Gazzari's sun. "Who's that over there?"

"Lord Bactra's people," Rusher said, looking back over the displays. "They delivered the arxeum. The, uh, *former* arxeum."

"And Odion's ignoring them?"

Rusher turned to face her. "I don't give history lessons, you know." Behind, someone on his crew muffled a chuckle. Rusher looked back and sneered. "Not right now, anyway."

Kerra ruminated. What she saw squared with what she knew from Republic intel: Bactra dealt with both brothers. Whatever deal he and Daiman had, he'd be unlikely to get involved in the fight—and they would likewise steer clear of him. That was it! "Make for over there," Kerra said, pointing to Bactra's forces. "Maybe we can hide among the neutrals."

"Maybe they'll adopt us and take us home," Rusher said, rolling his eyes. He threw up his hands. "Do it," he instructed his helmswoman.

Diligence quaked, lurching to the right so quickly that Kerra had to steady herself against the window. Listening to the metallic groan as the ship yawed, she looked down at the colossal cross-shaped cargo lander that served as the ship's right foot and wondered whether it would stay attached. Any shipwright in the Republic would call this slapdash.

The navigator spoke. "We're made, Brigadier!"

Rusher looked up to see blue laserfire zinging past the port window. A second later orange fire arced past the viewport on the Kerra's side. "Who's got us?"

The Mon Cal looked up. "They *both* have, sir." Several of Odion's and Daiman's ships had broken off to follow them toward the nebula.

"Rear turret?"

"Damaged in the shelling, sir."

Rusher shrugged and walked up the steps. "Won't be long now," he said, looking down. Bactra's ships were up ahead, tantalizingly close—but they'd never get there at this rate. *Diligence* didn't have the speed or shields to survive an engagement.

"This is crazy!" Confronting Rusher, Kerra waved toward the window behind her. Another ray lit the space outside. "You can fight! This ship's bristling with weapons!"

"This ship's weapons are on pallets in the hold, lady," Rusher said, glaring. Grabbing her arm, he turned her abruptly to face outside. "Those gun barrels out there are just *cargo*—and half of them are gone."

Kerra's face fell as she looked where he was pointing.

"Our aft gun's out. That leaves us with a couple of fixed rock-crumblers that fire forward," he said. A barrage echoed through the ship, causing Rusher to reach for a vertical support. "They've got us. We slow for a second to turn around—"

Kerra looked blankly down at the control pit. There had to be something she could do—but her mind, usually crackling with ideas, failed to produce. Looking back, she saw the brigadier. Arms crossed, Rusher leaned against the column and stared out the window at the rest of his ship. The laser blasts were coming closer now, mirroring off the shine on the window.

"Thanks. For . . . for getting us this far," she said.

He didn't look back. "Sorry we couldn't get your kids clear."

Kerra started to step toward the window. "They're not exactly my kids—"

Kerr-rraannng! The view outside the window abruptly changed, laserfire and nebulosities becoming black steel and screaming red lights. *Diligence* rocked violently, knocking both Kerra and Rusher backward from the bulkhead.

"They hit us!"

"No," Rusher said, scrambling to his feet, looking up at his ceiling. "They *bumped* us!"

Kerra joined him back at the viewport. Odion's dark gunships soared by on the right, barely clearing *Diligence*'s body. To the left, Daiman's tri-pronged pursuit fighters jetted past. Firing away—firing ahead.

"They're not targeting *us*," Kerra said. "They're shooting at *Bactra*'s ships!"

Rusher's jaw dropped. Ahead, in the nebula, two of Bactra's crescent-shaped cruisers had just erupted into flames. "What in the—"

"Incoming message," the comm operator announced from behind. "Hologram!"

Suddenly the holographic image of Daiman was beside them, fluorescent in the darkness. "All irregular units, attend to me. This operation has entered a new phase . . ."

Rusher shook his head. "What . . . just happened?"

His bridge was silent.

The message had been as terse as the one on the parade grounds, days before. Daiman had commanded *Diligence*—and, Rusher presumed, any other mercenaries surviving Gazzari—to follow on a particular hyperspace route.

Rusher saw the warrior woman perched at the farthest point forward on the command deck, kneeling as she studied the nebula ahead. There wasn't much left to see—save debris.

Daiman and Odion's forces had together torn into Bactra's surprised flotilla, laying half of it to waste in less than a minute. Bactra's largest vessel and the other survivors had leapt abruptly for hyperspace, followed by several of the warring-until-a-minute-ago brothers' capital ships. And leaving just now were the two large cruisers, one Odion's and one Daiman's, that had landed untouched on Gazzari shortly before.

"He mentioned coordinates."

"Right here, Brig." The comm operator read what they had been sent. "You're not gonna believe this."

Rusher was nearly struck dumb. "This—this is in Bactra's space. *Jutrand.*"

"It's his capital, isn't it?" Kerra's voice came from up ahead. She was still rocking gently on her knee, looking out into the nebula to a point far beyond the burning wrecks. "It's Bactra's capital."

"I don't know," Rusher said. "Maybe not for long."

Rusher tried to put the pieces together. He had to think that Odion would have sent the same message to his own forces. Why else would they have attacked Bactra at the same time? But that only raised another question: why would Daiman and Odion have done anything at the same time, besides try to kill each other?

His visitor looked back, every bit as confounded as he was. "I've been away for a while," she said. "Is there any precedent for Daiman and Odion collaborating?"

"None. You just saw it," Rusher said. "If I hadn't seen it, I wouldn't have believed it."

Kerra stood. "There's nothing here I can't believe." Her voice was lower than he'd heard it before.

Rusher looked back to the Mon Calamari. "Anyone targeting us?"

"No, Brigadier. Daiman still has forces lifting off from Gazzari, but all Odion's people appear to have followed him."

To Bactra's homeworld. Rusher looked up to see Beadle Lubboon in the doorway, holding a datapad. The kid looked as if he had gotten lost at least once heading for the bridge. *That's all right,* Rusher thought. *We're all a little lost right now.*

"I have your head counts, Brigadier."

Rusher climbed the steps from the command pit to take the datapad. "Master Dackett?"

"The medics had to strap him to the table, sir, to keep him from coming up here when the shooting started."

Exhaling, Rusher took the datapad. His relief over the news lasted until he saw the numbers.

"One thousand seven hundred and seventeen."

Kerra looked back. "That's your crew?"

"No," Rusher said. "That's *yours.*"

Rusher's crew looked back at him. How could so many refugees have fit on *Diligence?* Their commander had the answer. "Our survivors are five hundred and sixty." He ticked off the numbers. Some percentage each of Ripper, Coyn'skar, and Zhaboka battalions—plus those whose assignments had kept them aboard *Diligence* on Gazzari.

He dropped the datapad to the carpet and stood in silence for a moment. Then he turned.

"Daiman gave us an order. Load coordinates for Jutrand."

On the other side of the bridge, Kerra nearly leapt out of her boots. *"What?"*

"We were hired to fight a battle for Daiman," Rusher said, gravely. "He says it's not over."

"It is now!" Kerra stomped down the steps into the command pit, walking behind the seated bridge crew. "What are you going to do, throw rocks at Bactra? I mean, you just said it. Half your crew is *dead* or—" She stopped herself and looked incredulously up at the brigadier. "No, no," she said, leaning over the navigator's chair. "Belay that order. Just—"

"Belay?" Rusher stormed to the railing. "Listen, lady, you're lucky to be here right now. I'm of a mind to dump you and your kids back on that ridge and go, while we still can!" He looked at the ships outside. At least no one was shooting any longer, but that didn't mean they were safe. "Whatever our condition, we're professionals. We've got a commitment. Daiman could still be in the system with us, for all we—"

"No. Odion and Daiman followed Bactra—on those cruisers that came to pick them up." Kerra looked up at him. "I don't sense them anymore."

"You use the Force?" Rusher stared at her. "The lightsaber's not just for fun?"

"I'm a Jedi."

Rusher rolled his eyes. This was surreal. "Some kind of Knight errant, running around in Sith space alone, is that it? Saving student bodies here and there."

"No, this is new," Kerra said earnestly. "Usually I save whole planets."

Rusher looked at her for a moment, expecting her expression to change. It didn't. *I was right the first time,* he thought. *She's crazy.*

Throwing up his hands, Rusher turned to walk off the bridge. "Okay, we're done. Plot us a way out of here."

"To where?" the navigator and Kerra asked in unison.

Rusher shrugged. "Just somewhere." They needed repairs. Reinforcements. Time to regroup. But they wouldn't be welcome in Daiman's space after skipping out on the Jutrand leg. They could try to argue they were too crippled to make the trip, but Rusher didn't put much stock in the odds of sympathy from Daiman.

And most of all, they had to rid themselves of their passengers. *One in particular.* "I'm going to go check on Master Dackett and the others."

Rusher paused in the doorway and looked back. "And for your information, *five-sixths* of my crew is dead or missing. Get it right."

The door closed behind him.

"Bactra is finished," Narsk said, relaxing on the sand.

The desert breeze was warm on his fur. Quality med-pacs were doing wonders for him, too. Odion's idea of medical care was amputating sore limbs and grafting blasters in their places.

It had taken mere days for the joint surprise attack to break the back of Bactra's regime. Narsk had left near the outset, as planned, fleeing to an outpost near Jutrand to observe and recuperate. Now he was making his final report. "Odion and Daiman are fighting over the remains, but that's to be expected."

A female voice expressed satisfaction. "The errand is complete, then. A bequest will be arranged."

Narsk bowed his head. "Certainly." This audience was almost certainly done. Two sentences were the most he'd ever received by hologram.

As he began to rise, another question came: "What . . . about the Jedi?"

Startled, Narsk straightened himself before the comm unit's cam. "Kerra Holt? She was on Gazzari," he said, "targeting Odion. I don't know if she escaped."

The words hung in the air for a moment. Narsk wondered whether he was supposed to have said something more—or something different.

"She did escape," the response came, at last. "I know exactly where she is."

Narsk didn't know how, but he knew not to ask. He swallowed hard, his throat only just now restored by the drinks of the oasis resort. He could feel his brief respite coming to an end. "What is your bidding?"

"Keep an eye on her. She could mean more to my plans than you know." The hologram began to fade into the rays of the double sunset. "And as for *you*, prepare for travel. I know another who needs the services of a specialist . . ."

Part Two

THE
DYARCHY

CHAPTER ELEVEN

Saaj Calician liked to look at the grand city, but he couldn't remember why.

He vaguely recalled first seeing the view from The Loft on his arrival, years earlier. It was then that he had found the metropolis *grand,* and it was that appraisal that he continued to rely upon, now that his facility for description was leaving him. Today, when the regent looked down, he saw only the geometry of life here; little beings in little hexagonal buildings, rising from the pale cerulean sea that surrounded his mesa. The ocean, too, he seemed to remember liking—but he couldn't be sure. It was just an impression, and Calician could no longer determine whether it was his thought or somebody else's.

The Krevaaki lingered at the window ringing the penthouse, letting the sun warm his tentacles. Even through the dark screen, it always helped his circulation. For a moment, he thought he almost had feeling back in all his limbs.

But the feeling was fleeting. Calician's glowing black eyes narrowed in irritation. Other Krevaaki, twice his age, had more range of movement than he had. Some days he couldn't even wiggle the feelers beneath his shell-like snout. There was nothing fair about it. The regent had *not* been living hard. He was *not* well traveled.

But he was, by vocation, the elder—and the job had made him old.

The robed figure writhed in anger. His upper limbs still worked, hidden in the folds of the beige fabric. The Krevaaki he had known, the ones so much more robust at his age: what were they, anyway? Nothings! They were out there now, within the polygonal communes on the horizon, carrying out his instructions. None of them had risen to anything like his position, even those touched, as he was, with the Force.

He'd heard their tales, back when tales were being told, of famous Krevaaki following the other side of the Force, as Jedi Knights and other fools. What had that brought them? Nothing, compared to what the dark side had made available to him—then, as a youthful adept under Lord Chagras—and now. It was so obvious, what the dark side offered. Great, powerful rewards, like . . .

. . . well, he couldn't remember right now. But he was sure there were some, and those selfless shell-heads back home would never share the benefits. It always felt good to think of the other Krevaaki. Comparing his lot with theirs, Calician knew who he was. Powerful, and real, and independent—

"REGENT!"

The Krevaaki tore from the window, robes billowing. Cramped tentacles tingled to life, suddenly animated by more than his spirit. Scaling the diamond-shaped dais, he faced the shadows without seeing. He was in the Presence, and it was wrong to look too closely.

"Regent-aspect will feed us," a scratchy female voice commanded.

"I will feed you."

As if on air, Calician glided from the great room and into the hallway, to pass on the command. The meals would be had. He would find the beings on the next level that understood the food dispensers, and if they weren't capable of fulfilling the request, he would operate them himself. And he could, too. Tentacles that didn't work for him, minutes before, were suddenly nimble now.

Calician didn't question it; there was nothing *to* question. He knew his role. To the Presence, *he* was the appendage.

"Brigadier Rusher's asleep," Beadle Lubboon said. "I was trying to tell him about the housing situation for the refugees and he dozed off again."

"Again?" Kerra stared at the young Duros, fidgeting outside the door to the barracks. "He does this often?"

"I am new here, myself, ma'am," Beadle said, apologetically. "But he seems . . . to be interested in what he's interested in."

That sounded like a more gentle description than she would have given. Kerra shook her head. "Wait until Master Dackett gets done in prosthetics," she said. "Maybe he can make something happen."

Kerra watched the recruit amble back to the turbolift and turned to the bustling dormitory. After having spent a few days aboard, she'd changed her view of Rusher's ship. It wasn't the luxury liner she'd been led to expect by the bridge; that was more an observation lounge where crew and cosmos alike were on display. It appeared that Devaronians—or at least, the bunch that had built the crew compartment—had a fairly stratified social system. Some of the accommodations were fine, if not fancy, individual rooms with views. But most riders traveled in large barracks located not so much "belowdecks" as "betweenwalls," in the innermost sections of the ship. Passengers were shelved in long rows of berths stacked three-high. There was barely enough room to walk between them— much less run, as many insisted on doing, despite her repeated warnings.

And it wasn't like there was anyplace for them to go.

Beyond their bunks, there was only an adjoining common activity area that doubled as a mess. When they weren't eating, they were trying to destroy it. The students weren't exactly younglings, but they were without Sith supervision for the first time in their lives—locked in a confined space, with nervous energy to spare. Even the young adults seemed to be devolving to the lowest maturity level in the room. Their activities were in real danger of doing lasting damage to the bolted-down furniture, if not the body of the ship. Kerra was glad they'd forgotten the way to where the artillery was stored.

And there were three more roomfuls on other decks, each demanding Kerra's attention. Even at that, there hadn't been enough space. While Rusher's ship had once carried more than three thousand warriors, the majority worked shifts and shared accommodations. Kerra had been forced to put several on the floor in the hallway outside—generally the older students she'd deputized as chaperones. Most of them were happy enough for the chance to get out of the big rooms and actually experience silence again.

It had been an exhausting period. She'd encountered problems she'd never imagined dealing with before, situations taxing all the logistical skills she'd developed under Vannar Treece's tutelage. Because another feature of Devaronian society meant that almost all its travelers were male, the refresher facilities on the deck were communal, offering none of the privacy that several of the species under her care required—herself included. She'd started running lines to the refresher on each deck. But even that had been a struggle to set up. She'd soon found that Industrial Heuristics had brought recruits from several of Daiman's worlds, not just Darkknell, to Gazzari. While the recruiters she'd met had spoken Basic—well, one of them had—several of the species on board didn't know a word. How did you tell a Wookiee to wait his turn to relieve himself?

There was more. They all breathed oxygen, but the living quarters were always too hot or cold for someone—usually too hot, as the trip dragged on. Some of the species couldn't be billeted near each other, for olfactory reasons or otherwise. And putting always amorous pubescent Zeltrons on a cruise ship with *anyone* had been a total mistake.

These were things Industrial Heuristics had already thought out, she was told; the arxeum was designed as a multispecies facility. More than once, Kerra found herself wishing one would miraculously appear.

Little help had come from the brigade members. People had assisted her on occasion under orders, but for the most part, few, beyond young Beadle, volunteered. Most stayed to their own decks. Kerra had wondered aloud about that before Novallo, the middle-aged human engineer. Kerra found the woman otherwise unburdened with the hardship of a personality, but nonetheless asked whether the crew members were always so hostile to civilians.

"Sometimes," Novallo had answered. "But that's not it. Your brats are sleeping in their dead friends' bunks."

Rusher had been little kinder, for the few minutes she'd actually seen him in the past week. She'd only caught him a couple of times in the days since Gazzari, always when he was on the way to someplace else. Everything involving the refugees he'd delegated, particularly to the spacey but well-meaning Duros. It was probably the most she could expect from someone who worked for the Sith. He was the wrong person to look to for assistance, much less compassion.

In stark contrast had been the old-timer named Dackett, who claimed to have a lifetime of experience in quartering integrated crews. Like the guns in the hold, the man seemed made of Sarrassian iron. When Kerra had first seen him, he was in medbay, loudly refusing to allow the medics to reattach his arm until worse-off gunners had been treated. It had been too late to save the limb by the time they'd gotten to him, but he was more concerned about making ship and crew whole again. He'd never been officially restored to his duties as far as she knew, but the droids had given up sedating him after the fourth futile day of trying to keep him confined. The man reminded her a bit of a friend she'd made on Chelloa: totally living for the people. It was good to have any help at all.

Dackett was more familiar with the species living in the Grumani sector, and in several cases had sent over gunners who could serve as interpreters. More important, he'd made the food situation their one bright spot. Rusher's Brigade ate better than anyone she'd met in the Daimanate—and even with the large number of refugees, they still numbered less than the ship's regular complement. Most of the students' dietetic needs had been addressed by what was in the larder; the gunners were a diverse bunch. But watching the teenagers, Kerra saw that many either gorged themselves, hoarded food in their berths, or both. The hardships of years of slavery weren't going away on a single starship ride.

The saddest thing was how many, amid all the tumult, sat in silence, shell-shocked by recent events. How could she explain everything that had happened to them, in any language? And when she did speak to them, all wanted to know one thing: What would happen to them *now*?

Kerra wondered, too. There were so many of them. She'd thought seriously more than once about taking them all back where they'd come from. But there were all sorts of problems with that. Even if she could get Rusher to agree—a prospect she put little stock in—they hadn't all hailed from the same place. And even if they did return to Daiman's territory, his forces simply weren't going to welcome their arrival. She envisioned going to one planet only to see the students forcibly redistributed again, perhaps as pawns in yet another deadly scheme. And that was unacceptable. Daiman's specter, she'd realized, was the unifying thread in the stories of the few refugees she'd gotten to know.

Like Eejor, the diminutive Ortolan, whose toddler sister had died from the poisons in Daiman's water. Eejor's parents had delayed reporting her death for a year in order to accumulate enough rations to buy a positive recommendation from his factory shift leader. Or Yuru, the Snivvian teenager, whose four older siblings had died in Daiman's slave armies. His look-alike father had attended work disguised as him the day Industrial Heuristics came to administer its tests.

The most heartbreaking case was Lureia, a human girl, ten years old at most. Her family had the misfortune to live on one of the frontier worlds passed back and forth between Daiman and Odion. After successive invasions, only Lureia's teenage sister remained from her family—until the day that her sister, too, did not return home. For a week, the child lived in panic, knowing nothing until corporate scouts arrived, seemingly convinced that Lureia was a budding expert in repulsorlift design. Now she sat all day in her bunk, folding and refolding the ragged blue headband that was the last connection to her sister.

Kerra had no answers for the girl—but her own question had been answered. Gub had been the first to suggest it, days earlier. He might have wanted to keep his granddaughter around—but it was more important to him that she be transported to a better place, with a better life. Kerra had thought to make Darkknell a better place for everyone by doing away with Daiman. If she'd failed at that, at least she could make sure that Lureia's sister and all the other guardians had not made their sacrifices in vain. She'd gotten Tan and the others out of the Daimanate. Now she had to make sure they wound up in a safe place.

If such a thing existed in Sith space.

"Don't move, Kerra! I've got you in my sights!"

Kerra looked over to the short ashen blur behind the mess counter. "If you want to be silent, Tan, you'd better turn the sound baffles on." Stepping over, she gave the amorphous shape a kindly swat. "And you've still got some growing to do, if you want to hunt Sith."

"Blast!" Tan Tengo pulled off the mask of the stealth suit, causing the system to deactivate. The Sullustan was a comical sight, binding the outfit in a dozen different ways just to get it to fit. The Bothan's mask was a better match for her bulbous facial features, but the rest of it was so scrunched that the baffles couldn't do their jobs. "I thought I had you that time!"

The suit had made Tan, now Kerra's bunkmate again, the life of what had once been the Sat'skar barracks. Kerra certainly had no interest in using the thing ever again, though she had wondered a few times if by turning it inside out, she might shut out the noise of the deck.

And Tan now clung to anything having to do with Kerra. Some of it was the situation, she knew, but not all of it. Just as a nanny and part-time tutor, Kerra already had been Tan's hero on Darkknell. Learning that the bedtime stories her human big sister had told her back then were true—and that Kerra was one of the Jedi Knights she'd described? That was heaven. Watching Tan strike a sequence of action poses in the comically large suit, Kerra rolled her eyes. Her comet had picked up a tail.

"Aren't you sleepy yet?"

"Darkknell time, Kerra!"

Kerra yawned. "That excuse won't last forever." She

looked over at the open door at the back of the galley. "Were you just wearing that thing outside?"

Tan giggled. "Just trying it out again."

"Again. Find out anything juicy?"

"Well, if you're trying to pin down the elusive captain, you'll find him two decks up in the solarium." Tan smirked. "I followed that skinny Duros."

"Good girl. Five Jedi points for you."

Rusher emptied another square glass. Lum ale wasn't his favorite, but he wasn't going to waste the good stuff. Not this week.

The solarium always seemed to have a silly name to him. The spaceliner part of *Diligence* went from stars, to stars. No one was going to get a tan watching hyperspace blur by. But they'd left the little room intact, partially because it gave Rusher a place to unwind and study his history holos.

Neither facts nor fermentation were working for him today. Rusher had been in constant motion since the first hyperspace jump, one of a series needed to escape Daiman's territory. Inventory and casualties, casualties and inventory. There'd been not a minute to think about where they were going, or what he might do then. He'd made sure of it.

The crew expected—no, *needed*—to see the same Jarrow Rusher they always had. Upbeat. Joking. Ready with a quotation or an alternate history in a millisecond. And he had given them that. On the bridge, in the ward room, and, most of all, in medbay. He'd learned that from his mentor Yulan, before the bad times. *"Units take losses. Leaders take charge."*

But he didn't know how to take this one. As they'd figured it, *Diligence* now had but two working battalions. One laser battalion—Ripper, fully outfitted and staffed with the merger of personnel from Coyn'skar—and one missile battalion in Zhaboka. He hadn't led so few in more than a decade. Four cargo ramps on each side seemed superfluous. Ripper and Zhaboka each had a side of the ship to themselves.

Running too small a crew in Sith space was perilous, even beyond the hazards of the battlefield. As he'd just seen with Daiman, Sith Lords absorbed independent operations into their slave armies all the time. Size meant effectiveness, which meant independence. And security—security they wouldn't have now. Historical knowledge, like power, was fragmented in Sith space. But try as he might, he couldn't remember any cases where enslaved units lasted long enough to be remembered, much less feted by later generations.

Love of history had, in fact, led to Rusher's independence in the first place. He'd had the relative good fortune to be born into the systems of Lord Mandragall. A real throwback, Mandragall had known more about the Sith of old than most of his rivals—and had used that knowledge to develop the scheme that had, thus far, kept Sith talons off *Diligence*. He'd found it, of all places, in the recordings of Elcho Kressh, whose father, Ludo, had figured in the Great Hyperspace War millennia before. Ludo had made his son sit out that disastrous conflict in a hidden location. But though frail of frame, Elcho was not one to take the Sith Empire's failure idly. Elcho spent years developing a counterattack plan, making the most of the small forces available to him. The concept, as Mandragall had learned from one of tentacle-faced Elcho's holocrons, was simple—and quite applicable to his modern world.

When most Sith Lords raised their armies solely from their enslaved populations, Kressh family rival Naga Sadow had fared better by absorbing outside cultures with different skills. Elcho, exiled outside the Stygian Caldera, saw an even wider variety of forces that similarly might be brought to bear against the Republic. Pirate bands, mercenary militias, species holding a grudge: any number of potential allies existed. Through them, a small number of Sith believers could project great force. It wasn't necessary to have Sith officers aboard every ship, Elcho reasoned, so long as bargains were constructed properly. Offering promises of operational autonomy and a share of the spoils, Elcho built an impressive force from spare parts.

But his counterstroke against the Republic was never delivered. For while Elcho's father had tried to shield his son from harm at every turn—even fashioning a protective amulet for him—no magic could save the young Sith from his own foolishness. Drinking deeply at revels on the eve of invasion, Elcho had suffered a ruptured stomach, killing him within hours. His invasion force, strung together only with his own agreements, soon dissipated. But his ideas lived on, in a holocron discovered by Lord Mandragall in his youth.

With neighbors on all sides declaring themselves Sith Lords, the friendless Mandragall found he didn't have the blaster fodder to throw at his opponents. When droids failed to protect his interstellar borders, he consulted the recordings and followed the long-dead leader's dictates to the letter. There was something slightly romantic about the notion, Rusher thought; nearly three millennia after his death, Elcho's grand plan finally got its trial.

Indeed, Mandragall made significant inroads against his opponents, flexing muscles that didn't really belong to him. More than three-quarters of Mandragall's combat forces were independent operations, fleeing from the threat of enslavement by other Sith Lords. Most were more than willing to fight in Mandragall's name in exchange for continued autonomy and access to the resources and recruits they needed.

But in the end, Mandragall, as mortal as Elcho surrendered to human foible. Twenty years earlier, Daiman and Odion's mother—a wretched monster by the name of Xelian—seduced the aging Mandragall and slew him in the night. Rivals pounced, only to discover that Mandragall's great army was mostly ephemeral. But the model had been created—or re-created—for Beld Yulan, and many who came after.

And for Rusher, although maybe not for much longer.

Human foible. He turned the glass in his hand. How many mistakes on Gazzari had been his? He'd known Death Spirals existed, if not on the scale that they saw. Should he have developed some tactic, just in case? How many of those who remained would suffer for his failure?

The door slid open, behind. "Master Dackett," he said, not looking back. "How's the arm?"

"Skinnier. And it smells like something that came out of a k'lor'slug."

"No wife number four this season, then. About time you gave the rest of us a chance." Rusher filled another glass and proffered it. "Anesthetic?"

"I won't take your pity," Dackett said, "but I will take your drink." Settling his mass into the second chair, he reached instinctively for the glassy cube—only to see that it was the robotic hand that he had raised. He glared at it. "Down, you!" Seemingly reluctantly, the cybernetic limb withdrew.

Rusher chuckled. "You two are going to have some negotiating to do."

"Yeah, well, we're not alone." Dackett seized the drink with his flesh hand and downed it. "You're going to have to do something about all of this. You've got a handle on the rest of it, but we don't have the bunks for all these refugees."

"Then put 'em on the floor."

"I can't walk the halls amidships now without putting

my boot into some someone's gullet," the master responded. "And we've got food now, but we're gonna run out of some stores pretty soon." He slammed the empty glass on the table. "And some of the people, Brig. I got Skrillings eating the trash, down there."

"Maybe we can ration that," Rusher said, knocking another swig back. "This isn't entirely new, you know. We *have* picked up riders before."

Dackett grew more animated. "Yes, but those were military. Infantry. Shock marines. People from other militias. And they usually gave us something for the ride." The refugees had nothing to give them at all.

Rusher looked at the shadows on the floor. If they were trying Dackett's patience after just a couple of days, Rusher was glad not to have gone near them. "Well, you know the score, Ryland. We haven't found a place to dump 'em off yet."

"Blast it, Brig! You're not even *looking*!" Dackett stood abruptly. "I don't get it. That buffoon kid—"

"Lubboon?"

"I know what I said. We were going to lose him on the first cinder that had a hyperspace buoy!"

Rusher looked up. "The kid saved your life, Dack!"

"Not before he ran over my foot with the cargo crawler!"

Rusher set his glass down and stared blankly at the bottle. "Maybe I don't want an empty ship just yet."

Dackett sat back down. "Now we're getting somewhere." He looked directly at his commander. "Look, I see it, too. My whole staff bought it on that ridge. But I can tell you now, there's nobody in this crowd you can make into a gunner, any better than you can that Duros kid." He placed the lid on the bottle. "The quicker we clear the decks, the quicker we can get some new people. Some new battalions."

Rusher glared. "Shooting what? Sharp insults?"

"Whatever we give them," Dackett said, "until we win enough fights to get more guns. But there's no room for anyone new, until you make it." He rose again, leaving a giant crease in the chair. "I'm not gonna tell you how you need to feel, Brig—but I am gonna tell you how you need to act. You can't let 'em just see you going through the motions. You've got to *do* something. Pull the trigger."

"All right," Rusher said, smirking. "How should we do it, then? Air lock or poison?"

"Maybe poison," Dackett said, opening the door. "He's ready to see you, ma'am."

Kerra Holt stood in the doorway. "It's about blasted time."

CHAPTER TWELVE

Kerra had been trained as a Jedi Knight. She excelled in tracking. She'd been living in Sith space for weeks with only her recollections of star maps to tell her where she was. And yet, somehow, Brigadier Rusher had ditched her again. She'd followed Tan's directions to the solarium, only to meet Master Dackett, who offered to go in first and smooth the way. Finally inside, she'd prepared to launch into her list of demands for the refugees when Rusher stood and excused himself to the refresher in the next room. Looking at the empty bottles, Kerra understood why—and seeing his cane still propped beside the chair, she thought nothing of the interruption.

Until Rusher never returned.

After banging on the door, she'd finally opened it, to find no facilities whatsoever. It was a service accessway leading to a ladder. It was *Era Daimanos* all over again, substituting only an eccentric Sith lackey for the eccentric Sith Lord. What was it with these men hiding on their spaceships?

Now, fully three hours later, Kerra had him pinpointed again: decks away, in the wardroom, in the middle of spinning a tale about some old battle for his underlings. She wondered if he had a secret twin. Combat Rusher had been headstrong, but somber; that was the version she'd seen in the solarium. This was the Mess-Table variety: joker and huckster. Storming in, Kerra was determined to get some answers out of one of those personalities.

"Stop!" she yelled, shaking his walking stick at him. "Move again, and you'll need this cane for real!"

Rusher looked at her, and then to the expectant faces around him. He let out a hearty laugh, which they joined in. "Duty calls," he said, rising.

Catching a few of the grimier gunners leering at her, she was suddenly glad they hadn't gone anywhere near her refugees. This Rusher was hardly running a Republic Navy vessel. But then, what could she expect from a Sith stooge?

Some answers. "Where are you running off to this time? An emergency on the bridge?" She followed him into the anteroom. "Another brewery to bankroll?"

"I *had* been drinking, young lady," Rusher said, reclaiming his cane. "I needed a walk to clear my head before attending to your very important problems."

"Thank you for patronizing me."

"It's my pleasure," he said, turning down the long hall toward the bridge. "So. *Jedi.* We don't get your kind around here. You're out here on official business?"

"Not quite." Kerra explained Vannar Treece's mission to the Daimanate, and how she'd gotten stranded. "You've heard of Treece, I'm sure."

"No. Should I have?"

Kerra chewed her lip. She'd have thought that all Treece's efforts would have made more of an impact. Intellectually, she knew that Sith space took in many sectors and untold numbers of systems—and that there was nothing like mass communications here. But Rusher seemed to know things—or, at least, he pretended to. It was disappointing.

But Rusher seemed to grow more interested as she spoke. He clearly understood the workings of the Republic, even if he'd never been there. "If you're not officially sanctioned by the Jedi Order," he said, "or by the Chancellor—then how did you get a ride out here?" He recounted what he knew of the Republic Navy's sometimes-tentative relationship with the Jedi. He'd met a couple of former commanders, cut off here decades earlier in Sith space. They wouldn't ferry a rogue Jedi to a cantina without someone's stamp of approval. "You don't break into Sith space flying commercial."

"We paid the way ourselves."

"Oh! So you guys are like Gell'ach going into Kabal— or Revan, before . . . what was it? Garr'lst? No, Cathar." He snapped his fingers. "I get my massacred cat people mixed up."

"Are you like this all the time?"

"I don't know—I'm not really around myself all the time."

Kerra began to walk away. "I'll come back when you've sobered up."

Rusher grabbed her wrist and chuckled. "No, I'm fine," he said, releasing her. "We don't get much news from the Republic here." He patted the bulkhead warmly.

"What's this thing's name, again?"

"*Diligence*. It's named for one of the *Inexpugnable*-class Republic ships from the Mandalorian Wars," he said. "Admiral Morvis's ship. You know, Dallan Morvis was very much misunderstood. People assume that because you're born to wealth, you don't know what you're doing."

Walking again, Rusher nattered on about the exploits of Morvis's crew—and then more about his ship. Kerra tuned him out. Soldered together out of spare parts, *Diligence* would never have been permitted in any Republic battle fleet. And yet Rusher was so proud of it. The man was a total mystery. He seemed to want to emulate the military leaders of old, and yet he had so little to work with. And the ship's name! That just seemed sort of sad, like a garbage scow driver naming his ship for one of the great exploration vessels.

". . . and I've always said, if Exar Kun had artillery at Toprawa, your Jedi Chancellor would be sporting yellow eyes today."

"Can we get to the subject?" Kerra stood in front of him, arms akimbo. "We have to deal with the refugee problem."

"Yes, you're right," Rusher said, nodding. "When can we get rid of them?"

"*What?*"

He pushed past her down the hallway. "You said we had a refugee problem. I agreed. I never really intended for you all to stay aboard this long." He looked up. "There was just more to take care of first."

Kerra steamed. "I'll say. And I've been taking care of it!" She stalked down the hall after him. "And '*get rid of them.*' That's just great!" She shook her hands as she walked. "I'm not sure what I should have expected from someone who works for Sith Lords!"

"Who else am I supposed to work for? The Republic?" Rusher laughed. "I don't know if you've noticed, but they closed all their branch offices." Pausing, he looked back at her for a moment, studying her.

Kerra flinched under his gaze. "What?"

"Just remembering what that kind of energy was like." He turned and began walking again.

"I've counted six hyperspace jumps. Are you telling me we haven't found a single suitable port since then?"

"Depends on what you mean by suitable," Rusher said, climbing the ramp toward the double doors leading to the bridge. "And whether I care about your definition. *Suitable* for me means a place where Daiman won't shoot at me on sight for fleeing."

Kerra gawked. "We're still not out of the Daimanate?"

"We couldn't very well cross into Odion's territory—or Bactra's. Not without knowing what in blazes is going on." He slapped the button to activate the doors. "It's required some detours."

Kerra watched the general half limping down the steps into the command pit. His leg really was giving him pain, she saw, but he kept forgetting to put the cane in the correct hand. *Huckster.*

Rusher stood behind the signals officer. "We've been trying to scan for any news at all, to see what the score is. We don't know. Maybe it *is* safe for us."

He looked up at Kerra, who shook her head. "Daiman wanted the kids for his military-industrial brain trust," she said. "He'd find them."

"And if there's the slightest chance Daiman and Odion have united, this is no place for them—or you."

She was glad he seemed to readily agree. "It doesn't make any sense," he said. "I mean, really, you have no idea how much blood has been shed between these two."

"I have an inkling." That was an understatement, she thought.

"Daiman and Odion have been at each other's throats—well, since Chagras died."

Chagras. Kerra knew the name from the intel reports and Vannar's stories. The Chagras Hegemony had been a relatively stable period in Grumani sector politics, during which the Sith made inroads against the Republic. The invasion of her Aquilarian home had come during the Hegemony. Luckily for civilization, it hadn't lasted long. Eight years earlier, Chagras's death, under reportedly mysterious circumstances, had touched off a new round of internecine fighting. Not just within his own realm, but seemingly everywhere in Sith space.

Rusher confirmed that Odion and Daiman's war had

broken out then—the creator of all things still in his late teens. But he had no idea what they were fighting over, or what had caused it all. Rusher knew of Chagras—he'd fought both for and against him in his younger days—but he'd never met him, and had no idea what had killed him. "What kills any of them?" He related the ends of Elcho and Mandragall. "I don't know where longevity comes from with these people, but it isn't lifestyle."

Kerra knelt and rested her head against the railing, stray ebon strands falling on either side. None of it made any sense. Why would Odion and Daiman team up, even briefly? She sensed an unseen hand at work. But she always sensed that, among the Sith. Exasperated, she moaned audibly. "Can't we just go to the Republic?"

"Who said anything about going to the Republic?" Rusher looked at the navigator. "Ishel, do you know how to go to the Republic?"

The Mon Calamari shrugged.

"I sure don't," the brigadier said. "Hey, how'd *you* get here?"

"There was a lane to Daiman's transport center near Chelloa," Kerra said, rubbing her forehead against the cool railing. A headache was beginning. "I don't think it's an option."

"I'll buy that." In the weeks since Odion and Daiman tangled over Chelloa, traffic from the Daimanate military hub had doubled. "I might amble by there with a shipful of Jedi, but not just one. Next time, bring some friends."

Kerra opened her eyes and glared through the railing. "What'd I say?"

"Nothing," she said. She stood, knee joints cracking. "Look, can you just get us *closer* to the Republic?"

"What are you looking for—convenient connecting flights? I don't think you understand. The hyperspace lane options out here are pretty limited." Rusher called up a holographic display and pointed to the glowing lines. Avoiding Daiman's and Odion's space, they'd have to make another six jumps to get appreciably closer to the frontier with the Republic—and a couple of times they'd have to double back. "And you've got different Sith waiting in between each of those jumps. They're not going to wave as we go past."

Kerra scowled. It was the chief difficulty she'd experienced since her arrival here. In the Republic, one could count on ready access to databases including most of the known commercial hyperspace lanes. The military kept some private, and some corporations tried to keep newly discovered lanes secret when it benefited their trade.

But in Sith space, everything was different. In shutting down its subspace communications relays here, the Republic had created a breakwater of ignorance between Sith space and the inner systems. No longer able to draw upon the collected knowledge of Republic spacers, Sith starship drivers were reduced to using the information they already had stored, plus whatever was in libraries and data centers in their territory. Repeated fragmentation of Sith power had greatly degraded what was available in the latter; as Odion had just done against Daiman, statelets often targeted each other's knowledge centers for destruction.

Aboard one of Daiman's fighters in the Chelloa episode before Darkknell, she'd had access to exactly one hyperspace route: the intended route Daiman had planned for that vessel to take. Maps meant options. Possible escape. Cartography was power, and, increasingly, Sith Lords were hoarding it.

Rusher clapped his hands loudly. "Okay, I've got it here. *Byllura*."

Kerra looked up at the display. "Byllura isn't closer to

the Republic. It's farther away," she said. "Farther away is not better."

"Sometimes it is, out here." Rusher touched a control, causing gridlines to appear in the air, delineating the latest territories known to the *Diligence* crew. "Byllura belongs to the kids."

"What kids?"

"I don't know," Rusher said, waving his hand through the display to move stars around. "I've never been back this far. But they say there's a Sith principality that's run by children."

"*Children?*" The idea sounded like a bad Republic holodrama. Kerra imagined playground kingdoms run by angry young Sith with tousled hair. "You don't mean that."

"Well, I don't know much about it. I always imagined it was some kind of regency deal, with the power behind the crèche and all of that."

Kerra stared at the pseudo-stars and breathed deeply. If there *was* someone running the realm for them, she couldn't imagine the situation lasting very long—not where Sith were concerned. "How recent is what you know about the place?"

"Heard from someone who went near there once. They've been in power for five years, at least," he said. "Sounds odd to me, too. None of these Sith underlings is very patient. I would think 'old uncle' would have done them in by now—or 'old aunt,' or the palace pastry chef."

Seeing Rusher smile, Kerra gave in. If he was pleased with his solution, moving him might take another week. "I don't see we have any choice," she said. "I guess, whatever happens, they can't be as hateful as the adults."

"There were other kids at that Jedi school, weren't there?" Rusher asked. "You *have* met some before." He glanced back toward the exit. "I mean, before this week."

Ignoring him, Kerra started toward the exit. There would be a lot to do, presuming the place was remotely satisfactory. Which she wasn't at all sure it would be. "None of them sets foot off this ship until I check the place out—*mercenary*."

Sounding amused at the label, Rusher called after her, "This is Sith space, Jedi. We're not going to find our way out—and we're not going to find the paradise you're looking for." Scaling the steps from the command pit, he found her in the doorway, glaring back at him. He shrugged and raised his hands. "You're just going to have to settle for the best we can find—and the best is the least-worst."

Kerra stared back at him, icily.

Rusher turned to his crew and smiled, again the jolly drunkard. "You know, I'm glad I got that out. I nearly said *least-beast*."

"No," she said. "That would have fit."

"Regent-aspect," the girl called.

It wasn't a command, this time. Calician woke from his daze and looked toward the pile of orange pillows at the center of the room. It was happening again. The boy atop the plush mountain was shaking, droplets of sweat streaming from his pale forehead.

The fever had returned. Quillan was seeing the future. The future, or something so far outside his frame of reference that it tested his understanding. Black eyes searched the room, as the human searched for—what? Words? Fourteen years old, and Quillan had never spoken once in Calician's presence.

Kneeling beside him, his sister, Dromika, fought to follow the boy's trembling movements. Making small, frantic motions with her hands before her frail sibling's face, she fought to capture his attention.

Calician stepped as close as he dared. Only the care

droids were allowed to physically approach the twins, and he was only supposed to address them from his dais. Standing anywhere closer disoriented Quillan too much. The teenager's perceptions were too strong. Everything that made Saaj Calician an individual was already shining through the Force, blinding the boy. Additional visual stimuli only overwhelmed him. It was the reason, he now remembered, for his robe, colored to match the walls.

Her brother calmed, Dromika spoke for him, as she always did. "Regent-aspect," she said, tracing in the air with her fingers. "Regent will sense the approach of new aspects," she said, voice wavering.

"I will sense the approach of new aspects," Calician droned.

The Krevaaki closed his eyes and tried to focus his mind. *Aspects*. It was how Quillan and Dromika referred to all agencies outside themselves, organic or electronic. Twins, separated in body, but conjoined through the Force—one being, that no power in science or Sith alchemy could separate. They had been just five years old when he met them—very young, as humans went—and they had never, in Calician's memory, set foot outside their Loft.

And yet, Calician had realized on meeting them that they represented that which he most desired: power. True power, beyond the imaginings of any of the neighboring Sith pretenders. Power that would one day rule the galaxy.

Dromika clenched her long blond hair in her fists. "Regent will find the aspects, and include them."

Calician repeated the command. His audience over, he stepped back outside the siblings' lair. The nanny droid passed, ready again to help Dromika in her hours of grooming. He had his own job to do.

Include. There had been a time, long ago, when he hadn't understood that instruction. He hadn't really belonged, then. His ego had still stood in the way of enlightenment. He was still thinking of other Krevaaki, and what his outfit looked like, and how he might be the one Sith to put down the Republic once and for all. All trivia. Such information was useless to his masters. It need not exist.

And soon, none of their rivals would exist, either. Gliding down the spiral ramp to a lower floor, the regent spied the creature that would help make it happen.

The giant brain floated, asleep, in its cloud. Calician stared at it. Adrift in its cylinder of deadly cyanogen gas, the grotesque alien form paid him no mind.

The Celegian was old. It had been the first one that Calician had captured and brought to The Loft, years earlier. Already two centuries old by then, the monstrosity had been no match for its abductors. The alien still bore signs of being brought to heel; several of its hanging dendrites were no more than stumps, severed by the torturers.

Calician hated Celegians. One of his few lingering memories was of being mocked as a child: "Saaj Celegian," the other Krevaaki had called him, jealous of his piercing intelligence. During his Sith education, he had finally encountered real Celegians at one of their colonies on Tramanos. If he hadn't already disliked them, he would have started then. The creatures flew about in their self-propelled gas envelopes, trying to participate in the world's commerce as if they weren't colossal floating brains. By never acknowledging their own ugliness, they seemed to expect others to ignore it, as well—an uncomfortable burden for their counterparts, to say the least. And while the Celegians had inborn telepathic skills, enabling them to surmount all language barriers, they seemed to have little interest in using their special abilities for influence and power. Ludicrous! What was an advantage if one didn't press it?

Calician had harbored no compunctions about using what they wouldn't. Within days of being appointed guardian of the twins, he'd arranged to have this first specimen—never known by any name other than "One"—brought in. The results had been so positive that he had worked to lure entire Celegian communities to Byllura. Thousands of the creatures had settled in the capital city of Hestobyll. But while One was old, it had proven itself unmatched at its job.

It was time for it to prove itself again. Calician raised his hand before the cylinder. "You will contact the defensive stations," he said, hammering at One through the Force.

For a moment, the mass of gray and crimson sat, unresponsive, in the foggy soup. But then the Celegian's chilly response echoed through the regent's mind: *I will contact the defensive stations.*

"You will report the appearance of any strangers immediately."

I will report the appearance of any strangers immediately.

Calician shivered as he watched the tendrils beneath the creature beginning to stir. Violet blood pulsated through thin membranes on the creature's pate. The being was coming to life, contacting the other minds in the facility. Its telepathy had a limited range—less than a kilometer—but that would reach all the intended parties on the island. And more.

The regent stared at the transparisteel container. Years earlier, he would have flinched, moving quickly to avoid seeing the repulsive thing in action. Now he couldn't remember what it was he had once found so nauseating.

He watched idly for a minute—until, moving, he caught

a reflection of someone he didn't recognize in the glass. He looked about for several seconds before realizing the image reflected was his own.

Facial tendrils drooping, he trudged back upstairs to his assigned place near the twins.

CHAPTER THIRTEEN

Rusher had said she wouldn't find paradise. The brigadier had clearly never been to Byllura.

The capital city, Hestobyll, was constructed on a waterfall. No—it had been constructed *as* a waterfall, or more precisely, a river delta carved into a steep diagonal slope. Kerra had seen the remarkable formation on their approach from orbit. Byllura's largest landform was a high plateau, separated from the sea by towering escarpments all around—everywhere but near the southern bay, where the drop-off to the ocean had been sculpted into terraces. A grid of canals cut in a hexagonal pattern broke each terrace up into hundreds of six-sided city blocks, with water cascading pleasantly down from one level to the next through dams. Raindrops from the tropical forests at the continent's center, high above, thus completed their long journey into a rippling blue sound, lapping at the edge of the geometrical shore.

Kerra turned toward the pinkish sun and inhaled deeply. Fresh ocean air filled her lungs, reminding her of her Aquilarian home, years earlier. Avian creatures drifted lazily across the sea. There were no ships in the harbor—that seemed strange—but quite a few landing pads, like theirs, constructed on platforms above the gentle surf and connected to the city, behind, by bridges.

At this distance, she couldn't see much detail to the

terraced city; Dackett had been called away before she could ask for a pair of macrobinoculars. Even as obviously engineered as the metropolis was, though, the shapes seemed in harmony with the surroundings. Low, featureless structures squatted on the hexagonal steps running up the embankment, with bridges running across the canals. Nowhere to be seen were the smokestacks of Darkknell or the mining pits of Chelloa.

The Sith didn't build this, she thought. *This was a Republic world.* She put it on her mental list of places to visit when they finally took it back.

The only thing marring the beauty of the scene was the mesa. A flattened mountain the same height as the mainland plateau perched in the middle of the bay, several kilometers from the shore. Kerra imagined it to be some granite remnant of erosion, or perhaps a chunk separated from the continent by whatever seismic event created the bay. There was something constructed atop it, she saw; almost a squashed dome, overhanging the mesa on all sides and making the formation resemble a giant balo mushroom. Occasional airspeeders buzzed back and forth from the mesa to the city. And there was something else, in the bay: buoys the size of starfighters, bobbing in concentric rings radiating from the mesa to the mainland.

Odd. And odder still, no one had come to meet them.

"Jedi, I think you made out better than you could have hoped."

Kerra turned to see Rusher at the bottom of one of the starboard ramps. Once it had become clear that no welcoming party was on the platform, she'd hit the surface first, followed by Novallo and her crews checking hull integrity. But Rusher had taken his time to emerge. "It's quiet," Kerra said.

"Nobody stopped us, anyway," Rusher said. Strange-looking fighters in orbit hadn't even moved when they exited hyperspace. Nobody had even hailed them until they were on final approach, when a guttural voice came on the comm system directing *Diligence* to one of the platforms ringing the bay.

"And we know we're not in Daiman's space," he said. The brigadier knelt and pointed to the tiled surface of the landing platform. *Diligence* was parked upon a colossal letter *aurek*, formed by chalk-colored hexagons. "No little flags. The alphabet's normal here."

"I don't know," Kerra said. "Maybe Daiman's 'revelation workers' haven't gotten around to stonework yet." But she likewise doubted that this was Daiman's territory. All those orderly rows of city blocks—and no holographic statues that she could see. Or real ones, for that matter.

And it definitely wasn't Odion's territory. There was still a city to see—even if she'd only seen a small number of figures moving about.

Rusher stretched, lifting his walking stick high into the air. "Well, it looks good to me," he said, turning to face the cargo ramp. He cupped his hand to his cheek and yelled, "Deploy!"

At once, the other seven cargo ramps clanked open. Metal plating rumbled, as the first batch of refugees came thundering down the ramp behind Rusher.

Kerra leapt toward the foot of the ramp, nearly knocking the brigadier over. "Wait! Wait!" She looked up. Dackett was leading the exodus, with Beadle Lubboon nearly lost in the stream of bodies.

The tromping continued over her voice until she ignited her lightsaber and yelled, *"Nobody move!"*

The puzzled crowd stopped in its tracks—although more students continued to descend the other ramps. Kerra shot an irritated look at Dackett. "So that's where you got called away to."

The master shrugged, nodding toward his superior's back.

Lightsaber shining, Kerra pointed it toward the brigadier's chest. "I told you, I needed to check the place out first!"

"I thought that's what you were doing, down here," Rusher said, looking down with annoyance at the glowing tip. "Were you just checking out the sea air?"

Kerra deactivated the lightsaber and stepped closer to him. "I need to do a proper recon, *Brigadier,*" she yelled. "Do you even know what that is?"

The man stared down at her, coolly. They'd played this game over the past couple of days on the way here, but he'd always chosen the battlefield. She could tell: bickering with the little Jedi girl was something that won him points with his soldiers. But he'd always had the upper hand, or been able to pretend whatever he was giving in about wasn't important. She wasn't going to let him get away with that now—even if she had to break him right here, in front of his top officers and all the refugees.

"I think," Rusher said, speaking slowly, "that there's shelter up in that city. Room for a lot more people than my ship has. And nobody's shot at us for being here." He counted on his fingers, ticking off the benefits of Byllura. "Shelter. Security. Sustenance. I win. Goodbye."

He began to move, but Kerra blocked him. "We don't know anything about the Sith that run this place! Why aren't they here yet?"

"Maybe they've gone swimming," Rusher said. "It's a nice day for it. Look, I've told you. On a datapad, this place has everything you need."

"These things are all theory to you!"

"Do I look like a theorist?" Rusher smirked.

Kerra saw he was playing to his crew again. She wasn't going to allow it. "I think you don't care. You haven't even come up to see the refugees the whole time we've been aboard." She gestured toward the crowd of students, listening on the ramp. "Is that why you're in artillery? So you never have to see who you're attacking?"

Rusher exploded. "Now, you wait a minute!" Abruptly grabbing her shoulders, he turned her behind one of the ramp hoists, out of sight of most of the crowd. Startled by his sudden movement, Kerra looked up at him.

"You think this isn't real to me?" The brigadier spoke quickly in Kerra's face, trying to keep his voice down. "I may not see who I'm shooting, little Jedi, but I always see who gets shot. I've got kids your Sullustan's age and younger that I've had to carry away from deployments in vials!"

Yanking a surprised Beadle from the line of escorts, he folded the kid's ear back to reveal an embedded chip. "I've got comm-frequency tags on all my people so I know who's where, and when," he said. "I don't leave anyone behind unless going after them is going to get more of my people killed than it saves. But when that's the case—like on Gazzari—I go!" He straightened and looked back at the ramp. "Carrying your people is going to get my people killed."

Kerra simmered. This was yet another side to Rusher—but it was clear he was serious this time.

Serious, she could deal with. "One hour," she said.

Rusher looked toward the bridge to the city—and stepped back toward the cargo ramp. Ripping the com-link headset from Beadle, he pitched it to Kerra. "One hour."

Kerra bolted across the tarmac toward the corrugated pathway. Rusher turned, gesturing to his troops to re-board the refugees. He was almost in their midst when he was interrupted by the Jedi, standing at the edge of the bridge and looking back.

"Oh, and Brigadier? Jedi don't leave anyone behind, either," she said. "It's a good trait."

She turned and ran toward the city.

The time was now!

Calician paced the perimeter of the circular penthouse, as excited as he had been in years. He could even feel the tips of his tentacles—without the animating power of Dromika's commands. After eight years of plotting, eight years of banal arrangements made in the name of his dual masters, all was coming to fruition. And it all had to do with the new arrivals, down below.

The regent returned to the northern window to study the strange-looking warship again. "One" had reported its arrival from hyperspace first, passing on word from the orbital sentries. Now it was clearly visible on its landing platform, separated from the mesa and The Loft, atop it, by a few kilometers of seawater.

According to plan, the starship's occupants had been allowed to debark without interference. Certainly, they would want to do so. Byllura was pleasing to the organic eye, even if Calician could no longer remember why. In the design he had implemented for his young charges, Byllura was the planetary equivalent of a Whinndorian gorsk-plant—a pretty flower with a paralyzing sting. Population, manufacturing output, military strength: all these things had grown steadily in the Dyarchy in the past eight years because when people came to visit, they stayed—whether they intended to or not.

And very soon, thanks to his efforts, Quillan and Dromika would export Byllura's brand of welcome to the other worlds within their space, and beyond. Planets controlled by the twins today would hew even more tightly to their commands—clearing the way for the Dyarchy to expand.

And now, at last, Calician knew what direction they would expand in.

The Dyarchy had several Sith neighbors, ranging from the watchful Arkadianate to the pretenders of the Chagrasi Remnant. But no border was wider than the one the twins shared with the accursed Lord Daiman. Like their other neighbors, Daiman had been reluctant to either ally with or declare war on their Dyarchy. Calician had spoken with him several times, always by hologram. The narcissistic Lord of Presumption had never seemed to understand his younger rivals, and what Daiman didn't understand, he dismissed. That was well, the Krevaaki thought; Quillan and Dromika lacked the forces for an all-out confrontation.

But now Daiman had made a critical error. A strategic move against Lord Bactra, in concert with his brother, Odion. Calician knew very well why they had done it; he had received the message on the special channel, too. But while the Dyarchy was too remote to share in the dismemberment of the Bactran territories, it did front a tantalizing number of systems in the Daimanate's rear. A rear now unguarded. Daiman would expand into Bactra's space only to lose his own.

The sorry warship below had been the harbinger. Word of Daiman's move against Bactra had filtered in, but the appearance of the vessel—*Diligence,* the commander had called it—served as confirmation. When asked, the mercenary had even transmitted his reasons for visiting Byllura: delivering student refugees from the Battle of Gazzari. Calician knew that Daiman would never have allowed the escape of any portion of his workforce, so long as he had ships in the area to stop it.

It was all the confirmation they needed. Quillan had already sensed it, of course; and when Dromika gave the command, it had taken Calician mere moments to put the plan into action. The battleships, under construction for years, were ready in their secret docks. Within a day—maybe within hours—all would be under way.

For the first time in months, Calician felt truly alive. Not as an individual, but as a *part* of things. Big things, as foreseen by his masters. It didn't matter that the mechanics of the plan were his. The Sith Code had it wrong. "Through victory, my chains are broken"? The chains *were* the victory. By binding the weak, the chains were the *victors*!

In the midst of his elation, a stray thought entered the regent's mind, passed on by the Celegian, downstairs. *Someone is approaching Hestobyll from the warship. And the students are reboarding.*

Calician stopped. That didn't make sense. *Diligence*'s captain had indicated readiness to off-load his passengers. What could cause him to change his mind? Nothing. Unless they weren't what he said they were. Unless they were part of some kind of Daimanite trick—

Calician lurched backward. He wasn't the only one who'd heard the One's thought. Tentacles flailing within his robe, the regent flurried, against his will, back onto the diamond dais before the twins.

Dromika faced him, green eyes glistening. He knew her command before she gave it. But he obeyed, nonetheless. As always.

Was it the salt? Or the wind? Kerra didn't know what it was about seaside settlements, but they never seemed to look as nice up close as they did from the ocean, or from above. The buildings of Hestobyll were mostly white and beige, many sandstone constructs drawing from what she guessed were local materials.

But for some reason every place she'd passed looked . . . dingy. Uncared for. Even the newer buildings had a light sheen of dirt on walls facing the harbor. Large reflecting pools built into several of the terrace levels had a coat of algae almost thick enough to walk across. The seams between the small tiles that made up the pathways were caked with mildew. There wasn't a lot of spray coming from the cataracts, but it looked like whatever hit the streets was never wiped away. Every walkway she found was slick, regardless of its proximity to water—and the bridges connecting the polygonal city blocks stank from their accumulated grime.

This wasn't a place for running.

Fortunately, she didn't seem to have a need to run—at least, not so far. Hestobyll reminded her of some sleepier ports in the Republic: people of various species drifted about, ambling from one uninspired stone igloo to another. Duros. Caamasi. Ithorians. Sullustans. None of them paid her the least bit of attention. Kerra looked down. No, she hadn't gone out wearing the stealth suit—but she certainly felt invisible.

Making sure her lightsaber was out of view in her vest pocket, she selected a wandering Ithorian to approach. Surely, she could engage her in a conversation about something. If nothing else, there was the gorgeous weather to talk about—and maybe Kerra might learn something about the state of things on Byllura.

"Excuse me," she said, stepping up to match the brown giant's lumbering gait. "Hey! I'm talking to you!"

The Ithorian barely looked down at all, continuing to walk toward one of the hexagonal silos that dotted the cityscape.

No good, Kerra thought. *Language problem.* She didn't know Ithorian. But *someone* had to know Basic.

Spotting an elderly Duros couple passing, she tried again. They actually stopped, but only to look at her with mute indifference. Kerra turned in disgust, scanning the crowd. The people looked as shabby as the buildings: old clothes, barely fitting in many cases. And all with the same vacant expression.

"I'm in a droid factory!"

Kerra's hour was nearly up when she chased down a female Sullustan on one of the lower levels. Sullust was in a nearby sector—and she *knew* they understood Basic there. If not, she understood a little Sullustese from her time with the Tengos. But again, she received the same sad stare. Kerra searched the Sullustan's bulging eyes. It was as if she wanted to respond, but couldn't remember the words.

"Remember our deal," Kerra's comlink crackled. It was Rusher's voice, right on schedule.

Stepping into an alcove, she spoke quickly, explaining what she'd seen. "This doesn't look right to me," she said.

"Somehow, I knew it wouldn't," the voice responded. "Well, you'd better hurry and find out whatever it is you're after. We just heard from Deep Voice again on the commset. The Byllurans saw the refugees on the platform—and they're sending people to help with our situation."

"Our situation?" Kerra goggled. "How do they know about that? You *told* them?"

"Hey, it's their planet. All the guy said was that they'd send someone by to direct the kids to a center."

"A center for what?"

"For assigning living quarters. Those are the exact words," Rusher said. "You've got to admit, it sounds innocent enough."

Kerra frowned. She agreed with the brigadier. As relocation practices went in Sith space, it was downright mild. Before she could say anything else, Rusher reported that his sentries had spotted someone's approach. "Be careful," she said.

"The word is *diligent,*" Rusher responded. "Oh, and be on the lookout—you've picked up a tail. Rusher out."

Kerra tapped the headset. "Hello? What?" *A tail? What does he mean by that?*

"Exasperating jerk," she grumbled aloud.

"He says the same thing about you" came a voice from behind.

Kerra spun, angry at being caught unaware. There was nothing but the sidewalk and canal there—until she looked down.

"Tan Tengo!" she growled. "You followed me?"

Before the young Sullustan could answer, Kerra heard another familiar voice coming from the stone staircase leading down.

"There you are!" Beadle Lubboon said, sweat streaming from his emerald skull as he topped the stairs and saw Tan. The Duros soldier fell to his knees, hyperventilating. "So . . . many . . . stairs . . ."

Tan looked at the Duros, and then up at Kerra. "Don't you know some kind of Jedi healing trick to help him?"

"Help him how? By making him run laps every day?" Kerra put her arm around the recruit's chest and helped him toward the canal. Beadle surprised her by abruptly plunging his head into the burbling water.

Kerra exchanged glances with Tan until Beadle emerged, gasping. "Thank you."

"What are the two of you doing here?"

Tan explained that she was in one of the groups that had come down the ramps from *Diligence*—but when the order came to re-embark, she had seen Kerra running toward the city.

"She bolted, Master Holt," Beadle said, fingering the water from his ears. "Bridgadier sent me after her."

Kerra clutched at her hair, sure it would fall out at any minute. She could see where the refugees ranked in Rusher's mind, if Trooper Lubboon was the rescue team.

"It's so drab here," Tan said, wandering and looking up at the city. "It's the same three buildings, over and over again."

"Darkknell wasn't exactly a colorful place," Kerra said. But she knew what the girl meant. Here on Byllura, all the bright colors belonged to nature. Architecture, fashion— everything suffered from a dearth of energy, imagination, newness.

Stepping to an outer wall long enough to confirm that *Diligence* wasn't powering up its engines yet, Kerra turned back toward another crowd headed for one of the hexagonal silos. This one was large, the size of a full Hestobyll block—and, from the sounds inside, evidently some kind of factory. She could see smoke now, rising from a chimney above.

Beadle and Tan in tow, Kerra pulled an elderly Duros from the line. As before, neither he nor anyone else responded to her action. Nor did he respond to her simplest questions. Holding the man's shoulders, she looked to Beadle. "Can you speak to him, Beadle? Show him we're friendly. Ask him his name."

The lanky Duros saluted and joined Kerra in front of the old man's face. "Sir, what's your name?"

Kerra glared at him. "I mean, in Durese!"

Beadle shrugged. "I don't speak Durese."

"Great."

Sitting on the canal ledge and splashing with her stubby feet, Tan chimed in. "Maybe there's something in the water."

"I don't think so," Kerra said, looking into the dull, wilted eyes of the old man. "And language isn't the issue." She could sense it. The Duros understood the words. It wasn't that he wouldn't respond; he *couldn't*. "He seems . . . *numb*."

Wait.

Kerra turned back toward the man and raised her fingers. She hated doing this, but if her hunch was right . . .

"You don't want to go into the building," she intoned.

The Duros elder froze. "I don't . . . I don't . . ." His arms began to shudder. "Go into the building."

Kerra held his shoulders and studied his eyes. There was something there. An emotion. *Confusion? No. Panic.*

Abruptly, Kerra released the Duros, who bolted ahead as if shot from one of Rusher's cannons. The green figure disappeared into the doorway, as he had always intended to. Or as someone else had always intended for him to.

"It's a Force-user," Kerra said. Daiman had his Correctors and his propagandist historians, but this was different. Here, the Sith were *directly* imposing their will on the people—*all* of the people. But how? Force persuasion was a one-on-one technique. To mystify a populace on such a scale required—what? She had no idea.

Kerra scrunched her nose, deflated. This wasn't a safe place for her charges at all. She'd been hoping that, outside the influence of Daiman and Odion, conditions might be better. If anything, they were worse.

Is every place out here insane?

Abruptly, Kerra stepped to the canal wall and lifted Tan by her shoulders. "Beadle, tell Rusher we're coming back."

"You've got my comlink," he said, picking his ear again.

Reminded, Kerra reached to activate her headset— when suddenly a booming alien voice echoed in her ears: *Dyarchy Fleet workers, you will commence loading operations now!*

Kerra looked around, surprised. The voice wasn't coming from the comlink—but from another mind. *Tenders, you will deliver the designated Celegians to their assigned vessels!*

At once the lazy pace of Hestobyll picked up around

her. Citizens who had been taking their time to reach their destinations suddenly began moving quickly, thundering toward the hexagonal buildings. Other residents poured onto the slippery streets from the white domes—housing, Kerra imagined—to join the march. It was Byllura's version of Darkknell's morning commute, all directed by a mysterious source: the same voice Kerra had just heard.

Celegians, the voice had said. Kerra had met a Celegian years before on Coruscant: hard to look at, but easygoing—part of a seemingly happy race of interstellar travelers. A natural phenomenon, their thought broadcasts "sounded" quite different from thought projections through the Force; and that was unmistakably what she and the locals had heard. It made sense as a form of public address, with listeners able to comprehend regardless of their lingual differences.

"Hearing" another announcement, Kerra looked around. No Celegians were visible—and they certainly would have been noticeable!—but that didn't mean anything. As she turned to face the direction where the sensation was strongest, her eyes locked on one of the large silos. From there, a Celegian could contact much of the city at once. That had to be it. Looking around, Kerra felt like kicking herself. City blocks radiated from silos all across Hestobyll. Those reflected the Celegians' range, she imagined. There had to be more than one.

But the quick compliance of the people seemed odd, and nothing explained the tremors she now felt in the Force. Apart from the famous Jedi Master Ooroo, millennia before, the Force had touched relatively few Celegians. Using the creatures for mass communication was novel, but signified no inherent danger. Pushing her way up crowded steps to get a better view, Kerra called out behind: "Beadle! Stay with Tan!"

Suddenly the crowd began churning faster. Fighting against the wave, Kerra struggled to keep her balance—and to see what was driving them. It wasn't the Celegian's words. Humanoid figures in skintight red suits descended across the cliffside city aboard silver multiperson airspeeders. Leaving their speeders hovering over the canals, a few of the scarlet riders leapt high into the air. Traversing several meters in an uncanny instant, the determined newcomers landed safely on the sidewalks and charged the crowd.

There's our Sith, Kerra thought. *So much for paradise.*

"Tan! Tan!" Kerra looked back. The girl had gotten lost in the crowd—and the Duros was gone, too. The Scarlet Riders, men and women of various species, were still on the move, hurrying stragglers along toward their work. They hadn't harmed anyone yet, but Kerra noticed baton-shaped weapons slung over their left arms. She swore. "Blast it, Beadle, I told you to stay with her!"

Forcing her way through the stampede, Kerra leapt atop the canal's retaining wall and looked down at the crowd. There was the Ithorian from earlier, surprisingly nearby—and face-to-stern-face with one of the riders. Despite the height difference, it was easy to tell who was in charge. The Ithorian seemed mystified. Feeling a twinge in the Force, Kerra realized why. Straining, she heard them:

"You will comply with your orders immediately!" the rider said.

"I will comply with my orders immediately," the Ithorian droned in Basic, before barreling forward.

Seeing the same exchange going on all along the thoroughfare, Kerra realized the truth. The Celegians only gave—or passed along—the commands. The Scarlet Riders enforced them, using Force persuasion. It made sense, now. The people of Byllura were indeed numb, worn down by constant mental manipulations by Force-users!

Alert, Kerra scanned the crowd for her companions. Suddenly she saw Beadle Lubboon in the crowd, confronted by two riders. And there, behind them, was Tan, being held by a third. They weren't trying to escape—and Kerra knew why. There was only one thing to do.

"Hey, Sith!" Kerra yelled, leaping atop a stone platform and igniting her lightsaber. A dozen faces in the mob turned toward her. "Yeah, that's right! I don't want to go to work! *Come and get me!*"

CHAPTER FOURTEEN

For the first time since Gazzari, Kerra's lightsaber tore into Sith flesh. That battle had been chaotic; multiple combatants heading after different targets. Here, even amid the workers scrambling to safety, there was a simple direction to events. Kerra, trying to chase Tan and Beadle's captors; and more Scarlet Riders than she could count trying to stop her.

Kerra bounded against a sandstone wall and leapt back into the fray, lancing toward her assailants. Their batons were alive with energy now, blades matching the color of their suits. But the weapons were only half the length of her lightsaber, the minimum required for herding workers. It forced her to abandon all the fancy lightsaber disciplines with names she could never remember anyway and fight free-form. That was the way she liked it. A female rider jabbed at her—and received a roundhouse kick followed by a deathblow. A hulking male rider leapt toward her from behind, stabbing downward; Kerra twirled and sliced backward, separating his sword arm from his body.

Withdrawing her lightsaber from her fourth attacker, Kerra turned back, only to walk into a maelstrom.

You will stop you will stop you will stop!

Four advancing Sith, speaking in unison, pounded at her through the Force. Dizzied by the mental onslaught,

Kerra felt her knees buckle. Rolling away on the sweaty sidewalk, she opened her eyes to see them advancing. Advancing—and speaking, their words pummeling her.

Wincing, Kerra looked behind them—and saw one of their airspeeders, hovering, unoccupied, over the scene. Reaching through the Force, she grabbed at it and pushed. The vehicle complied, slamming violently down onto the canal retaining wall behind her surprised attackers. Their psychic attack momentarily broken, Kerra pushed again, causing them to lose their footing on the slick surface. Regaining her feet, she bounded toward them . . .

. . . and past them, leaping over the speeder's debris to the top of the retaining wall. She broke into a run toward the sea, relieved that the mental pressure had abated. Force persuasion was a discipline almost every Force-user learned, even if she loathed using it. But she'd never felt such power behind it before—excepting perhaps Odion's coaxing call to self-destruction. The only thing that was keeping her alive was that, at least as far as she could tell, the Scarlet Riders had learned mesmerism to the exclusion of other, more physical skills. She could take them in a direct duel—but now was not the time. She spied her real goal, ahead. Tan and Beadle's captors had loaded them aboard one of the airspeeders, the first in a row of three readying to head across the bay.

She'd have only one chance to catch them.

Speeding up as she approached the trailing airspeeder, Kerra remembered her headset and punched a button. "Rusher, this is Kerra! Whatever you do—don't let the rest of the refugees off the ship!"

Tell me something I don't know, Rusher thought, pocketing his comlink as he dashed across the once-lush carpet of the ready room. One didn't go very far in Sith space without seeing a suspicious mind trick now and again. From what he could tell, the characters in red that had ridden up had worked more than a few of them.

The brigadier had been getting ready to kick back in the solarium when he saw them through the skylight: the first fliers coming across from the mesa in the bay. By the time Rusher reached the top of Starboard Three, he'd seen Novallo and her fix-it team standing, hypnotized, in the middle of the metal bridge. In between them and *Diligence,* riders representing Byllura's government stalked across the platform, rounding up everyone they could find.

Rusher cursed himself. He'd advised the sentries not to challenge any arrivals too strongly, figuring that the locals were coming to escort the refugees away. Either that, or the Jedi or Trooper Lubboon would be back with the Sullustan kid. But the Sith who ran the planet evidently weren't going to settle for just his passengers.

It wasn't the first time a Sith Lord had reneged on Rusher's independence; not everyone respected the way forces from Mandragall's former empire did things, and even if they did, they were Sith. Cheating was in their nature. But as far as he knew, the faceless masters of Byllura didn't even know who or what Rusher's Brigade was. It was just a crew to enslave, a warship to be grabbed.

A warship where most of the weapons are on the inside, Rusher thought, running onto the bridge. At least the deckwatch had the presence of mind to close the ramps before anyone boarded. But the options from here were limited. This was going to be a close one, if they got out of it.

"Hailed from below, Captain!"

Rusher stepped down into the command pit to see the view from the cam beneath Port Ramp One. A gaggle of red-suits was there, including one toothy monster of a Trandoshan who looked none too comfortable, strapped into his light jumpsuit. Looking up at the cam, the Trandoshan waved a meaty green hand and hissed, "You will open this vessel and report for assignment."

"It doesn't work over the comm, pal!" Rusher snorted. These weren't Sith Lords, or even the higher-quality Sith adepts he'd seen. They were specialists, like him—trained at one thing.

And it wasn't going well for them. The rider repeated his command.

"Talking louder doesn't help!" Rusher sat down at the Besalisk's comm station. "Now can we talk about you returning my crew, or—"

"The Dyarchy has spoken! Open this vessel!"

"If you say so," Rusher said, pointing to his helmsbeing. "Drop anchor!"

With a metallic crack, Port Ramp One dropped open, smashing the Trandoshan and two of his cronies flat. The ramp lifted back shut less than a second later.

"Good hydraulics, baby!" Rusher said, patting *Diligence*'s command console and smiling.

A brief respite. His reverie halted when the Mon Calamari navigator spoke up, pointing to another monitor. "Master Dackett's down there."

"What?"

"Other side, sir." Rusher looked at the view from the underbelly. Dackett and several more of the sentries stood, motionless, before another red rider.

"Blast!" Rusher sat back in the chair, flustered. The fat man was going to get him killed one day. "Probably saw the shore and went out looking for the women."

As Rusher stared, the Trandoshan walked into the scene, rubbing the fresh dent in his rubbery skull. "You *will* submit, mercenary!" He ignited a short crimson lightsaber. "Open up or we'll cut you out!" The Trandoshan shot a look at his stupefied hostages. "Or maybe we'll cut something else!"

Rusher stood, tapping vainly on the comlink. "This is your department, Jedi! Where are you?" *Diligence* could use a rear-guard action, Jedi-style. "Kerra Holt, come in!"

Nothing.

"Blast and blast!" Rusher said, tossing the comlink to the floor and stomping up the steps to the big window. Their lurch ratio was shot to blazes, anyway. "We're on our own." He looked down at the helmsbeing. "Can you lift off without cooking them?"

"Sir, you're going to *leave* Master Dackett?"

"He'll find a way back," Rusher said, looking back outside. "We've still got his old arm."

Kerra had gone cliff diving a few times as a child on Aquilaris. But never as an adult, never as a Jedi—and never from a ledge that stood not over water, but over a city. Running atop the retaining wall, she saw the permacrete ledge run out just ahead, where it guided the water down a hundred meters to the next level of Hestobyll.

She sped up. *Boy, this had better work.*

Leaping, Kerra stretched her arms wide, reaching for the rearmost airspeeder as it pulled away. If she was shocked that she'd tried it, she was even more surprised when she overshot it, crashing down upon the suddenly idling vehicle's hood. Rolling over, she saw the crimson-clad driver struggling with the control yoke. Feeling the impact, the Rodian looked up at her, puzzled.

"Engine problems?" Kerra asked, putting her boot through the windscreen and into the driver's snout. Scrambling across the shattered remnants, she leapt atop the bewildered Rodian. Crowded from the driver's seat, the Sith lackey struggled to find his baton. With an inviting target in the creature's green proboscis, Kerra grabbed him by the scarlet collar and punched repeatedly.

Hanging halfway outside the speeder, the pummeled Sith turned his glassy eyes on her and focused. *"You will release me!"*

"Okay," Kerra said, pulling her hands back into the airspeeder. The stunned Rodian plummeted out of sight.

Kicking out the remains of the windscreen—no transparisteel factory here, she saw—Kerra settled into the driver's seat. Up ahead, the airspeeder bearing Beadle and Tan rocketed away, climbing above the edge of Hestobyll and out over the harbor. It was making a direct line for the mesa at the center of the bay; she set her speeder on a course to follow.

Confirming that she wasn't being pursued, Kerra looked down and to the left. Something was going on with *Diligence*, but from her elevation it wasn't clear what. More people were out on the tarmac and bridge, and she could see some airspeeders and red outfits. But at least she didn't see any shooting. Kerra couldn't imagine that Rusher would endanger his own people on the dock by putting up a struggle—but, then, she never knew with him. If the red-suits down there were as powerful as the ones she had faced, they might have already shown him a thing or two about fast-talking.

Kerra faced a decision. The refugees would certainly be in jeopardy. But just as clearly, *everyone* who lived on Byllura was in danger: danger of losing their sanity, as they had already lost their independence. This scheme was something Daiman could have dreamed up. The workers weren't simply enslaved here; the rulers of—what had the Celegian called it?—*the Dyarchy* were actually turning the people into automatons, one command at a time. Darkknell had been a place where art and other forms of leisure had been discouraged as unnecessary. Byllura had taken Daiman's notion a step farther. The place was colorless not because the people weren't allowed to decorate their lives; in fact, they probably weren't even aware of what things looked like. Or much else, for that matter. Not under that kind of psychic duress. Strong-willed beings could resist Force persuasion, but here there was simply too much of it going on. Wills were being broken before anyone realized they were under attack.

Kerra remembered thinking the harbor mesa and the building overhanging it resembled a balo mushroom. Now that first impression seemed prophetic. One of her early assignments as a Padawan had been shutting down a ring of Core World smugglers shuttling shipments of the fungi to Coruscant for processing. Mere busywork for a new recruit; neither the Jedi nor the Republic had much time for spice interdiction, and between war and plague, the population had plenty to forget. But on that assignment, she'd gotten to see people in the grip of narcotics: still functioning, but no longer the masters of their own lives.

That's who the people of Hestobyll had reminded her of. And whoever—or whatever—was on that vertical island was controlling them in the same way. The Byllurans were still independent beings, but with no will to resist when the call came. And increasingly, no identities of their own.

And there was more going on, she noticed now. Accelerating, Kerra looked down at the buoys leading from the mesa across the bay to the city, behind her. They appeared to be evenly spaced, just like the silos in the city.

"More Celegians," she murmured, passing over one and getting a closer look. There, visible through the transparent roof of the buoy, bobbed a Celegian in its protective cylinder. Kerra's mind raced. The Celegians on the mainland weren't simply public address announcers. These poor creatures were all links in a telepathic communications system—a chain that reached, unbroken, all the way across the water to the mesa and its retreat, high above. She'd heard of ancient signaling methods that used line-of-sight signals instead of electronics. Whoever was running this place had put the entire bay on his telepathic grid. There wasn't a need for a comlink anywhere.

Except in her case. Reminded, Kerra activated her headset and prepared to call in her destination. The mesa and its metallic cap loomed before her. "Another sanctum," Kerra groaned, shaking her head. *I just hope they don't use Daiman's architect!*

"They're putting holes in us, Brigadier!"

Rusher's nostrils flared. This was worse than mynocks. The second *Diligence* hit the thrusters and began to hover, several of the red raiders from outside had leapt onto the ship. Now monitors showed the Trandoshan and several of his buddies clinging atop the massive retro-rockets, jabbing at anything they could find with their short red lightsabers.

"Give 'em a spin, helm!"

The tentacle-faced Khil complied, her light green fingers a blur across the console. Around them, *Diligence* lurched and spun, forcing Rusher to grab on to chair backs for balance. Outside, the scenery of Byllura blew past—and on the monitor, so did several of the Sith climbers.

"Still a couple left, sir!"

"Cut thrusters!" Rusher yelled.

Diligence slammed violently to the platform, just in time for Rusher to yell another command: "Thrusters on!"

The tentacle-faced helmswoman got the picture, making *Diligence* hop like a Zeltron veil dancer. Bracing himself, Rusher watched the underside monitors. This time, even the muscle-bound Trandoshan lost hold.

Rusher signaled a return to midair. "Good work, Zussh!

Next time someone tells me they've been to Corellia, I'll believe them!"

"I'd sssay it's a good thing we got the hydraulicsss fixed," the Khil hissed.

"And that Novallo isn't here to break my neck for that stunt." Reminded, Rusher walked up the steps to the viewport. "Where are our people?"

Diligence swung over the bay, turned aft, and tilted. Looking down at the platform, Rusher spotted Dackett and Novallo standing with thirty or so crew members, backed toward the far edge of the raised dock. However strong the Sith lackeys' power of suggestion was, it wasn't enough to keep victims standing around when all blazes were breaking loose. Rusher saw that the Trandoshan and the few other goons who hadn't been thrown into the water were out of commission, lying in the huge cracked imprints *Diligence* had pounded into the tiled surface. But others were coming across the bridge from the city.

Boy, it'll feel good to shoot something. "Make it an island!"

With a jolt that rocked the bridge, the turbolasers mounted left and right of the crew compartment blasted downward at the metal bridge. Rated for nothing more than clearing asteroids, they were more than sufficient to send the structure—and quite a few of the baton-toting thugs—into the bay.

"Brigadier! The airssspeedersss—"

Rusher saw it—and felt it—before Zussh finished hissing the words. A flash of gray filled the viewport before him, sending a tremor through the bridge that knocked him to the carpet. Several of the airspeeders that had brought the trouble to the landing platform were still out there. If he'd forgotten about them, they were reminding him now, slamming against the upper decks and trying to rupture the windows. He'd never be able to bring the ship's weapons to bear against them. Too bad they didn't—

Wait, Rusher thought. *Weapons, we've got.* From his position on the carpet, he turned to face the crew in the command pit. "Spin us again—and hit 'em with the long cannons! The Kellies!"

Zussh's dark eyes blinked. "Sssir, thossse are in the hold."

"The carriages and generators are. The barrels are attached to the hull!" Rusher stood, gloves flush with the window. Three airspeeders buzzed past, trying to find a safe means to approach the spinning ship, spinning in place. Spying a red rider making a run, Rusher yelled. *"Hard to starboard!"*

Diligence yawed violently, its protruding Sarrassian iron cannon barrels cleaving the air like a massive rotor. The stern metal tore through the first of the shoddily built airspeeders as if it wasn't there. While the second speeder avoided that fate, its pilot didn't, flung nearly over the horizon by the spinning muzzle.

Well, that's a new one. Rusher watched the third airspeeder hurtle into the bay, struck by a glancing blow. What would he name this tactic? It wasn't something they could try against a larger ship or a fixed obstacle without snapping off their attachments. *The Rusher Just-This-Once Maneuver, maybe.*

"Visual on Master Dackett, sir."

"What's he doing?"

"Beating the Trandoshan to death with his new arm."

Rusher smiled. "Put us alongside the platform and drop Starboard Ramp Three. Just like a regular evac." *Well, nothing at all like one. But it'll do.*

Diligence dropped into position. Rusher looked for his cane. His sprain from Daiman's palace had healed, but he might need it for defense when Prenda Novallo boarded. Mesmerized no longer, *Diligence*'s hull doctor would have just seen him using her precious ship like a battering ram.

But as he watched his crew board on the monitor, he realized that inevitable confrontation would be the least of his troubles. They'd won a few minutes' respite from the Sith, but the refugees were still aboard, and their nursemaid hadn't returned. Rusher found his comlink, on the floor.

"Holt! Come in! *Jedi!*"

The light on it blinked. She'd sent a message, during the chaos. But before he could play it back, a call came from the helmsbeing.

"Brigadier, we've got new contacts from the north. A lot—and they're big!"

Rusher gritted his teeth. *Now what?* "Bigger than the airspeeders?"

"Bigger than *us!*"

Rusher dashed to the viewport facing Hestobyll and gaped. Steam was rising from the giant stone pools built into several of the terrace levels. Steam—and something else, something they wouldn't be able to overcome with a couple of rock-chasers and a few stunts.

His eyes widened. "Little Jedi, wherever you are—I think we've made them *mad!*"

A Jedi!

Calician marveled as he shambled away from One. A Jedi Knight was less than ten minutes away from The Loft. There was no need to consult any electronic scanner, nor even any reason to look out the window. The network he'd developed had brought the news instantaneously to him and his young masters.

Part of the inspiration had come from watching jornisae spiders, accidentally and unwisely imported from Cularin to his homeworld. Even when he blinded the creatures, they could sense the approach of others, feeling vibrations in their webs. The arrayed Celegians created their own web, constantly broadcasting status reports back and forth to one another. The same individuals who provided them the reports were charged with forcing them to send them: the red-clad Unifiers.

Quillan and Dromika hadn't understood the need for the Sith adepts to wear uniforms; they never expected to see them, anyway. In the body of Dyarchical power, the Unifiers acted both as regulating agents, ensuring that orders were followed—and as antibodies, killing or co-opting pathogens. The biological metaphor was Calician's, too, straight from his writings about how the pinnacle of Sith power might be achieved.

The glorification of self? The subjugation of others? Clearly these ancient precepts pointed to only one solution. For just one Sith being to rule a system of lifeforms the size of the galaxy, those *others* would have to be part of the *self*. Constituent parts of a larger whole, self-regulating; acting on the direction of the mind. There wasn't any other way. Governments, despotic or republican, were too inefficient. As long as any other will had force, a leader could not force his will on all.

It had required bringing the twins into his scheme, but he'd done it. Daiman and his Correctors were pikers compared with what they had achieved. To a degree, Byllura operated as a single living being—and, as he could hear from the rumbling outside, the hatchling was about to leave the nest. But that was also the problem.

He remembered it now, as he entered the turbolift and headed to the penthouse. Quillan and Dromika had been necessary. No Sith he'd met, Lord or adept, had the boy's natural talent for far-seeing; and likely no Force-user, anywhere, was the girl's equal when it came to giving strong hypnotic commands. But the regent had assumed *his* will would remain intact. He would serve as the ego, working as the conscious mediator between the out-side world and the siblings in their cocoon. To them, the world beneath their comfortable floor was a theoretical place. A realm they would imagine and influence, but never enter. That role would be reserved for Calician.

Only it had gone wrong. Emerging onto the top floor, he remembered it all. The excitement had restored some of his faculties, some of the independent spirit he once had. It wasn't possible to mediate between someone of Dromika's power and the rest of society without losing one's own identity. He wasn't strong enough. He doubted anyone was.

And yet, there wasn't anything to be done about it. He stole a glance toward the twins as he walked toward his place by the window. Sandy-haired Quillan sat and stared, mouth unwiped, wearing his night-clothes at midday, as he did every day. Dromika lay on her back, braiding and unbraiding her hair as she pawed at a pillow with her bare toes. Calician quickly looked away. There was no defeating power such as theirs.

Hearing more thunder across the bay, Calician realized the rest of the galaxy would soon learn the same. The battleships were ready and rising from their construction hangars, secreted beneath Hestobyll's just-drained reflect-ing pools. Mammoth, two-pronged affairs of precious imported durasteel, the fourteen vessels had been con-structed quietly over five years in preparation for this day.

And each, critically, included an important passenger: a Celegian. The same training centers on Byllura that had turned raw Sith adepts into masters of persuasion had worked their ways on the few Celegians they'd found who were receptive to the Force. None of them would ever rival the hated Master Ooroo for power. But en-sconced at the heart of a battleship, each would ensure that orders from Byllura were followed exactly. Unlike their cousins in the harbor and up in the city silos, they wouldn't simply pass commands along. They'd ensure they were followed, forcing their will on crew and escorting fighter pilots, alike.

Some had taken convincing. The Celegians were an accursedly independent lot. But, as here on Byllura, there would be Unifiers present to ensure their participation. And if that failed, the threat of harm to their fellows in captivity had always worked.

There weren't many of them, but they would be enough. They would be the first wave, claiming Daiman's rearward systems. Calician hoped they might even be able to win space engagements and land battles without a shot fired. Any Daimanite that approached within half a kilometer of the ship-brains would be vulnerable to their attack. The twins would command them—and thus command all. Nothing would be able to stop them.

"Regent-aspect . . . will protect us," Dromika said.

Calician turned, puzzled. The girl was sitting up now, looking at him plaintively as she calmed Quillan. The boy was in a fetal position again, as he often was when confronted with something new. "I will protect you," the regent said, belatedly. Dromika's uncharacteristically tentative question hadn't had her usual strength of psyche behind it.

But the next one did. "You will tell us how to destroy a Jedi," the girl said, green eyes flaring with orange fire. "You will tell us, *now.*"

Mindlessly, he repeated her demands—and then found he had nothing to say. He had faced plenty of Jedi Knights while learning the Sith ways. But none had come to Byllura and its neighboring systems in the eight years since its founding.

The Grumani sector had been too far gone by then, Byllura too far into the Sith interior. While he'd heard rumors of Jedi stabs into Sith space, they'd always attacked elsewhere. But he knew he had faced them once. He just knew . . .

Chitinous eyelids flipping closed, the Krevaaki sank his head in shame. "I . . . I don't know how, Lord Dromika. I don't remember."

"You will destroy the Jedi!"

"I will defeat the Jedi," Calician said, whirling with renewed vigor back toward the turbolift. The words he had spoken were Dromika's, but also his. He had created the perfect Sith command structure. As horrible as it was to lose his place in it, that paled before letting a Jedi take it down, in its moment of triumph. Better to lose to another Sith than a Jedi.

He might forget the rest, but no Sith could forget that.

CHAPTER FIFTEEN

The trick with invading hidden fortresses, Kerra thought, was picking a strategy and sticking with it all the way. She hadn't dealt with enough to declare herself an expert, but given her recent experiences, it seemed a truism. You could sneak in, evading detection at all costs and shying away from all encounters; or you could just barge in, leaving nothing standing, including the doors. Hopping back and forth between the approaches simply clouded the issue. Once you had a trail of bodies behind you, it really was past time to consider a subtle approach.

Looking back at the trail of bodies behind her in the hallway, Kerra decided she wouldn't worry about who had seen her or whether they might be sending for reinforcements. Skittering off in search of a path of less resistance would just take longer and, ultimately, endanger more people.

Besides, this way was more satisfying.

All those days on Darkknell wanting to strike back— strike *something*—she'd imagined a day like this. She'd been careful not to desire it too much; that way led to the dark side. But in all her sneaking around, she'd wondered if she would ever get to confront Sith oppressors directly. It was true these weren't Daiman's people; the lack of statues on every city corner said that. But she'd seen enough of the Bylluran brand of Sith oppression in two hours to make the Dyarchy, whatever that was, her target of choice. *Bring them on.*

More were coming, for sure. Since arriving in the airspeeder bay gouged into the side of the granite tower, Kerra hadn't heard any sirens or seen a single surveillance droid or cam. But the Celegians in the facility hadn't stopped chattering in her mind, alerting more Scarlet Riders—now Scarlet Runners—to her movements. The baton-wielders had tried to block her entry from the start, and had kept her from seeing where Tan and Beadle's captors had taken them. They'd tried to keep her from entering the main tunnel leading into the strata, and they'd waged a massive effort to keep her out of the one turbolift she'd found. The minions—if that's what they were—were getting stronger now. More capable. She had guessed that would have been the case, but not a lot else on Byllura had gone as she'd expected.

Seeing that, Kerra had begun using their ferocity and numbers as a guide. The Celegians' mental ululations were coming from so many different directions inside the facility that she couldn't use their strength as her homing beacon. But the most recent wave of attackers had one thing in mind: preventing her from ascending higher within the mountain complex. As with real balo mushrooms, the active ingredient had to be up in the crown.

Just like the perverse to imitate nature, Kerra thought, pushing out the corpse that was keeping the lift door from closing. Looking at the controls, she saw only two higher levels. Directing the car to the topmost, Kerra calmed herself and entered a defensive stance, lightsaber at the ready.

The door opened to reveal more red-suited protectors, also in defensive stance, their lightsabers ignited. In unison, they raised their free hands and screamed through the Force: *You will leave you will leave you will leave!*

"Okay," Kerra said, punching the control and closing the door. She hadn't intended to switch to taking the path of least resistance halfway through, but there wasn't any sense being doctrinaire about it—especially not when they were giving her such a headache. Spying a hand-hold above the doorway, Kerra sent the car to a lower floor and extinguished her lightsaber. Leaping for the slot above the door, she dangled by one hand and raised her weapon. There was no access hatch in the ceiling centimeters above her head, but there would be in a few moments.

Scurrying up the service ladder inside the shaft moments later, Kerra could still feel the psychic pressure from the defenders through the lift door. But their tactics confused her, more than anything. Their defense had seemed one-dimensional—two, at most. Mesmerize and fight. Fight and mesmerize. The mesa garrison was more powerful at suggestion and more formidable at fighting, but other tasks seemed to be beyond them. Scaling past the floor she'd fled, she heard people throwing themselves violently against the door. *Who can't open a stuck turbolift?*

Finding a ventilation tunnel leading up and away from the shaft—so much for avoiding them—she remembered the Rodian back on the airspeeder. He seemed to have no inkling at all how to restart his stalled-out vehicle. And the pattern of defense, too, seemed strange. She'd heard the Celegians' psychic calls, directing her opponents to defend hallways she was only considering entering. Were they using the Force to predict her movements? Or was it someone else?

Someone's controlling all this, Kerra thought, spying light at the end of a side shaft. She'd found the metal roots of the mesa-top structure now, driven into the rocky base; ventilation ducts brought in air from outside. Shimmying the long meters toward the illuminated grating, she looked up to find what she'd expected: a short stretch of shaft above, providing entry to the squashed dome.

But it was what she accidentally saw between the sunlit slats that gave her pause. Outside, across the bay, great battleships were on the rise, rumbling from housings within the terraced city. Suddenly she realized what the workers had been preparing. But for what purpose?

Slicing a larger aperture with her lightsaber, Kerra squinted at the harbor, trying to find *Diligence* and its platform. Her eyes crossed the shoreline twice before she spotted the dock, apparently cut off from the mainland— and empty.

Fumbling for the headset around her neck, Kerra found the mouthpiece. "Rusher! You'd better have a good explanation for this!"

Looking down at the sea, Rusher thought it didn't seem nearly as peaceful as it had when they'd landed. Perhaps it was because the water below was now dotted with people who'd been trying to enslave him—and more airspeeders were rallying from the coast, trying to reach the weaving spacecraft.

The battleships weren't paying them any mind—at least, not so far. The first three had made for orbit almost immediately; they certainly had someplace to go in a hurry. The presence of several others lingering in the stratosphere was the only reason he hadn't flown higher. Evading the airspeeders had taken them barely half a kilometer from the rearmost behemoth.

Seeing it, Rusher felt a faint twinge at the back of his skull. A slight spark, associated with a feeling.

A feeling that he should order *Diligence* down.

Rusher shook his head. A strange thought, but his hunches were like that sometimes. Standing at the viewport, he looked down at the ocean again. How would heading back down now protect them? It didn't make any—

You will set your vessel down.

Rusher's cane fell to the floor.

"Are you feeling something?" he asked.

"Yes, sir!" Master Dackett stood in the open double doorway to the bridge. "It's just like what those little cretins were doing down on the platform."

"It's stronger near the battleships," Rusher said, staring out the window. He looked to Zussh, at the helm. "Let's . . . be somewhere else."

He scraped at his hair, flicking sweat to the carpet. His eyes followed the droplets down. Going back to the surface had seemed like such a good idea—for a moment. Landing, and debarking, and giving his ship over to the red-clad Sith flunkies, just as they'd asked . . .

Rusher looked up. The ship hadn't moved. Looking back down at his helmswoman, he noticed the Khil's hand shaking over the controls. He stepped down into the command pit and placed his gloved hand over hers. "It's okay, Zussh. I felt it, too." Together, they pressed the switch to move *Diligence* clear.

"Very sssorry, sssir."

"That's enough of this," Rusher said, rescaling the steps. "Get us out over the ocean and head for space."

Refugees or not, Byllura wasn't a place to stick around. This happened so often in Sith space, he thought. Things were so fluid, and many of the warlords so secretive, that one never really knew what to expect from system to system. But they'd find another world quickly enough. Maybe in the Chagrasi Remnant—that wasn't very far away. Any place would be better than this.

"We've still got a missing man, Brigadier," Dackett said, standing at the railing.

"Lubboon?" Rusher looked incredulously at the ship's

master. "We *were* talking about dropping him off on top of the nearest hyperspace buoy." He'd half hoped the kid would wind up staying on Byllura with the refugees; it was why he'd sent him in search of the Sullustan, instead of someone more competent. "Blazes, Dack, *you* were talking about it!"

"I know. But that was before we knew what kind of junk they were pulling here."

"And that matters how?"

"It doesn't," Dackett said, scratching his fleshy neck with his artificial hand. He sighed. "But he pulled me out of that hole on Gazzari. It's the least I can do."

He slapped the back of his hand against the viewport. "Nobody pulled *me* out of a hole! People have just been getting me *into* them!" Rusher looked down at the heaving ocean, livening up as the *Diligence* flew farther from the mainland. Reminded, Rusher looked to his comlink again. The light was flashing; another message had come in while they'd been enraptured by the battleship. "Hang on. Message from Her Craziness." Putting it to his ear, he listened.

From beside the command pit, Dackett watched as his commander stood. "Anything?"

"She's swearing at me. And cutting out." He chucked the comlink to the floor and looked to the Besalisk at the comm station. "Morrex, do you have any more?"

"No, sir," the verdant giant said, tapping his massive headset. "But they know some new words in the Republic."

Rusher turned back to the window. The airspeeders that had been flying alongside, looking for an opportunity, were long gone. No one had challenged their flight across the open ocean. He looked back to see his helmswoman looking at him.

"I have a clear path to orbit, Brigadier," Zussh trilled.

"And nothing between this hemisphere and the nearest hyperspace lane."

Rusher folded his arms, made a command decision, and kicked the wall repeatedly with his good leg.

"Pull up the comm-tag records," he said, looking down at the Besalisk. "Lubboon. Rank, Major Disaster." With any luck, the Jedi would be where he was. He looked over to see Dackett, smiling gently. "And you quit grinning, or I'll have your other arm."

"Just indigestion, sir."

Rusher! Would the man ever check his comlink? She wished he'd told her what channels *Diligence* monitored. At least that Besalisk comm operator seemed to know what he was doing.

But it probably wasn't Rusher's fault, she thought, running through the darkened hallway. Between climbing upward through a granite tower and the mountaintop building she'd entered, she hadn't been able to get a signal outside since the air vent.

And given how they communicate in this mynock's nest, it's hardly a surprise, she thought. More of the red-suited acrobats had assaulted her, more urgently than before. Whoever was directing them seemed to have changed strategies midcourse. Instead of predicting where Kerra might go and trying to intercept her, the defenders had begun setting up roadblocks in the facility. Armed warriors lurked behind hastily constructed barricades in some hallways; in others, like the one she was in now, there were just the physical barriers. Dusty desks and computer equipment stood in heaps, haphazardly piled in front of the doorway.

"It's like a child barring the door to his room," Kerra said aloud, picking her way past. She didn't know quite where the comparison had come from; Rusher had spoken of children running Byllura, but she'd seen no sign of any on the whole planet. Just more of the scarlet warriors.

She needed answers—answers she hoped to find in the dim light of the round room, up ahead. The place was huge. The spare desks and consoles had come from here, she realized; it had clearly once been a command center of some kind. All that remained in operation were seven large video monitors, hanging from the ceiling in a circular pattern and silently cycling through maps of Hestobyll. But instead of facing outward, the screens had been turned to face the transparisteel cylinder at the room's center. And its monstrous occupant, floating in a pale yellow cloud and emitting a steady psychic hum.

Kerra had never imagined Celegians could grow so large. Even if it were mobile, it never could have fit through any of the doorways here. She didn't know what Celegians ate or how, if they even did at all. But this creature appeared to have gorged, now a flabby mass of drab dotted with bloody boil-like knots. And unlike the animated figure she had met on Coruscant, this one had root-like tentacles that dangled, damaged and limp.

She stepped toward the container carefully, remembering that the gas inside was as deadly to her as air was to the Celegian. The creature remained motionless and unresponsive. Kerra crinkled her nose. It didn't make sense. This being was clearly the nerve center—it was impossible to avoid such references when looking at a giant disembodied brain. The telepathic messages back and forth to the city began and ended here in a cacophony she had to struggle to ignore. And yet the Celegian seemed nothing like a Sith overlord, an evil answer to ancient Master Ooroo. In fact, it looked dead. *A specimen in a vial.*

Touching the side of the cylinder, Kerra was surprised

by a somber voice in her head, different in volume and tone from the others. *What is your message?*

"Message?"

What is your message?

"I don't know what you mean," she said, aloud again. She didn't remember whether Celegians had normal hearing, or were strictly telepathic, but the creature seemed to stir when she spoke. And the background buzz of outgoing telepathic communications had ceased. *It's listening.* "Those people out there—they're following *your* instructions. You're the one enslaving people." Kerra looked around, warily, expecting the Celegian to call for its enforcers.

But the creature simply sat, frozen in the gas. The buzz of background communications resumed, continuing between the Celegian and—what?

"And the battleships," Kerra said, remembering the sight from outside. "You're running them, too. With Celegians aboard, is that right?" She glowered at her reflection in the container. "You send them messages. You're spreading this madness."

For another long moment, there was no response.

Kerra knelt beside the cylinder's base. There, at the bottom, were flashing controls. She couldn't rupture the tank, but she could deactivate its circulation system. Within minutes, enough waste gas would build up inside to quiet the creature's commands to its minions once and for all.

"I'm sorry," Kerra said, reaching for a switch. "But you're Sith."

She looked up, one last time, for any reaction. Again, nothing.

And then a whimper.

It sounded like nothing she'd ever heard before—a thin, sonorous moan no louder than a whisper. But it felt like an ancient sadness had passed by, barely caressing her mind as it went. The thought, if that's what it was, wasn't directed at her. It was directed at the universe.

Like a whimper.

Kerra looked up at the beast towering in the haze behind the transparisteel. The facility was rife with emanations from the dark side of the Force. But none, she now realized, was coming from the Celegian.

Abruptly, she yanked her hand away from the switch. She'd been too quick, so busy listening to the telepathic noise that she hadn't been minding the Force. The Celegian wasn't using it at all, for good or ill.

Tentatively, Kerra placed her hand on the cool surface of the container and reached out through the Force. The second she touched the Celegian's mammoth mind, emotions overwhelmed her. Fear. Anger. Joy. Hatred. Love. All of them at once, confused and intermingling.

Breaking contact, she realized the feelings were all hers, brought forward in self-defense against a mind that had become a null. A nonentity. The Celegian's mind was alive and percolating with the messages it was conveying—but all that activity, she realized, was autonomous. The creature's judgment centers had been bypassed, if they functioned at all. Independent reason had no place in its waking mind.

It spoke, but it didn't know the words anymore.

Taking a breath, Kerra renewed her contact with the strange mind. This time, she focused her approach, trying to find her way through the wreckage of the Celegian's psyche. Most conscious beings whose minds she had touched had a spark, a fire that drove them. Here only an ember remained, and what she felt chilled her.

The creature seemed . . . bereft. Its whole life was a timeless agony. An independent mind, reduced to a conduit and controlled by others. *Others.* Kerra reached for a visual image, but found only a single, shadowy figure, all scaly forearms and facial shell-platings.

"A Krevaaki? That's who's controlling you?"

Controlling . . . who?

Surprised to hear a response, Kerra looked around the base to find an identification plate. "One? That's your name?"

The Celegian stirred, emitting a gentler version of the same sound. Kerra perceived that the creature had had another name, at one time, but that time had long since passed. She pressed for more detail on the Krevaaki— and on the others. But the wretched being had no understanding of space and time anymore. It understood there to be a greater power ruling the Krevaaki, but it could be on the next floor or in the next galaxy.

Hearing a thump on the other side of the room, Kerra quickly looked away. Seeing nothing, she looked down at the container's base. "One, do you want me to free you?"

Free . . . who?

Kerra huddled up close to the plating. There wasn't time for an existential debate. "Look, I need your help. I know what you're doing—all of it." One was responsible for Byllura—and for coordinating the defense of the mesa. Her talking to it had probably bought the quiet moments she'd had. She hadn't sensed any commands relating to the fleet; from touching One's mind, she'd understood that another Celegian, elsewhere in the building, was relaying commands to the ships through Sith comm system operators. They wouldn't be able to link far-flung Celegians telepathically without intermediaries. But the quivering mass before her could make a difference for everyone. "Do you know where my friends are? Can you to tell the people chasing me to leave me alone?"

Tentacles shifted. It wasn't understanding.

"They'll listen to you, One," Kerra said. "That's how they decide to do anything. Just tell them to—"

She stopped. The warm colors on the Celegian's frontal lobes began to dim. She was losing it again.

Realizing what she had to do, Kerra bit her lip and stood. Lifting the two fingers of her right hand before her, she spoke in a monotone: "You will command the sentries to return to their barracks."

Life returned to the Celegian. *I will command the sentries to return to their barracks.* And then it did.

"You will command *one* sentry to deliver the Duros and the Sullustan prisoners to the airspeeder bay." She could get them out from there, she figured; hearing it comply, she continued. "You will order the people of Hestobyll to their homes," she said. "You will stop sending messages for others."

One paused for a moment, seemingly puzzled, before finally repeating the commands.

For a moment, Kerra thought she felt another of the whimpers again. She smiled. She might have broken the Sith hold on Byllura only temporarily—they did have more Celegians—but One would no longer be a part of it, provided she could protect it from its masters. "I'll get you out of here, somehow," she said, patting the side of the container and looking around. The tank was bolted to the floor, and the doors weren't wide enough. But at least Rusher had a team of engineers, presuming she could find them.

Walking toward the entrance, she reached to pull her headset back into place—only to hear the beep of an incoming call. She activated the comlink. "Where have *you* been, Rusher? I hate to break this to you, but we're going to have another guest!"

"I am not Rusher," a scratchy voice said.

Kerra stopped running. She didn't have time for guessing games. "Look, I don't care who you are, as long as you're with *Diligence*—"

The speaker didn't let her finish. "We met on Darkknell—twice. The first time, you stole something from me."

Kerra stared into the dim light. She'd barely been able to get a signal before. But this voice was pure and clear. And familiar.

"The Bothan?"

"You do remember."

"I—I'm surprised to hear from you." Kerra didn't even know his name. "Are you here?"

"I wouldn't be talking to you at all," came the curt response, "but I have my instructions. And here are yours," he continued. *"Divide and conquer."*

"Wait! What?" She looked around the darkened control room. The only thing here was the Celegian in its tank.

"Where are you?"

"I am here, *Jedi*," responded a much different voice from behind her. Seeing red light reflected in the container, Kerra felt fire lash her back. Rolling forward, she looked back to see six of the lightsaber-batons—all in the tentacles of a single attacker.

The Krevaaki!

I will destroy the Jedi!

Dromika's command rang in the regent's cavernous ears. It helped to remember it. Every syllable stirred his body to action, restored his lost youth and vigor. The teenager's commands had always had that effect, but never so much as now—now, when he had just set his emerald eyes on his first living Jedi in years.

"I will destroy the Jedi! I will destroy the Jedi!" The Krevaaki's tentacles whirled into motion, making deadly rotors of the weapons they held. He had discarded his robe in the turbolift—and on seeing the human woman dawdling, had pounced.

He'd only torn into the back of the dark-haired invader's jacket when she dived forward, tumbling out of the way. She was a Jedi. She had to be, to move like that.

And Quillan, upstairs, had already sensed that she was, and told Dromika, who had ordered the regent-aspect—

"I will destroy the Jedi!" he said, whirling ahead into the command center.

The woman leapt an overturned chair, left from the days when the Celegian wasn't handling communications. There was the creature, up ahead, in its tube. Calician remembered that he hated it, this time. He would have to put it back to its tasks once he had dealt with the interfering Jedi Knight. "I will destroy the Jedi!"

"Shut up!"

The Jedi raised her hand and sent one of the chairs tumbling through the air toward him. *A strange skill,* Calician thought as he cut the furnishing to pieces in a blur of lightsabers. He vaguely recalled once knowing how to levitate things, but it had been more than a decade since he had exercised the power.

But combat, his body remembered. And Dromika's command had unlocked talents he'd never had. Krevaaki were formidable fighters. But even the greatest Krevaaki Jedi, Vodo-Siosk Baas, had only used his two uppermost limbs to hold his battle-staff. Now tentacles that could not lift a cup for Calician that morning were wielding lightsabers of their own.

The Jedi stood, meters from him, her own weapon ignited. An emerald lance in the darkness. She looked at him, warily. "The Krevaaki, I take it."

Calician didn't deign to respond as he zigzagged through the maze of furnishings on the shortest route to the woman. The Jedi Knight backed off, leaping from desk to upended desk. She seemed to want to parlay, to find something out about him and the operation. Calician charged ahead. He had his orders.

And now he had his chance. Seeing the Jedi duck in front of the Celegian's gas chamber, the regent twirled one of his lightsabers and hurled it at her. The woman started to move, just as he'd expected—only to halt, knocking the thrown weapon to the floor with her own. Charging, Calician threw another, aiming at a spot over her head.

"No!" the woman yelled, leaping to knock the small-ish lightsaber away before it struck the tube. "What are you doing? You'll smash the chamber!"

"*I will destroy the Jedi!*" Calician yelled.

"And you, too, you idiot!" She jabbed a thumb against the transparisteel.

Calician froze for a moment, watching the giant brain bobbing in the toxic gas. He looked down at the four remaining lightsabers curled in his tentacles. Yes, rupturing the tank would have killed them both. And yes, he didn't care. He was destroying the Jedi.

The regent slithered back a meter, shifting the weapons to different limbs. This wasn't supposed to be the Sith way—not the one that he remembered learning about. Sith weren't self-destructive. He'd thought he was part of something larger, earlier, something worth surrendering his identity to. But Dromika's implanted command had urged him to his own demise, in order to protect her and her brother.

Not this way, he thought. He gestured invitingly for the Jedi to engage him, well away from the Celegian's chamber.

"Now you're thinking," the Jedi said, leaping a table and entering a defensive stance.

Calician lurched forward, tentacles whipping the lightsabers back and forth in a weaving motion. The Jedi lunged powerfully downward, glancing off the up-per sabers before yanking her weapon back upward, singeing his facial tendrils. The regent advanced again, only to find her leaping nimbly to his right, forcing him to turn to follow. The more he turned, the farther she moved. The regent snarled. Moving in a circle kept him from bringing more than two of his weapons to bear at any one time.

The Krevaaki turned back the other direction suddenly, hoping to catch the Jedi off guard. But instead, she moved inward, grabbing one of his weaponless limbs with her spare hand and yanking. Knocked off balance, Calician fell—

—and found himself looking up at one of his tentacles, dead and unmoving in the Jedi's gloved hand. She'd severed it on the way down.

No pain, Calician noticed. It was one of the limbs from his middle carapace; that morning, he hadn't been able to feel a thing in it, either. Only Dromika's power of suggestion had restored its movement. Now the thing was dead again.

And so would he be, if he didn't move. Calician skittered backward as the Jedi advanced. The woman was too strong. He had the skills to destroy her, deep in the recesses of his memories. But he needed direction, just as his withered limbs had needed life. There was only one place to get both.

"Jedi!" he said, moving back toward the lift he'd descended in.

"So you can say something other than—"

Calician ignored her. "You came looking for children, Jedi. I heard the Celegian pass your command to the sentries." He stepped inside the lift. "If you care to see children, follow me!"

The doors closed behind him. Byllura would, again, be a trap.

CHAPTER SIXTEEN

"You're not going to believe this, Brigadier."

Waiting on the cargo deck, Rusher stared blankly as the image came up on the monitor. Defying all sense, they'd crossed over kilometers of ocean back to the mesa where the Dyarchy airspeeders had come from. And there, below, was Beadle Lubboon, sitting in the middle of an airspeeder and waving to the sky like a castaway outside a life pod.

Rusher looked over to Dackett, standing by at the dropgate. "Now if we only had audio, we could hear your savior yelling like an idiot."

Dackett rolled his eyes. "Are we clear to open or not?"

"Oh, by all means," Rusher said, patting the master's shoulder and stepping to the other side of the cargo door. "But remember, if you want to keep him, he's your responsibility."

Ignoring his elder aide's response—something about brigadier generals and their mothers—Rusher flipped the switch to lower the ramp.

The Duros stood, alone, in an airspeeder floating just outside the speeder bay. No one contested his presence; in fact, nothing had impeded their own approach. From their level, they could see the Sullustan girl sitting on the ledge of the landing port, kicking her legs.

"Why didn't you pick up the girl?" Rusher yelled down to the bobbing airspeeder.

Beadle gestured meekly toward the vehicle's steering yoke. "I started the speeder before she got in," he said. "I only know forward and stop."

Directing his bridge crew to bring *Diligence* down closer to the sea, Rusher started to concoct a response. But the ship's master got his attention first.

"Great suns, Brigadier. Look!"

Bodies littered the garage behind the nonchalant Sullustan. At least a dozen of the scarlet-clad sentries, like those who had hassled them at the dock, all chopped down at various points in the huge room. Here and there, wrecked airspeeders still burned, remnants of a colossal melee.

Dackett looked down at Beadle, struggling to climb the line they had dropped to him. "Do you think he fought all those people to get her out?"

"I haven't got the slightest idea." Rusher looked at Dackett—and in unison, they both pulled on the rope, hauling up the wayward Duros.

"Where's your headset, recruit?" Rusher asked, watching him clamber onto the ramp. "You see what comes of going out without your comlink."

"Begging the brigadier's pardon, Brigadier," Beadle said, "but if the brigadier recalls, the brigadier gave it to the Jedi."

Rusher pursed his lips. "Oh." He looked back into the airspeeder bay, and the corpses strewn across the floor. "You did this?"

"Kerra Holt came after us," the Sullustan yelled from her perch.

Rusher stepped aside so two of his troopers could leap down into the floating airspeeder. "Look—what's your name?"

"Tan!"

"Tan, we're going to back this speeder up to you so you can get on. My ship can't land here, and we can't get any closer." The airspeeder bay was meters below, and cargo ramps would never reach it without the stowed cannon barrels jabbing the cliff wall. "Hop in when they get to you!"

"No!"

"No?"

"She's here inside the mesa, somewhere. You have to go in after her."

Rusher looked at Dackett. *I'm going to die,* he mouthed.

"I'm sorry, kid," Rusher said, looking down and attempting to appear kindly. "We just don't know where she is. This is a huge place, and we don't know how much time we have to go searching for—"

Suddenly scrap metal struck *Diligence* from above, ricocheting off the starboard cargo assembly and raining down past Rusher.

He was almost afraid to ask. "What was that?"

"Droids, sir." Dackett pointed to more of the stuff, coming down. Arms. Legs. The odd torso. All were part of a larger shower of transparisteel shards, falling from the cantilevered facility atop the mesa.

"She's up there, Brigadier!" Tan squealed, standing on the ledge and jumping up and down. She pointed to the building, hundreds of meters above.

Rusher straightened. "I stand corrected. Just stop jumping, before you fall in!" He glowered at Dackett. "Or before I *jump* in."

Another locker opened—and another droid launched forward, hurtling toward Kerra. As she had with the last five, she used the Force to hurl the bulbous thing through the shattered window.

This was getting old.

Kerra had followed the Krevaaki upstairs in a service turbolift. She wasn't about to follow in the same car. It didn't seem likely that the Krevaaki would kill her with a booby-trapped lift, but she wasn't willing to put it past him.

Stepping out of the lift had confirmed her location. The room was vast, easily the full diameter of the squashed dome she'd seen from outside; spacious living quarters perched high above the bay. *They always nest on the top floor,* she thought. You could usually tell a Sith Lord by the real estate.

An opaque dome rising nearly to the ceiling sat in the room's center, well away from her. The curved window went all the way around the penthouse, its path interrupted every twenty meters by small rooms jutting inward. Some held nothing but multicolored storage bins neatly shut and stored away. Others held banks of lockers—and as soon as she passed, she learned what was in them.

Nanny droids. Big, chubby spheres-on-spheres, tumbling around on their repulsorlift bases. She'd seen their like before, in the Republic; the BD series had cared for generations of aristocratic young, teasing and tending with metal tendrils not unlike the Krevaaki's.

And like the Krevaaki, they had thrown themselves at her in a most un-tender fashion. As each locker burst open, its metallic occupants sailed into the room, encircling the colossal upside-down bowl at its center in a whirlwind of protection. The droids were unarmed, but at a hundred kilograms each, the hurtling mamas were weapons themselves. With every step Kerra took into the room, another droid broke from the swarm, throwing itself at her. She'd beheaded the first three with her lightsaber—and while she kept it handy still, she had long since lost patience with this game. Now, when one lunged, she simply waved her free hand, angling the writhing projectile through the windows. If the living occupants of the room were here, they wouldn't be able to miss the noise.

With the last droid tumbling down into the bay outside, Kerra surveyed the room. Still no Krevaaki; just the strange onyx hemisphere, a dozen meters across, sitting silently. The room around it had a playroom feel, but it seemed long since out of use. Brightly colored furnishings peeked out from beneath drab sheets. All the toys were tucked away. It reminded Kerra of the spare room in a neighbor's house in Aquilaris, years before. A child had lived there, but childhood joy did not.

Instead, she only felt the angry presence of the dark side. She'd felt it elsewhere in the facility, but here in the loft—that was a good name for it, she thought—it permeated everything. And it was more than anger, she realized; it was *furor*. Furor over being trapped. Over the loss of something never known. Whoever lived here had sat on that resentment, letting it grow into a thick hate that made her heart sink with every step.

And at its center: the black dome. Lightsaber at the ready, Kerra circled it. Was it a prison? Or a *lid*? She heard rustling from within. Wrecking the place hadn't drawn anyone out. Would anything?

Then she noticed a slightly raised platform in the shape of a diamond, just steps away from the dome. The carpet leading to it was worn; whoever stood there only ever approached from the outside, facing the dome. Gritting her teeth, she did the same.

As soon as both her feet were on the dais, Kerra saw the half orb ahead shudder. Recirculated air whooshed from its base as a gap opened between it and the floor. It *was* a lid, rotating on a horizontal axis and sinking back into the floor behind. A raised round stage sat within—but this was no amphitheater. Light from the shattered windows fell across a mass of orange cushions, piled high in the largest bed-fort she'd ever seen.

Near the center sat two teenage humans. A boy rocked with his hands around his knees, glancing furtively at Kerra and then looking quickly away. For someone just a few years younger than she was, Kerra thought he dressed younger still, sitting in bedclothes in the middle of the day. But his dark eyes looked old, set back in his bald head above heavy bags.

He, at least, seemed to notice her. The blond girl beside him sat endlessly brushing her hair, paying Kerra no mind whatsoever. Kerra wondered for a moment whether the well-fed pair were indeed the Krevaaki's prisoners—until she realized that they were the focus of the dark side energy she'd felt. She looked up at the lid, tilted backward. A meditation chamber, the largest she'd ever seen.

The boy looked again at Kerra, eyes searching for familiarity. Just as Kerra started to speak, the girl noticed her, too, dropping her brush and speaking to the air. "Regent will address the Jedi-aspect."

A strange statement from a stranger source. The girl dressed in the oversized nightshirt was well on her way to womanhood, and yet she had the wide eyes of a youngling.

"You are in the presence of the Dyarchy" came a voice from behind the round lid. The Krevaaki emerged from behind the half dome, bearing his four shortened lightsabers. His stump of a tentacle hung, limp and unbandaged. "This is Lord Quillan," he said, gesturing to the boy, "and his sister, Lord Dromika."

Kerra remained on the dais, looking warily at the pair. "And I call you—?"

The Krevaaki seemed to stall, fumbling for words.

Looking back at the human couple, he finally answered. "I am regent here."

The scheming regent, Kerra thought, remembering Rusher's joke. But it wasn't clear who was in charge here. "You've taken my friends," she said. "I've ordered them freed."

Quillan simply bobbed back and forth and looked away, while his sister looked angrily at Kerra. Dromika seemed eager to blurt something—but, glancing back at her brother, she said nothing.

"The Lords do not understand what you speak of," the regent said. "They do not interact with the universe as you and I."

Looking to the siblings and receiving no rejection, the Krevaaki explained. Twin children of a powerful Sith Lord, Quillan and Dromika had never perceived reality as others did. Quillan lived entirely inside his expansive mind, sensing other organics as phantasms moving in his personal dreamworld. No one could contact him, save Dromika, connected to him on a level no Sith scholar or physician understood.

But she, too, had a unique situation. Since learning to speak, Dromika's only form of communication had been Force persuasion. And her talent for it was immense, acting on levels beyond the vocal. Even in infancy, before she knew the word for hunger, Dromika had possessed her human caretakers to get whatever she and her brother needed. "Now we use droids for their immediate needs when I am not present," the regent said. Dromika's power had been so great that she burned out less prepared minds.

They had Daiman's problem, Kerra realized—only worse. Much worse. Daiman had come into his Force powers and his Sith philosophy at a later age, after he'd already been socialized to some degree. He may not have *believed* that others were sentient beings with free will—and he certainly perceived the environment around him through a strange prism. The universe was the playing field of some game on an astral plane. But Daiman at least interacted with that environment; he understood it, and accepted it as a given. The twins only acted *through* their environment, making other beings extensions of their own will.

It was exactly, she realized with horror, what Daiman had been trying to accomplish back in the camp with the Woostoid aide.

"I have been asked to explain this so you will cease your activities and submit to inclusion," the regent said.

"Inclusion?" Kerra stepped down from the dais and walked, wary of coming too close to the now-watchful twins. "Like you included the Celegians? Did they ask to be part of this?"

"They were useful. They needed to be first."

"First of how many?" Kerra waved toward the window and Hestobyll, across the harbor. "You've already got a planet in thrall. How long are you going to let this go?"

They're Sith, she realized, answering her own question. But could you be *born* Sith?

She faced the Krevaaki again and pointed to the siblings. "Listen, Regent—how is it they came to be the center of all of this? Why isn't someone trying to help them?"

"I *am* trying to help them. I . . . have orchestrated all this. I have built it for us all. We will realize our destiny—as one."

To the side, Quillan glowered at the Krevaaki. His sister followed suit. The regent seemed to shrink under their gaze.

Kerra noticed. "I don't think they feel your role is as central as you do," she said. "You're just another Sith flunkie—just another tool."

The regent shuddered with rage. "You will join us—join *them*—or be destroyed."

"No."

Expecting an attack from the Krevaaki, Kerra was startled to see movement from another quarter. The boy knelt atop the pillows and shakily raised his hand. The child had never exercised, she thought—if he had even left the room at all. But with his feeble motion, his sister stood and raised her hand.

"You will kneel," Dromika said, facing Kerra.

Kerra stumbled. She'd fended off attempts to mesmerize her all day, but this was on another scale entirely. The younger girl's words stabbed into her brain, raking at her free will. Kerra's brow furrowed, her mental shields going up too late.

"You will kneel!" Dromika boomed, clenching her fists.

Kerra locked her knees together, fighting against the weight pushing down on her. It was more than simple suggestion. Dromika appeared to have mindlessly worked other forms of Force manipulation into her commands, acting out upon the physical world to force Kerra's muscles and bones to comply.

Still, the Jedi fought. "I . . . will . . ."

"YOU WILL KNEEL!"

Kerra's knees went out from under her. Hitting the floor with a painful thud, her hands struck the ground palm-first. Her weapon, extinguishing itself, clattered away.

Eyes tearing up, Kerra tried to crawl toward her lightsaber, just meters ahead of her. But immense pressure continued to bear down on her. The only way to keep from having the life crushed out of her . . .

. . . was to kneel.

"Regent-aspect," Dromika said, much quieter. From the side, the Krevaaki glided toward Kerra, his quartet of mini lightsabers raised.

Sweat pouring, Kerra looked up and tried to speak.

Tried to move. Tried to do anything against the executioner now looming above her. Tentacles curled, bringing the four glowing instruments of death centimeters from her neck on all sides.

Feeling their burning presence, Kerra had a fleeting thought of all the close calls she'd escaped, through sheer cussed stubbornness.

Now, at the end, that will had finally failed her.

Calician looked down at the Jedi, completely at his mercy. It had been so long, he thought, savoring the moment. So much had been lost to him. But this moment would be *his*, and his—

The regent saw his limbs flexing before him, ready to plunge their weapons into his victim.

"No!"

At the last moment, Calician had realized *he* wasn't the one bringing the lightsabers to bear. "Let *me* do it!" The regent looked back to see Dromika standing there, at the edge of the pillows, her hands raised, willing him ahead.

"You will destroy the Jedi!" the girl yelled. She jabbed with clenched fingers, trying to make Calician move. *"You will destroy the Jedi!"*

Calician shuddered, the lightsabers pausing a hair's breadth from the Jedi's neck. "Yes—*I* will destroy the Jedi! Not you! *Me!*" He fought the force animating his tentacles. "Release me!"

The girl simply glared.

Incensed, the Krevaaki fought back, directing at his young master the psychic power he'd so often utilized in her name. *"You will release me!"*

Seeing the Krevaaki hesitate, Kerra fell flat to the floor and reached through the Force. Her lightsaber clattered between the regent's legs and into her hand. Before a single second expired, Kerra ignited it and rolled to the right, depriving the regent of one of the tentacles that gave him footing. The Krevaaki screamed, doubling over and dropping his weapons.

Momentarily freed from Dromika's control, Kerra regained her feet and started running. The girl shifted, beginning to react. Kerra couldn't allow that. Reaching forward, she swept with her left hand, scooping up the droid-debris in her path and blindly launching it toward the siblings' roost. Dashing in a circle around them, she wasn't going to be able to strike them with anything. But she wasn't trying to spread destruction—just distraction. To enforce the twins' wills, Dromika had to get her attention, or at least concentrate.

Kerra wasn't letting that happen. Out of the corner of her eye, she saw the teenagers reacting to the sudden shower of scrap. Quillan clasped his hands together and let loose a mournful howl, while his sister stumbled around on the cushions, trying to keep her body in front of him as Kerra turned.

The Jedi widened her circle, dousing her lightsaber and snapping it to her belt in a single, smooth move. She needed both hands as she ran ever-wider circles around the pair. It felt to her almost like a game in a gymnasium as she yanked storage containers from the open closets, hurling their contents into the penthouse. Toys. Food. Clothing. It all came out, rocketing to her left as she dashed. Through the miasma of junk she could see the boy standing now, balancing on shaky legs and wailing while his sister yelled something inaudible at the floored Krevaaki.

The regent wasn't going anywhere, Kerra saw—but now Dromika was on the move. Kerra saw the girl clamber off the pile of pillows and onto the floor, into the stream of the hurled objects. As canisters and utensils clattered past, Dromika raised her hands and mimicked

Kerra's hand motions. Kerra skidded to a stop. Grabbing one of the nanny droids' tubby abdomens from the floor with her hands, Kerra heaved, bowling it toward Dromika. Struck by the bouncing ball, the girl fell.

Quillan screamed—and as he did, Dromika leapt from the ground, reinvigorated. Kerra started running again, this time sweeping with the Force to rip window shards from the floor. She had to keep shifting strategies, keep them on the defensive. The twins' only understanding of combat, physically or through the Force, came secondhand, through their minions. They couldn't be accustomed to this kind of thing.

But she was quickly running out of things to throw. Changing tactics again, Kerra bolted across the diameter of the room, leaping onto and over the pile of cushions. Quillan lurched away, waving for Dromika to return. The girl moved faster this time, traversing the platform quickly. Kerra looked back, trying to find the turbolift she'd entered through.

That was a mistake. Dromika, running up behind her, reached out through the Force. Turning to run again, Kerra stumbled across an empty drawer from one of the cabinets she'd hurled. Falling before a shattered window, she reached instinctively for her lightsaber. But looking up, she saw the Sith girl, meters away and approaching with her hands raised. Dromika began to speak . . .

. . . and screamed, instead. Behind her, Quillan had seen something she hadn't. Dromika's head snapped to the right, looking out the window—and into the muzzle of a Kelligdyd 5000 cannon, racing toward her. The girl dropped as thousands of kilograms of Sarrassian iron stabbed through the window, driven by the movement of the warship outside.

Rolling away, Kerra looked back in surprise. *Diligence!*

The warship lurched away from the building, withdrawing the colossal makeshift battering ram and taking part of the window frame with it. Looking to see Dromika reviving, Kerra regained her feet and started running. Reminded, she reached for the comlink and yelled, "Is that you, mercenary?"

"Silly question" the response came.

Kerra couldn't argue. To her left, she saw the Krevaaki trying to rise on his remaining tentacles. Only one of his lightsabers was lit—but looking back, she saw Dromika holding one of the others. Kerra winced. She should've put the regent down before this, she thought. And did the girl know how to use the lightsaber? She didn't relish another confrontation.

Bounding across the room, Kerra looked back to see that *Diligence* was no longer hovering outside the window. Boots skidding on the rug, she heard the reason.

"We can't get a ramp to you like this!" Rusher's voice crackled. Kerra saw the ship bob outside the window and drop again. "We're going to slip under where the building juts out. You'll have to jump!"

When don't I? Kerra wondered. She looked back. The regent had foundered, unable to make his remaining limbs obey. But Dromika continued to advance, green eyes now an empty red, matching the weapon burning in her hand. Behind and to her right, Kerra saw Quillan meekly backing toward the window, hands raised to mimic Dromika's motions.

Or was it the other way around?

Divide and conquer, the Bothan had said. Kerra looked at Quillan's eyes, as alive now as his sister's were vacant. *Dromika's not the puppeteer. She's just another puppet—for Quillan!*

"*Stop!*" Dromika yelled, raising her free hand. Facing her, Kerra shuddered under the psychic command—

—and bolted, dashing straight between Dromika and the regent, heading straight for Quillan. The boy looked at her in wordless panic, his hand raised just like his sister's. Charging, Kerra saw Dromika wilt, no longer animated by her connection to her brother's mind.

"Ngaaah!" Quillan yelled. Tucking her head beneath his armpit, Kerra wrapped her hands around the boy and shoved toward the window where she'd seen *Diligence* last. With a mighty heave over the crunchy bottom of the pane, she carried Quillan over the side.

Tackle becoming a tumble, Kerra saw the lower levels of The Loft whisking by—and the luxury-cruiser-sundeck-turned-spotters'-nest of the warship rising up to meet her. Tucking her left leg under the terrified teenager, Kerra slammed violently into the hull. White heat shot from her ankle to her eyes in an instant.

Dazed, Kerra rolled, Quillan still partially on top of her. *Diligence* rolled, too, the harbor air currents pitching the vessel's nose upward. Kerra and the boy slid backward, toward the deck-top railing and the bay, hundreds of meters below. Kerra clawed, desperately seeking a handhold.

A metallic hand grabbed her instead. "We've got her!" Master Dackett yelled.

"Move us out!" Kerra heard. Dragged along with Quillan by Dackett and two other troopers, she spotted Rusher standing, partially visible, in the hatchway.

"No," she yelled, pushing futilely against her bearers. "Tan and Beadle are still down there!"

"We've got them," Rusher called, making a hole for his crew members to pass her into the hatchway. He regarded Quillan, feebly pushing at the air. "You didn't think we had enough kids along?"

Kerra fought to wrest away from those relaying her down the ladder. So Tan and Beadle had made it out. But they weren't the only ones in jeopardy. The Celegians were back there, still living a life of unimaginable agony out in the buoys. And what of everyone else on Byllura?

In the whole Dyarchy? "We can't leave!" she said, wincing as the crew set her down on the deck. "You don't understand. *I* can't leave."

"Not a chance, Holt," Rusher said, gesturing for the hatch above to be closed and speaking into his comlink. "Orbital velocity, now."

"You can't make me go with you!"

"The cargo I'm carrying is yours," Rusher said, descending the ladder toward her. "Until it's delivered, you go where we go."

Feeling the sudden impulse driving the vessel forward, Kerra lay back against the deck, defeated. Rusher stepped past the medic tending to her and headed down the hallway. Kerra glared. "Leaving people behind again. This isn't going to help your lurch ratio."

CHAPTER SEVENTEEN

"He's just a kid!" Rusher rapped the head of his walking stick against the railing to the command pit. "And you're telling me he's Sith?"

"A Sith Lord," Kerra corrected.

"Oh, well, *that* makes sense," the brigadier said. "We didn't have a Sith Lord in the collection. Glad you brought him on board!" He glared at the Jedi, sitting on the plush carpet of the bridge and nursing her wrenched thigh. Her attention was where his was: on the boy huddled in the nook, far forward. Rusher had posted armed guards to either side of the teenager, but it hardly seemed necessary. The kid was a mess. Since arriving with Kerra on the bridge, he'd alternated between fevered looks through the viewscreen at Byllura, below—and howling fits with his head tucked between his knees.

A Sith Lord in his pajamas, Rusher thought. *I've seen it all now.* "He's never been in space before?"

"Quillan's never been out of his *room* before," Kerra said, edging closer—and then back. She seemed to alternate, too: between sympathy and wariness. Rusher understood from her that, minutes earlier, the boy had been trying to kill her. But "Lord Quillan" didn't look powerful. If anything, he seemed . . . mentally challenged.

Kerra looked around at the cosmos filling Quillan's

sight on all sides. "It's this blasted observation lounge of a bridge. Can't you polarize the viewports, or something?"

"Not under attack, I can't," Rusher said, eyes sweeping the space from port to starboard. The Dyarchy battleships he'd seen leaving Hestobyll were all out there, part of a serious space force that included cruisers and snub fighters. He even spotted some troop transports in the mix, all clustered near the battleships. The Dyarchy meant business for someone.

But not *them*—at least not so far. Despite his words, *Diligence* wasn't under attack. Since they'd reached orbit, the Dyarchy fleet had simply sat there, in between them and any hyperspace jump points. Leaving the Bylluran system for anywhere required negotiating this field of predators, poised to strike. And unlike Gazzari, Rusher didn't figure the ships would suddenly leave on another appointment.

"You say this kid's their boss," he said, gesturing toward Quillan. "Is that why they're not attacking?"

"I don't know," Kerra said. All her efforts to reach the boy had failed. "I think they're waiting for orders."

"From him?"

"From anybody." The Jedi stood, looking out at the sea of motionless spacecraft.

Rusher waved to the Besalisk in the command pit, ordering a complete scan of all channels coming from Byllura. If any word came up, he wanted to know it first. "Look, Holt, if this kid's the boss, can't he tell them to knock off?"

Kerra looked at the teenager, peeking at her with reddened eyes as he quaked. "I don't think he can tell anyone anything," she said. "Not without his sister."

Rusher waved his arms. "Well, let's get her on the comm then!"

"*No!*"

The brigadier rocked back on his heels, surprised by the urgency of her response.

"I mean," Kerra said in a more composed tone, "no, I don't think it works that way. She speaks for him, but he only speaks to her through the Force."

"I thought you people could fire your jibber-jabber a long way."

"It's not easy, if you've never done it before," Kerra said. "And Quillan's never *had* to do it before."

Rusher's head swam. Agitated, he raked the head of his cane against the metal railing, causing a *clackety-clack* that set the Sith boy moaning again.

"Yeah, that's right," Rusher said. "I feel like crying, too." He stomped toward the Jedi. "I don't want *either* of you here!"

Flinching at the pressure on her leg, Kerra tried to stand. "You've made that clear."

"There's never been a Sith aboard *Diligence* for a *reason*," Rusher said, eyebrows flaring. "It keeps me and my crew safe—and them away from the heavy artillery." He waved at the fuzz of stars beyond one of the Dyarchy's fleets. "Don't they teach you your own history out in the Republic? Maybe you've heard of a little thing called Telettoh's Maxim. It goes—"

"*Never let Malak aboard,*" she finished.

"You're blasted right!" Generations of military professionals knew the tale of the Republic admiral who'd let a Sith-in-Jedi's-clothing come along for the ride. He'd spent the rest of his career trying to undo the damage. "We'll take their jobs. We'll take their fuel. But we won't take a Sith across the street. Not if I—"

Morrex called from within the pit. "We got fire, Brigadier!"

"At us?" Rusher dashed back to the railing, distracted from his anger.

The comm officer responded by pointing to the monitors. Lights shone on Byllura's surface, where Hestobyll and its continent were now slipping into nighttime. But it wasn't artificial illumination.

Fire.

Kerra limped away from the teenager toward the port window. Studying the surface of the world slipping past, she pointed to locations all along the terminator into night. Rusher joined her, bearing a pair of electrobinoculars. Plumes were rising from several levels of the capital city. "Riots?"

"People are waking up, I'd imagine," Kerra said. "And waking up *angry*." There had been a constant stream of commands coming from the mesa to all of the twins' minions on Byllura, she explained. Now that Quillan's sister had no commands to relay, order was collapsing.

Rusher rubbed his forehead. "And the first thing they do is set their place on fire? That doesn't make any sense at all!"

"How should I know?" Kerra asked. "People have been telling them to work, sleep, and eat for years. This is the first time they've had any options." She paused. "Granted, it's an odd way to spend your first night off."

"Don't ask me," Rusher said. "I blow stuff up for a living." He looked back over his shoulder at the warships outside. "If this is our chance, maybe we'd better slip past now—before they realize how fun it is."

"Yeah," Kerra said. "I think you're—"

"Incoming transmission, Brig!"

Just as Daiman had appeared to them days before, now another Sith materialized in the dim light. A dour-looking Krevaaki, Rusher saw, tentacles draped in a cape. "Who's this?"

"The regent," Kerra said. "I don't know his name." Forward, the boy squealed, mystified by the strange image.

"My name is Saaj Celegian," the figure in the image

responded. The Krevaaki coughed and looked down. "I mean, Saaj *Calician*." He paused, his posture straightening. "I know that now."

Rusher looked at the image, puzzled. "So he knows his name. What's the big deal?"

"I think it *is* a big deal," Kerra said. "Quiet." She hobbled over to address the hologram. "What do you want?"

Kilometers below, Calician stood downstairs in the control room of The Loft. Beside the sleeping Celegian in his tube, the Krevaaki looked up at the seven video monitors, showing images from across the bay in Hestobyll. It was one of the few surviving parts of the surveillance system the floating brains had not replaced—and now it gave him his only detailed view of what was going on.

As commanded, the workers at the secret underground shipyards had started work on more battleships the instant their recently constructed fleet was safely away. Unfortunately, the knowledge of metal-casting procedures lay not with the workers on the scene, but with a small group of experts on one of the lower floors of the mesa complex. Normally, the Celegians carried their instructions to scarlet-clad Unifiers in facilities all across Byllura, allowing them to run many operations at once. But when the hub Celegian stopped routing messages, the factories were caught without know-how at a critical moment. At six Hestobyll sites, molds filled uncontrolled with molten durasteel, overtopping and setting off chains of explosions. He could see that something similar had happened to three of their munitions factories as well.

Heavy lids drooped as Calician watched the chaos spread. Byllura had been a model of Sith centralization, a nonelectronic system centered on a single Lord's will.

Now the former regent saw it all ending. A body could survive without a thinking mind only while the organs knew their function. Without One, the network was damaged. Without the will of the twins, it could never be repaired.

"—I said, why are you calling us?"

Hearing the Jedi's voice, Calician shambled back to the holographic setup as best he could on his remaining tentacles. "I am simply calling to learn whether the boy Quillan yet lives."

"Why?" The dark-haired Jedi in the crisp image appeared to grow more reserved. "Are you looking to parley?"

"No, it's too late for that," the Krevaaki said, briefly explaining the mounting industrial disasters spreading across Byllura. He redirected the cam toward a monitor showing Dromika, who had collapsed into a faint after her brother's disappearance through the window. "She cannot tell a physical presence from one she observes through the Force. She cannot see him, so she does not search for him," he said, looking at her motionless body.

"She was the only one who could reach him—and for it, she became as much his slave as I did." Calician refocused the cam on himself and snorted. "Kill him, if it pleases you," he said, lifting a singed stump that once held a lightsaber. "It might please me."

The comment caught the Jedi speechless.

Another explosion came from across the bay, this one so loud it was audible through the control room's windowless walls. "That would be one of the power stations," Calician said.

The woman crossed her arms, her brow furrowed. "You can't just send instructions over a comlink, like anyone else?"

"Our minions have none. A secondary communications system provides a potential avenue for dissenters," he said. "And before you ask, the other Celegians have rebelled, just as One here has. I cannot use them."

"I wasn't going to ask," she said. "But I would ask that you free them."

"That, Jedi, is the last thing I would do," he said. "But I can do no more, anyway. I will leave that to the others, when they arrive." He glanced back at another monitor. "And it seems, now, they have."

"Others? What are you—"

Before Kerra could finish her question, the skies around *Diligence*'s bridge came alive with motion.

One after another, colossal white vessels leapt in from hyperspace, surrounding the planet and orbiting fleet. Long and majestic, the crystalline warships—like snowflakes on a skewer, Kerra thought—swiftly opened fire on the Dyarchy's battleships.

Kerra stumbled toward the command pit, where Rusher and his crew were only beginning to react. So were the battleships, she saw out the starboard viewport. They didn't need guidance from Byllura to be jolted into defensive action, but they moved sluggishly compared with the cruisers and similarly shaped fighters.

"Get us out of here!" she said.

"Which way?"

"Any way!"

Diligence tossed, banking away from Byllura on a vector through the combat. Watching, Kerra saw the precision with which the newcomers were striking. Two flaming battleships were out of commission—but salvageable. The arrivals were taking care not to destroy their prey.

"I've never seen them before," Rusher said, stepping up to the window beside her.

"I thought you lived around here!"

"I live on this ship," he said, fumbling nervously with

his cane. "I work all over. But nobody knows how many Sith Lords there are—if these are even Sith."

Kerra scowled. *Someone else would sure be nice, for a change.* But out here, nested within competing Sith statelets, it couldn't be anyone else.

Grabbing onto Rusher's arm as *Diligence* weaved— she'd nearly forgotten her injury in the excitement— Kerra foundered emotionally. This was her worst nightmare from Darkknell, realized. It was exactly what she was afraid would happen in the Daimanate, had she caused a collapse from within *that was visible from without.* She looked over her shoulder to Byllura. There wasn't any time to get any of those people free. The whole Dyarchy was collapsing—and, somehow, the twins' rivals had seen it. But how, so quickly?

With a start, Kerra realized the Dyarchy bordered Daiman's territory. Were these ships his? What could Daiman do, she wondered, if he knew the power the twins held? His greatest desire was to subjugate absolutely, to render other organics literal extensions of his will. But the twins had accomplished something he hadn't.

For whatever reason, Daiman still counted his own ego, his own individuality too important. He wanted to subsume others, yet at the same time he enjoyed dominating them too much to truly allow a merger of will and matter. But Quillan and Dromika didn't understand the concept of "other." As near as Kerra could tell, from infancy they'd treated the Force as another of their senses—and they had no clear understanding of where they stopped, and others began. For all his bluster, Daiman had come to his Force powers too late. He had already known who he was by then.

What could Daiman do if he captured the twins now? Could he co-opt them?

Learn from them?

Kerra looked back to the tactical display. They weren't

anywhere near escaping the battle zone yet—and there was another vessel, still larger, up ahead. The flagship, hanging back and observing everything.

And at the moment, blocking their path.

Behind, she saw the hologram, still there. "Calician, can't you do something?"

The former regent shook his head, sadly. "This is not my house." He paused, then looked up. "The *dowager* will decide our fate."

The image disappeared.

"Tractor beam's got us, Brigadier!"

Rusher looked at Kerra, mouthing the words unbelievingly. *The dowager?*

"That's her," Narsk said, standing in the doorway of the flagship. "That's Kerra Holt." The Bothan looked at the hologram and smiled, toothily. *No more running, little Jedi.*

And it had been easy, just like the rest of this job.

Narsk had arrived on Byllura just a day earlier, traveling aboard a special stealth fighter contributed by his latest employer. Quickly locating the video surveillance system left over from early in the twins' reign, he'd installed a secret transmitter and left for higher ground, atop the cataracts, to monitor it.

He'd been surprised—but not alarmed—to see the Jedi and her warship appear that morning. But it had worked out well: the artillery carrier's communications were even easier to crack from his position. From them, he learned that Kerra was indeed at the center of the chaos being wrought below; when he'd seen her chasing across the bay to the mesa, he'd directed his client to be at the ready.

And when he'd ascertained that she was in the sanctum, he pulled the trigger, cutting in and giving her the information she needed. He didn't even wait to learn the result, heading back to space—and a rendezvous with the arriving flagship.

Easy. The Jedi had not disappointed.

"Very good, Narsk Ka'hane. Take a seat."

Narsk settled back in a hide-covered chair and watched his own breath as he exhaled. She kept it so cold here. Through the shimmering frost particles, he focused on his employer. She was the best looking of all the Sith Lords he'd worked for, he thought. Daiman tried to look like the center of attention. This woman earned it.

Human and just a few years older than Kerra, the woman struck a noble warrior's pose in white furs and armor. Her skin was clear, freckled with frost. Golden eyes, narrow and fiercely intelligent, looked back at him.

He wasn't human, but if he were—

"Thanks for the good work, agent," she said, stepping past him onto the upper deck of the bridge. "And for the thought." She looked down and addressed the hologram. "So you're the Jedi."

"You . . . have the advantage."

"Yes, I do," she said. "My name is Arkadia Calimondra. I'm a Sith Lord—and I'm here to help."

Part Three

THE
ARKADIANATE

CHAPTER EIGHTEEN

Hyperspace had become a haven for Kerra; her only one, since arriving in Sith space. Suffering might hold sway on either side, but the weird region between stars was something even the Sith could not ruin.

In the past, when she had traveled between worlds under duress, Kerra had always chosen to make the journey. *Diligence*, instead, had been compelled to follow the crystalline flagship and part of its fleet into the hyperspace lane, under threat of disintegration. She'd wanted to object, but Rusher wasn't about to deviate from the course he'd been provided. The day in the Dyarchy had simply been too much. The fight had gone out of everyone— herself, included.

They hadn't been boarded. But before jumping, they'd been ordered to provide information about how many warriors and refugees were aboard *Diligence*. Kerra disliked admitting there were hundreds of students on board, but she was more worried the invaders might destroy their warship outright. The woman in the hologram somehow seemed to already know their situation anyway.

The new Sith Lord was a puzzle: serious and direct. Kerra had spent part of the hours in hyperspace parsing Arkadia's few words. Rusher seemed to know nothing of her and her realm. What had the woman's comm officer called it? *The Arkadianate.* Another would-be warlord with an eponymous empire. Just what the galaxy needed.

But while Rusher had not recognized the emblem on her flagship—seven interlocking chevrons, one for each color in the visible spectrum—he had recognized the vessel's name. *New Crucible* related to Ieldis, a peculiar ancient Sith Lord who was the favorite of a number of philosophical descendants—including, of all people, Odion. The Crucible of Ieldis had been a novel military institution, created by him to transform peaceful subject peoples into talented warriors; several Sith Lords in more recent times had tried to put their own spin on it. Kerra's heart had sunk on hearing Rusher's explanation. *From one slave pit to another.*

Early in the journey, Rusher had gone to his quarters for sleep, or perhaps back to his solarium for fortification. Kerra didn't know. Fearful of leaving Quillan alone—*Diligence* had no formal brig—she'd tried to rest on the plush floor nearby, where she could keep an eye on him. She'd found it impossible to sleep for more than an hour at a time, given the bustle of the command pit. But at least one person had remained quiet: Quillan had calmed down with every light-year *Diligence* put between itself and Byllura.

Kerra gave partial credit for that to Tan. Visiting the bridge to see her former roommate, the Sullustan had spied the distraught Quillan, curled up at the front of the room before his yawning guards. Before Kerra could object, Tan had plopped down on the carpet near the boy, assuming he was just another refugee. In a sense, of course, he was. And as Tan sat chattering away about the sights and sounds of hyperspace around them, Quillan had stopped quaking and started watching her instead.

Kerra had initially feared that the boy was trying to find another potential puppet, but she'd perceived nothing of that in the Force. Rather, the young girl simply seemed to be a calming influence for the troubled teen. Tan was close to Dromika's age, Kerra realized—and just as child-like, in her own bubbly way. From studying in the shadows of the Tengos' apartment one week, to serving as playmate to a Sith Lord the next; it made as much sense as anything else.

The rest of the trip had been an exhausted slide. Momentum had carried Kerra far from that first trip to Chelloa all the way to Byllura. But as *Diligence* and its escorts emerged from hyperspace into a bluish pocket of newborn stars, she was filled with dread. She hadn't been in control of her destination during the flight to Gazzari, but at least she'd had a plan for after her arrival. Seeing the white world laced with pink striations looming ahead, she knew nothing but the planet's name. And that had come from their captors.

Syned. Reading what passed for star charts aboard his ship, Rusher had said it rhymed, roughly, with *lie dead*. She'd thought that was a strange choice of expressions until they got closer. It fit. Syned was a frigid lump. Near to but little warmed by its adolescent star, the globe spun quickly, weak sunlight racing across its surface of water and carbon dioxide ice.

But while that surface had seemed smooth and featureless from orbit, on approach Kerra had seen mammoth slabs tilted diagonally, remnants of tectonic fractures. Elsewhere, bright smears marred the surface, evidence of ancient cryovolcanism. Syned might be lying dead now, but it hadn't always been a quiet place.

Diligence had been directed to land near an icy outcropping just across a wide basin from what appeared to be a small cluster of greenhouses. Several other starships sat on the ice nearby. *New Crucible* didn't follow them down, instead expelling a shuttle to the A-frame building across the frosty plain.

That had been their cue. Now Kerra and Rusher stood, as commanded, on the surface of Syned, both wearing the space suits the brigadier had produced from the hold. A whisper of oxygen clung to Syned's surface, but given the temperature, removing the environment suits would have been the first step in a slow suicide.

Weary from her broken sleep, Kerra looked across the terrain for any clues. The basin was one big parking lot. Tracked vehicles had been out on the ice, running between the ships and the hothouses—if that's what they were. Warmth and Syned didn't seem to go together.

But neither did the pair at the foot of *Diligence*'s ramp. Kerra had simply thought it before; now she knew it for certain. Rusher was no ally. She glared at him, holding that silly cane of his, even out here. His space suit was clunky and copper-colored, just like hers—and both would have been considered antiques in the Republic. The man shifted back and forth on the ice; Kerra thought he was trying to find which footing would make him look the most statuesque. *No wonder he was working for Daiman.*

He looked up at Syned's tiny star, visibly traversing the sky. "Join Rusher's Brigade and see the galaxy," he said over the comlink.

Another joke. Kerra took a step forward, keeping her back to him. "I'm not talking to you," she said.

"And yet, you are."

"We didn't have to follow these people," Kerra said. "We could have dropped out of hyperspace before getting here!"

"You know that's not true," Rusher said, poking his walking stick against the pink ice at his feet. "We had no idea who else was in the lane. We could have collided. Or worse."

Kerra exploded. "Worse? We've just gone from one Sith Lord to another. *Again*." She turned to find Rusher chipping at the ground and trying not to chuckle. "Tan and her friends hate to go to sleep anymore! Another day and they could wake up . . . *gaaahh!*" Rage outpacing her mouth, Kerra shook her fists theatrically. "They might be running Odion's deathmills. Or back where they started, shining statues for Daiman!"

Rusher shook as he laughed. "I like this whole not-talking-to-me part," he said. "Look, kid—*Jedi*—we were never going to find a place that wasn't run by Sith. Let's just be patient and check this one out."

"I'd like to check it out! I can't," Kerra said, opening her fists and looking at her hands. *New Crucible* had ordered Kerra and Rusher to wait outside, unarmed. Using the hated stealth suit wasn't an option, either. The Mark VI had a remarkable operating range, but Syned's temperature was well outside it.

Kerra looked back toward the west and squinted. Just a few minutes earlier, it had been noon in this high latitude; now Syned's sun was dropping behind the settlement. The two conical tractor beam generators they'd spied from orbit cast the longest shadows, reminding her that, whatever else might happen, *Diligence* wasn't going far without permission. Its external weapons were simply too weak.

Squinting against the icy glare, she made out movement. The brigadier had seen it, too. Stepping forward, Rusher flipped the cane into a surprised Kerra's hands and raised his macrobinoculars. Kerra looked at the stick and smoldered. *I'd like to crack that faceplate with—*

"Wow," Rusher said, lowering the unit. "You have to get a load of this!"

Curiosity trumping annoyance, Kerra reached out and yanked at the macrobinoculars, still looped around Rusher's armored neck. Pulling the brigadier down, she angled the glasses toward the approaching blur.

Lord Arkadia Calimondra rode across the ice sheet toward them, looking every bit like one of the winter warrior princesses Kerra had seen in her story-holos as a child. Above the furs and armor from before, Arkadia now wore a silvery cape that caught the frigid air as her mount loped across the tundra. The great three-limbed reptile bounded along on clenched fists, its forked tail snaking back and forth behind it.

And amazingly, Arkadia's face and forearms were exposed to Syned's cruel climate. Even the creature she rode had a heated air supply, Kerra saw. Arkadia's sole nod to the elements was the addition of the cape and a museum relic of a headdress. Pulling at the reins with one hand, Arkadia seemed to be enjoying just a brisk day out.

Kerra released the macrobinoculars abruptly, causing Rusher to nearly pitch over. The woman was halfway to them, now. Kerra tried to wipe the fog from her faceplate, to no avail. "What was it the Krevaaki said? A *dowager*. What's a dowager?"

"A widow," Rusher said. "An old woman who owns her late husband's property, like an estate."

"She doesn't look like a widow to me."

"Maybe. I sure don't think I'd survive a shore leave with her," Rusher said, rubbing his gloved hands together. "But it wouldn't be a bad way to go."

"Please," Kerra said. "Try to grow up."

Before them, the ice-lizard slid to a stop, splaying its palms wide to get a purchase against the ice. Towering above them, Arkadia yanked at the reins. As the Sith Lord twisted atop the creature, Kerra spied a meter-long, ornamented staff, bound to Arkadia's back.

"Sorry about the circumstances," Arkadia said, her words precipitating into snow. "Our landing bays aren't yet large enough to accommodate vessels like yours." She leaned over and patted the chuffing creature's snout. "And I can only get the beralyx out for a ride in the summer."

This is summer? Kerra stared at the newcomer. The woman was twenty-five, maybe thirty at most—and healthy. And for the first time among the Sith Lords she'd met here, Kerra saw face paint: light silvery streaks beneath her eyes, setting off her frost-speckled cheeks and completing the whole warrior-queen look. It was quite a getup.

Arkadia seemed equally bemused. She looked down at Kerra and smirked. "I said no weapons, Jedi."

"What?" Kerra looked down to see Rusher's cane, still in her left hand. "Oh," she said, lifting it in both hands. "Fine." Abruptly, she brought the care down over her space-suited knee, snapping it in two. She pitched the halves to Rusher, who glared at her and tossed them to the ice.

Arkadia noticed him. "Kerra Holt of the Republic, I spoke to earlier. But who are you, sir?"

"Jarrow Rusher, of Rusher's Brigade." He saluted. "That's my ship you forced down. *Diligence.*"

"*Diligence,*" Arkadia repeated. "Like Admiral Morvis's vessel?"

"The same," Rusher said, visibly impressed.

The Sith woman spoke matter-of-factly. "His exploits in the First Battle of Omonoth were a fraud, you know."

Rusher's smile froze. "You must know something I don't, then."

"Probably."

With thigh-high boots, the woman kicked the reptile into motion. As it loped in a studious circle around the pair, Kerra watched Rusher. The man was dumbstruck, for a change. Arkadia had punctured one of his historical heroes and sounded authoritative in the process.

I'm going to have to study up so I can do that, Kerra thought.

"You wanted us here, ma'am," Rusher said. "What can I do for you?"

"It's what I can do for you," Arkadia said, bringing the beralyx to a stop. "It's as I said. I'm here to help. You were leaving Byllura when we found you. I understand you have refugees aboard."

Kerra studied the woman as she dismounted. The Jedi only came up to Arkadia's chin. "The refugees weren't from that conflict," Kerra said. "We're just passing through."

"I know," Arkadia said, raking ice from the nodding beralyx's eyes. "You told us that. And I am aware of what happened in the Daimanate. To the arxeum they were bound for," she said.

Rusher looked at Kerra, puzzled. They hadn't mentioned where their passengers had come from in their transmissions.

Arkadia continued, not looking at them. "I am willing to help your students—and to provide for your ship's needs, Brigadier. But I need something first."

Abruptly, she turned toward them. "You do have a refugee from Byllura," she said, piercing eyes focused on Kerra. "What I really need right now . . . is to see *Quillan.*"

Kerra stiffened. "I'm sorry?"

"Don't toy with me, Kerra Holt," Arkadia said, looking down. "I know you have Lord Quillan of Byllura aboard your ship. I am prepared to render aid, but only if the boy is produced first."

Rusher started to move toward the ramp, but Kerra grabbed his arm. "Hold it," she said. Eyeing Arkadia, she waved her hand. "Look, whatever the boy once was—

he *isn't* now. I saw what your people did to the Dyarchy ships. I know he was a rival. But he's not a threat to you now." She wondered what she was doing, speaking for a Sith—but the pathetic creature under guard didn't seem to be that. Not anymore. "You don't have to kill him."

Arkadia looked down at Kerra, her face betraying no emotions. After an icy moment, she burst into laughter.

"Kill him? Of course, I'm not going to kill him!" she said, smiling broadly. *"I'm his sister."*

Still under construction, Arkadia's citadel had been built inside a series of connected ice calderas. With the collapsed underground reservoirs' contents having long since boiled off to space, Arkadia's builders had simply erected a thatch of ice pillars above, topped with a layer of transparisteel. The result had been a massive airtight compartment inside the ice, far larger than it appeared on the surface and roomy enough for an entire city. *A creature hiding under a shell,* Kerra thought.

And Calimondretta, as Arkadia called it, was as alive as the surface was dead. Emerging from the cab of the trundle car—the tracked ground transport Arkadia had sent to *Diligence*—Kerra surveyed the great atrium. Hundreds of workers thundered past, crisscrossing artificial flooring stacked with orderly piles of supplies. With Arkadia's starships forced to park outside, Patriot Hall served as a massive depot. Several ramps led gradually downward from the main floor to large galleries hewn into the glacier.

Only stars shone through the transparent ceiling; night had fallen for the second time in four hours. Syned was the complete opposite of Darkknell and its endless days and nights. But the place was bright, nonetheless, thanks to long tubes embedded in the ice walls. Effervescent blue liquid coursed through them, giving off a warm light. "Our lifeblood," Arkadia said, turning over the beralyx to a wary green-skinned handler. "Synedian algae." The seas under the ice sheets were full of the stuff, she explained, drawing energy from thermal vents. Whole sections of Calimondretta were devoted to cultivating and processing the algae, which provided both fuel and food for the settlement. "We use every molecule of it. Nothing is wasted."

Kerra observed her own breath. "It still doesn't keep it very warm here."

"Some guest you are," Rusher said, stepping out of the trundle car. "Don't criticize someone living in an icehouse for not turning on the heat."

At least he had that overcoat of his, Kerra saw. He hadn't bothered to find anything more for Kerra to wear, nor had he spoken to her on the ride over. She figured he was still stinging over the cane incident. But at least she hadn't done that in front of his crew. What was he upset about?

Her eyes darted to the foot traffic, now flowing around their parked vehicle. After the dismal streets of Darkknell and the robotic misery of Byllura, Syned had plenty of energy to it. The citizens in Patriot Hall looked up and around as they walked, not down at the floor. And most of their clothing was brand new: uniforms of varying colors and styles. Those clearly didn't all come from the algae.

"We have something for you," Rusher said, slapping the side of the trundle car. Trooper Lubboon emerged from inside, pushing Quillan down the ramp in a brown hoverchair. His hands fastened to the handles of the antiquated model, Quillan appeared nearly catatonic.

Stepping to the foot of the ramp, Arkadia looked down at the teenager. No trace of emotion crossed her face, and Quillan didn't respond, either—not even when Arkadia knelt beside him, cape flowing on the chilly floor. Kerra studied the two together. Beyond the high foreheads, she couldn't see much resemblance—nor a lot of big-sisterly warmth coming from Arkadia. But at least it was a peaceful meeting. Arkadia had assured her earlier that not all Sith siblings were like Daiman and Odion.

"Still hiding in there, little Quillan?" Arkadia said, searching his eyes.

Suddenly the boy moved in his chair. Arkadia appeared startled for a moment before noticing that Tan had scampered up behind her. "Ah. Hello, girl," Arkadia said. She looked up at Kerra. "Why is she here?"

"I didn't want to bring her," Kerra said, grabbing at Tan's shoulder and pulling her back. "She's one of the students—I mean, the *refugees*. But we need to calm Quillan down to move him, and she seems to help."

Arkadia nodded to the girl and stood, directing Beadle toward an ice portal where her aides waited to take care of Quillan.

"Why did you bring Beadle?" Kerra whispered to Rusher.

"We're trying to be as unthreatening as possible, remember? The worst thing Lubboon might do is run over her foot with the chair."

"It's a hoverchair."

Rusher rolled his eyes. "Believe me, he'd find a way."

At least he was talking again, Kerra thought.

Returning from seeing her brother off, Arkadia addressed the military man. "You became part of history yesterday, Brigadier. I hope you appreciate that."

"He does," Kerra intervened. "But what do you mean exactly?"

"The Dyarchy has fallen. After eight years, Quillan and Dromika's realm has become part of the Arkadianate."

By replacing the commanders on the Dyarchy's ships of the line with Celegians, Arkadia said, Quillan could have made them an organic extension of his planet-bound command. But there had always been a fatal flaw. The bobbing brains aboard the cruisers had to get their orders, somehow, and that had required technology. While Arkadia said she could imagine trained Force-users transcending space with their telepathy, the method seemed impractical to her. Such feats were difficult and rare, not something to be relied upon. "An error of youth and inexperience," she called it. "Quillan always would have been dependent on a physical linkage, somewhere. And that linkage could be attacked."

Arkadia explained that she had just dispatched an agent to Byllura seeking to compromise that connection when Kerra suddenly appeared, disrupting Quillan's communications at the source. "It was then that we thought to help you," she said. "And you did your work well. You triggered our invasion."

"Help me?" Kerra felt the pain in her leg coming back. "What do you mean?"

"Divide and conquer" came a familiar voice from behind the trundle car. Around the transport strode the Bothan, wearing a brown parka matching his fur.

Kerra gawked. She hadn't seen the spy since Daiman's castle on Darkknell. But it had definitely been the Bothan's voice back on Byllura. "You—"

"I take it you know each other?" Rusher said, eyeing the new arrival with puzzlement.

"Yes, I know him! This is—this is . . ." Kerra stopped, stymied. She'd never learned his name.

"Narsk," the Bothan said, looking up at the brigadier.

Rusher scratched frost from his beard and smiled. "I got it! You're the guy from Daiman's torture wheel!"

"Well, thanks for the help," Narsk said, little regarding the general as he stepped past. "Here is your final report, Lord Arkadia."

Arkadia took the datapad from the spy and read.

Narsk described the contents as she did so. Even now, her forces were landing on Byllura, taking control of the whole regime.

Kerra grabbed at his sleeve. "I thought you worked for Odion!"

"I'm an independent contractor," Narsk said coolly, "much like your friend here who doesn't help people. Arkadia is the highest bidder." He paused. "Of the moment."

"This is why I like you, Narsk," Arkadia said, not looking away from the datapad. "I always know where I stand with you." Reading, a faint smile crossed her face. "This is good."

"Your forces have taken Hestobyll without a shot fired, my lady," Narsk said. Arkadia's advance guard had installed itself in The Loft, and was sending forces across the planet to free the Celegians from their prisons. The Dyarchy's network would be dismantled, and all its citizens—floating brains included—would become contributing members of the Arkadianate.

Kerra looked in the direction Quillan had been taken. "What . . . will happen to Dromika?"

"She will remain in her mountaintop home, supervised and tended to," Arkadia said. "Far away from her brother. They should never see each other again, given their curious connection. I don't know what kind of life it will be for Dromika, but I expect it'll be superior to what she had." She paused. "I'll visit her later, to check in."

"And Calician?"

"*Dead,*" Arkadia said, slapping the datapad on Narsk's chest.

The Bothan nodded and took the device. "The regent was executed just before I received the call. They said he met his end quietly."

Kerra stepped back. The figure she'd fought had acted

as one possessed, but in the hologram, the Krevaaki had seemed almost tragic. "Why did he have to die?"

"Quillan was the mind," Arkadia said, "but Calician was the *mastermind*. He built the system. Maintained it. He made possible all that my brother wrought."

Another enabler, Kerra thought, looking over at Narsk and Rusher. *I'm surrounded by them.*

"Every Sith sees a different path to rule of the galaxy," Arkadia said. "But once a strategy has been shown to fail, the strategist must pay the price."

Kerra looked back at the Bothan. "And when exactly did you stop working for Odion and start working for her?"

Arkadia regarded Narsk civilly. "Agent Ka'hane is someone I've worked with before," she said. He'd contacted her just after the Battle of Gazzari morphed into a war on Lord Bactra, claiming that he'd had enough of Odion and Daiman for a while. "One can hardly blame him, really. I dispatched him to Byllura. And the rest," she added, smirking gently at Rusher, "is history."

"You thought you could get me to do your dirty work," Kerra said acidly.

"You *did*," Narsk said with a sneer.

"Actually, once he told me you were there, we didn't know *what* you might do," Arkadia said. "But you've tended to be a destabilizing factor, wherever you've gone. We expected an opportunity might arise this time."

Narsk bowed to Arkadia. "Is there any other service I can perform?"

Arkadia studied Kerra for several seconds. "Perhaps. Stick around, Narsk. I'm sure there's something you can do."

The Bothan looked back at Kerra. "There is something. She has property of mine—back on her ship, I suspect."

The stealth suit, Kerra thought. "Oh, that! I gave it to a little girl. Good luck getting it back." Suddenly reminded, she looked up, startled. "Tan! Where'd she go?"

Rusher pointed down one of the huge blue-lit hallways. "She went with Beadle and the boy."

"Here we go again," Kerra snarled. "Does anybody ever make it back to your ship?"

"Hey, you brought her. You lost her."

A hand touched Kerra's shoulder, chilling her. "Don't worry," Arkadia said. "She's no doubt excited. There is a lot for her to see in our city—and for you, too."

"Me?" Shrinking from Arkadia's reach, Kerra looked around. She'd been expecting guards to show up to cart her away to wherever they kept captured Jedi, presuming they had such a place. But everyone she'd seen had seemed like a civilian.

"This isn't a concentration camp, Kerra. It's civilization. An enlightened community, which will welcome your refugees."

Kerra's jaw set. "No guards?"

"Well, you won't be left alone," the glistening Sith Lord said. "But all members of the Arkadianate have some kind of combat training. And all of them will act to protect it, if you try to disturb it."

Before Kerra could respond, Arkadia clapped. A Twi'lek aide in mauve stepped forward. "Take Brigadier Rusher to requisitioning. I'm sure his crew and passengers have some immediate needs."

As Rusher nodded genteelly and saluted, Kerra glared at him. *Still looking for a job.*

"And call for Seese," Arkadia yelled, heading off in a different direction. "There's much that we want from the Jedi—but there is much she should learn first!"

Seeing Rusher depart with the Twi'lek, Kerra looked back across the atrium to Arkadia. An aide had taken her headdress, revealing hair as light as Kerra's was dark. Another aide stood nearby, waiting on her every word.

Kerra's head swam. This was like no welcome a Jedi had ever received from a Sith Lord. And none of the dozens of people around seemed to take the least note of it.

No one but the Bothan, who leaned against the trundle car, eyes shifting back and forth between the two of them.

CHAPTER NINETEEN

Arkadia had wanted Kerra to walk in the shoes of her citizens. Touring Calimondretta, Kerra figured she could have fit her entire body comfortably inside a single one of her guide's boots.

And yet the Herglic moved through the thoroughfares of the ice-hewn city with amazing speed, forcing Kerra to march double-time just to keep up with her. One of the larger members of a once-aquatic species, Seese was a lumbering gray behemoth measuring two-plus meters in all directions. Clad in her bright yellow vestments, the guide could have been seen from orbit, Kerra thought.

Still, the Sith city seemed to have done more to accommodate larger species than many Republic trading centers had. All the doorways were wide enough for the Herglic, and even the escalators had long, graduated steps. "There will be Celegians joining the Arkadianate," Seese said, riding down to a lower level. "It'll be nice to have someone the same size around!"

Kerra nodded. She noticed the steam rising from the blowhole atop the frost-covered Herglic's head. "Aren't you cold here?" she asked.

Seese let out a thunderous laugh. "A body that stays in motion doesn't notice," she said, launching into a discussion of her life as they emerged from yet another factory. Seese had been in the Arkadianate just six years, but had found time to familiarize herself with all operations on Syned, as well as several other of her leader's worlds. "And I still had time to have four children—can you believe it?"

Indeed, Seese seemed to know everything about every place they entered. The alga-processing plants, without which there would be no life on Syned. The reclamation facilities, finding metals vital to Arkadia's cause one milligram at a time from the waters deep underground. Even the education centers, where the youth of Syned were turned into productive and committed citizens. Seese had found her first assignment as a teacher there, just after Arkadia had conquered her homeworld.

But if her guide harbored any ill will about that, Kerra had seen no indication of it. In fact, she'd been able to get little specific about Arkadia out of the Herglic, save some platitudes about the Sith Lord's keen mind. Early in the tour, Kerra, remembering Calician's statement, had asked if Arkadia was a widow. Seese thought for a moment, but didn't remember her master ever taking a mate. That line of conversation had resulted in yet more gushing about Arkadia.

"Of course," Seese boomed, "it would be a clever mind indeed that could hold our lady's attention!"

Now, entering their sixth factory off Progress Plaza, Kerra found herself wearying of the victory tour. That's what it was, she realized; a show, proving Arkadia's path to power superior to that of any other Sith. She'd initially imagined the names of the great underground halls to be ironic, but apparently, the people bought into them. There were no Correctors, no scarlet-clad straw bosses. Instead, about one worker in twenty wore a blue sash and a blaster; members of the Citizen Guard, responsible for peace and order. "We have more volunteers than we need, actually," Seese said. "Many take the added duty to help their own advancement. But there's rarely much to do."

Certainly, the system seemed less oppressive—no one, anywhere, seemed to be working under any threat of pain. But something still seemed wrong. In the hydroponic gardens, where they raised silkenfronds for thread; and here, in the textile mill, whose produce helped warm the citizens. Everyone seemed just a bit *too* devoted, somehow.

"Wait," Kerra said, spotting a green-skinned male across the factory floor. "That guy!"

Seese looked across the mill, whirring with activity. "The Falleen? That's the manager's station. He's the manager here."

"But I've seen him," Kerra said. "Back when I arrived. He was Arkadia's beralyx handler!"

The Herglic stared blankly at the mop-topped figure. "That may well be." Barging forward, Seese got the manager's attention. "You, citizen. Do you come fresh to this?"

"Promoted this very work cycle," the Falleen said, exhibiting a rumpled smile. He turned back to his control board, flashing frantically.

Kerra watched the new manager struggle. She'd thought his expression was halfway between pride and terror.

Walking away, she quizzed her host. "He was working the stables. Now he's *here*?"

Arkadia was, as ever, the answer. "She always likes us to come at a project *fresh*," Seese said, rocking on mighty stumped feet. "With new eyes."

The rest of the hour passed in much the same way. Why did the mill turn out clothing in so many bright colors? To help Arkadia's citizens become noticeable, memorable individuals. Why had no one, to Seese's memory, ever left

the Arkadianate? No Sith Lord offered anything comparable to the life found here, under the frigid wasteland.
Why had Arkadia been so slow to bring the rest of the
galaxy under her protection? She knew that speedy conquest came at a price to the existing civilization. A meal
had to be digested, before eating again.

"But make no mistake," Seese said, seeing commotion
up ahead. "Arkadia will rule the galaxy, and we along
with her."

Kerra looked far down the hollowed-out hallway to
see Arkadia, dressed more lightly in a silvery tunic and
cape, leading Beadle and Tan through the Promisorium.
Tan seemed excited to be touring Arkadia's academy;
Beadle seemed to be rubbing his forehead.

"My time with you is done, I see," Seese said. Giant
lips pursed, the Herglic female looked down at Kerra.
"If I may take the liberty, Kerra Holt, you do not seem
like a bad person. I do not understand why they say the
Jedi hate the Sith."

Kerra looked up, tongue-tied. "I don't know what to
say to that."

"Well, maybe there are different kinds of Jedi—just as
there are different kinds of Sith." Turning on a massive
heel, Seese began to depart.

But Kerra placed a hand on the creature's mighty arm.
"Wait, Seese. I do have one more question."

"Certainly."

"How was it you knew Celegians would be coming
here?" Calimondretta seemed to have an open society,
but Kerra had seen no hint of any kind of mass media.

"Why, I was at the battle," Seese said. "I was a tactical officer aboard *New Crucible* just yesterday."

"And now you're a *tour guide*?"

"New eyes," Seese said, smiling broadly.

But looking into the glowing yellow slits, Kerra thought

Seese's eyes seemed very old. The Herglic trod away, perhaps a bit slower than before.

"Kerra! Kerra! Kerra!"

The Jedi found she had something attached to her leg. "Hello, Tan. How was your . . . your tour?"

Tan bounced up and down, describing the sights that she'd seen in the Promisorium with Arkadia, from the classrooms to the dining halls. Kerra's attention, however, was on Beadle, and his bleeding forehead. "What happened to you?"

"He tripped on his boot and fell down one of the escalators," Arkadia deadpanned.

Kerra looked to a moving staircase behind her. "Every step's two meters long! How could you fall down one?"

Arkadia smiled primly. "I wasn't there, but I am told that it was something to see."

Beadle smiled weakly at Kerra. *If he's an ad for Rusher's services,* Kerra thought, *they might as well fly back to the Daimanate now!*

Tan chattered on about the wonders of Calimondretta's educational system, becoming almost a tiny version of the Herglic tour guide. As she spoke, doors opened to the left and right, discharging younglings of all species from their lessons. Kerra wondered if their release had been timed to accompany Tan's message, to reinforce the healthy state of the local youth.

If so, Arkadia's point was made. Kerra scanned the small faces milling past, all on their way between classes. These weren't the grease-covered child laborers of Darkknell; whatever they might build in the future, right now, they were building themselves. Her attention shifted to a Gotal couple, standing off to the side with a tiny child. Touching head-cones, the mane-faced parents saw their son to his classroom door.

As the Gotal adults picked their way back through the

crowded hall, Kerra closed her eyes. Something about the scene both warmed and chilled her. Similar moments were happening all around. All akin, in a way, to Gub's parting with Tan, days earlier: parents sending their children off to find better places in life. Was that universal? She'd seen identical sights in the Republic, every time a Padawan entered the Jedi Order.

She'd never had an experience like that. The Sith had robbed her of her family. And yet, these partings seemed temporary. Arkadia hadn't ripped these families apart.

What had Seese said? *Maybe there are different kinds of Sith.*

Walking in the stream of students just her height, Tan grew ever more effusive. And the thing she seemed most excited about was the range of subjects the students here learned, from calculus to genetics to stellar cartography.

"Your ward told me of the life she was bound for," Arkadia said, nodding to the awed younglings she passed. "Tan and your other passengers were going to be chained to one subject for the rest of their lives! Preposterous. This was Daiman's idea?" She searched for Kerra's gaze. "Come, you can at least answer me that."

"It was a corporation," Kerra said, looking away. "Industrial Heuristics."

Arkadia nodded. "One of Lord Bactra's holdings. The *former* lord," she corrected herself. She'd been apprised of events on Gazzari. "My last information is he was hiding in a Quermian retirement colony, somewhere. Well, he should be safely out of the fray there."

Kerra wondered how Arkadia had heard, all the way out here. *That Narsk, maybe.* That made sense.

Strolling back toward Patriot Hall, the main atrium, Arkadia described for Kerra how Tan and the others would be educated in her realm. Students would work to become as versatile as they possibly could—so that, as adults, they could contribute in as many ways as her

state might need. Other Sith Lords treated sentient beings as just another raw material: basic elements, un-
workable and immutable. Miners taken captive in the
territory of one became miners in the next. But what if
the victor needed physicists? An empire's strategic needs
changed with the mix of neighbors on its borders. How
would it do for a state that suddenly needed nothing but
fighter pilots to have only a token few?

Before Kerra could respond, Arkadia spied someone up
ahead and stepped up her pace. Rusher and the Twi'lek
stood in a loading zone near a massive magnetic gateway
to the frigid outside world. Beside them, several workers
loaded a mountain of containers and cylinders onto a trio
of trundle cars. Arkadia swept toward them. "Did my assistant find your supplies, Brigadier?"

"Everything I could have asked for," Rusher said,
studying a datapad. "Should replenish all the stocks the
refugees drew down. I'm surprised at the variety of food
you have here."

"We don't live by algae alone—not with so many different palates. What we don't grow here, we ship in."
She looked at Beadle. "It will probably take your crew
longer to unload it than we took to grow it."

"We're pretty good with loading," Rusher said, passing
his recruit the datapad. "One of our specialties, in fact."

Arkadia smiled politely. Looking down, she reached
for Tan's hands. "Go, girl, and tell your friends aboard
Diligence of the kind of life that awaits them here."

Kerra winced as Tan hugged the Sith Lord good-bye.
Arkadia accepted the gesture, appearing to regard the
expression as novel.

"I'll be across later," Kerra told the Sullustan, walking
her to the ramp. "I don't think Arkadia is done with me."

"She'll let us stay here, won't she?" Tan asked, black
eyes hopeful in the doorway. "Please try to convince her,
Kerra."

Kerra's heart caught in her throat. Looking back, she saw Arkadia standing confidently as she chatted with Rusher and the Ithorian aide. "Whatever she wants to do, Tan. I'm pretty sure she's already decided," Kerra said. "Stay safe." Stepping back, she saw Beadle approaching the transport. "Make sure she gets safely back to *Diligence*."

The recruit nodded. "Master Jedi, do you think this could really be a home for us?" Flustered, he corrected himself. "I mean, for *them*?"

"Not sure about a mercenary life, Trooper?" Kerra patted his shoulder and smiled weakly. "Well, I hope you make the right decision."

"You, too," Beadle said, needlessly saluting her. Stopping in the hatchway, he looked back. "I'm sorry, I don't know why I said that." Shaking his head, he disappeared inside the trundle car.

Kerra turned to see Arkadia looking with obvious satisfaction at the work the Twi'lek's team was doing.

"You have mastered this office quickly, Warmalo," Arkadia said. She looked the Twi'lek in his narrow eyes. "I should like to challenge you further."

"I . . . appreciate a challenge," the aide said.

"Report to the foundry. You are the new director of metallurgical operations."

The pasty-skinned figure rocked, seemingly unsure how to respond to the news. At last, Warmalo bowed his lumpy head. "Thank you, my lord."

Kerra watched the newly promoted aide stalk off. "Does he know anything about metallurgy?"

"He has the same grounding I expect from all my people," Arkadia said. "But he had been at the same assignment for nearly three months. I think he can do more. I *expect* him to."

As the loaded trundle cars revved up behind her, the

din reverberated throughout the atrium. And yet Rusher and Arkadia couldn't miss noticing it when Kerra suddenly burst out laughing.

Rusher looked at her, puzzled. "You take these spells often?"

"I get it!" The floor rumbling with the departure of the trundle cars through the magnetic seals, Kerra knelt and clasped her hands. "I get it. I understand what you're doing here!" She looked again at the Twi'lek, shrinking into the distance. The Herglic. The Falleen. And now him. It was the common thread. She looked up at Arkadia. "Your whole society. It *looks* orderly. But it runs on chaos."

Arkadia stared down at her for a moment before her expression softened. "Your perceptions are sharp, Jedi," she said. "I knew that they would be. You've learned, in your day's journey, what I have spent a lifetime learning—how to forge an effective society under one person."

Rusher looked at her with interest. "I don't follow."

"Organizations decay from the moment they're created, Brigadier," Arkadia said. "All Sith want to rule, and rule forever. But to rule forever, there must be constant revival." Seeing Kerra stand, she gestured to the stars through the ceiling panels. "You've seen much chaos at work in Sith space. I have harnessed chaos. Organized it. I have made a slave of change."

Kerra explained to Rusher what she had seen. "It's like the way you run your crew. She expects people to be able to do any job," she said.

"Flexibility. Versatility. These are the traits I'm looking for," Arkadia said. "I don't assume my subjects have only one kind of potential, only one destiny. I challenge them to find more in themselves."

The Jedi responded with a canny smirk. "But I bet

Rusher doesn't take his best gunners out of the field the second they get good at what they're doing. Do you, Brigadier?"

Rusher straightened his collar, seemingly unsure of the tack he should take. "No. No, that wouldn't make sense." He looked at Arkadia. "Don't you have a competence problem?"

"Don't *you*?" Arkadia pointed in the direction Trooper Lubboon and the trundle cars had gone. "At least I'm guaranteed all my workers have the same starting knowledge about the things I care about. And those who knew life under regimes before mine have a great incentive to see that we all succeed."

Kerra studied Arkadia. The Sith woman's philosophy was less deranged than others she had heard in Sith space—but she was still Sith. There was always an angle. Kerra just had to find it.

Arkadia watched her working it out. "You can say what you're thinking."

"I'm thinking all this moving everyone around keeps *you* safe, as much as anything," Kerra said. "Your more skilled underlings never become rivals, because they've always got something new to do. They're always having to scramble to get reestablished." She looked directly at Arkadia. "Your philosophy is an *insurance policy.*"

"And reducing wasteful conflict is bad how?" Arkadia rested her chin on the back of her hand. "You've seen what it's like out there. Can you really say rivalry among Sith is *good* for the galaxy?"

Kerra's grin faded. The woman was right. As proud as Kerra was of her insight, it didn't change the fact that, from all she had seen thus far, the Arkadianate appeared to be a safe place for those who lived in it. If this was Arkadia's worst secret, it was hard to find an objection to it. But she wondered why the Sith Lord had wanted her to come to the realization on her own.

"I did," Arkadia said, catching the thought through the Force. "Because it's important to me that we understand each other—and that you understand what I have to offer." Stepping to the middle of the atrium, she spread long, silver-clad arms. "I'm offering sanctuary to all your students, here on Syned."

Kerra stared. "How do I know you won't put them to work making weapons?"

"You don't—and I will," Arkadia said. "I have my own borders to protect and wars to wage. But that will only be *some* of the time. With me, they have some hope of doing something else, besides. And in relative safety," she added.

Rusher shook his head. "I'm sorry, Lord Arkadia," he said, "but your neighbors do things a lot differently. If you want the kids—and, hey, if you do, just ask—why don't you just take them?" Catching Kerra's angry glare, he added: "Not that you should."

"Because I want Kerra's goodwill," Arkadia said. "The hospitality I am offering is genuine, and I need her to know that—before I can ask something in return."

Here it comes, Kerra thought. Agreeable demeanor or not, Arkadia was still Sith. The students weren't enough. "What, do you want *Diligence*, too?" Kerra could almost hear Rusher's teeth grinding at the mention.

"Nothing like that," Arkadia said, gesturing deferentially to the man. "I'm sure Brigadier Rusher is talented, but *specialists* don't really fit into my scheme. Their thinking is too . . . narrow." She smiled primly at Rusher. "No offense."

"No defense," Rusher said, breathing easier. "I'd be a goner the second you decided I'd serve you better as an accountant." Rubbing his gloved palms, he added, "We are available for hire, though."

Kerra ignored him. "Then what do you want? Why would you possibly want my *goodwill*?"

Arkadia didn't answer. Another aide had delivered a datapad that the Sith Lord was scanning with interest. Looking up, she said, "I have something to attend to, but I will call for you both. Until then, I hope you'll remain here as my guests."

Kerra looked back to see several members of Arkadia's Citizen Guard stationed before the magnetic seal. Arkadia might offer hope, but she didn't take chances with her own.

CHAPTER TWENTY

Life was like a cannon, Beld Yulan had always said. "You've got to clear the empty casings before you can fire again."

As with most things—at least, up until he went Odionite—Rusher's old mentor had been right. Depression had nearly claimed Rusher, aboard *Diligence* after Gazzari. But in a strange way, the Jedi and her brood had been the distraction he needed to get his bearings again. The escape from Byllura had woken him up. He still had a crew that needed his protection and guidance.

But that shell had been fired. It was time to move on. Here, in just a few hours in Calimondretta, he'd gotten interested in starting over again. Arkadia's people had done amazing things with fabrication, feats that might make future artillery pieces lighter. Watching the Twi'lek supply master work—while he had still had that job— had also been instructive. Rusher saw three ways he might reorganize *Diligence*'s cargo pods, to speed weapon deployment. He didn't expect Arkadia would allow him to recruit here, but his visit would result in a better future for Rusher's Brigade.

Reaching that future meant clearing the barrel. The refugees had to go. And there, the casing was stuck.

Entering Calimondretta, he'd realized why nothing larger than a fighter was allowed to enter the facility: the place was an icehouse for real. The roof panels in the atrium might be transparisteel, but the rafters and frame were solid ice. Not a place to light up engines—or even land near, given the shaking he'd felt when the trundle cars rolled out. Most of the city might be safely ensconced in the great tunnels, but its exit to the outside world had to be protected. *Diligence* could come no closer; the refugees would have to cross the ice sheet.

But bringing seventeen hundred students across in trundle cars would take days. The airtight cabs held only four passengers, with cargo following behind on sleighs. He didn't even want to think about trucking space suits for a thousand aliens of different sizes.

A sticky problem, but one that Arkadia's people had been working with him in earnest to solve. Now the solution was nearly in hand. Making notations on a datapad, Rusher descended an escalator into a bluish grotto. The locals were big on their algae, he saw; colossal tubes filled with the bubbling stuff rose thirty meters around an interior plaza, serving as both light source and living art for Arkadianites dashing off to work.

Blue goo in an ice cave. Well, it beat Daiman and his statue, Rusher thought. But the coursing bubbles didn't seem to be calming anyone. Syned never slept. Everybody had something to do, someplace to go.

Almost everyone.

"Hey," called a voice from below.

Rusher looked down. There sat Kerra, elbow propped on one of her knees, at the foot of one of the massive foaming cylinders lighting Reflection Prospect.

He had to look twice. That nervous energy was gone. Since meeting Kerra, he'd only seen her in action. Even after he'd spirited her away from Byllura, she'd stayed on the bridge, fidgeting and quizzing him about their destination. He'd finally retired, just to keep her from straining her injured leg. Jedi healing didn't seem to be a class everyone took.

Kerra simply slumped, drinking from a container like a beggar outside a cantina.

"A little early to start, isn't it?" he asked. "The sun just came up."

"For the fifth time today," she responded, opening the lid. "It's water."

"Your loss." Rusher looked from side to side. The only other people not heading off somewhere were a couple of Arkadia's Citizen Guard, watching Kerra from a respectful distance across the hall. He thought he spied another up on the balcony, above.

Kerra snapped the lid shut. "What's she got you doing?"

Rusher explained the work he was doing to bring his passengers into the city. "They've got a big icecrawler that'll do the trick, but they need my help on a bushing we can marry to one of our cargo ramps," he said. "That's the problem when we mounted the spaceliner atop the cargo pods. All our doors on the ground are for heavy equipment."

"It's not your only problem," Kerra said, tucking the container in her vest pocket. "I haven't decided they should go."

"What, the doors?"

"The refugees!"

"You sure that's water? Because you're not making sense," Rusher said. "It's my ship and it's Arkadia's planet. Who are you, again?"

Kerra straightened against the tube and shook her fists in the air. "I knew she'd take you in! I'm surprised your drool didn't freeze to the floor!"

"What are you talking about?"

"Ever since you met, you've been orbiting *her* like a satellite."

Rusher chuckled, despite himself. "Well, *her* is a handsome woman," he said. *Striking* was more like it, but the kid seemed agitated enough. "And she's created all this. You don't see anything to admire there?"

"She's a Sith."

"Yeah, but she also knows stuff. A lot of people out here don't know their own history, much less anyone else's," he said. "I like a woman who keeps up on current events . . . a thousand years ago."

Kerra stood, and as she did, her Arkadianite shadows across the plaza stapped to attention. She waved her hand, dismissively. "They're always watching me. I'm in a box until she needs me—for *whatever*."

"Well, whatever she's up to, she doesn't sound like she's going to hurt you," he said, "or she'd have done it by now."

"Terrific."

Rusher laughed. "I don't know what you're expecting, but this looks like a pretty good deal. We didn't have any idea how to get you back to the Republic, anyway, and a lot of routes just lead somewhere worse." Kerra started walking away, but he went on. "Tan seems to like it here. And not only do we get to leave—they're helping us!"

Kerra spun, yelling up into his face. "So you're just going to go somewhere else? Serve another Sith Lord?"

"There aren't many other customers," Rusher said. He didn't know many of the neighboring Sith Lords, but Mandragall's practices had spread a long way. Someone would be willing to use an independent operator.

"You could do something else!"

"Like what?" He looked at the commuters, dashing to their assignments. "I'm a little old to start tending to riding animals."

"Something real," Kerra said, shoving aside his trench coat collar and grabbing at the medals on his chest. "Look at you, Rusher. You're wearing insignia that you've just *made up*. You're not part of anything real. You don't fight for anyone."

"I'm wasting my life, is that it?" Taking her arm, Rusher edged her out of the foot traffic and into the glow of the towering alga vial. "Look, what exactly did you think would happen? That I'd carry you all across Daiman's creation and more to get you someplace I've never been? This sector is my home," he said. "This is my *job*. I'm not some scoundrel with a heart of gold that you can sweet-talk into joining your . . ."

"Don't say it!" Kerra tried to force past. "This conversation is over!"

Rusher blocked her path and grabbed her wrists. "Look, you've got a lot of opinions—but not a lot of facts. You don't understand anything."

"Let me go." Hazel eyes blazed with hate.

"In a minute—once you understand what it is that I do," Rusher said. "Yes, I'm a mercenary. Yes, I work for the Sith. But there's no one else to work for."

"That's not true," Kerra said. "You could work for the *people*!"

"Fine. You tell me how," Rusher said. "You want me to be a part of something, but you don't know *what*. It's all good to set your own course when you're just one person, carrying around a shiny stick. But I'm a cannoneer. Those artillery pieces weigh tons! Some take sixty operators to set up, fire, and withdraw! How am I supposed to feed those people, to fuel that ship, while working for your you-don't-know-what? On the grift?"

"That's how you do it now!"

"Yeah, with the permission of the Sith whose territory I'm in. How many places do you think I could land *Diligence* if I were a renegade?" Rusher shot a glance back toward the watchers and lowered his voice. "They'd enslave every person in my crew, and they wouldn't care what happened to them. You've got a galaxy of people to worry about. I've got five hundred and sixty. And I'm not going to lose any more," he said. "So before you go deciding what other people's responsibility to the galaxy is, maybe you'd better take a closer look. They might have responsibilities already."

Kerra stared angrily at him. And then he saw her eyes widen, just a millimeter, those black eyebrows beginning to arc. For the first time since meeting her, Rusher saw something new in that small, determined face.

Doubt.

He released her hands and let out a deep breath, surprised and a little ashamed by the intensity of his outburst. He kept forgetting: Kerra Holt was just a kid, not much older than those refugees of hers, and the same age as many of his own recruits. He'd traded fire with her because she'd seemed to be able to handle any barrage.

But this was her Gazzari hillside.

Kerra looked away, sullen. "I don't even *have* my shiny stick."

Rusher remembered. The lightsaber was back on *Diligence*, where they'd been ordered to leave it. "Well, you broke mine."

One of Arkadia's minions stepped around the alga column to address them. "Kerra Holt, you have been invited to meet Lord Arkadia in her museum."

"Museum? Sounds interesting," Rusher said.

"And you should await our lady outside, Brigadier, once you've finished your work with our engineers."

Somberly, Kerra began to follow the minion through the crowd. But before she left Rusher's sight, she turned.

"It's true," she said, looking down at the cerulean shadows on the floor. "Arkadia hasn't asked for anything—yet. She's only given. And she looks like the best option we have." She looked up. "But she's still Sith. And that means something."

Rusher looked at her. "I don't know what that means."

"It means keep your eyes open, Jarrow. For my kids—and yours."

From the balcony of the level above, Bothan eyes watched as the humans parted.

Narsk hadn't been able to keep track of the Jedi the entire time on Syned; Arkadia had given her surprising freedom of movement. It hadn't mattered. Kerra had been easy to find, roaming the great ice halls listlessly. She seemed deflated, wholly contained.

But while he knew where the Jedi was, Narsk still had no idea what Arkadia was trying to accomplish with her presence. He didn't care, despite a personal interest in seeing her suffer. But observing Kerra was part of the instructions he had received in the desert, instructions he would carry out. Thinking back on that short, sunny respite, Narsk shivered. Why couldn't Arkadia have picked a planet like *that* for her citadel?

After his work on Byllura, he'd expected Arkadia to bring him into her confidence about her plans. That hadn't happened, but the fact that he was still in Calimondretta suggested that hope wasn't lost. Another assignment might be in the offing—and he knew what would more than likely prompt it.

The Bequest was finally happening.

He'd received word of the upcoming event just an hour earlier, via his implant. Seven long pulses, transmitted by a system that remained a mystery to him. They meant that today would be a special day. They always were. How could they not be? When power consorted with power, the galaxy shook.

Walking back from the chilly balcony railing, Narsk imagined the preparations being made in capitals across the sector. The conversations with advisers, the secret side deals already being considered.

The Bequest was on.

And if his eyes could be trusted, Arkadia had just summoned a Jedi to her presence. What was she *up* to?

Narsk bolted for the escalator. It was time to have a talk with the mercenary.

Kerra had rarely gotten around to visiting Coruscant's museums. It was always something for another day. She'd hardly imagined that her first museum since Jedi Knighthood would be under an ice sheet in a Sith Lord's redoubt.

Arkadia's aide had led Kerra up several flights of stairs into a rotunda, open to the stars above through a small transparisteel aperture. Synedian algae cascaded through fixtures around the room's circumference, giving the place a cool glow. A heptagonal pylon half a meter high sat at the room's center, focal point of floor tiling leading to the seven equally spaced exits.

A lot of empty space, she thought, watching her guide depart. *More planetarium than museum.* The only exhibits were on the walls, sitting in small elevated alcoves between the doors.

She'd expected to see the usual Sith relics—as if there could be anything "usual" about sinister instruments of mayhem. Instead, many of the items seemed commonplace, although their vintage was clearly ancient.

Here, according to the captions, was a translation device used by an aide to Chancellor Fillorean during negotiations with the Duinuogwuin. A diamond bit used by a nameless slave to mine crystals in the Great Hyperspace War. A holorecorder used to interview the philosopher Laconio—but not the famous recordings themselves. A fusioncutter used by a Sith trooper to board *Endar Spire*. All were critical to history—and yet all seemed mundane, as anonymous as the people who used them.

Looking up at the organic light fixtures, she realized the common element. These things were all *tools*. Arkadia shared something else with Daiman besides a liking for sevens in interior design: there was no art in her realm. Everything was functional, even the display in the plaza where she'd left Rusher. The pretty tubes simply routed Synedian algae from the pumps to the final destination. Some of Calimondretta's architecture was remarkable, but as with Daiman, it served mainly to fete Arkadia, rather than soothe the people.

And they needed soothing. They were all so frantic. Kerra thought back to the family of Gotals she had seen parting in the hallways of the academy. She'd thought there was something missing from the scene at the time, but she didn't realize what it was—until now.

Joy.

The Arkadianites didn't suffer from the same kind of oppression that Daiman's slave laborers did, but they lived under a cloud nonetheless. People didn't have to be threatened with physical danger to be afraid. And Arkadia's system kept them fearful. Fearful of loss of status, should they underperform. Fearful of being shifted to occupations they didn't know anything about, should they perform too well. Arkadia kept them in perpetual motion. Perhaps they *were* happier than Darkknell's hopeless residents; certainly, they weren't as bad off as the drones of the Dyarchy. But in their own way, the people here suffered.

Kerra's eyes fixed on a single item, just over a meter long. It was another implement, but different from the rest. A branding tool carved from the bone of some monstrous creature, it had a metal tip worked carefully into hand-polished grooves. Carvings in its curved length depicted the story of the owner's family.

"It's beautiful, isn't it?" Arkadia asked.

Kerra looked to see the Sith Lord behind her. She was in her war regalia again, just as she'd been when aboard her flagship. "It's very nice work," Kerra said.

"Even I can see that," Arkadia said, stepping past her to the display. "The crafter who made it toiled thirty long years at creating such pieces. They were signs of status, prized by heads of households." She lifted the branding tool from its stand. "This was from the end, near the apex of the woman's skills."

"The end?"

"Trading vessels from one of your Republic corporations arrived on Odryn to launch a trade in prefabricated goods. They were able to replicate existing tools at a hundredth of her price. The artisan, who knew nothing else, threw herself into sea and drowned."

Arkadia's hands clenched, snapping the branding tool in half. "Beauty is meaningless against the wave." She threw the fragments to the floor.

Kerra looked at the broken tool, dumbfounded.

"Such a thing would never have been allowed here," Arkadia said, "because the craftswoman would have had other skills to rely upon." The idea of spending a lifetime in a single pursuit was a recipe for stagnation, for obsolescence.

"But the cost is the masterpiece."

"Then it is worth paying."

Kerra knelt and picked up the pieces. "There's more cost than that," she said, gently replacing the fragments on their stand. "Your people. You keep them running. But you're going to run them to death."

"What about the Republic?" Arkadia said. "Your society—even your beloved Senate—is driven by commerce. You create occupations, but you don't guarantee them. You allow competitors and new technologies to disrupt them, without so much as a thought to those whose livelihoods are impacted."

"But we choose to face those challenges," Kerra said.

"Do you?" Arkadia walked to the pylon at the center of the room. "With me, they know change is coming. But that change has meaning. It serves a cause. It happens to be mine."

Kerra stared, perplexed. The woman wasn't anything like she'd expected. Misguided as she was, Arkadia was . . . *logical.*

Noting her expression, Arkadia laughed. "Did you expect all Sith Lords to be murderous, knuckle-dragging villains? You can't run a galaxy that way."

"Then let the students go."

"I can't do that," Arkadia said. "Understand, Kerra. If I seem reasonable, it's because I value reason. But I'm still Sith—and I am not going to release lives I control just to gain the trust of a Jedi." She walked behind the pylon and touched a hidden control. "But I will offer them refuge—and I have something else that I think will be of even greater value to you."

Around them, the living lighting dimmed—and above, the skylight went opaque. The sides of the heptagonal pylon slid down, revealing projectors that cast images of stars and nebulae around the darkened rotunda. Kerra looked up, straining to find a point of reference. She couldn't.

"You came here to strike a blow against the Sith," Arkadia said, "and perhaps to help some of the people under our sway. But I sense that you also want something else. Something you haven't been able to get from anyone, on any of these worlds."

Drowning in a sea of stars under Sith domination, Kerra closed her eyes. There *was* something she wanted. *An explanation.*

"An explanation," Arkadia repeated. "An explanation for all the wars, all the destruction you've seen. How brothers came to war. The strange ending to events on

Gazzari. And how all this chaos rests within a larger order."

Arkadia stood before dual projector lights, shadows falling before her. "I need something from you, but for you to help me, you have to know something no one outside Sith space knows. You have to know *why*."

CHAPTER TWENTY-ONE

Kerra sat, a student again in stellar cartography just as in the Jedi academy. Only this was a lesson no Jedi Knight ever had—from a teacher none would suffer to live.

And yet she was spellbound. The stars above had meaning now, painted in colors and outlined. There was Chelloa, where she'd arrived. There was the winding path to Darkknell. And there was the refugees' flight path, leading through Byllura to Syned. Symbols hovered in the air, marking Arkadia's best guesses at who controlled what.

The Jedi rubbed her eyes, unbelieving. She wanted to memorize it all as quickly as possible. But there was so much. Far more systems were under Sith control than anyone in the Republic imagined. And from the snaking maze of territories and the jangle of colors and emblems, it was clear there were far more players, too.

"You know of the Sith Lord Chagras," Arkadia said.

Kerra nodded. Chagras had controlled Darkknell before Daiman.

"Chagras and Xelian were brother and sister—two of the seven children of Vilia Calimondra."

Kerra hadn't heard the latter name. But Xelian, she knew, was Daiman and Odion's mother. Chagras was Odion and Daiman's *uncle*? That was something the

Sithologists of the Republic had never heard. The researchers she'd studied under weren't clear on who Odion and Daiman's father was—just that he had been out of the picture for many years. But neither brother acted or looked much like the popular image of Chagras. His empire had been reasonably orderly.

"I think you're going to have to start at the beginning," Kerra said.

"The fountainhead," Arkadia said, teeth glinting in the shimmering light, "is Vilia. My grandmother. Over the years, my grandmother acquired several dead husbands—and a sizable empire." Above, large blocks of space blinked into icy blue, one section after another.

"The dowager," Kerra whispered.

"Well, I hope you didn't think that was *me*," Arkadia said, smirking. "But Vilia had a problem. Each of her marriages produced offspring. And those seven children, grown, each claimed the right to be her sole heir." Above, seven worlds dripped red. "So she proposed a contest. The *Charge Matrica*. Whichever child expanded her holdings the most would have her whole legacy, when the time came."

Kerra stood up, mesmerized by the display. "When—when was this?"

"Thirty-four years ago. Before you, or I, or the so-called creator of the universe was born," she said. "So the challenge began."

Above, the blue areas swelled, sprawling across sector borders and filling in gaps. Every world, Kerra realized, was one of the many that lost its freedom—one of the planets Vannar Treece had fought to save.

"It worked," Arkadia said, "for a while. But Sith don't play fair. When her bid began failing, Xelian—Odion and Daiman's mother—declared war on Chagras. *My father*." Arkadia clasped her hands together and looked down at them.

Kerra looked at her, stunned. *Chagras's daughter.*

"That broke it," Arkadia said. "All of Vilia's children went to war against one another. My grandmother seemed . . . strangely unwilling to referee. And our joint cause suffered." In the holographic display around them, the blue mass of space stopped growing and began to fragment, breaking into multicolored zones. "For years, Sith conquests in this region stalled due to the infighting. Until only Chagras was left from his generation—and peace came."

"I know," Kerra said. She had been born into that island of relative silence. No one had ever known why the internecine violence had stopped. Her parents were simply glad that it had, so they could stop fleeing. "Did your father win Vilia's legacy?"

Arkadia stiffened. "Yes. And no." She began pacing around the flickering pylon. "He was sole heir. But Vilia yet lived, and so retained most of her holdings. All my father was guaranteed was the cooperation of his many nieces and nephews in restoring all that had been damaged. Ten years ago, Chagras was ready to face the Republic anew."

"Aquilaris," Kerra said. "Chagras sent Odion to conquer Aquilaris." *My homeworld.* She glared at Arkadia.

Arkadia returned her gaze. "You lost your family, I take it. Well, we are joined in sadness—for before many more worlds fell, Chagras died suddenly, eight years ago. And eight years ago . . ."

"A second *Charge Matrica* began," Kerra whispered. "Among the grandchildren?"

"Among the grandchildren."

Arkadia let the words sink in as, above, the star map showing took on a leprous aspect. The Chagras Hegemony shattered into five shards. Then ten. Then more.

"Daiman and Odion went to war first," Arkadia said. "They barely needed the excuse. On Byllura, where my father had placed my troubled brother and sister for safe-keeping, Calician took control and began to build a state around Quillan and Dromika. There are others," she said, almost somberly. "I can't even remember them all, sometimes."

Kerra's head spun. "Wait a minute. You're telling me every Sith Lord who's warring out here is related?" It was just too fantastic—and something no one, not even Vannar, had ever heard. "You're all *cousins*?"

"No, not by any stretch," Arkadia said. "Not even all the human Sith Lords trace back to Vilia. But it is a big family. There are also half-breeds—and some outsiders, like Calician, who try to figure in," she said. "It's all about impressing Grandmother."

"So she'll remember them when she *dies*?"

"She favors them now, too," Arkadia said. "Vilia doles out assets from her holdings occasionally as rewards."

Flabbergasted, Kerra sagged against the wall. Looking at the patchwork of color suspended in the air, it seemed too incredible. "Who would believe this?"

"*You* will," Arkadia said. "It's time." Pressing a control on the pylon, she watched the starfield disappear. The Sith Lord walked through the darkness toward Kerra, stopping in a semicircle on the floor. "Stay in the shadows," she said. "Watch—and say nothing. If you're noticed, I'll have to kill you immediately." She looked back. "And your students."

Chilled, Kerra looked toward the pylon. In place of the floating star systems, a constellation of images flickered into being. Odion, as large and hateful as life. Daiman, in his gaudiest fineries. And there were others. Men. Women. More teenagers. Robed or in battle dress. Mostly human, but some strange faces. More cyborgs, like Odion. A figure in a chair. An odd wraith-like entity in a hood. Kerra's eyes jumped from one to the next. She didn't know where to look.

And every one of them postured, trying to look as menacing—or regal, or wise, or aloof—as possible. Daiman seemed completely disinterested, not even deigning to look at the others. Which was hard, given how many there were. Kerra had seen seven markings on the floor: locations for standing. She assumed there were similar rooms elsewhere. But there were far more than seven images sharing the circle.

It was like the Jedi Council.

A council *of hate*.

"Greetings, my children," came a soft voice from the center.

Kerra looked past Arkadia. There, hovering above the pylon, was the image of a white-haired woman in a gossamer yellow gown. *The Dowager. Vilia.*

Human, and in her seventies, at least—wrinkled, but not worn. Kerra watched as the woman caressed a strange alien flower; she appeared to be in a garden, somewhere.

Clearly enjoying her retirement, Kerra thought. *Just letting the star systems roll in.*

"I wish to offer you all my congratulations on the liquidation of Lord Bactra," Vilia said.

"Us *all*?" Odion smoldered.

"Yes, Odion," the woman said. "The Quermian was an outsider. He was a friend to our family for many years—but he couldn't change what he was." She turned, as if seeing all the dozen-plus Sith Lords in virtual attendance at once. "I felt the need for Bactra was past—and he gave us the opportunity to do something about it."

Kerra clasped her hand tightly over her mouth, muffling her gasp. *Of course.* Daiman and Odion had truly been fighting on Gazzari—until they suddenly stabbed Bactra in the back. She'd just never imagined they'd done so on command.

And least of all at the behest of someone who looked so kindly. Vilia swept her hand gracefully through the air. "You have *all* done very well since we last spoke," she said. "And the time has come for the assignment of bequests."

A murmur went up from the collected holographic Sith Lords. Half approving, half resentful.

"Bactra's territories have already fallen to those nearest: Daiman, Odion, Lioko, and Malakite," she said, gesturing to a couple of Sith Lords whom Kerra hadn't seen before. "That is as it should be. But his greatest assets are his corporate holdings, which call no single world home." She reached to the side, out of the projected image, to retrieve a small parchment. "I now dispose of these. Industrial Heuristics and all affiliated enterprises, I give to Daiman."

A laugh went up from Arkadia's left. Kerra could only see Daiman's back from where she was kneeling; he was definitely paying attention now. Off to the right, Odion was stiffening against the muffled laughter of some of his virtual cousins.

"The bequest doesn't change anything," Odion said, his scarred face filling with rage. "I occupy Bactra's capital. If the little snot wants these—these *merchants*, he can come and get them!"

"The award has been made," Vilia said, turning toward the image of her massive grandson. "The planet is yours, my Odion, but you will give the executive staff time to relocate to a position behind Daiman's borders."

"I'll send the corpses!"

"That is *enough*," Vilia said.

The room instantly quieted. For the first time, Kerra saw the eyes in that kindly face clearly: bright and red. Suddenly self-conscious, she scooted farther back against the wall.

"Far be it from me to preach to you on philosophies, Odion," the old woman said, softening. "You each have your own approach—and I respect that. I applaud that, in fact. But corporations are not to be destroyed lightly."

"They're a tool of the Republic," Odion snarled.

"And the Republic is a tool of the corporations," Arkadia interjected.

Vilia smiled, recognizing Kerra's hostess for the first time. "Very good, Arkadia. I know how you all were taught. You recognize power when you see it."

The dowager looked away for a moment. "But perhaps something from my own complement will balance the accounts for you, Odion," she said, lifting a datapad. "Here. Two legions of Trandoshan slave-warriors, from my forces. I award them to you. They'll arrive in your territory in three days—just as the Industrial Heuristics corporate staff leaves your space for Daiman's. Understood?"

Odion bristled. Finally, ever so gently, the glistening head nodded.

Kerra placed her hand over her mouth to stifle her gasp. *The destroyer of the universe, brought down by his grandmother!*

"Listen, Bothan, unless you're looking to enlist, get away from me!"

Marching down the narrow hall behind Arkadia's guide, Narsk stepped faster to keep up with Rusher. Mercenaries were so frustrating. Never willing to be diverted from the course they'd set for themselves—even when others had really set their courses.

"This is important," Narsk said, boots grinding on the crunchy floor as he tried to keep up. "There is a pouch on your ship that belongs to me."

"So you keep saying. The Jedi stole your stealth suit," Rusher said. "I believe she also brought along a walking tank from the Battle of Mizra. I expect it's hiding underneath her bunk."

Narsk sidled up and grabbed the warrior's sleeve. "I asked her about it back in the atrium when you arrived. She said a little girl had it," he said. "Maybe the Sullustan you brought over?"

"Maybe." Rusher yanked his arm away. "But I can't leave to go fetch anything. Lord Arkadia's ordered me to wait here, same as you."

"You've got a comlink, surely."

Rusher charged ahead after the guide. "Look, Snark—"

"Narsk."

"Whatever. I'm not going to annoy a Sith Lord by asking to make side trips. All the refugees will be coming across in the icecrawler later. If your gizmo exists, we'll send it back with Tan then." He shook his head. "And then I'm out of here!"

"That may be too late," Narsk said, entering the anteroom outside Arkadia's museum. No one was here, apart from two Wookiee Citizen Guards posted at either side of the golden portal. He checked the chrono as the guide parted. The Bequest was on, right now.

And the Jedi was witnessing it. She had to be. The guide who had escorted Kerra from the grotto had taken her up the same hallway, a corridor with no other outlets. In a third of a century, no Jedi had been allowed to see a Bequest taking place. The only possibility was that Arkadia intended to show off her catch—but the Jedi Knight would have to be executed immediately, as all the other Sith Lords watched. That was decorum, or the Sith equivalent.

What is Arkadia trying to prove?

The Bothan's fur rippled, his ears perking up. Someone was coming up the entry hallway: another of Arkadia's aides pushing Quillan, still in the hoverchair from the mercenary's ship.

Of course he'd be invited, Narsk realized. The boy had every right to attend the Bequest, even in his current state. But the teenager seemed oblivious to everything, his head tipped awkwardly onto his shoulder.

Watching the great door open to allow Quillan's chair to pass, Narsk wished again for the stealth suit. All the answers were in that room, with Arkadia. But Quillan wouldn't be paying any attention!

Where's a holorecorder when you need one?

Inside the darkened rotunda, Kerra looked from face to strange face as Vilia rattled off a list of Bactra's captive corporations, doling them out. Kerra gritted her teeth. She couldn't keep track of the names. Guy-next-to-Odion looked like an evolutionary throwback. No hair care in *his* realm. Woman-on-Arkadia's-right hid behind a crimson mask barely visible beneath an ornate cowl. And one figure kept fading in and out, as if underwater.

Craning her neck to see better, Kerra slipped suddenly against the icy wall. Putting force on her injured leg, she fought to keep from making a noise as her bottom hit the ground. Above, the pieces of the branding tool tumbled from their holder. Kerra reached out with the Force to catch them, millimeters above the floor.

"What was that?" Vilia asked.

"Nothing," Arkadia said, tossing her head back and shooting Kerra an evil look. The ice queen straightened herself. "If the Bactran affair is concluded, there is something more to take up. I have custody of the twins, Quillan and Dromika."

Another sound of surprise, louder this time, went up from the circle. From Kerra's right, one of Arkadia's minions walked Quillan's hoverchair into the room. Arkadia brought the chair and its unresponsive passenger into the holocam's view, beside her.

"Is . . . he well?" Vilia asked, looking with concern. "Is she well?"

"They are apart, but I have them both," Arkadia said. "They are safe."

"That's good to hear." As the old woman spoke, Kerra thought she could see Quillan perking up. There were too many images in the room for him to focus on—Kerra couldn't keep track of them all, herself. But he seemed to recognize his grandmother's voice.

"I claim their world and territories as mine," Arkadia said.

To her left, Daiman's eyebrow went up. "And the corporate interests?"

"They didn't have any."

Vilia sighed. "I see no objection to this," she said, glistening in the darkness of the room. "Just rewards, fairly won." She paused. "But the twins, themselves. What is to become of them?"

"I think it would be best if they were cared for separately," Arkadia said. "Dromika remains on Byllura, and I think she will thrive there—alone. But Quillan should have more attention. I was thinking," she said, "I was thinking that *you* might provide it."

Vilia seemed surprised. After a moment, she smiled broadly. "What a wonderful idea. Yes, that makes perfect sense," she said. "Have him delivered to me immediately. I will send coordinates of my current home on a secure channel. You have done well, Arkadia."

"Thank you, Grandmother."

Kerra looked from one to the other. She could see the resemblance now. Both in their clear, precise manner of speaking—and in their appearance. They shared the same searching, intelligent eyes.

Vilia turned again, as if admiring the flowers in her garden. "And I thank you all. It's so nice to see you again. Following your progress, watching you grow like this—it helps me keep going. Hopefully there'll be an opportunity for another bequest, soon." The old woman nodded to her brood and vanished.

And so did they.

Kerra gawked at Arkadia as the lights came back up.

"You're all a family," she said. "You fight with one another—but she can make you stop." She shook her head, mystified. "Why doesn't she make you stop? You can talk to one another like this—and you work together when she asks. Why don't you all work together all the time?"

"This meeting was ten minutes long," Arkadia said. "The span of *actual* cooperation against Bactra probably wasn't much longer than that. But Vilia does hold leverage, in all the resources from her own conquests and from her various marriages."

Vilia sat upon an enormous pile of material wealth, military power, and corporate holdings. Passing them out like presents kept everyone in line, everyone playing the game. The strongest Lords had every reason to see it through.

"No one wants to fail the *Charge Matrica*. No one wants to fail Grandmother." Arkadia looked down at her brother, who seemed to be totally detached from reality once more. "I told you I needed something from you, Kerra. Well, this is it. I want you to carry Quillan to my grandmother."

Kerra looked at the siblings, stunned.

"And when she receives you," Arkadia said, deadly serious, "I want you to *kill* her."

CHAPTER TWENTY-TWO

"Kill her?" Kerra couldn't believe her ears. "She's your grandmother!"

Arkadia didn't blanch. "Yes. And she's grandmother, biologically or through adoption, to every person you saw just a moment ago. And it is because of them—because of her madness—that these sectors churn with conflict."

Kerra shook her head. It didn't make sense. But for a couple of flashes, the woman in the holographic image had seemed . . . *nice*. The Jedi looked at Quillan, sleeping in his chair. Vilia had seemed genuinely concerned about the boy. And the others, too; she seemed interested in advancing all her grandchildren's lives.

"What Grandmother is concerned about is *delaying* the day a successor will arise," Arkadia said. "It's the reason she staged the first *Charge Matrica* a generation ago. And now, this one."

Vilia Calimondra had accumulated so much in her youth that she never could have protected it all, should even a couple of her many offspring rebel. And that seemed a certainty, Arkadia said, for jealousy and hatred ran freely among Vilia's children by her three late husbands.

"Without the contest, sooner or later, she would have been forced to take sides," Arkadia said. And the side she really cares about is her own. If Vilia's children were just expanding her holdings by attacking the outsiders she suggested, like Bactra, I would have no argument. But she's been allowing—no, subtly *encouraging* us to attack one another. These little arbitration sessions are for show, just so she can throw some scraps of bloodied meat on the floor for us to fight over."

Dizzied, Kerra looked from one artifact on the wall to another. What Arkadia was saying squared with the history she knew, but it seemed so incredible. And one part didn't make sense. There had been a winner to the first contest. "Your father. Chagras."

"And my father died," Arkadia said. "That time of stability you remember, when Chagras lived as the sole heir? Vilia lived in constant fear of assassination from him."

"Did he give her any reason to worry?"

"Did he feel as I did, do you mean? I don't know. I only know," Arkadia continued, "that he died. *Poisoned.* The weapon was a potent nerve toxin, so powerful it overcame all his abilities to heal himself through the Force. I looked for his murderer for a year, but he had so many enemies." Golden eyes focused back on Kerra. "A *convenient* number of enemies."

Kerra grew animated. "You think she had her son killed?"

"Well, she certainly had her son *kill*," Arkadia said. "I'm not sure how far a jump it is in your world, but among the Sith . . ."

Shaking her head, Kerra stepped from the wall and eyed the pylon. She hadn't seen any kind of communications system like it in Sith space. Without the Republic's relays, no one was around to maintain a network allowing so many so far apart to converse.

Sensing her interest, Arkadia explained that it was yet another part of the family legacy, provided by Vilia as a means of staying in touch with her grandchildren. And only she could activate it. "It's another way Vilia keeps control. I couldn't call on the others with it if I wanted to. My top technicians have been all over it. They can't figure it out."

Your top technicians were probably cooks last week, Kerra thought. "Why do you want me involved in this, anyway? If you feel like this, why don't *you* do it?"

"I can't go with Quillan," Arkadia said. "Grand-mother's paranoid. She has dozens of secret retreats. This is the first time I've known where she was—and I guaran-tee, she won't be there next week. Vilia's bodyguards con-stantly scan for familiar presences. I wouldn't be able to get off the ship, uninvited. I have second choices—but they are weak compared to you."

"And fail or succeed, a Jedi assassin means your hands are clean."

Arkadia paused. "Something like that. But this isn't just about me. It's about you, and the reasons you're here. You should *want* to do this." She looked to the sky-light, now transparent. Syned's sun was passing above. "You said Odion struck your home. Aquilaris, was it?"

Kerra nodded.

"A free settlement outside our space, if I recall. In the margins. Now, Chagras sent Odion to conquer Aquilaris," Arkadia said, repeating Kerra's words from earlier. "That's true. At the time, his nephew still worked on his behalf. But Chagras was following orders, too." She stared Kerra down. "*Vilia* ordered the invasion of your homeworld."

Kerra stood her ground. Arkadia was working on her, to be sure, using logic and words to motivate her just as the twins' minions had used the Force. She wasn't going to have it. "Making this personal isn't going to make me kill your grandmother," Kerra said. She'd already foresworn her chance at revenge against Odion weeks earlier, on Chelloa.

"I think you sell yourself short," Arkadia said, stalking around the pylon like a vordebeast. "I've searched your thoughts—and I've seen your actions. Everything you've done. You're quite the guerrilla operative, for your own cause." She gestured toward sleeping Quillan. "Weren't you ready to assassinate Daiman—to attack the twins—just to ease the suffering of the common people?"

"Daiman's a warlord," Kerra said. "And killing one old woman won't solve anything. The rest of you—you're still Sith Lords."

"And we'll still squabble. But it won't be a contest. It won't be a *race*."

Kerra looked to the napping teenager, then back up to the skylight. She had been looking for some way to make a real impact, something that would help all the people under Sith rule. But there were limits to what one person could do.

Or maybe not. Vilia had shown otherwise. And there had been that moment, that flash of ire during the Bequest. Kerra had seen it. Vilia was Sith, and a Sith was quite capable of the things Arkadia said.

But Arkadia was Sith, too—as was everyone at the Bequest. What kind of chaos might a sudden change unleash? Kerra had worried about a power vacuum in the Daimanate. What if killing Villa set loose something worse?

The decision was easy.

"I'm not going to do it," Kerra said. "I don't know what would happen. But I'm a Jedi. *I don't work for Sith*—and I won't help you, either." She gestured to the items on the walls. "Find another tool."

Arkadia shook, anger rising. Almost imperceptibly, the meter-long staff strapped to her back slipped through the air into her right hand. She touched the crystal at its center—and two brilliant shafts of crimson light extended from either end of the rod. "You were my best option," she said, raising the double-bladed lightsaber before her unarmed guest. "And you've just taken that away."

Stepping back toward the door she'd entered through, Kerra glanced toward the walls, looking for the tools that could be used as weapons. But as she did, the six other portals opened, revealing Citizen Guards carrying hefty blasters. Her options were gone, too.

Where's a torture wheel when you need one? Rusher leaned against the ice wall and tried to tune the Bothan out. The fur-face kept going on about wanting his silly stealth suit. Maybe Daiman had just wanted to get a moment's peace.

The more aggravating thing was the great door, tantalizingly shut just to his left. Arkadia's museum was in there, he'd been told. Rusher could only imagine what historical treasures might be inside. A real museum? In Sith space? He knew Arkadia had only summoned him here to discuss the refugees. But still, he wished the door would open, and that Arkadia would give him even a minute to look around . . .

Suddenly the door *did* open. Lightsaber gleaming, Arkadia strode out, followed by a small parade of warriors. In the middle of the group marched Kerra, barely visible past their armored frames. Her forearms were bound together behind her back in a single black cylinder, Rusher saw.

Catching a furtive glance from Kerra as the marchers passed, Rusher called after her. "Hey, wait!"

Arkadia interposed herself, allowing her sentries to pass with their prisoner. "I want your passengers here now, Brigadier. Are they fabricating the bushing?"

"Yes, but—"

"Then report to the main atrium," the Sith Lord said. "They'll bring the icecrawler in from the south garage bay when it's ready. Board it and bring me your refugees."

"And then we can leave?"

"Only then," Arkadia said, sternly. "I still don't need specialists in my organization." She spied the Bothan, lurking behind Rusher. "Narsk, we'll be able to do business after all. Are you up for some more fieldwork?"

Narsk nodded. "Always, Lord Arkadia."

Arkadia deactivated her dual lightsaber and gestured toward the open doorway. A human aide emerged, pushing Quillan in his hoverchair. Taking a datapad from her assistant, Arkadia ran her fingers quickly across the device. "Narsk, follow Quillan and Enbo here. I'll be along shortly to fill you in." Turning, she shoved the datapad at Rusher.

"What's this?" Rusher's eyes were still on the guards, disappearing down the long hallway.

"These coordinates will take you out of my space. Use them. Maybe the Chagrasi Remnant can use your services." Arkadia spun to follow her detachment.

"What . . . what will happen to Kerra?"

Not looking back as she walked, Arkadia responded. "She'll get the same treatment due any Jedi in Sith space."

Rusher gulped. Seeing the Bothan's attention fixed on the chair-bound teenager, he inhaled and headed down the hallway after the group. Kerra was out of sight now, somewhere in that mass of mayhem. The kid had been a problem, but she didn't deserve the punishment of a Sith Lord. Few did.

"Listen, there's no need for you to go to the trouble," he said, searching for his best sales smile. "I can take her offworld with me."

Arkadia whirled angrily. "And have her charging around demolishing things here, just like she did in the Daimanate? Thank you just the same, *Brigadier*." Her voice dripped venom. "She'll be drained of her intelligence about the Republic and the other Sith Lords she's seen. Then I'll destroy her personally."

Rusher's arms slumped.

From behind him, the Bothan called out. "Lord Arkadia," Narsk said. "For me to serve you, I require the return of some property from the warship. Something the Jedi stole."

"Make it happen, Brigadier," Arkadia said. "I don't care how."

Every bit of this was wrong, and Narsk knew it.

He watched as Arkadia and her coterie disappeared down the long hall. The brigadier stood up ahead, gawking. The human didn't appear to know what to make of Arkadia's actions. Well, neither did he. The Jedi had been condemned to die—but she shouldn't still be alive in the first place.

Narsk looked down at Quillan, being pushed past him by Arkadia's aide. There was no doubting what had happened in the museum. Kerra Holt had seen a Bequest, with all members of the great family present. She had to know about the *Charge Matrica*. Narsk knew the rules, shrouded in mystery though they were: Kerra should have been executed without delay in order to protect the family's greatest secret.

That they are a family at all.

With their states so far-flung, the descendants of Vilia had been largely able to keep their familial connections private. The deactivation of the Republic's subspace communications relays had dried the interstellar ocean of knowledge, leaving many unconnected pools. Few knew the genealogy of their local Sith Lords in any detail—save perhaps for the subjects of Odion and Daiman, whose leaders' kinship had been worked into their personal mythologies. To a large degree, the Charged, as Narsk thought of them, had prospered from the secrecy. It had made coordinated stabs against outsiders like Bactra possible; it had also protected them against being seen as a common enemy by other Sith Lords.

The Jedi's blood should be on the museum floor.

And now, his implant was buzzing again.

Narsk thought back on his codes. One long burst was *Call in.* Seven short bursts signaled an impending Bequest. What did alternating short and long pulses mean?

Beware your employer.

Narsk staggered, nearly slipping on the icy floor. His superior had directed him to serve Arkadia. Now Arkadia was a threat, as seen—or, more precisely, *foreseen*—by those with resources far greater than his. Whatever Arkadia had in mind likely meant trouble for his true employer—and now the icy Sith Lord expected him to be a part of it.

It was, at once, a thrilling and terrifying place to be. Yes, he'd know her intentions firsthand. But what if he couldn't stop them? Even if he had access to the comm systems in Calimondretta—which he didn't—Arkadia might not give him the chance to get a warning out. What if he became trapped in her scheme, forced to be part of whatever it was with no way of getting out of it?

Beware your employer.

"Are you coming, sir?" The bald-headed aide looked at him, searchingly.

"Lead the way."

Narsk fixed his eyes on the aide's boots as he walked. He had to have an exit strategy.

"This isn't right."

Looking up, Narsk saw the mercenary leader up ahead, muttering and seemingly looking for anyone to talk to. "This isn't right," Rusher repeated.

Narsk silently agreed. "Then you need to do something, Brigadier."

"What?" Rusher asked as the aide went past, pushing the hoverchair. "I can't risk everyone for one person." He looked to the end of the empty hallway. "Even if she risked herself for all of us back on Byllura. I don't have the right to put everyone else on the line." He looked down at Narsk and straightened, composing himself. "Anyway, it's not my job."

Narsk looked at the human. Another specialist, saying things he could've said himself. He chose his words carefully, walking just slowly enough to allow Arkadia's aide to edge out of earshot. "I understand that, Brigadier. But I think whatever happened in that museum may have changed things. Your crew could be in danger if you follow Arkadia's orders."

"Maybe. But they'll *definitely* be in danger if I don't." Rusher shook his head. "I need more than that." He swore under his breath. "It doesn't matter, anyway. You've seen those tractor beam emitters. We're not making orbit while they're there—and I doubt they'll let us just turn them off."

Narsk nodded. The redundant stations were a kilometer apart and unconnected. Striking one, deactivating one, would do nothing. "It is a problem," he said. "But there might be a way. We're both in the same business."

"What's that?"

"*Demolitions.*"

Walking beside Rusher, Narsk quickly discussed ideas he'd had since first seeing *Diligence* from the bridge of *New Crucible*. At first, the redheaded general listened reservedly. But as Narsk continued, he could see the color draining from the man's face. "Are you ill, human?"

"No, but *you* might be," Rusher said. "These are some of the craziest ideas I've ever heard of. What do you know of ships and munitions, anyway?"

"I worked for weeks in Daiman's top testing center."

"Well, you must have spent them in the ventilation

shaft," Rusher said. He snorted. "I won't have a ship left if I do what you ask."

Narsk shrugged. "You may not have one if you don't. And there's another part," he said, "one that can't wait. It'll require someone on your crew, completely beyond Arkadia's suspicion."

Rusher looked at him for a moment, calculating. "Yeah. Yeah, we've got that."

"You have a comlink?"

Rusher produced one from his pocket and smiled. "Modern encryption and everything."

"Yes, I cracked it on Byllura," Narsk said, grabbing it. He worked the controls. "Use this channel, and no other. Arkadia shouldn't be able to hear your transmissions to your ship." Seeing the aide approaching a fork in the hallway up ahead, Narsk shoved the comlink in Rusher's hand. "I have to go. You need to decide now."

Rusher shook his head. "There's nothing to decide, Bothan. What you're talking about is crazy. And I can't do all this for no reason."

Narsk understood. The mercenary worked just as he did. There was only one way.

"Fine," Narsk said. "I want to *hire* you."

Rusher did a double take—and let out a belly laugh. "*You* want to hire *us*?"

"Is that so novel?"

"Our Brigade has only ever taken jobs from Sith Lords."

"And you would be now," Narsk said, "in a sense. And let me tell you about the payment . . ."

Gub Tengo's apartment had only felt like a coffin. Now Kerra was actually in one—or its Sith equivalent. Arkadia wasn't one for wasting space on prisoners.

While being marched deep in the icy depths of Calimondretta, Kerra had expected to see something like a traditional detention block. But Arkadia's facility looked more like a data-processing center, with tall rows of stacked horizontal metal cabinets rising into the chilly air. On approaching, she'd realized the contents of the cabinets were alive: prisoners, being fed air and nutrients through tubes. Kerra could see interrogator droids on floating platforms, mining data from the poor beings trapped in the boxes. It was a filing system for organics.

Hefted by the guards into one of the chambers, Kerra had wondered who else might be trapped in the pods around her. Surely, they couldn't all be people Arkadia had captured from her neighbors' territory. Was it a reconditioning area, too, for dissidents? Or, perhaps, a place to punish those who had failed in too many of their ever-changing jobs? Arkadia had never been clear about what happened to those who never measured up.

With the breathing mask strapped over her mouth, Kerra had been shut inside the case. But it had been dark inside only for a moment. Within seconds, the tiny confines had been lit from within by blinding strobes—and shrill, high-pitched sounds had replaced the silence. Either light or sound faded at irregular intervals, only to have the other increase in intensity. It was unpredictable, and meant to be that way. There was no meditation, no chance to reach out through the Force for anyone or anything.

Her only relative peace came in those moments when one of the droids came over the internal speakers, demanding answers about the Republic. Some of the questions she'd expected. *What were its most recent frontiers? What is the state of Republic warship technology today?* Others had surprised her. *What is the biology of the species closest to the frontier? How much has the Republic invested in toxicology studies?*

She hadn't answered any of their questions, of course, earning more punishment for her ears. At least she could close her eyes, leaving her seeing nothing but the backlit blood vessels in her eyelids—and plenty of regrets. She'd been wrong to consider Arkadia's "hospitality" for a second, just as she'd been wrong to think that Byllura could have been any kind of a haven. In both cases, she'd said to herself that she really wanted the students to leave Sith space entirely. But, in truth, she would have accepted a passable alternative in Sith space for Tan and the refugees, had one existed. Gub and all of the parents and guardians who placed their children with Industrial Heuristics and Rusher's Brigade had hoped their children would go to a marginally safer place. She'd fallen into the trap of thinking a slight improvement was acceptable, just so she could get back to thwarting Sith Lords.

"Blowing things up is easy," she had told Rusher earlier. "Mercy is hard."

She'd been hard on him, she realized, in part to keep pressure on herself, to keep *her* from settling for less for the students. As Sith-serving mercenaries went, he really wasn't that despicable. He definitely seemed to care about his crew. She envied him in that his job was finite. There were so many who needed help—her *personal* help—that she could barely conceive the scale of hers. There were seventeen hundred refugees aboard *Diligence* relying on her. But that wasn't a seventeen-millionth of the number who would remain in jeopardy. Was it right for her to focus her efforts on making things perfect for a select few when there was so much more to do?

Yes. Kerra only needed to recall the image of Lureia, the little girl with her missing sister's headband. She—and so many of the others just like her—had suffered too long to merit only half measures. Yes, being the only Jedi Knight in the sector gave Kerra other responsibilities. But those didn't absolve her of her duty to those who had put their faith in her. She was beholden. There was no such thing as a "safer place" in Sith space. One way or another, she had to get them the blazes out of here!

The interrogators started in again, droning on about the number of Jedi and where they were stationed. Hearing their questions, Kerra realized she was learning more about what Arkadia knew—or didn't know—than they were learning from her. The Jedi's great trump card, their reputation, lingered after their departure, but many beings she'd met in Sith space seemed to know nothing about the Jedi at all. Rusher had admitted that his knowledge came mostly from his history studies. Even some of the Sith Lords she'd encountered seemed to have little idea how to deal with Jedi. Arkadia had thought Kerra could be bargained with. Odion, in the Chelloa affair, had thought Kerra could be persuaded to see suicide as a rational choice. The twins seemed to have no knowledge whatsoever of what she was.

Indeed, of all the Sith Lords and minions she'd encountered, only Narsk had seemed to immediately have a handle on what the Jedi were all about. *"You Jedi are supposed to be about fair play and decency!"*

Kerra opened her eyes. The Bothan was right, of course.

But how did he know? Who *was* he?

CHAPTER TWENTY-THREE

Narsk stood patiently in the tiny round hangar. The place lacked one of Arkadia's lofty names: Embarkation Station 7 was one of a cluster of domes on the surface of Syned, connected to Patriot Hall and the rest of the city through a long series of underground corridors to the south. But the small structure was, in its own way, Arkadia's Black Fang—and the unique silver craft being prepared inside meant more to her efforts than all Daiman's wild starship concoctions meant to him.

And Narsk had simply been invited in. Or commanded to attend, rather. For this ship was for *him* . . . now.

Shining before the renewed darkness outside the magnetic field, the shuttle was little more than a fighter with a longer crew cabin. A droid pilot sat in the cockpit, its torso fused to the frame of the ship. The passenger section appeared slightly more comfortable; wide enough for the new hoverchair Arkadia's techs had constructed to replace the shoddy brown one from *Diligence*. The floating throne sat, soft and resplendent in regal burgundy, at the edge of the gangway.

"The boy will be here soon."

Narsk looked behind to see Arkadia in the doorway to the dome. No longer in her showy Bequest finery, she had surrounded herself in a flowing turquoise shift. Gone were the fur accessories and the great headdress; now, her silvery tresses hung before her in long braids. In the hours since leaving the anteroom, she'd gone from anger to complete ease. Amazing, given what she'd just ordered him to do.

"Your technicians have been showing me the vessel," Narsk said. "I can see where Lord Quillan sits. Where will I be?"

Arkadia walked aft to the three cylindrical engines, each pointing backward. When she twisted a hidden control atop the central rocket, the exhaust port cycled open to reveal a hollow area inside, just large enough for a small human. Or a large Bothan.

Stepping to the back, Narsk peered inside. There was an oxygen mask and water supply; not a cubic centimeter of space had gone to waste, and yet Narsk could see a passenger riding inside without too much discomfort. "Won't they realize the engine isn't lit?"

Arkadia cycled the cover shut and waved to a technician. Suddenly a furnace-blast of flame and noise came from the false exhaust port, singeing Narsk's whiskers.

As the din subsided, Narsk patted the ship's frame. Such a difference from what he'd seen in the Black Fang. Arkadia's people knew their design.

"We've calculated that the jump to the target's world will take seven hours. You'll have oxygen in the compartment for eight."

"That's not a lot of extra time," Narsk said.

"If you take extra time, you will already have failed," Arkadia said. "As I told you, the target is a Sith Lord—elderly, but not to be trifled with." She studied the spy's face. "You've studied the visuals. I'm guessing you have some sense of who Vilia is, Bothan."

Narsk tried to appear indifferent. "I hear things."

"Then you know I am entrusting you with a great deal."

"And you know my reputation," he said. "It's why

you hired me, to enter the Dyarchy. Even if the Jedi hadn't happened along, I would have given you the opportunity you needed."

The Sith Lord stared. "And if you're captured?"

"Ask Daiman what I reveal when I'm captured," Narsk said. "I never say more than I need to say. Besides," he added, "as far as anyone off this planet knows, my last employer was Odion."

Arkadia smiled. "That could work for me."

Narsk nodded. He hadn't known what had come of the Bequest, but it was likely that Odion now had a grievance against the dowager. Nothing pleased him.

Arkadia crossed the packed-snow floor to the front of the shuttle, explaining how the ship would automatically carry Quillan and the hidden Narsk to Vilia's hideaway. She was describing the secret passcodes that would bring the vessel safely through her planetary defenses when Narsk noticed movement out on the tundra, beyond the magnetic field.

"What?" Arkadia said, seeing Narsk's expression. Turning, she saw a space-suited figure ambling aimlessly on the ice. "What in the—"

Seeing the Sith Lord reaching for her weapon, Narsk stepped forward. "I think this is the delivery you called for." Stepping to the shimmering aperture, the Bothan waved to the newcomer. Spotting him, the figure waved back excitedly and loped across the wasteland toward their structure.

"It's the fool Duros!" Arkadia stared as Beadle Lubboon approached in an environment suit clearly fitted for a Wookiee. The transparent helmet, barely secured, wobbled around his green head. His armored left arm hung limply at his side as the trooper stumbled across the slick surface. Looking to Arkadia for approval, Narsk stepped to the controls and allowed the young Duros to enter.

Beadle lumbered into the dome, boots clapping against

the deck plating. The Duros fumbled awkwardly with his free hand for a pouch slung over his right shoulder. Failing miserably, he began chattering an apology—or, at least, that's what Narsk imagined. The helmet had fogged completely over inside. "Turn your speaker on or take your helmet off, Duros."

With Narsk's help, Beadle unlatched the helmet, which clattered to the frozen floor. "Thank you, sir. If you're Narsk, I have something for you."

Narsk pulled the pouch over the recruit's shoulder. He unzipped it and peeked inside. After many days and several planets, the Mark VI was his again.

Arkadia eyed its courier. "Why did you *walk* here? Rusher could have sent you across on the back of one of the trundle cars."

"He did, ma'am. I fell off."

"They move four kilometers an hour!"

"Really? The one that hit me felt like it was going faster," he said. "I think I broke my arm."

Arkadia rolled her eyes. "Pride of the mercenaries." She pointed to the exit. "Your commander should arrive shortly with the refugees, Duros. Wait for him in Patriot Hall." Seeing Beadle shuffling in the doorway, she growled, "The big room with the door leading outside!"

Beadle smiled meekly. "Is your infirmary open? I'd like to have something for the pain, if I could."

Arkadia nodded, gesturing for an aide to lead the recruit.

Narsk watched the door close behind them. "Hopeless," he said, shaking his head. "Well, he'll be gone, soon." He paused. "You're really going to let the mercenaries leave?"

"They can leave," Arkadia said. "They just won't *live*. Those hyperspace coordinates I gave the brigadier will drop them into the Nakrikal Singularity."

"Why not simply seize his ship?"

"Why bother? He said they were down to just a couple of artillery pieces. And if I want a cannon carrier, my people can build a much better ship than that from scrap." She looked down at the pouch. "Is that the great Narsk Ka'hane edge?"

Narsk pulled out the stealth suit and displayed it, trying to hide his dismay. The Jedi had put it through a lot of punishment. It indeed looked as if a child had been playing with it. He'd be lucky to buff out the smudges before he needed it.

At least Arkadia seemed impressed with it as it was. She ran her hand inside the seam, marveling. "How did you come by such a device?"

"If I revealed all my sources and methods, you wouldn't have much of a need for me, would you?" Narsk said. "But it will get me close to this Vilia, easily enough."

"She's still Sith. She'll sense you coming."

"One doesn't challenge Sith Lords as I do without learning how not to be sensed."

Watching Narsk meticulously return the suit to its container, Arkadia turned back to the shuttle, where the workers were removing the hoverchair after its fitting. His mission would be a simple one. When the vessel arrived on Vilia's world, Narsk would slip out unseen, shadowing Quillan. Once he confirmed that Quillan was in Vilia's presence, he would kill the old Sith Lord.

Narsk looked around uneasily. "You have a weapon for me?"

"It's right here," Arkadia said, walking to the hoverchair. Tipping it on its side, she opened a hidden panel to reveal five orbs of bluish gas. The pods were attached to a detonation device.

"A bomb?"

Arkadia chuckled. "Not up on everything, are you, agent?" She gestured to the alga light fixtures, above. "I meant it when I said we use all of the Synedian alga. One of the organism's little-known by-products happens to be an incredibly potent nerve gas." She jabbed her thumb at Narsk's pouch. "I'd wear the oxygen mask underneath that thing, if I were you."

Narsk's eyes widened. "Your . . . brother will be in the chair."

Arkadia looked at the chair coldly. "There are losses in war." Facing Narsk, she folded her arms. "Had the Jedi gone in your stead, I might only have needed this as a backup. But whatever your talents, you are no Jedi. Thus, *you* are the backup." She passed him a small remote control. "This triggers the gas."

Narsk looked at the device and nodded. So Arkadia had tried to recruit the Jedi—and failed. Arkadia was clearly her cousin Daiman's equal when it came to scheming.

"When the trap activates and you've confirmed that she is dead, you will find the location of your payment inside the chair." Producing a small tablet from within the folds of her garment, Arkadia showed it to Narsk before tucking it above the central gas canister. "The datachip contains all the intelligence I have gathered about all my neighbors—enough information to make you very popular with your future employers for years. But you and I will never meet again."

Narsk smiled weakly and turned toward the exit. He would be expected to leave within the hour.

Crossing the threshold, Narsk froze when Arkadia called after him.

"Bothan. If the suit allows you to do anything, why didn't you assassinate Daiman? And why didn't the Jedi, when she had it? It sounds as though you would have had the opportunity."

"I can't speak for the Jedi," Narsk said, turning in the doorway. "I'm not sure anyone can. She's clearly insane.

And I won't speak of my orders from Odion, except to say that, had I been ordered to kill Daiman, Odion would be an only child today." Seeing Arkadia studying him, he continued. "I do owe Daiman a debt for his treatment of me. But as much as I might like to punish him for that, I don't do things for the sport of it."

That much was true, he thought, backing up. "I'm sorry, but I need to visit your infirmary before the flight. Your algae don't agree with the Bothan system."

"Follow the useless Duros," Arkadia said, turning back to study the vessel.

"I'll do just that."

Whoever claimed ice was smooth had never been to Syned. The icecrawler's treads amplified every bump, sending vibrations through the cabin and along a path that terminated in Rusher's molars.

The rumbling rhombus was enormous, easily half the size of *Diligence*. Rusher looked back down into the cavernous cargo compartment. Arkadia's staff had suspended several levels of seating on metal scaffolds toward the rear of the vehicle, more than enough room to accommodate all the refugees. The Sith Lord was going to get this done in one trip.

"We're here, mercenary," the shiny-eyed driver said.

Rusher had seen the hairy-headed Nazzar before. "Weren't you driving the rumblecar that brought us over?" he asked.

"Promotion."

Rusher looked through the viewport. The icecrawler loomed above *Diligence*'s starboard arm, edging closer to its giant clawed base. His team had removed the jutting cannon barrels on one side to permit the crawler's approach.

Turning back, Rusher leaned across the back railing to the driver's compartment and called down to the Citizen

Guards, waiting by the enormous door some forty meters below. "We're extending the bushing! We need you guys in the hole, ready as the door opens, in case there's any breach!" Obediently, the space-suited figures set down their weapons and disappeared into the short tunnel. Seeing them appear on the cockpit's video display, Rusher lifted his comlink. "We're here, Dackett. You know the drill."

A different kind of rumbling rocked the icecrawler's frame as the corrugated door began to open. Seeing the long-faced driver release the controls, Rusher spoke again. "Hey, I think they're going to need help down there."

"Not my job. And if you did your part, they shouldn't be having any trouble!" The flinty-voiced driver looked idly up to the security monitor. Seeing commotion on the screen, he began to rise . . .

. . . only to have his head snap backward. A clump of the Nazzar's mane in each glove, Rusher yanked the driver's head back before slamming it forward against the console. An agonized groan came from the stunned creature's throat as the brigadier pulled him from his seat and shoved him over the railing, into the yawning cargo area behind the cockpit.

Turning quickly back to the security monitor, Rusher deactivated the feed just before the unlucky driver's body hit the grating. "Sorry, pal," he said, hearing blasterfire below. "Not every promotion's a step up!"

Rusher looked down into the cargo area. The Nazzar's body was only one of several now. Zeller and the armored troopers of Team Ripper were in the tunnel, blasting away. The icecrawler's Arkadianite crew was dead before the pressure equalized between the two vessels.

Spying her superior officer above, Zeller yelled, "Master Dackett sends his regards. And—begging the brigadier's pardon—he says you're crazy!"

"He's not the only one!" Already sliding down the ladder from the upper level, Rusher called out, "Did our runner make his delivery?"

"Yes, sir!"

"Get the cutters in here to bring down this decking!" Rusher scanned the cargo compartment. They'd need all the room they could get. "We're going to have to do this in record time!"

Kerra could feel her energy failing. The lights and sounds continued to hammer at her—but even without them, she felt like she'd reached the end. For weeks, she'd been fueled alternately by compassion and outrage. But now she was the lone quadractyl, just like the one she'd seen as a child, struggling to stay afloat in the icy waves.

She could barely move in the tight compartment; her awkward position was cutting off the circulation in her arms and legs, and she felt her muscles were going soft. If she didn't get out soon, she'd be no risk for escape at all.

She should have struggled more against the jailers, she thought. Anything would be better than this. The screeching died down again, in advance of more questioning from the droid. Kerra winced. It was all too much. How many days, how many weeks, would they keep her here? Was *this* the execution Arkadia mentioned? *Just kill me already!*

But this time, the voice was different. An organic whisper. "Hold fast."

Kerra opened her eyes into the blinding light. *The Bothan!*

Long minutes passed, during which Kerra wondered if it was all a joke, one more method of torturing her. The Bothan worked for Arkadia, after all. But finally, she felt movement, as the entire chamber around her slid outward. Cool air rushed in.

Pawing at the oxygen mask, the Jedi forced herself to sit up. Light-headed, she struggled to make sense of the whirling world outside. It was dimmer, and the space directly outside her metal vault was churning.

Kerra lanced out with her hand, grabbing at anything. She caught something. "Hello, Narsk."

The Bothan deactivated the Mark VI and removed his mask. "Sorry," he said. "It took a while to figure out which drawer you were in. And I had some company to deal with." Floating beside Kerra's prison on a hoverlift, Narsk pointed to the remains of the interrogator droids, smashed on the floor meters below. "Evidently, droids can't see you coming in this suit, either."

"Not unless you've been on Gazzari," Kerra moaned, rolling out of the box and onto the Bothan's platform. She coughed. "If you're here for revenge, I was already locked in a bin all day."

"Happy to hear it." Narsk quickly shut the door to her cabinet and lowered the hoverlift. "It makes letting you go now a little easier."

Slumped against the railing, Kerra glared suspiciously. "Why do you want to help me?"

"I don't," Narsk said, pulling the pouch from his back. "Let's just say I represent someone who wouldn't appreciate Arkadia's plan. And to complete my mission, I'm going to need a diversion—more than the mercenary alone can provide."

The mercenary? Kerra wavered. "Rusher?"

The hoverlift touching down, Narsk unzipped the pouch and fished for an object inside. Successful, he handed it to Kerra.

"Wait. This is my lightsaber!"

"Observant."

"But this was on Rusher's ship," Kerra said, staring at the weapon. She looked up. "You've been there?"

"No—but it arrived with the person who returned my property." Narsk removed a writing instrument from the pouch before slinging it over his shoulder. "I was lucky to get it to you at all. He hid the lightsaber in the arm of his space suit—but it got stuck between his elbow and the joint ring. He couldn't move his arm the whole time he was walking here."

Kerra gawked. "Beadle? He sent *Beadle*?"

"I told Rusher to send someone Arkadia would never think to frisk," Narsk said. "I think it actually improved the trooper's balance." The spy opened the side gate to the hoverlift. "We've got to move."

Scrambling after him, Kerra found staying upright difficult. Fortunately, Narsk didn't want to go far, directing her to a sheltered alcove between stacks of prisoner cabinets. Arkadia was busy preparing for something big, he said, something that required her full attention.

"The assassination," Kerra offered.

"The assassination is the first chapter," Narsk said. "I've only had a short time to scout the city in the Mark VI, but I've already seen half a dozen war parties preparing to head to Arkadia's various borders, poised to act. Should her plot succeed, chaos will follow, all across this sector and more. Knowing it's coming, she likes her chances."

And Arkadia had something else: the organophosphate distilled from the Synedian algae. *Chagras's Blood*, as it was called, evaporated instantly, killing at a rate that made the Celegians' atmospheres seem healthy by comparison. Narsk waved to the towers of cabinets on either side of them. "From what I can see, this place isn't so much a prison as another *testing center*. When they're done asking questions, they see what their gas does to various species."

And now, he said, that nerve toxin was being loaded

into shells for delivery to Arkadia's warships, moored across the tundra.

No wonder she didn't need Rusher's brand of artillery, Kerra thought. "But Rusher's helping you?"

"Helping *us*," Narsk said. "You and your refugees."

"Why would he care what happens to the kids? To me?"

"I don't know that he does," Narsk said. "But he knows you have *this*." Grabbing her wrist, he pushed her sleeve back and scrawled several numbers on her arm with his static pen.

"These—these are hyperspace coordinates," Kerra said. "But it's only half of a location."

Narsk slid her sleeve back down. "He has the other half—half payment for what I've asked him to do. If your gunner general wants them, you two are going to have to reconnect. He has to give me my diversion, one way or another."

Kerra shook her head. "He can find a way out of Arkadia's space," she said. "He'd never come here for this!"

"Possibly not. But these lead to a jumping-off point in uncontrolled space—the beginning of another lane. *Leading to the Republic*." Tossing the pen to the floor, Narsk started to turn away.

Kerra, dazzled by his revelations, grabbed at his arm. "A route to the Republic?" Rusher had never come across anything like that in all his travels. "How did you get such a thing? Who *are* you?"

Narsk glared at her. "I told you when we met. I'm not Sith. I just work for them."

"Evidently several at once!"

"No," Narsk said. "Not really. Just one." Stepping to a security monitor, he tuned to a scene of the tundra outside. The icecrawler was on its way back, right on schedule. "We have ten minutes, at most. Head for the Patriot Hall—and I'd find a space suit."

Anxiously, Kerra looked back and forth at the metal prisons lining the aisle. "I've got to free these people!"

"You're wasting valuable time," Narsk said. "Most are already dead." Even though the toxin went inert after a few minutes, Kerra would have to open a lot of cabinets to find anyone alive—and anyone she found would be in worse shape than she was.

Reminded of the toxin, Kerra thought of the factories she'd toured, producing shell casings. The so-called Chagras's Blood could wreak immense harm on the innocents neighboring Arkadia's realm. But there were so many factories—and so little time. Desperate, she dashed to the security monitor, looking for a map.

"You can't do everything, Jedi," Narsk said, watching her search. "There's no time."

"People are counting on me!"

"Which people?" Narsk barked. "Look, I don't care what you do now. Free the prisoners! Charge the factories! Blow yourself up! It's the diversion I want, either way." He stepped from the alcove. "But decide whether you want to die helping *every*body—or live helping *some*body."

Footsteps echoed in the halls, far away. Kerra looked back at the stacks of cabinets in anguish.

"You landed here with a mission, Jedi. You want to do more? Do it on your own time." The Bothan pulled the mask over his snout and spoke, his voice muffled. "If you want to survive out here, you focus on the job."

Kerra turned her attention from the monitor to the lightsaber, back in her hand at last. *Focus.* It was one thing she knew how to do. *One of several*, she thought, gripping it.

Rounding the corner, Kerra realized something with a

start. Narsk had had the same employer all along, and there was only one person it could be.

She called out. "Narsk! If you're protecting Vilia, why are you letting a Jedi who knows about her live?"

The shrouded figure at the end of the aisle looked back at her for a moment. "Because I wasn't ordered to kill you." Pressing a control, he disappeared.

CHAPTER TWENTY-FOUR

"Good luck to you, sir!"

Passing Citizen Guards as he strolled to the Embarkation Station turbolift, Narsk nodded casually and waved, feeling like an explorer leaving on a mission of discovery. That's what it was, for all they knew; with the mask removed, the Cyricept system resembled the jumpsuits he'd seen Arcadia's test pilots wearing. They knew he wasn't one of them, but he was a specialist working for their cause.

If they'd known how fast he'd just been running, they wouldn't have been smiling. Narsk gasped for breath as the lift doors closed. It had taken too long to find the Jedi. He'd just trusted to the Mark VI and hoped for the best, bolting headlong across Calimondretta. He hadn't stayed long enough to learn anyone's reactions, but surely a phantasm had been seen that day. At least no one had raised an alarm. He didn't need that.

Not yet, at least.

The lift doors opened to reveal the hangar dome at the end of a long hallway. Narsk could hear the shuttle's preflight preparations under way. Time was short. He stepped quickly, wondering if he had done the right thing. Freeing the Jedi had been a calculated risk. He'd only been ordered to watch her, and releasing her went a great deal beyond watching. But even before he'd heard

Arkadia's plans for Vilia, he'd known he would need a diversion. He couldn't count on the cannoneer alone. Mercenaries could be bought off. Jedi couldn't.

If Narsk dealt in backup plans, the Sith Lord did so doubly. The Bothan remembered what he'd seen earlier, when Arkadia had slipped the datachip beneath the gas canister assembly in the hoverchair. There was a second device, in addition to the receiver for his remote detonator: a timer. He'd seen enough in his work to recognize it immediately. Arkadia had planted a fail-safe. If Narsk didn't trigger the poison gas trap in Vilia's presence, it would go off anyway, at some period following the shuttle's touchdown at his destination. How long would he have? He didn't know. But it ruled out simply stealing away with Quillan and never triggering the bomb.

Quillan. Where was he? Narsk scanned the hangar floor for the hoverchair. The boy was supposed to have been brought here by now for transport. If he wasn't, the whole scheme could unravel in a . . .

"What kept you?"

Narsk turned to see Arkadia, just inside the doorway, wearing her battle armor again. Her hair bound in a metal cap, the woman stood beside Quillan, the young man still huddled in the brown hoverchair. To their right, Narsk saw the swanky new chair, innocent and ominous as he'd remembered.

"I had to run the suit through some diagnostics," Narsk said, bowing to Arkadia. "The Jedi had not been taking care of it."

"Hmm." Arkadia looked Narsk up and down before returning her attention to her brother. Carefully, she used the Force to levitate Quillan's body from the dingy, battle-scarred chair. The boy sagged in the air before gently coming to rest on the new, velvety model.

"I'm just saying good-bye," Arkadia said, shooting

another annoyed glance at Narsk before returning to her private moment. She knelt beside Quillan, stroking his soft hand. "I'm sorry, my brother. You never had a chance in life." Bowing her head, she spoke in low tones. "But in death, you may avenge our father."

Narsk studied Quillan. There was no hint of comprehension in those eyes at all. Without Dromika at hand, he was truly nothing positive or negative—but he was still a living thing. *Tragic,* he thought.

Her steely gaze returning, Arkadia pointed to the tail section of the shuttle, its secret compartment in the rear open to view. A technician zipped across the room, depositing a small stepladder for the Bothan's use. Arkadia looked down at Narsk. "Well?"

Narsk stammered. "I—I thought you might have more pressing business, right now." He tugged at his collar.

"It's all in hand," Arkadia said. "This is an important day. I'm not going to miss this moment."

"Very well," Narsk said, looking fearfully at the vessel. Walking toward it, he looked past the magnetic field up ahead to the surface of Syned, in long afternoon shadows again. Nothing was happening out there—or in all Calimondretta, so far as he could tell. There was nothing else to do. He ground his teeth and stepped on the ladder.

Mercenaries! Looking inside the cramped compartment, he wondered whether anyone else had any respect for a job anymore. *I paid for a diversion! Where's my diversion?*

"This is Calimondretta Control. Protective field is open, 'Crawler One. Welcome home."

The magnetic barrier across the great doorway shimmered and vanished, permitting the icecrawler access to the thatched atrium. The massive vehicle lumbered forward, its lofty nose just clearing the top of the entrance to Patriot Hall. "Thanks, Cali Control," its driver said over the communications system. "It's been a fun ride. Won't be long now."

No, it won't, Rusher thought, shutting off the transceiver. It was good that Arkadia had brought him into the process when it came to transferring the refugees; it had given him access to the command deck, and nobody in the ice city seemed to have thought it odd that he'd been the one speaking to them.

Rusher reached to the side and grabbed his space helmet. This was insane. Challenging a Sith Lord on one's own was crazier than anything Beld Yulan had ever ordered near the end—and he'd run half his people off. And yet, as Rusher had described his crazy plan over the secure channel earlier, he'd gotten immediate agreement from Dackett and all the section chiefs. Even engineer Novallo had bought in, grudgingly.

Maybe it was the news of the Bothan's payment. When Narsk had offered a series of jump coordinates leading safely to the Core Worlds, Rusher had laughed out loud. But then the spy claimed the proof of his knowledge was aboard *Diligence,* of all places: in the alleged stealth suit. Soon Rusher had Dackett on the comlink describing the amazing piece of technology in Tan's possession—a product, according to the micro-tag inside, manufactured on Coruscant, four months earlier.

Perhaps seeing Tan demonstrate the suit had made everyone sign on: a trip to the Republic would be the shore leave of a lifetime for some, and a chance for escape for others. A chance for a real refit, beyond their endless jerry-rigging.

Or maybe it was because he was finally doing what Dackett had said, back in the solarium days earlier.

You can't let 'em just see you going through the motions. You've got to do something. Pull the trigger.

Rusher could see their greeters gathering on the depot

floor, far below the icecrawler's overhanging cockpit. Arkadia's Citizen Guards were out in force, ready to receive the vehicle and its passengers. Judging from the weapons some of them carried, it didn't appear that they expected all the students to come willingly.

Well, good for you, Rusher thought. *Makes me feel better about what we're about to do.* Clambering onto the ladder, he yelled down to his companions. "Get set, brigade! We're about to make some history!"

The Houk Citizen Guard at the intersection of the frozen passageways waved his blaster at the workers clamoring for his attention. "I don't care how many of you saw this—this *phantom,*" he yelled, brown jowls shaking. "Don't you have jobs? I know I do!"

Kerra slipped from one doorway to the next, thankful for the distraction. The interrogation facility hadn't been guarded like a prison, but evidently Narsk's departure from it had attracted attention all along his route. Personal stealth technology wasn't much help when forcing your way through a crowd of commuters.

Still, Kerra found herself wishing she had the hated suit now. Her muscles stinging, her head still ringing, she forced herself forward. The fact that Arkadia's workers didn't wear identical uniforms had given her a chance to move anonymously through the halls, but slowly. *Too* slowly.

Ten minutes, the spy had said. She didn't even know why she was supposed to go to Patriot Hall, or what he meant by a diversion. How in blazes was she supposed to know when ten minutes were—

"Lockdown! Lockdown!" A pair of beefy blue-sashed sentries dashed past her alcove. "Hold everyone! There's been an incident at the Impound!"

So that's what they called the place. "I guess we're doing this," Kerra said, stepping into the ice tunnel and igniting her lightsaber. "Hey, guys!" she yelled to the guards up ahead. "I'm your incident!"

In the hangar, Arkadia raised her hand, preparing to close the compartment door behind Narsk. "You have my encrypted channel programmed into your datapad," she said. "Contact me when you've succeeded."

Before she completed the motion, sirens reverberated through the dome. Narsk could hear them resonating all the way up the long hallway from the lift.

Arkadia looked angrily to a speaker on the wall. "What's going on?"

"The Jedi has escaped the Impound," a tinny voice responded.

Narsk wriggled from his confines. "The Impound? Is that a prison?"

"It's more of a morgue," Arkadia snapped. "Or it should have been, for her. She couldn't get out alone. Somebody let her out!"

Reflexively, Narsk drew his arms back inside the false engine. His eyes darted to Quillan and his hoverchair, being walked toward the ramp for loading into the passenger compartment. "I . . . think you should attend to this problem, Lord Arkadia," Narsk said. "I thank you for seeing us off, but matters are well in hand."

"Yes," Arkadia said. "That's because it's *my* plan."

Storming toward the exit, Arkadia called one of her Wookiee Citizen Guards from his station by the wall. "You there!" She pointed to the tail section of the shuttle. "Make sure the Bothan shuts that chamber tightly. We don't want him asphyxiating in space!"

Narsk's heart fell as the sash-wearing tower of hair took station behind the engines. Behind the glaring Wookiee, Arkadia was already gone.

Narsk smiled weakly at the guard. "Nice day for a flight, isn't it?"

* * *

The chubby depot manager pounded on the gate of the icecrawler. "We don't have all day! When are you going to open up in there?"

Definitely not yet, Rusher thought, watching through the small viewport. Far behind the pasty-faced manager, he saw Arkadia and several of her minions crossing the atrium floor from north to south in a big hurry. Watching them vanish down one of the side ramps into the glacier, Rusher turned back to his team, waiting in place behind him inside the vehicle.

"Would have been nice to have seen that museum," he said, his hand raised. "Drop the gate!"

Outside, the manager stumbled backward, nearly crushed by the falling drop-gate. Shaking his fist, he bellowed. "What do you think you're—"

The manager's jaw dropped. Instead of seeing the expected refugees inside the massive cargo hauler, he was staring down the long barrel of an ancient laser cannon, crewed by a team of determined-looking space-suited cannoneers.

"We'd like to have you meet Bitsy," Rusher said, standing nonchalantly to the left. Looking at the wide-eyed Citizen Guards ahead of him, he lowered his hand. *Rough day to be you, friends.* "Fire!"

The ground beneath Embarkation Station 7 shook, causing flecks of ice to flutter from the hemispheric ceiling. Lodged inside the shuttle hidey-hole, Narsk looked wanly at the Wookiee guard. "Don't you think you should go do something?"

The Wookiee snarled. Kicking away the stepladder, she grabbed Narsk's snout and shoved him painfully backward into the compartment.

Narsk sputtered, coughing on his own whiskers. "That's not what I meant, you idiot!"

*   *   *

Terrified workers stampeded through the carved-ice halls leading to Reflection Prospect. Kerra's initial assault had caught the sentries who had raised the alarm by surprise. But the hulking Houk guard had thought nothing of the safety of his fellow citizens, firing his blaster as he charged through the crowd. The Houk had actually shot both the hapless Citizen Guards in the back before Kerra could strike them.

Flipping her lightsaber to her left hand, she pulled one of the fallen sentries' weapons into her right hand with the Force and returned fire. Kneeling, she targeted the sheer crystalline wall to the Houk's right, knocking him from his feet with the ricochet.

Several more combatants entered from side hallways, responding to the screeching siren. Holstering the blaster in her belt, Kerra charged ahead, raking from side to side with her lightsaber.

There wasn't any release in lashing out this time. Not like on Byllura, with its crazed mesmerists. The Citizen Guards of Syned weren't Sith hopefuls, but instead people devoted to—or stuck within—Arkadia's military-industrial system. As another guard fell before her, Kerra was glad she hadn't seen Seese in one of the blue sashes. It was always harder killing someone you knew.

Seeing an opening in the opposition line, Kerra leapt toward it. There, ahead, was the giant grotto with its balcony and escalator, surrounded by giant burbling pipes of Synedian algae. But no one was reflecting in the cave plaza now. A dozen guards had taken station near the other exits, and several snipers were on the overlook, the balcony leading back to Patriot Hall.

Alarmed at the numbers, Kerra drew her blaster and took aim at the tube where she and Rusher had quarreled so many hours earlier. "Let's see what you think of this," she yelled, firing.

Nothing happened.

Kerra rolled, avoiding return fire. She'd hoped to inundate the grotto with the blue slop—only the by-product was toxic, Narsk had said. But the towering cylinders were made of something tougher than transparisteel. Tossing aside the blaster, she went back into action with her lightsaber, deflecting fire as she tried to advance. But with the snipers firing from up above, Kerra could only retreat to the doorway she'd entered through. *What I'd give for a concussion grenade,* she thought. The plaza was the only route she knew to Patriot Hall.

Suddenly there was a break in the firing from the balcony. Kerra thought she heard thunder now, reverberating faintly above the klaxons. Atop the upper floor, the snipers parted to allow a new arrival to approach.

Lord Arkadia looked down from the ledge. "The errant Jedi," she said, seemingly undistracted by the noises far behind. "You're surrounded. It's time to die."

He'd thrown everything in. Rusher had Bitsy on the atrium floor now, tearing a new hole in the glaciated wall. After its first deadly shot, it had taken ten bearers and twenty seconds to get it out of the icecrawler and into action. Now Team Zhaboka fanned out to the left and right, slamming their missile launchers to the surface and firing anchor bolts into the floor. Behind, Zeller and her Team Ripper crewmates were rolling out the brigade's last good Kelligdyd 5000, its crushing bulk crashing noisily over the drop-gate.

Deploying fast was easy when you didn't expect to get your weapons back.

Rusher opened up again with Bitsy. No need for spotters in this battle. Every shot hit something. Arkadia's welcoming committee was long gone. And every shot sent seismic waves through Patriot Hall. Through all of Calimondretta, it seemed.

On to stage two. "Zhabokas high!" Rusher yelled into his helmet comlink to troopers not ten meters from him. "Quickfire, quickfire!"

With synchronized precision, six mortar launchers tilted and chuffed, firing at the transparisteel covering atop the atrium. The shells' sonic splitters activated on contact, pulverizing the screen protecting Patriot Hall from Syned's frigid temperatures. Instantly, the atrium's atmosphere ballooned outward, buffeting the metallic powder that had been the transparent roof and shearing it harmlessly outside.

At once, automatic durasteel doors shuttered the pathways into the city, protecting it from loss of heat and air. Dozens of Arkadia's hapless soldiers, exposed now to both laserfire and Synedian ice, pounded on the barriers, clamoring to enter.

"Help them crack those doors," Rusher ordered, not so helpfully. Bitsy spoke again, slamming the western barrier with such force that it snapped right off its durasteel gudgeon. The cavern ahead was open now, a gaping, smoke-filled maw leading into the underground city. Slapping the back of one of his troopers, the brigadier gestured for the team to pivot the weapon to the north. Kerra had been taken south, earlier—and much farther west led to the Promisorium, and Arkadia's own younglings. He'd never before led an assault on a fortress from *inside* the fortress. This would take finesse, as much as could be managed with heavy artillery!

Still, they'd already seen some success. He looked up at the cloud of destruction that had been the ceiling and marveled. Clean shots, all. The massive ice timbers still mostly stood, holding nothing but framing a view of the new night, outside.

Outside. Stage three. He tapped his helmet again. "*Diligence,* this is Rusher! Dackett—get moving!"

*   *   *

The Wookiee flinched. The ice sheet rumbled gently, causing loose items in the hangar to quiver. But Arkadia's appointed guardian simply growled, staring down the Bothan stuffed into the tail of the shuttle.

"Oh, blast it!" Fumbling in the cramped space, Narsk yanked the mask back down over his head and activated the Mark VI, vanishing.

"Wurf?"

The female Wookiee stepped closer to the chamber, tilting her head left and right as she stared at the seeming nothingness.

Until she came too close. "Sorry, lady!" Narsk's gloved hands shot out, grabbing a handful of hair on each side of the Wookiee's face. Yanking, he slammed the guard's forehead hard into the metal frame.

Narsk shot forward, tumbling over the back of his dazed victim. Hitting the floor, he stumbled behind one of the landing gear, out of sight of the technicians.

More thunder came from the south. Fearful of the visible effects of the snow falling from the shaking ceiling, Narsk curled up underneath the fuselage and strained to find Quillan. The boy sat placidly at the bottom of the ramp, surrounded by three technicians who were considerably less calm.

Join the club, Narsk thought. *She's not paying me enough for this!*

Kerra pulled her lightsaber from one body only to embed it in another. Arkadia was letting her guards have their chance at her. Reflection Prospect had gone in a couple of minutes from a place of peace to a killing zone.

She struggled to find somewhere to stand. New attackers replaced every one that fell. And deflecting blaster shots into them wasn't effective, she'd discovered. The fancy sash wasn't the only thing Arkadia issued her Citizen Guards; the electromesh tunics under their clothes took the punch out of blasterfire.

The Jedi leapt, winging another attacker. The accursed tunics were no match for her lightsaber, but they made it more difficult for her to withdraw it. She couldn't do this with body shots. This was messy enough work already.

The floor shook. There was no mistaking it now: there were explosions coming from the north, in the direction of Patriot Hall. Shooting a look up to the upper floor, Kerra saw that Arkadia was noticing it, too.

"That's enough," the Sith Lord said, directing her snipers back to the ledge. "No blasters. Thermal detonators!"

A Citizen Guard looked up at her. "But our people are down with her—"

"And doing their job! *Now do yours!*"

From his perch on the track of the parked icecrawler, Rusher could see *Diligence* climbing into the thin Synedian air toward Patriot Hall. Red lights glimmered on the great conical tower to the north, one of the two tractor beam emitters he'd seen on landing.

"That's it," Rusher whispered. *Make them think you're coming for us.*

The warship had covered half the length of the ice sheet outside when the lights on the north tower suddenly went green. *Diligence* seemed to struggle against an unseen force, urging the transport and its attached cargo pod clusters toward the parking area, already littered with ships. The ship wobbled, straining to rise higher over the tractor beam emitter.

Rusher tapped his space helmet to activate the comlink. "That's it! Cut it loose!"

Diligence dipped and yawed—and suddenly the entire starboard cargo assembly separated from the ship, plummeting like a colossal bomb toward the emitter and Arkadia's parked fleet.

KRAKKA-BOOOM!

CHAPTER TWENTY-FIVE

Syned shook!

Narsk grabbed the landing gear and held on. He looked out through the magnetic field to the inferno beyond. The mercenary had signed on all right. With a vengeance. The northern tractor beam emitter was a memory. And even as the deadly blossom of exploding ordnance rose and expanded, it fell in on itself, creating another caldera in the ice where the landing field had been.

As the surface ice beneath it distributed the kinetic energy, Embarkation Station 7 rode up and down as if on an uncoiling spring. Above, massive chunks of ice fell from the ceiling, narrowly missing the stumbling Wookiee. Around the quaking shuttle, technicians staggered toward the walls, away from Quillan in his deadly burgundy chair.

Narsk leapt from behind the landing gear and lunged for the teenager. Half visible in the shower of ice, the Bothan forced his arm underneath the heedless boy's shoulder and heaved.

"Hang on, kid. This is for your own good!"

Farther south through the tunnels, the explosion rocked Reflection Prospect, knocking Arkadia and her snipers to the ground. From beneath the balcony, Kerra saw it: reverberating through Calimondretta's glacial skeleton, the shock wave ripped the icy pillars suspending the second floor to pieces.

She dived for the only shelter she could see—the threshold of the hallway she'd entered through, littered with bodies. At once, up ahead of her, the entire second floor of the grotto heaved and gave way, shaken by subsidiary blasts as it went down.

Kerra shielded her face against the rush of chilly debris. *Those were the thermal detonators,* she thought. But no thermal detonator could shake an entire city!

"Boy, that was pretty," Rusher said gleefully.

"I don't know," Dackett responded over the comlink. "Novallo's gonna take my other arm for this."

Rusher had told the Bothan right: it had been an insane idea. All *Diligence*'s armaments were deployed on the floor of Patriot Hall around him; not nearly enough weapons to consume all the munitions socked away in the ship's clawed, four-chambered cargo clusters. Neither Rusher's ground team nor the ship had any way to fire those.

But *Vichary Telk* had once been a ship to itself, before being welded to the cargo pods. Severing one of the two cargo compartments that served as *Diligence*'s feet had been a simple matter of sealing the accesses and setting off the explosive bolts holding the hydraulic system in place. The engineer had, indeed, invented some new words on hearing Rusher's plan in the secure comlink exchange. But the plan had worked, making an astounding impact.

"You're beautiful, Bothan—whoever you are!"

Now *Diligence* looked stunted, half its footing amputated. The ship would never land again in this condition. "Losing lateral control, Brig!" Dackett called over the comlink.

"Hang on," Rusher said. Opening a pack on his belt, he looked at the homing sensor. Nothing. "Dack, you got anything on our wanderers up there?"

"Negative. The tags aren't strong enough to penetrate the ice!"

There goes that gambit, Rusher thought. Beadle had delivered more than just the stealth suit and the lightsaber. They'd welded a comm-frequency tag just like the one all his troopers wore to the base of the Jedi's weapon. But neither Beadle nor the lightsaber were showing up on his register. "We're going to have to do this the hard way. Let me make my call!"

Switching from the secure channel to the one he'd used to contact Calimondretta Control, Rusher slid down off the icecrawler and placed his call. "Lord Arkadia, this is your deliveryman," he said. "Give me the Jedi—or I'm gonna crack your city open and let you all die!"

In the rapidly disintegrating hangar, Arkadia's technicians listened as the brigadier repeated his message. Or tried to listen—as the blasts kept coming from the south. The intruders in Patriot Hall were shooting again, doing their best impressions of the miners who had originally hollowed out Calimondretta's tunnels.

Abruptly, a muscular human mechanic turned to see a surprising sight in the frigid haze: a bipedal snowman, pushing Quillan and his hoverchair up the ramp to the shuttle. "Hey!"

So much for this, Narsk thought, slapping a wrist control and deactivating the stealth suit. Suddenly appearing in the shower of ice crystals, Narsk yelled back through his mask to the mechanic. "Saboteurs!" he implored, pushing the chair higher. "Hurry, we've got to complete the mission!"

"I don't think we should do anything without asking—"

Narsk faced the mechanic, the suit and mask serving to make him look menacing and mysterious. "Look around!

Don't you know your job?" He jabbed his gloved claw toward the shuttle. "Now help me load him up!"

Befuddled, the mechanic dashed to the top of the ramp, pushing Quillan and his conveyance inside the hatch. Seeing the worker secure the passenger section, Narsk dashed down the ramp, headed for the hidden compartment he'd tried so hard to escape from just moments earlier.

The stepladder gone, Narsk leapt, grabbing hold of the tail section and pulling himself up. Straining, he reoriented himself and backed his body, serpent-like, into the chamber. Reaching for the compartment's tube-like oxygen feed, he routed it under his mask. The vehicle shook around him, beginning to taxi toward the exit. The droid pilot had been given the go signal.

Reaching for the control to cycle the compartment shut, Narsk saw chaos on the receding floor of Embarkation Station 7. The Wookiee guard and two of the techs were there, screaming at the seemingly paralyzed mechanic. After a second the man realized his mistake and began yelling at Narsk.

"Wait a minute! You've got the *wrong hoverchair*!" The mechanic dashed past the booby-trapped chair, still parked on the hangar floor, its rich color obscured by frost. "Quick! Raise the magnetic field! Order the droid to stop the ship!"

Feeling the sluggish shuttle lift from the ground, Narsk found the remote control Arkadia had given him and pressed the button.

The last thing he saw before his hidden compartment cycled shut was the burgundy chair spiraling into the air, riding a volcano of blue gas. And the bone-chilling screams were the last thing he heard, before the sound of the accelerating engines on either side of him claimed his hearing forever.

*   *   *

Kerra puffed, sprinting the long meters up the hallway. Arkadia's guide had led her this way earlier, on their way to the museum. It was the only path out of the grotto now; the collapse of the second level had ruined the route up to Patriot Hall. And while she'd seen Arkadia on the terrace before, she hadn't seen her fall. Kerra was taking no chances. No more than she already had, anyway.

Although the pumps no longer worked, the algae still lit the way, fluorescing in their tubes. Even back in the ruins of Reflection Prospect, the giant pipes had held, although several now tilted at dangerous angles. Arkadia's society really was formidable in its accomplishments. She represented a great threat to everyone around her—and the Jedi and the Republic didn't even know she existed. Kerra had to change that, had to stop Arkadia.

But she already had a job. She had to get the refugees out.

Reaching the anteroom, Kerra dove toward the opulent museum door. Cracking it open, she found what she expected inside: Arkadia's museum, in all its vast circular majesty. Several of her prized artifacts had fallen to the floor, shaken by the tremors in the ice.

Kerra searched for exits. The stars shone through the skylight twenty meters above—far too high to reach, even jumping from the pylon at the room's center. But there were six other entrances. One of them had to have—

Arkadia.

The Sith Lord stood in the doorway to the left, her ornamented staff in both hands, her face smudged with smoke, her once-proud armor scratched and singed.

"I don't know what you've done or how you've done it," Arkadia said, activating the control transforming her staff into a double-bladed lightsaber. "But it stops here."

*   *   *

Rusher swore. Minutes had passed, with no response. He'd held his fire on the city, but the city had nothing to say to him. Only Team Zhaboka was still firing; Rusher had sent them and their more portable weapons out onto the tundra to target land vehicles approaching over what was left of the ice sheet.

Certainly someone could hear him; he heard the panicked chatter on the comlink channel. But none of it seemed directed at him. If Arkadia was out there, she was probably busy.

And if Kerra was out there, that's where Arkadia was, too.

"Stop shooting! Stop shooting!"

Rusher looked to the north, where the tunnel leading into the glacier had collapsed between their fire and their impromptu bomb. A space-suited figure clambered awkwardly through a tight gap between the crushed gate and several ice boulders.

"Lubboon!" Rusher dashed across the crunchy depot floor. Two of his troopers pulled chunks away, helping the recruit past.

"I gave the Bothan the lightsaber like you said, sir," Beadle said, breathlessly.

"The Jedi, trooper! Did you see her?"

"No, sir. But the Bothan gentleman did go after her," Beadle said, pointing ahead of him. "North."

"That's south."

Rusher stalked the debris-strewn floor, trying to remember. The big grotto was directly south, at the juncture of passageways leading east, to Arkadia's museum, and farther south, down a series of escalators. The Citizen Guards had taken Kerra that way, deeper into the bowels of the glacier. With the damage they'd done to the passageways, there was no reaching the grotto, much less anything leading down from there.

No, if Narsk had reached Kerra, the Jedi would have tried to go up. That meant either Patriot Hall—or up the long, climbing hallway to Arkadia's museum. Was there some exit at that end? More important, could they ever find it? There wasn't any time for picking through the rubble. If Arkadia had any other ships in the system, they'd be on their way by now.

A call on the secure channel interrupted him. "The other tractor beam's got us, Brigadier!"

"Give 'em the other barrel, *Diligence*," Rusher said, waving to his crew to stop firing. Looking south, he clicked the comlink again. "You can't land, anyway, until you do. We'll assemble outside."

"You don't sound happy. No Jedi?"

"No," Rusher said, "and no route to the Republic."

"Let's use the coordinates the Sith lady gave us," Dackett said. "We've got 'em punched up and ready to go as soon as we recover everyone. I don't think we're going to be very popular here after this."

As usual, the ship's master made sense.

Rusher sighed. He'd tried.

Kerra parried one lightsaber stroke after another, backing toward yet another doorway in the circular room. All the exits were locked from the outside, including the one she'd entered through. Arkadia had her trapped.

"You're little more than a Padawan," her opponent said, weapon whirling in her hands. "You don't know what you're dealing with. You've never known!"

The ruby blade came down, streaking against the ice floor. Leaping, Kerra bounded past the holoprojector pylon, which now provided the only cover in the room.

"You're not the first Sith I've faced," she said, fighting for time. "You're just another petty dictator, like the rest. You're not special."

"Don't compare me with them," Arkadia snapped. "Mine is an enlightened regime!"

Kerra laughed. "Well, it's true then, what I've always heard. An 'enlightened' Sith would kill her own grand-mother!"

Ignoring the taunt, Arkadia raised her weapon high over her head and charged. Kerra darted out of the way, causing the tip of the Sith Lord's lightsaber to spark off the pylon.

"I'm just taking what's mine. What *should* have been mine!" Pressing a control on her weapon, Arkadia detached the ends from the meter-long staff, dropping the ornamented bar to the floor. One weapon had become two.

Kerra leapt, only to be repelled by Arkadia's gleaming defense. Incredibly, the woman seemed as coordinated with two lightsabers as with one, using the first to parry while preparing a counterstroke with the other. Forced back, Kerra fell, stumbling over the raised tiles set in the icy floor. Pressing her advantage, Arkadia brought both lightsabers forcefully against Kerra's green blade.

Straining in the crackling battle of strength, Kerra looked into her atatcker's eyes. The calculating intelligence remained, but anger was taking hold.

"I was a fool to expect you to help," Arkadia said, mashing her lightsabers against Kerra's. "Too smart by half. But it's done. The assassin is on his way." Shimmering red light danced across her face. "They're *both* gone."

Eyes transfixed on Arkadia, Kerra suddenly caught a feeling through the Force. *Both gone.*

"You . . . you sent Quillan to die. Didn't you?"

Arkadia froze—and the world around her rumbled. The Sith Lord looked up to see a flash of light over the skylight. The stunted *Diligence* screamed overhead, releasing something from beneath. Kerra recognized it: the port-side cargo cluster, fully a quarter of the ship's mass, spiraling toward the surface.

Syned shook again, harder than before. The southern wall of the museum erupted, forced inward by the cataclysmic meeting of megatons of explosives and ice. Arkadia staggered with the impact. Kerra kicked out, taking the Sith Lord's legs out from under her.

Abruptly, the floor itself fractured, two-thirds of the ice jutting upward. Forced to the northern wall, Kerra deactivated her lightsaber and clambered across the icy rubble, looking for an open passageway beyond the askew doors. Aftershocks and secondary explosions continued to shake the dome. Clouds of frost fell from above.

And there, in the snowfall, she saw Arkadia, bruised but advancing.

"How could you?" Kerra yelled, reaching in vain for some handhold to climb the wall. "You sent your brother to die—in a trap against your grandmother? *How could you?*"

Stepping over a crevasse in the floor, the Sith Lord waved her hands. Both lightsabers returned to her from the rubble. She ignited them. "There can be only one Sith Lord," she said. *"And no Jedi."* Arkadia leapt . . .

. . . and above, the sky ripped away in a blinding flash.

Kerra struggled to open her ice-crusted eyes. The top third of the dome was gone. Arkadia's museum, shattered from above and below, was open to the stars and Syned's deadly cold.

Hearing creaks as she tried to move, she couldn't tell whether they came from the collapsed pit around her or her own bones. Fumbling in the ice, she found a metal bar and jabbed it into the snowy wall, using it to pull herself up. A tool, from what had once been a museum of tools. Slamming the makeshift piton into the wall again, she scaled the frozen slabs, desperate to escape. Something was moving in the debris behind her.

With a heave, Kerra lunged onto the surface of Syned and inhaled. Frigid air, only barely laced with oxygen, stabbed at her lungs. Around her, she saw only devastation. Most of the buildings on the surface were gone, and majestic Patriot Hall was now a leaning frame of pillars. The tractor beam emitters were gone. The field once strewn with ships heaved, tossing and refreezing.

Hearing footsteps in the ice behind her, she tried to run, only to stumble and fall, choking at the cold.

Diligence was gone. But she had seen it in the air, earlier. Was it escaping? Cheek against the ice, she decided to think that it was.

It had been a good fight. She'd done her part.

She closed her eyes.

CHAPTER TWENTY-SIX

The light of the medbay was warm and reassuring, everything one would expect from a classy spaceliner. Kerra blinked at the room through her oxygen mask.

"Looks like she's thawing out," a familiar voice said.

Stretching against the pillow, Kerra watched a medical droid remove her mask. The silver model stepped aside to reveal Rusher, leaning inside the doorway. Overcoat gone, the redhead wore a black shirt beneath a worn rust-colored jacket.

"What happened?" Kerra croaked, voice raw from exposure.

"You went for a walk outside without your space suit," Rusher said, grinning.

Kerra struggled to sit up. "No, I meant to the dome. I was fighting Arkadia—and then half of it vanished."

"Oh," Rusher said, stepping inside the room. "Thank Bitsy for that." He explained that while he'd been waiting to be picked up by what was left of *Diligence,* he'd spied a telltale knob alone on the ice out to the east. Catching the faintest trace of a signal from the tag on Kerra's lightsaber, he'd sent his ship on a flyover to confirm it was the top of a deep and massive dome. Then the brigadier, along with Lubboon and the Rippers, had heaved the massive weapon onto a cargo sled behind one of Arkadia's trundle cars. One final shot across the tundra had leveled the dome.

"You thought I was in there—and you *shot* it? You could have killed me!"

"We're a precision crew," Rusher said. "We shaved it like hair off a bantha."

Pouring himself a cup of something medicinal, he recounted how he'd tricked his way into Calimondretta with his remaining artillery pieces. He was fortunate that Arkadia had sent the icecrawler to get all the refugees in one trip; it had allowed him to put all of his munitions into action.

"We'd never deployed inside a building before, but we hoped if we got in there and shot enough stuff, they'd give you to us—or you'd scurry out somewhere." He drank. "That's how it worked."

"How'd I get back to the ship?"

"I . . . arranged transportation."

"You carried me?"

"Barely," Rusher said. "You're heavier than you look." He smiled. "All muscle, I know."

Kerra rolled her eyes. "What about that bad leg of yours?"

"Well, I had to keep my lurch ratio perfect this mission. And as has been brought to my attention, the walking stick was always just for show."

"I'm sorry I broke your old one."

"Oh, I don't mind. I like the new one you brought me better." Rusher lifted something from a shelf, behind her.

Kerra recognized it with a start. "Arkadia's lightsaber?" Looking again, she realized it was the detached, ornamental middle. *So that's what the stick was that got me out of the museum,* she thought. "But it's too small for a cane."

"But dandy for a swagger-stick," Rusher said.

Kerra rubbed her eyes. "The refugees?"

"All aboard *Diligence,* all safe. All twenty-two hundred of them."

The Jedi's dark brow furrowed. "But we had . . ."

"One thousand seven hundred and seventeen," Rusher said. "I can't believe I'm saying this, but we picked up some more riders on our way out. A bunch of laborers found environment suits and dashed across the ice to us, begging to be taken along. Apparently, they weren't as patriotic as Arkadia wanted them to be. You remember that Twi'lek—the supply-clerk-turned-metallurgist? Evidently it wasn't much of a promotion."

Rusher shared some of what they'd been told by the new arrivals, including details about Arkadia's chemical weapons program. He smirked. "Sounds like we took part of that operation out during our little rampage."

"By accident," Kerra said. "You didn't even know it was there!"

"I'm in artillery. Everything we hit, we hit on purpose—even if we don't know what it is!" He patted the bulkhead. "Anyway, there was plenty of room here on *Diligence* for them, although we're kind of back to being *Vichary Telk.* Only ugly. With the cargo pod clusters gone, the spaceliner was a spaceliner again, more or less.

"Might as well put it back to its service," he said.

Kerra shook her head. "You tore apart your ship to save me?"

"My engineer isn't very happy with me, but what else is new? Besides," he said, reaching for Kerra's arm and pulling up her sleeve, "you were carrying our destination."

Kerra looked at the numbers on her arm, scrawled there by the Bothan. She wondered what had happened to him. The last thing this part of the galaxy needed was him out there, working his mischief in his stealth suit. And yet, for some reason, he had helped her—and helped

Rusher. She wondered if Narsk knew the reason why, himself.

A thought struck her suddenly. "Your artillery pieces! You left them on Syned?"

"Well, we couldn't very well bring them with us with no cargo pods. You know how it is with those things. Lightning-fast to deploy, forever to get moved out. And we were a little busy."

"But they're your whole business."

"We're going to the Republic, Kerra. Shopping is the official sport, from what I hear. I'm sure we can find a manufacturer willing to deal." He looked to the walls. "And it'd be nice to get some new holos."

"The Republic!" Remembering, Kerra slapped her knee enthusiastically—only to wince in pain. "I shouldn't have done that," she said. "But I think you'll like to hear this."

Quickly, she recounted some of what she learned from Arkadia about the Sith family and the *Charge Matrica*. As she tried to recall every face, every name from the Bequest, Rusher leapt in with details, filling in the blanks. He seemed to brighten as the pieces fell into place.

"That's astounding," he said. He'd known about some of the relationships, but not all—and while there were a lot more would-be Sith Lords that weren't in the family, Kerra's find had made many of the encounters he'd seen make sense.

"Get a recorder in here. I'll document everything," she said. "You want to meet a real Republic Chancellor? I think you're about to get your chance." Kerra warmed inside. The first time she'd sent others back to the Republic, they'd had to convey the sad news about what had happened to Vannar Treece and his band. This wasn't good news, but it was something direly needed in the Republic: light, shone into the darkness.

Rusher scratched his beard. "This does sound pretty valuable. You know, I've been itching to do a refit on the old tub," he said. "If this info's worth knowing, maybe they'll pay to give *Diligence* four cargo clusters, instead of two." He watched her face. "What? Don't they use the barter system there, too?"

Kerra smirked. "Don't make me go with you."

Rusher laughed. There was more laughter in the halls, she heard. The ship, morose after Gazzari, had been full of glee since the news of their destination spread, he said. Tan might never sleep again.

"She barely slept before." The Jedi sighed. *Mission accomplished, Gub.* "I'm pretty sure Beadle will be happier in the Republic, too."

"Actually, he wants to stick with us," Rusher said. "A few of your kids, too, want to stay on as part of the new brigade when I come back. Don't blame me—I didn't recruit 'em. But with their folks still under heel out here, they'd rather stay here, doing something."

I bet they won't feel that way after they've seen the Republic, Kerra thought. *Then again, maybe they might.*

"Sixty-three thousand," she mumbled.

"What's that?"

"Hmm?" She looked up, blowing a strand of hair from her eyes. "Oh. I was just adding up how many people I've sent back. Between Chelloa and what I've done since then, I've brought sixty-three thousand refugees to the frontier. About."

"That's a lot of traffic," Rusher said.

"Especially when you're not really trying to lead some exodus," she said. "It just happens. Sixty-three thousand down, billions to go."

Nodding, Rusher took his new swagger-stick and stood. "I guess you've got your own lurch ratio to worry about. That's what I came up here to tell you. We've got a quick stop coming up in a few hours—Tramanos, I think. I'm sure there's someone unpleasant there to keep you busy."

Kerra watched the man head to the door. For someone she'd thought a tool of the Sith, he'd surprised her. But that was the thing about tools. They could be used for another purpose. A better one.

"Rusher," Kerra called. "When you get to the Republic—I'd stay there, if I were you."

"No, you wouldn't," he said, grinning. "You're going to do what you came here to do—one system at a time."

Kerra laughed. "Me and what army?"

"You never know, kid. Maybe I'll cut you a rate."

The garden stood on a grassy hilltop, overlooking a green sea that stretched beneath towering pink clouds. Nothing from the morning rain lingered beyond a cool breeze, rustling the fronds of the plants lining the walkway.

Scaling the stone steps to the piazza, Narsk paused to sip from a fountain. Even the water here tasted sweet. For all the harshness of its masters, Sith space held enormous beauty. It was hard to believe this was only one of several such retreats, prepared and tended by the dowager's trusted orderlies.

The place was alive with natural sounds. Narsk could hear them now, through the prosthetics implanted in his ears earlier that day. Arkadia had secured the shuttle compartment against the dangers of space, but not the sound of the engines. Even activating the Mark VI hadn't done any good against the sonic bombardment; the receptors overloaded, burning out the suit forever. Just another of the trade-offs in his line of work; Narsk thought his new ears would make him a more effective spy.

His nose twitched. A multicolored butterfly perched on it, before flitting dizzily to an exotic flower on the trellis.

Ahead, a withered hand cupped the blossom. "Welcome to my nursery," the gardener said to the insect. "And you, as well, Master Ka'hane."

At the top of the steps, Narsk knelt. "Thank you, Vilia Calimondra."

He waited patiently as the snow-haired woman tended her garden. She always amazed him. Vilia Calimondra, the Evening Star. Conqueror of Phaegon and head of three houses. Bowed by time, but once tall and proud; what a warrior she must have been, Narsk thought. Hands that once held lightsabers were now mottled and wrinkled, well before their time—and yet, her golden eyes were still so alive. The Sith power did that, sometimes. The mind took a toll on the flesh.

Narsk had expected her to depart as soon as she learned of Arkadia's plot in full. But Vilia had taken the news of her granddaughter's plot calmly, and without surprise. Her seers had expected something, hence the brief warning he had received via his implant.

And if it had unsettled her in the least, she didn't show it. Here she was, in her simple amber gown, tending to nothing but her plants—and now her grandson. Brought here since Narsk's last trip up the hill, Quillan sat off to the side under a portable shade. No hoverchair this time; the bearers had carried the chair themselves.

Avian creatures soared over the ocean. Quillan grew animated, seeing past them to galaxies unknown. Head lolling against the chair back, he spoke syllables to the air.

"Yes, Quillan," Vilia said, sitting down at a bench beside the boy. She folded his hands. "Grandmother understands."

Narsk understood now, too. The teenager was the center of it all: everything that had happened since Gazzari. While Narsk had been on the battlefield, seeing to it that Odion and Daiman got her directive to attack Bactra, Vilia had grown concerned about someone else: Arkadia. Somehow, Vilia had learned of her granddaughter's interest in seizing not just the Dyarchy's territory—that was to be expected—but also the twins themselves. Had Vilia learned of it through the Force? Or through other assets like himself? Narsk hadn't asked. But Arkadia's particular focus on the children had concerned Vilia enough that she'd assigned Narsk to look into it.

His reputation had earned him a position key to Arkadia's plans on Byllura. It was sheer coincidence that the Jedi had gone to Byllura, too; it had certainly surprised him. But Vilia had known about it as soon as *Diligence* approached a populated world in the Dyarchy. Vilia had been able to track Kerra's location ever since her initial theft of the stealth suit—because Vilia had been Narsk's source for it. Her technicians had obtained the Cyricept system and modified it so that she could track Narsk—and, he imagined, whatever other minions she had given them to. The Mark VI may have been a hole in the spectrum while activated, but once a day while deactivated, it had silently pinged the secret communications network Vilia used to stay in touch with her family.

So Vilia had always known the Jedi would play a role in her future. She just hadn't known what it was. Kerra Holt had, in fact, saved Vilia's life by refusing to play assassin for Arkadia. Once Narsk learned exactly what Arkadia had in mind, he took the opportunity to free her. Vilia always liked her debts paid.

"You are here with news?"

"It should please you," Narsk said. Two of Vilia's other agents had used the moments of confusion in the Arkadianate to spirit Dromika away from Byllura. The girl would be kept far from her twin brother in the future— they had all learned that was for the best—but also out of the hands of opportunists who might exploit them, as Calician had. And Arkadia, for that matter.

There had been no communication from Arkadia. Another of Vilia's kin might have sent a mawkish message, playing the innocent and probing to see what the widow knew. Arkadia had remained silent to her grandmother. But she had spoken to Narsk, when he messaged pretending to be in hiding on a neutral world. From her, he had learned his spur-of-the-moment plan had worked better than he'd had any right to expect.

The damage done by *Diligence* had caused the floor beneath the hangar to collapse shortly after Narsk's departure. All Arkadia had found in the icy rubble were fragments of the booby-trapped hoverchair and the bodies of several of her technicians. Realizing they'd been killed by nerve gas and not the cataclysm, Arkadia had concluded that her aides had somehow loaded the wrong chair aboard the shuttle in the excitement, only to have the tanks in the correct chair rupture during the bombardment. Last seen climbing into his hideaway, Narsk had been able to claim ignorance when he communiated with Arkadia. He was a victim, too, he'd said, arriving on Vilia's world with the wrong hoverchair.

She'd responded curtly to that before cutting off the exchange. He knew she had other worries. Other sources had reported major damage to Arkadia's capital, and the recall of significant forces from the Dyarchy. It would be some time before Arkadia could consolidate her hold over any new territory.

Vilia liked her debts paid—but she seemed willing to let her granddaughter live with the embarrassment. One didn't want to be an outcast from *this* family.

"Chagras doted on the twins so," she said, patting Quillan's hand. "It was so hard, when he was taken away from them."

Narsk looked to the ground.

Rising, she looked searchingly at the Bothan. "You have something to ask, I sense. You wonder if I had something to do with my son Chagras's death," Vilia said, "as Arkadia claims."

"My lady, I had no—"

"You would as well ask if Arkadia had anything to do with it," she said. "An ambitious daughter, fearful her father's legacy would go to younger, more favored siblings? And an expert in nerve toxins, the very weapon that felled Chagras in his prime? You could construct a case against her as easily as you could against me, and it would be every bit as horrible." Vilia looked back from the hedge. "So why would you want to? A family is defined by its shared illusions, as much as by its blood."

Narsk shrugged. Gathering his courage, he straightened. "I have only had reason to doubt myself," he said. "I freed the Jedi. She won't leave Sith space—not if I know her. And now she knows about your family and the *Charge Matrica*. She could take that information to your enemies. Including the Republic."

Vilia waved off his concerns. There were no mass media to disseminate that information in Sith space, no authorities that would be believed. And the Republic had authorities proven itself ineffective even when it had good, recent intelligence about the Sith. "For the moment," she said, "young Kerra remains the only Jedi around."

"She could still be a danger to you and your family," Narsk said.

"I look on her as something else," Vilia said. "She's just like you, Narsk. She's a *learning experience*. For all of them. One day, the Sith will again turn upon the Republic—and we again will be facing the full roster of Jedi Knights. My grandchildren need to at least know how to deal with *one*."

Narsk had performed a dual role for years, she said. By serving her grandchildren, he was at the same time creating challenges for them. As far as Vilia was concerned, Kerra was just one more agent out there, testing her children's children.

"I am sorry, dowager," the Bothan said, looking down. "I know there are things that are beyond me. How does sowing discord strengthen your house?"

"You don't have children, do you, Master Ka'hane?"

Wooden, Narsk managed to shake his head.

"Well, I have had many—and they have had many. You expect them to fight with one another," she said. "I happen to expect them to fight well."

She turned to the chair, where Quillan continued to stare vacantly at the sea. "You always want them to succeed at whatever it is they set out to do. To strive," she said, stroking the boy's hair, "and to thrive." She smiled gently at the boy. "But when you see that some cannot, you pull them aside."

"This . . . this is a Sith philosophy?"

Vilia laughed. "The Sith are ancient, Narsk, but there were grandmothers long before that. We have our own function. You could call it a philosophy—but it is part of being what we are."

Seeing the woman return to her gardening, Narsk bowed and turned to depart.

"Oh, and Narsk?" Caressing a thorny flower, Vilia looked back and smiled. "If you do see Arkadia again, tell her I send my love. As always."

Read on for a preview of
Star Wars®: The Old Republic: Deceived
by
Paul S. Kemp
Published by Del Rey Books

Fatman shivered, her metal groaning, as Zeerid pushed her through Ord Mantell's atmosphere. Friction turned the air to fire, and Zeerid watched the orange glow of the flames through the transparisteel of the freighter's cockpit.

He was gripping the stick too tightly, he realized, and relaxed.

He hated atmosphere entries, always had, the long forty-count when heat, speed, and ionized particles caused a temporary sensor blackout. He never knew what kind of sky he'd encounter when he came out of the dark. Back when he'd carted Havoc Squadron commandos in a Republic gully jumper, he and his fellow pilots had likened the blackout to diving blind off a seaside cliff.

You always hope to hit deep water, they'd say. *But sooner or later the tide goes out and you go hard into rock.*

Or hard into a blistering crossfire. Didn't matter, really. The effect would be the same.

"Coming out of the dark," he said as the flame diminished and the sky opened below.

No one acknowledged the words. He flew *Fatman* alone, worked alone. The only thing he carted anymore were weapons for The Exchange. He had his reasons, but he tried hard not to think too hard about what he was doing.

He leveled the ship off, straightened, and ran a quick sweep of the surrounding sky. The sensors picked up nothing.

"Deep water and it feels fine," he said, smiling.

On most planets, the moment he cleared the atmosphere he'd have been busy dodging interdiction by the planetary government. But not on Ord Mantell. The planet was a hive of crime syndicates, mercenaries, bounty hunters, smugglers, weapons dealers, and spicerunners.

And those were just the people who ran the place.

Factional wars and assassinations occupied their attention, not governance, and certainly not law enforcement. The upper and lower latitudes of the planet in particular were sparsely settled and almost never patrolled, a literal no-being's-land. Zeerid would have been surprised if the government had survsats running orbits over the area.

And all that suited him fine.

Fatman broke through a thick pink blanket of clouds, and the brown, blue, and white of Ord Mantell's northern hemisphere filled out Zeerid's field of vision. Snow and ice peppered the canopy, frozen shrapnel, beating a steady rhythm on *Fatman*'s hull. The setting sun suffused a large swath of the world with orange and red. The northern sea roiled below him, choppy and dark, the irregular white circles of breaking surf denoting the thousands of uncharted islands that poked through the water's surface. To the west, far in the distance, he could make out the hazy edge of a continent and the thin spine of snowcapped, cloud-topped mountains that ran along its north–south axis.

Motion drew his eye. A flock of leatherwings, too small to cause a sensor blip, flew two hundred meters to starboard and well below him, the tents of their huge, membranous wings flapping slowly in the freezing wind, the arc of the flock like a parenthesis. They were heading south for warmer air and paid him no heed as he flew over and past them, their dull, black eyes blinking against the snow and ice.

He pulled back on the ion engines and slowed still further. A yawn forced itself past his teeth. He sat up straight and tried to blink away the fatigue, but it was as stubborn as an angry bantha. He'd given the ship to the autopilot and dozed during the hyperspace run from Vulta, but that was all the rack he'd had in the last two standard days. It was catching up to him.

He scratched at the stubble of his beard, rubbed the back of his neck, and plugged the drop coordinates into the navicomp. The comp linked with one of Ord Mantell's unsecured geosyncsats and fed back the location and course to *Fatman*. Zeerid's HUD displayed it on the cockpit canopy. He eyed the location and put his finger on the destination.

"Some island no one has ever heard of, up here where no one ever goes. Sounds about right."

Zeerid turned the ship over to the autopilot, and it banked him toward the island.

His mind wandered as *Fatman* cut through the sky. The steady patter of ice and snow on the canopy sang him a lullaby. His thoughts drifted back through the clouds to the past, to the days before the accident, before he'd left the marines. Back then, he'd worn the uniform proudly and had still been able to look himself in the mirror—

He caught himself, caught the burgeoning self-pity, and stopped the thoughts cold. He knew where it would lead.

"Stow that, soldier," he said to himself.

He was what he was, and things were what they were.

"Focus on the work, Z-man."

He checked his location against the coordinates in the navicomp. Almost there.

"Gear up and get frosty," he said, echoing the words he used to say to his commandos. "Ninety seconds to the LZ."

He continued his ritual, checking the charge on his blasters, tightening the straps on his composite armor vest, getting his mind right.

Ahead, he saw ahead the island where he would make the drop: ten square klicks of volcanic rock fringed with a bad haircut of waist-high scrub whipping in the wind. The place would probably be underwater and gone next year.

He angled lower, flew a wide circle, unable to see much detail due to the snow. He ran a scanner sweep, as always, and the chirp of his instrumentation surprised him. A ship was already on the island. He checked his wrist chrono and saw that he was a full twenty standard minutes early. He'd made this run three times and Arigo—he was sure the man's real name was not Arigo—had never before arrived early.

He descended to a few hundred meters to get a better look.

Arigo's freighter, the *Doghouse*, shaped not unlike the body of a legless beetle, sat in a clearing on the east side of the island. Its landing ramp was down and stuck out of its belly like a tongue. Halogens blared into the fading twilight and reflected off the falling snow, turning the flakes into glittering jewels. He saw three men lingering around the ramp, though he was too far away to notice any details other than their white winter parkas.

They spotted *Fatman,* and one waved a gloved hand.

Zeerid licked his lips and frowned.

Something felt off.

Flares went up from the freighter and burst in the air—green, red, red, green.

That was the correct sequence.

He circled one more time, staring down through the swirl of snow, but saw nothing to cause alarm, no other ships on the island or in the surrounding sea. He pushed aside his concern and chalked his feelings up to the usual tension caused by dealing with miscreants and criminals.

In any event, he could not afford to frak up a drop of several hundred million credits of hardware because he felt skittish. The ultimate buyer—whoever that was— would be unhappy, and The Exchange would take the lost profits from Zeerid in blood and broken bones, then tack it on to the debt he already owed them. He'd lost track of exactly how much that was, but knew it was at least two million credits on the note for *Fatman* plus almost half that again on advances for Arra's medical treatment, though he'd kept Arra's existence a secret and his handler thought the latter were for gambling losses.

"LZ is secure." He hoped saying it would make it so. "Going in."

The hum of the reverse thrusters and a swirl of blown snow presaged the thump of *Fatman*'s touching down on the rock. He landed less than fifty meters from Arigo's ship.

For a moment he sat in the cockpit, perfectly still, staring at the falling snow, knowing there'd be another drop after this one, then another, then another, and he'd still owe The Exchange more than he'd ever be able to pay. He was on a treadmill with no idea how to get off.

Didn't matter, though. The point was to earn for Arra, maybe get her a hoverchair instead of that wheeled antique. Better yet, prostheses.

He blew out a breath, stood, and tried to find his

calm as he threw on a winter parka and fingerless gloves. In the cargo hold, he had to pick his way though the maze of shipping containers. He avoided looking directly at the thick black lettering on their sides, though he knew it by heart, had seen such crates many times in his military career.

DANGER—MUNITIONS.
FOR MILITARY USE ONLY.
KEEP AWAY FROM INTENSE HEAT
OR OTHER ENERGY SOURCES.

In the crates were upward of three hundred million credits' worth of crew-served laser cannons, MPAPPs, grenades, and enough ammunition to keep even the craziest fire team grinning and sinning for months.

Near the bay's landing ramp, he saw that three of the four securing straps had come loose from one of the crates of grenades. He was lucky the crate hadn't bounced around in transit. Maybe the straps had snapped when he set down on the island. He chose to believe that rather than admit to his own sloppiness.

He did not bother reattaching the straps. Arigo's men would have to undo them to unload anyway.

He loosened his blasters in their holsters and pushed the button to open the bay and lower the ramp. The door descended and snow and cold blew in, the tang of ocean salt. He stepped out into the wind. The light of the setting sun made him squint. He'd been in only artificial light for upward of twelve hours. His boots crunched on the snow-dusted black rock. His exhalations steamed away in the wind.

Two of the men from Arrigo's freighter detached themselves from their ship and met him halfway. Both were human and bearded. One had a patched eye and a scar like a lightning stroke down one cheek. Both wore blasters on their hips. Like Zeerid, both had the butt straps undone.

Recognizing neither of them rekindled Zeerid's earlier concerns. He had a mind for faces, and both of the men were strangers.

The drop was starting to taste sour.

"Where's Arigo?" Zeerid asked.

"Doin' what Arigo does," Scar said, and gestured vaguely. "Sent us instead. No worries, though, right?"

No Scar shifted on his feet, antsy, twitchy.

Zeerid nodded, kept his face expressionless as his heart rate amped up and adrenaline started making him warm. Everything smelled wrong, and he'd learned over the years to trust his sense of smell.

"You Zeerid?" Scar asked.

"Z-man."

No one called him Zeerid except his sister-in-law.

And Aryn, once. But Aryn had been long ago.

"Z-man," echoed No Scar, shifting on his feet and half giggling.

"Sound funny to you?" Zeerid asked him.

Before No Scar could answer, Scar asked, "Where's the cargo?"

Zeerid looked past the two men before him to the third, who lingered near the landing ramp of Arigo's ship. The man's body language—too focused on the verbal exchange, too coiled—reinforced Zeerid's worry. He reminded Zeerid of the way rooks looked when facing Imperials for the first time, all attitude and hair trigger.

Suspicion stacked up into certainty. The drop didn't just smell bad, it *was* bad.

Arigo was dead, and the crew before him worked for some other faction on Ord Mantell, or worked for some organization sideways to The Exchange. Whatever. Didn't matter to Zeerid. He never bothered to follow who was fighting whom, so he just trusted no one.

But what did matter to him was that the three men standing before him probably had tortured information from Arigo and would kill Zeerid as soon as they confirmed the presence of the cargo.

And there could be still more men hidden aboard the freighter.

It seemed he'd descended out of atmospheric blackout and into a crossfire after all.

What else was new?

"Why you call that ship *Fatman*?" No Scar asked. Arigo must have told them the name of Zeerid's ship because *Fatman* bore no identifying markings. Zeerid used fake ship registries on almost every planet on which he docked.

"'Cause it takes a lot to fill her belly."

"Ship's a she, though. Right? Why not *Fatwoman*?"

"Seemed disrespectful."

No Scar frowned. "Huh? To who?"

Zeerid did not bother to answer. All he'd wanted to do was drop off the munitions, retire some of his debt to The Exchange, and get back to his daughter before he had to get back out in the black and get dirty again.

"Something wrong?" Scar asked, his tone wary. "You look upset."

"No," Zeerid said, and forced a half smile. "Everything's the same as always."

The men plastered on uncertain grins, unclear on Zeerid's meaning.

"Right," Scar said. "Same as always."

Knowing how things would go, Zeerid felt the calm he usually did when danger impended. He flashed for a moment on Arra's face, on what she'd do if he died on Ord Mantell, on some no-name island. He pushed the thoughts away. No distractions.

"Cargo is in the main bay. Send your man around. The ship's open."

The expressions on the faces of both men hardened, the change nearly imperceptible but clear to Zeerid, a transformation that betrayed their intention to murder. Scar ordered No Scar to go check the cargo.

"He'll need a lifter," Zeerid said, readying himself, focusing on speed and precision. "That stuff ain't a few kilos."

No Scar stopped within reach of Zeerid, looking back at Scar for guidance, his expression uncertain.

"Nah," said Scar, his hand hovering near his holster, the motion too casual to be casual. "I just want him to make sure it's all there. Then I'll let my people know to release payment."

He held up his arm as if to show Zeerid a wrist com-link, but the parka covered it.

"It's all there," Zeerid said.

"Go on," said Scar to No Scar. "Check it."

"Oh," Zeerid said, and snapped his fingers. "There is one other thing . . ."

No Scar sighed, stopped, faced him, eyebrows raised in a question, breath steaming out of his nostrils. "What's that?"

Zeerid made a knife of his left hand and drove his fingertips into No Scar's throat. While No Scar crumpled to the snow, gagging, Zeerid jerked one of his blasters free of its hip holster and put a hole through Scar's chest before the man could do anything more than take a surprised step backward and put his hand on the grip of his own weapon. Scar staggered back two more steps, his mouth working but making no sound, his right arm held up, palm out, as if he could stop the shot that had already killed him.

As Scar toppled to the ground, Zeerid took a wild shot at the third man near the *Doghouse*'s landing ramp but missed high. The third man made himself small beside the *Doghouse,* drew his blaster pistol, and shouted into a wrist comlink. Zeerid saw movement within the cargo bay of Arigo's ship—more men with ill intent.

No way to know how many.

He cursed, fired a covering shot, then turned and ran for *Fatman.* A blaster shot put a smoking black furrow through the sleeve of his parka but missed flesh. Another rang off the hull of *Fatman.* A third shot hit him square in the back. It felt like getting run over by a speeder. The impact drove the air from his lungs and plowed him face-first into the snow.

He smelled smoke. His armored vest had ablated the shot.

Adrenaline got him to his feet just as fast as he had gone down. Gasping, trying to refill his lungs, he ducked behind a landing skid for cover and wiped the snow from his face. He poked his head out for a moment to look back, saw that No Scar had stopped gagging and started being dead, that Scar stayed politely still, and that six more men were dashing toward him, two armed with blaster rifles and the rest with pistols.

His armor would not stop a rifle bolt.

A shot slammed into the landing skid, another into the snow at his feet, another, another.

"Stang!" he cursed.

The safety of *Fatman*'s landing ramp and cargo bay, only a few steps from him, somehow looked ten kilometers away.

He took a blaster in each hand, stretched his arms around to either side of the landing skid, and fired as fast he could he pull the trigger in the direction of the onrushing men. He could not see and did not care if he hit anyone, he just wanted to get them on the ground.

After he'd squeezed off more than a dozen shots with no return fire, he darted out from the behind the skid and toward the ramp.

He reached it before the shooters recovered enough to let loose another barrage. A few bolts chased him up the ramp, ringing off the metal. Sparks flew and the smell of melted plastoid mixed with the ocean air. He ran past the button to raise the ramp, struck at it, and hurried on toward the cockpit. Only after he'd nearly cleared the cargo bay did it register with him that he wasn't hearing the whir of turning gears.

He whirled around, cursed.

In his haste, he'd missed the button to raise the landing ramp.

He heard shouts from outside and dared not go back. He could close the bay from the control panel in the cockpit. But he had to hurry.

He pelted through *Fatman*'s corridors, shouldered open the door to the cockpit, and started punching in the launch sequence. *Fatman*'s thrusters went live and the ship lurched upward. Blasterfire thumped off the hull but did no harm. He tried to look down out of the canopy, but the ship was angled upward and he could not see the ground. He punched the control to move it forward and heard the distant squeal of metal on metal. It had come from the cargo bay.

Something was slipping around in there.

The loose container of grenades.

And he'd still forgotten to seal the bay.

Cursing himself for a fool, he flicked the switch that brought up the ramp then sealed the cargo bay and evacuated it of oxygen. If anyone had gotten aboard, they would suffocate in there.

He took the controls in hand and fired *Fatman*'s engines. The ship shot upward. He turned her as he rose, took a look back at the island.

For a moment, he was confused by what he saw. But realization dawned.

When *Fatman* had lurched up and forward, the remaining straps securing the container of grenades had snapped and the whole shipping container had slid right out the open landing ramp.

He was lucky it hadn't exploded.

The men who had ambushed him were gathered around the crate, probably wondering what was inside. A quick head count put their number at six, so he figured none had gotten on board *Fatman*. And none of them seemed to be making for Arigo's ship, so Zeerid assumed they had no intention of pursuing him in the air. Maybe they were happy enough with the one container.

Amateurs, then. Pirates, maybe.

Zeerid knew he would have to answer to Oren, his handler, not only for the deal going sour but also for the lost grenades.

Kriffing treadmill just kept going faster and faster.

He considered throwing *Fatman*'s ion engines on full, clearing Ord Mantell's gravity well, and heading into hyperspace, but changed his mind. He was annoyed and thought he had a better idea.

He wheeled the freighter around and accelerated.

"Weapons going live," he said, and activated the over-and-under plasma cannons mounted on *Fatman*'s sides.

The men on the ground, having assumed he would flee, did not notice him coming until he had closed to five hundred meters. Faces stared up at him, hands pointed, and the men started to scramble. A few blaster shots from one of the men traced red lines through the sky, but a blaster could not harm the ship.

Zeerid took aim. The targeting computer centered on the crate.

"LZ is hot," he said, and lit them up. For an instant pulsing orange lines connected the ship to the island, the ship to the crate of grenades. Then, as the grenades exploded, the lines blossomed into an orange cloud of heat, light, and smoke that engulfed the area. Shrapnel pattered against the canopy, metal this time, not ice, and the shock wave rocked *Fatman* slightly as Zeerid peeled the ship off and headed skyward.

He glanced back, saw six, motionless, smoking forms scattered around the blast radius.

"That was for you, Arigo."

He would still have some explaining to do, but at least he'd taken care of the ambushers. That had to be worth something to The Exchange.

Or so he hoped.

EXPLORE THE GALAXY WITH STAR WARS BOOKS

Whether you yearn for **YODA,**
dig the **DARK SIDE,**
or pine to be a **PADAWAN,**
reading can transport you faster
than the ***MILLENNIUM FALCON.***

Follow us on **Suvudu, Facebook,**
and **Twitter** and keep up to date on
all things **STAR WARS Books.**